# Bello:

## hidden talent rediscovered

Bello is a digital only imprint of Pan Macmillan,
established to breathe new life into previously published,
classic books.

At Bello we believe in the timeless power of the imagination,
of good story, narrative and entertainment and we want to use
digital technology to ensure that many more readers
can enjoy these books into the future.

We publish in ebook and Print on Demand formats
to bring these wonderful books to new audiences.

*About Bello:*

www.panmacmillan.com/bello

*Sign up to our newsletter to hear about*
*new releases, events and competitions:*

www.panmacmillan.com/bellonews

*Kate Hatfield*

Kate Hatfield, who also writes crime novels as Natasha Cooper, is fascinated by relationships: how they work; why they go wrong; how they change people's lives. Born in London, she worked in publishing for ten years before becoming a writer. She now divides her time between the city and the Somerset Levels.

*Kate Hatfield*

# MARSH LIGHT

BELL

First published in 1997 by Transworld

This edition published 2012 by Bello
an imprint of Pan Macmillan, a division of Macmillan Publishers Limited
Pan Macmillan, 20 New Wharf Road, London N1 9RR
Basingstoke and Oxford
Associated companies throughout the world

www.panmacmillan.com/imprints/bello

ISBN 978-1-4472-3876-8 EPUB
ISBN 978-1-4472-3875-1 POD

A CIP catalogue record for this book is available from the British Library.

Printed and bound by CPI Group (UK) Ltd, Croydon, CR0 4YY

Visit **www.panmacmillan.com** to read more about all our books
and to buy them. You will also find features, author interviews and
news of any author events, and you can sign up for e-newsletters
so that you're always first to hear about our new releases.

*For Doris Brown Hobbs*

# Chapter One

Gold has no smell. All the other materials Helena used in her work had their own comfortingly familiar scents, from the throat-catching pungency of the chemicals and varnishes to the warm mustiness of sawdust and the freshness of the water-based fillers and paints. Only gold left no evidence of itself in the air.

She bent forward to touch the dampened parchment size she had applied over the repair to her client's eighteenth-century girandole. It was a lovely piece, with holders for a trio of candles in front of an oval mirror in a delicately carved and gilded rococo frame. Having checked that the size was properly tacky against her fingertips, she took a sheet of twenty-four-carat gold leaf from its cardboard envelope and laid it lightly on the size.

There was a long buzz from the front door bell. Helena paid no attention, not even raising her eyes to the screen over her workbench. The sheets of gold leaf were so fragile that it always took all her concentration to apply one without tearing it or leaving any wrinkles. It was far too expensive to waste.

When she was at last satisfied with the smooth perfection of the patch, she did look up at the screen and smiled at the sight of the man patiently waiting under the wisteria that hung around her door. The grey and white image was sharp enough for her to identify her half-brother but not much more than that. It smudged his features and made him look much squatter than he was, almost ordinary; and if there was one thing Ivo was not, it was ordinary.

Reaching across to the intercom, Helena pressed a switch and said: 'Ivo? What a treat! Sorry about the wait. I'm in the shed, gilding. I'll buzz you in.'

He looked up towards the discreet camera over the door and nodded. 'Great, thanks,' he said into the grille beside the bell.

Having stripped off the old-fashioned cream linen carpenter's apron she wore over her loose khaki shorts and black T-shirt, Helena brushed some of the dust from her espadrilles and removed a blob of size that was stuck in her hair.

By the time she reached the door of the shed, Ivo was already opening the french windows. He waited at the top of the iron steps, standing in full sunlight between cascades of frothy-looking white and pink Clematis montana, which grew entwined with climbing roses. He was an inch or two under six foot, but he had had the luck to inherit the best features of both his parents. With his mother's thick dark hair, expressive black eyes and almost golden skin, he also had his father's infinitely more delicate bones and slim, straight figure. He was dressed, as usual, in faded jeans and an old cotton shirt that had been washed and worn to a silky softness that was much more important to him than its fraying collar and cuffs.

Helena was different from him in everything but their shared disdain for expensive clothes. She took after her mother, and was slight and fair, with the kind of thin skin that freckles easily and large greenish-grey eyes. Her slithery blond hair was casually bunched out of the way on top of her head in a rubber band the postman had left around a bundle of letters that morning. There was no makeup on her face to disguise the freckles, and the old army-surplus shorts she was wearing had been chosen for their comfort and the ease of movement they gave her as she worked. Her slender legs were bare and she had black canvas espadrilles on her narrow feet. She wore no jewellery of any kind and her nails were cut very short.

'Are you very busy,' Ivo asked, sounding almost wistful, 'or might you have time to knock off for a bit?'

Helena locked the door of the shed without bothering to answer. They both knew that he had not needed to ask; she had always given him everything he wanted and would have dropped the most urgent piece of work in order to spend time with him.

'Let's go indoors,' she said, pocketing the key. 'It's too hot and bright to sit out here; at least it is for me. And you must be boiled if you've come all the way from Oxford. What are you up here for?'

'Helena,' he said, mock severity banishing all the softness from his voice. 'Come off it. You know perfectly well I'm going to this dinner the parents are giving for Geoffrey Duxford. I thought you were, too.'

'I suppose I am,' she said, sighing. 'I'd managed to forget it for a blessed few minutes. Silly of me. Never mind. You must be thirsty. What would you like to drink? There's plenty of beer in the fridge or fizzy water, orange juice, elderflower cordial – but perhaps that's too girly for you.'

'Not at all. It sounds great. You know, I think you really had forgotten the dinner. What a very good thing I dropped round in time to remind you!'

Helena laughed and brushed past him on the way into her narrow kitchen. The fridge provided a welcome blast of cold air as she opened its door, and she stood gratefully in the coolness for an extravagant minute before reaching to the back of the bottom shelf for the bottles she needed.

'I hadn't really forgotten. But I have been trying not to think about it – or the rows it must have been generating.'

Ivo casually stroked her thin back as she poured their drinks. She wished she was not so sweaty and hoped her T-shirt did not feel damp under his hand. If it did, Ivo showed no signs of revulsion, and his voice was as lightly friendly as usual when he said: 'You take the parental fratching far too seriously. You're as bad as Jane. Be like me and ignore it.'

Helena turned with the two cool tumblers in her hands.

'But how can you? Don't they try to suck you in when they start savaging each other?'

'Sometimes,' said Ivo with all the confident tolerance she envied so much. He took one of the glasses from her. 'I just don't let them.'

Helena drank some of the prickling, sweet elderflower cordial and then said: 'I wish I knew how you managed that.'

'It's not exactly hard. You just have to remember that they choose to carry on like that. When something happens to make them want to stop, they will. You didn't make them start . . .'

Didn't I? thought Helena, but she did not say it aloud. '. . . and nothing you could possibly say or do would make them stop. You'd do much better to keep out of it all. They don't really want you involved – whatever they say – and it wouldn't get to you so much if you left them to it.'

'Perhaps,' said Helena, envying him his detachment almost more than any of his multifarious talents.

Everything seemed to come easily to him. He had been born with brains as well as confidence, and he had learned to make the most of them. Helena had watched his smooth progress through life with amused admiration, not in the least surprised when he had come top in every exam he had ever sat or when the dons had positively begged him to stay up at university to take a second degree after his stunning success as an undergraduate.

Like almost everyone else, she loved him. She had done so from the moment she first saw him, when she was a skinny, anxious seven-year-old, admitted to her stepmother's room only a few hours after his birth.

'They did tell you the dinner was to be black tie, didn't they?' she said in a ludicrous attempt to assert her seniority.

Ivo's glinting smile told her that he knew exactly what she was doing and did not mind it in the least. She slid back in her chair and smiled with him.

'Yes, dear,' he said as though to a fragile, elderly relation, 'and I washed behind my ears this morning.'

'Oh, shut up!'

'That's better. You really do need to lighten up, old girl. What are you going to wear tonight?'

'A rather glamorous long skirt,' she said, obediently trying to relax. 'I think it's going to look pretty good.'

'I'm sure it is. In the charming phrase of a well-known crime writer whose novel I was reading the other day, you always do scrub up well. What's the skirt like?'

4

'Sort of triangular, made from some spectacularly over-the-top ancient Florentine damask – black and grey. I bought it at a textile auction when I was in Amsterdam, meaning it for some chairs I was doing up.' She laughed again. 'It turned out to be much too flamboyant for them, but I thought it would do for me. I'm planning to wear it with a black scoop-neck body and that gold locket Geoffrey gave me for my christening. I hope it'll all go down all right.'

'Don't be such a wimp. Why shouldn't it? And anyway, why should you care? I never have understood why you mind so much about what other people think of you.'

'Haven't you?'

'No. You need to remember that you're an independent woman with your own thoroughly successful business and, I may say, a surprisingly high reputation among people who matter.'

'What on earth do you know about my reputation?' she asked, sitting up straighter.

'Aha!' he said. His black eyes looked thoroughly mischievous. 'Quite a lot actually. There are some important antique dealers who think you're positively brilliant at what you do and, in their words, "bizarrely honest" about it. I'm not quite sure what that means, but it sounds pretty good.'

'Well, maybe. But how did you hear it?'

'I've been spying on you for weeks,' he said casually.

'What?'

'Don't look so horrified. It was what we frivolous chaps call a joke, Helena. You know, one of those things that's supposed to make people laugh.'

'Ah.' She manufactured a smile, feeling uncomfortable. Ivo's jokes were usually much funnier than that. 'But where *did* you come across these gossiping antique dealers?'

'At an auction I was at last month.'

'You?'

'Don't sound so surprised,' he said. 'I know chemists are supposed to be boringly wedded to their labs, but it's not an essential qualification.'

'No, I suppose not. All the same . . .'

Her voice dwindled, but it did not matter. Ivo was already starting to say, 'In fact it was having seen how peculiar some of my colleagues had got that made me realize I must get away from the test tubes sometimes. Those who don't seem to end up like stale specimens themselves: deeply unattractive, rather smelly, and not much use to anyone.'

Helena laughed, feeling better.

'I can't stand sport,' Ivo went on cheerfully, 'and I can't sing a note, so it was going to have to be either acting or art of some kind. I thought I'd try the latter first and get my eye in by doing all the available exhibitions and auctions.'

'Well, good for you, Ivo. I had no idea.'

'No? Well, I've been to quite a few sales now, and I've come to the conclusion that I'm not all that keen on pictures or silver, but I think I might seriously enjoy collecting old furniture.'

Helena raised her fair eyebrows. Successful and charming Ivo might be, but it was going to be some years before he was rich enough to start buying antiques.

'In fact,' he went on, 'that's what's made me come up so early this afternoon. I was wondering if I couldn't commission you to do something for me.'

'Of course I will,' she said at once. 'I'd happily bid for anything you want, but, Ivo, anything good is going to be frightfully expensive.'

'I know that,' he said, looking amused. 'And I'm not asking you to bid for anything. I'm quite capable of doing that myself, thanks. Anyway, I've already acquired my heart's desire. But it does need some restoration. I hoped you'd help.'

'Acquired it? What?'

'A desk. I think it's rather a find, but it's pretty tired and needs a fair amount of work. Will you come out and have look at it and see what you think?'

'You mean you've got it with you?' said Helena, feeling as though her mind were working much more slowly than usual.

'Yes. I borrowed a van from a mate at Oxford. It's parked out there. Come on.'

'All right. Let me get rid of these first.' She took both glasses back to the kitchen and then followed him out of the house. A shabby white van was parked behind her much neater, smaller, red one.

Ivo unlocked the dented back doors and leaped nimbly up into the van. Helena followed him hardly less agilely and squatted down in front of the desk, which was swathed in coarse grey blankets and strapped to the struts that ran along the side of the vehicle. She peeled away the blankets and caught her breath at the sight of Ivo's heart's desire.

It was a simply shaped walnut kneehole desk in the style of those made during the reign of Queen Anne. Helena could not believe that it could possibly be genuine, although she noticed at once that the veneer had the right soft and silky look with appropriately faded markings. The proportions gave it a kind of unshowy elegance, and, as she ran her fingers over the beading and pulled out one of the drawers, she saw that it was exceedingly well made.

She made a quick visual check of the usual danger points. The veneers were thickish, nearly an eighth of an inch, and correctly quartered on the top. There were three drawers beneath the top and three on either side of the kneehole.

'Well?' Ivo said, sounding as though he thought she had had quite enough time to come to a conclusion and was bored with her silence. 'What d'you think of it?'

'Superficially it looks good, but real ones are frighteningly rare and I'd hate to give you any false hopes. I don't quite ...' She looked up at him over her right shoulder, frowning and worried. 'Ivo, I don't understand. Even fakes of this quality cost a fortune. How are you going to pay for it?'

He laughed, leaning against the side of the van with his hands in his pockets. 'You sound terribly worried. Are you mixing me up with my spendthrift, debt-ridden sister?'

'No,' said Helena, twisting right round so that she could see his face properly. 'You couldn't be as irresponsible as Jane if you tried. But I don't understand where you're going to get the money to buy something like this.'

'Unlike poor old Jane,' he said, '*I*'m lucky enough to have an understanding bank manager.'

'But what collateral could you possibly offer him? You didn't pretend that Father would . . . ?'

'Helena, don't be silly. I'm not completely mad. I went to my bank with a business proposition and they thought about it and eventually accepted. The desk is its own security. They could see that it was worth a great deal more than I paid.'

She was still frowning.

'Look,' he said, 'a rather philistine friend of mine with a juicy job in the City inherited it from some batty spinster aunt and had it delivered to his flat. As soon as he got it there, he realized it looked absolutely ghastly with all his modern Italian stuff and so he decided to flog it. When he told me what he was thinking of asking for it, I knew I couldn't pass up the chance. Between the two of us and my bank manager, we came to an arrangement.'

Helena was silent for a moment, thinking that the purchase of the desk was yet another piece of the astonishing luck that had always been visited on Ivo. She had been trawling antique and junk shops for years, attending many of the big auctions and looking in at antique markets all around the country, and she had never seen anything so good that was not priced at its full value – or more.

'If it's what I think it is, you've done well. You've obviously got a good eye, Ivo. But I'm still puzzled about the bank manager. For someone not yet earning, it's . . .'

'Now, stop it, Helena. You are not responsible for my finances and you don't have to worry about them. You've got plenty of other things to worry about, God knows. If you must know, I've been doing some tutoring since the autumn and accumulated just about enough for the bank man to think I'm a fair risk.'

'Oh, I see.' She reminded herself that even though Ivo was her younger brother his financial affairs were no business of hers. If he got himself into debt, he was probably quite capable of getting out again. 'And did he just accept your view of what it was worth?'

'Of course he didn't. He's not a fool. I got a valuation from an Oxford dealer.' Ivo looked at her with a smile of indescribable affection. 'I thought it would be better not to involve you at that stage. I can just imagine the state you'd get in if you thought you might've been leading me astray.'

'You know me too well,' she said, reaching out to touch his arm. 'That was generous.'

'So you will patch it up for me then?'

'I'd love to. I won't be able to get to it straight away, I'm afraid. I've got quite a few things stacked up and I don't want to antagonize faithful clients, even for you. Shall you mind waiting?'

'Not at all. But have you got room to hang on to it until you can do it? I don't want to lug it all the way to Oxford, only to bring it back again.'

'Sure. Let's take it in now.'

When the desk was safely stowed at the back of the carefully damp-proofed workshed, once again wrapped in its blankets, Ivo looked at his watch.

'I suppose I'd better get going; and you ought to start the scrubbing-up. It looks as though it may take some time.'

'Wouldn't you rather change here and stay the night?' Helena said, ignoring his insult. 'Mike won't be here and there's plenty of room.'

'Sweet of you,' said Ivo, blowing her a kiss. He was already halfway out of the door of the shed. 'But I'd better not. I told my mother I'd be with her as soon after seven as I could manage and with rush-hour traffic I'll be pushed to make it before half past. See you later.'

He had gone, moving as gracefully as ever and leaving as big a gap. Helena reluctantly went upstairs to wash her sticky, dusty hair.

# Chapter Two

Irene Webton stopped on the steps of her gloomy house in Herbert Crescent in Knightsbridge. She had been out to the hairdresser to have her long dark hair put up for the dinner that evening and she still had a great deal to do, but for a moment or two she could not force herself even to put her key in the lock.

She had always, disliked the look of the house with its clumsy gables and pillars, all built in the ugliest of ugly red brick. It was, she thought, like cheap tinned tomato soup gone stale and edged with dirt. The inside was little better, in spite of all the things she had done to cheer it up over the years. The long hall was still panelled in dull, coarse-grained oak, which seemed to drink up what little light reached it, but her husband had always refused even to consider having it removed or painted.

He was the only child of intensely ambitious parents, who had driven him unmercifully throughout his childhood. They had been determined that he should climb out of the frustrating, poverty-stricken world they had had to inhabit, and he had done everything he could to fulfil their dreams, except allow himself to be known as Godolphin, the Christian name they had chosen to fit his future eminence. He had changed it to Fin on the day he first went to school, and no-one had ever persuaded him to change it back, even when he was called to the Bar.

His steady climb towards success had pleased his parents, he had once told Irene, but they had never expressed real satisfaction in anything he did until he had scraped together enough money to get a mortgage for the house in Herbert Crescent. He had achieved it only just in time; four months after he had moved in his mother had died.

Irene understood something of what the house must have meant to him then, but she thought he ought to have grown out of it. He was in his sixties and had been a High Court judge for years, unassailably secure in every way. In the early days of her marriage she had sympathized with his need to keep the house decorated in the fashion his parents had found so satisfactorily grand but which to her seemed not only stifling but ugly. As the years passed her sympathies became less easily aroused, and for some time she had been doing her best to introduce subversive bits and pieces to dilute the closed-in pomposity of the place.

She had concentrated on richness of colour and texture rather than trying to pretend that any of the rooms could ever be light or pretty, and she had improved things a little, but she would infinitely rather have lived in her stepdaughter's much less luxurious but almost luminous house.

Pushing her key into the lock at last, Irene felt a familiar swoop of envy at Helena's life. There she was, aged thirty but still blissfully alone and independent. She had a small, beautiful, easily run house that was positively drenched in light on all but the gloomiest of winter days. Her income was not large but it was absolutely her own; she had earned it all, and no-one had the right to ask how she spent it or criticize her extravagances. Her whole life was her own. Never subject to anyone else's whim, she had a lover who came and went without asking anything of her that she did not want to give, and she had no-one to tell her what she should or should not be doing. Irene did not grudge her any of it, but there were times when she had to work hard not to think it seriously unfair.

The air inside the panelled hall was fresh with scent from the artlessly arranged bowls of lilies and roses she had put there earlier in the day. It was also much cleaner than the dust-laden stuffiness of the street, and yet Irene hated it. Reluctantly she let the heavy door shut behind her and listened to it bang, allowing herself to think melodramatically of cells and clanking chains and gaolers' keys because only by laughing at her life could she make it bearable.

She had no responsibility for the food that evening; it was being cooked by two old friends of hers who had a catering business. The tables were already laid, but she had still to concoct a seating plan that would not offend her husband's sensibilities or put any of the well-known enemies next to, or opposite, each other. She also wanted to give Ivo at least one person who might be interesting to talk to, and herself one of the few men who was not a lawyer.

Geoffrey Duxford would have to sit on her right since the dinner was in his honour. That would be pleasant enough, since he was always an entertaining talker and should be on particularly good form that evening, but it would be good to have someone who knew nothing of the law on her other side.

As she thought of Geoffrey, Irene grimaced, hoping that Fin's liking for him would survive what had just happened. They had been called to the Bar together and they had taken silk at the same time fifteen years later, but Geoffrey had been made a judge earlier than Fin and was probably now out of his reach. Irene shrugged. Even Fin could not blame her for that.

She risked getting in the way of the caterers to make herself a cup of tea and took it into the dining room with a pad and a list of the twenty-two expected guests. The dining room table had been dismantled and stored in pieces in her study to make room for two round tables she had hired, which would take twelve guests each. It meant the study was unusable, but that did not matter much. Her own work had been in limbo for weeks and could not get any further until after an important meeting the following day.

The plans for each table took more than half an hour to get right, but eventually she finished.

'What a waste of time!' she said aloud.

Normally she loved entertaining. Filling the house with interesting people, dressing up, producing lavish food and wine and talking for half the night were among her greatest pleasures. But any more than eight people meant that it was not possible to talk to them all; hiring caterers took most of the pleasure out of offering food to friends, and the whole thing became an expensive exercise in conventional flag-waving. Worse than that: the dinner had been designed to show the people who mattered in the legal world that Fin did not mind having failed to become a Law Lord himself. They all knew quite as well as Irene that he minded like hell.

Wanting to be dressed and out of their bedroom by the time he came home, she carefully checked the two tables, aware that Fin would dislike the vibrant red flowers as much as the ruby-coloured goblets she had recently bought to cheer up the chilly white and silver of their usual dinner tables. There were pristine crystal glasses for each of the three wines they would be drinking, but she thought that the guests could damn well drink their water out of something more colourful, whatever Fin thought about it.

As she went upstairs to dress, Irene did ask herself whether she might perhaps be being unnecessarily provocative, but by the time she reached her first-floor bedroom she knew that she was not. It was essential for her to stand up for herself if she were not to be completely wiped out by Fin, whose strength of will was phenomenal and whose visceral belief in his own superiority had been reinforced by his years in the High Court.

She had moved in with him when she was only eighteen and he thirty-four. In the early days she had let him order her about and tried to pretend that she did not mind. But those days were long over. At forty-six she was determined to become her own woman at last. She had taught herself to challenge Fin whenever he started talking to her as though she were a skivvy or a pupil, and she kept her end up pretty well, but it could be wearing. There were times when she wished that they did not have to argue about every trivial subject that arose, but she was going to carry on fighting until he acknowledged that she was not subject to his control, and that her ideas and wishes were quite as important as his even when they did not coincide.

If he did not like that – and he demonstrably did not – he would have to learn to put up with it. Irene knew that she could not spin out the rest of her days in quiet obedience. After all, she might survive another forty years or more, and she would go mad if she did not find a way to live as herself: not *for* herself, she often said when she was working it all out in the privacy of her mind, but *as* herself.

She had recently been noticing small physical changes and believed that she must be on the brink of the menopause. That was something she was eagerly awaiting, in spite of all the horror stories she had been told of lunacy, night sweats, insatiable sexual appetites, and ungovernable rage and misery. Not at all sure whether she believed the stories, she was entirely convinced that once the change was over she would have become a tough, confident woman who said what she meant, did what she wanted, felt fulfilled, and – with luck – scattered the irritating before her in abject terror. It had never crossed her mind that to outsiders she already appeared to be exactly that; it had often occurred to Helena.

Irene turned on her bathtaps and undressed, no longer avoiding the long mirror as she had done for so many years after her children were born. As part of her journey towards her ideal of confident and forceful serenity, she was trying to train herself to accept both her body and her character as they were, and she no longer pretended that her waist was not disappearing and her upper arms swaying when she moved. Her thighs could be described as fleshy at best, and, however much she reminded herself that they were thinner than those of Rubens's models, she could not quite manage to share his taste for such dimpled amplitude.

Sticking her tongue out at her reflection, she admitted that there was no doubt at all that she looked a great deal better in clothes.

'So what?' she said out loud as she stepped into the hot water. 'No one but Fin sees me without them and he doesn't count. Anyway, he couldn't care less.'

She lay back in reasonable contentment, soaping her arms and breasts and wondering whether it was a sign of good maturity or bad pessimism that she no longer fantasized about demon lovers or felt a frisson of tingling delight when she half-accidentally tweaked one of her nipples.

'Oh, Mum, get real!'

She could almost hear her daughter's derisive voice and felt a treacherous moment of relief that Jane had decided she could not afford either the time or the money to come south from Durham for the dinner. Irene had never believed she would come, but Fin had insisted that she should be asked, pointing out quite reasonably that Jane would have a justified cause of resentment if she discovered that Ivo was going to be there when she had not been invited. Accepting that, and not in the least wanting to hurt her difficult daughter, Irene had written at once. Jane had left it until the last possible moment to ring up and say casually that she would not be coming. Irene could not help thinking that she must have done it on purpose to cause the maximum inconvenience.

It was extraordinary how different her two children were, she thought, making certain that the water was not creeping up between her back and the bath to spoil the expensive arrangement of her hair. They looked fairly similar, although Jane went out of her way to disguise her attractiveness in baggy, uncomplimentary clothes, whereas Ivo, however casual his jeans and shirts, always managed to make himself look good. But in character they were completely different. Ivo was all ease and funniness and sensitive gratitude. Jane was spiky, difficult, argumentative, always in debt, resentful, interfering, and – not to put too fine a point on it – a nuisance; even a bloody awful nuisance sometimes.

Irene often reminded herself that she loved her daughter, and she usually managed to believe it, although she was honest enough to admit that it was much easier to love her from a distance than face to face. When Jane was at home, the irritation she set up in her mother was hard to ignore. Even when she was away she could still cause trouble.

Irene was dreading the scene that was bound to blow up when Fin read their daughter's latest letter. Since it was addressed to him, she had not opened it, but she knew from Ivo's last telephone call that it was likely to contain yet another plea for more money. He had told Irene that Jane was in quite serious debt again and would need at least a thousand pounds to bail her out.

Hearing the unmistakable sound of Fin's car drawing up outside the house, Irene sloshed water over herself to rinse off the soap and got out of the bath, glad that she could still move as easily as she had always done even though she was probably much too heavy. She did not approve of scales and so she had no idea what she weighed, considering that while her bigger skirts and trousers still fitted that was all that really mattered. She heard Fin unlock the front door and knew that he was turning aside into the small cloakroom to change his shoes. He always did that when he came in, even if he were about to change them again for the patent leather ones he wore with his dinner jacket.

He had come out of the cloakroom and was standing still, probably eyeing her huge bowls of flowers and disapproving of something about them, the extravagance probably. He walked a few paces and stopped again. He must have been picking up Jane's letter, which Irene had left for him beside the lilies on the hall chest. There was silence for a moment, then a sigh, and then his footsteps as he started up the stairs.

Irene put on her dressing gown and sat at her dressing table to deal with her makeup. She was still good-looking. There was no doubt about that and it would be silly to pretend otherwise, she decided, peering at her face. With its heavily marked brows, the flashing dark eyes that both Ivo and Jane had inherited, broad cheekbones, wide mouth and firm chin, it had a look of strength and generosity. At least she hoped it did. Her skin was reasonably good, too, even if it did tend to sallowness in the winter. Luckily the first sun always tanned it to a smooth fine gold, and that year it had been sunny since early April. Her nose was less satisfactory, being rather bulbous about the nostrils, but the way the hairdresser had piled up her hair took attention away from that.

Altogether, she admitted as she patted moisturizer into her skin, her face was coarse; magnificent perhaps in some moods, but coarse and best seen from a distance. It would have looked good on a sculpture, or even a stage. She felt the usual sharp regret at the sacrifices she had made before she had any idea how much they were going to cost her.

'Good day?' she asked, smiling politely as Fin's reflection loomed at her in the mirror.

He blinked and turned down the corners of his mouth in an expression that was so excruciatingly familiar that she wanted to swear. 'It could have been worse,' he said as usual. 'Yours?'

'Busy but all right. They took ages doing my hair, but I think I rather like it.'

'Good,' he said, deliberately withholding the compliment that she thought was her due.

'What do you think?' she asked, sternly telling herself that if she wanted something she must, ask for it directly and not try to cheat it out of him. She should have been much too old and sensible to flirt. 'About my hair, I mean. Attractive?'

'It looks fine.' He sounded surprised. 'Quite restrained.'

She wished she had not bothered to ask. Restrained indeed. She leaned nearer the mirror and stroked foundation over the moisturizer. He did not move. She could see that there was no letter in his hand.

'Ivo here yet?'

'No, not yet,' she said. 'But there seems to be a hell of a lot of traffic and so he was probably held up on the M40.'

Fin frowned and she knew that it was because he hated her swearing. Tough, she thought. Get real, Fin, or bugger off. It was hard to suppress a smile but she managed it.

'Isn't he coming by train?' said Fin as though Ivo's lateness must be her fault.

'Apparently not. He's borrowed a van to take some piece of furniture or other to Helena for mending.'

Fin grunted and pulled off his tie. Irene, still waiting for him to mention Jane's letter, was determined not to raise the subject first. That would give him an advantage in the battle that was undoubtedly to come. She painted smooth, fine black lines above her eyelashes, before highlighting the browbones with barely coloured shadow, and then turned her attention to her lips.

She liked her face again by the time she had finished making it up and was hooking some heavy Victorian garnet and gold earrings into her ear lobes. Fin had given her the earrings when they were first married, and there was a matching pendant. The whole set had seemed too big and ornate in the old days and she had not worn it then. Feeling that she had grown into it at last, she had had a dress made especially to go with it. When she was ready, she stood for a moment in front of the mirror admiring herself.

Made of heavy satin the colour of redcurrants, the dress was cut with a high waist and very low neck. A plaited rope of the satin mixed with flat gold cord joined the bodice to the long, tulip-shaped skirt. There was one thing to be said for the gradual sagging of a woman's flesh after forty, Irene thought as she settled her breasts within the dress; given an efficiently uplifting bra, it produced a wonderful cleavage.

She hung the pendant around her neck and straightened it against her skin. Letting her shoulders relax, she lifted her head and smiled regally at herself as Fin emerged from the bathroom, wrapped in his towel.

'What on earth are you wearing?'

Irene's shoulders stiffened again, but she hoped she was managing to keep the regality as she turned slowly away from the mirror.

'Isn't it good? I had it made to go with your glorious garnets. Look.' She touched the heavy pendant.

Fin grunted.

He could never understand why she had to get herself up so theatrically. She had given up all thoughts of acting when she married him and the fact that she had written a play that was about to be staged did not seem to him to be a reasonable excuse to drape herself in suggestively cut, exotically coloured frocks that showed off far too much of her front.

He rubbed his thin frame energetically, shaking his head slightly and wishing that he could fathom what it was that drove her to cause him so much trouble. He supposed that other people might say that it was his fault for having married someone so much younger than himself, but he knew that was nonsense. None of his colleagues' wives had ever been as embarrassing as Irene, even when they were her age.

'What's the matter with it?' she said in the all-too-familiar belligerent voice she had taken to using whenever she intended to make a scene.

Fin tried not to sigh. The last thing he wanted was a wholly unnecessary, manufactured quarrel before their guests arrived. He straightened up.

'Didn't it occur to you that it might be a little flamboyant?' He saw her mocking expression and, stung, said sharply, 'All right, if you must know, I think it's an absurd thing for you to be wearing at your age, far too brightly coloured and immodest. It looks like fancy dress.'

He turned his back and started to pull on his clothes.

'For a man who gets himself up in the sort of idiotic sub-medieval frocks and breeches and patent leather pumps that you wear, my dear,' she said, pretending to sound amused, 'not to speak of your ludicrous wigs, I think that's pretty rich.'

'Judicial dress is completely different, as you very well know,' said Fin coldly, keeping his back to her.

She said nothing and a moment later he heard her leave the bedroom. He hoped that she was going to behave herself during the evening and not talk too much, too loudly, or too unsuitably. That was probably past praying for. He decided that he would settle for her avoiding both smutty jokes and the customary diatribes about the alleged failings of the judiciary.

There had been many occasions on which he had tried to believe that it was not Irene's ludicrous flamboyance and unsuitable conversation that had blocked his career, but he still could not quite manage not to blame her for it. When he looked at Geoffrey Duxford – whom he liked and respected; he really did – he knew that there was nothing Geoffrey had that he, Fin, did not have except for a well-behaved, modest, calmly dressed wife.

Elizabeth Duxford was enchanting. Fin realized that he was smiling as he thought of her. She was getting on, of course; she must be nearly sixty herself, but she was still so pretty with her slender figure, sweet face and impeccably controlled silvery hair, and she never put a foot wrong. Everyone liked her, even Irene, who did not like many of his friends' wives. Elizabeth never caused trouble or made too much noise or showed off, and her clothes were always perfect for the occasion. It was not that she was a goody-goody either; she could flirt with the best of them, but always in such perfect taste, so gently teasing and sweetly affectionate that no-one could take exception to it.

Fin shook his head again and sat on the edge of the bed to pull on his shoes. He hated the fact that his bunions made the patent leather shoes hurt, just as he hated the worsening of his digestion, his increasing inability to sleep properly, and all the rest of the evidence that he was getting old.

After all, he was only sixty-two, and that was no age nowadays. And he still had a memory as sharp as it had ever been. There were some of his colleagues whose difficulties with names and facts made them almost as embarrassing as Irene, but he was still perfectly all right. He heard the sound of a well-used but not at all well-maintained engine outside and walked stiffly across to the window to look down into the street. A battered, filthy, once-white van was being parked just behind his gleaming Rover. His lips tightened in annoyance until he saw Ivo emerging from it and then he smiled. He could not help it. Everyone smiled when they saw Ivo.

He closed the front door without the bang the rest of the family could never resist. Even from the bedroom Fin could hear the boy's traditionally kind greeting to his mother.

'Mama! My God, you look stunning. What a superb dress!'

Irene was standing at the foot of the staircase, glowing under one of the few lights in the hall. She forgot her anger, the following day's meeting, and her dislike of pompous entertaining.

'Your father doesn't like it at all,' she said lightly.

'He'll come round when he sees everyone else fainting in admiration,' said Ivo more quietly, leaning forwards to kiss her. 'You smell delicious, too. What is it?'

'Madame Rochas. I decided it was suitable to my age and station.' Irene laughed at herself. 'It's nice, though, isn't it?'

'Very.'

'You'd better get on and change. They're due any second, Ivo.'

'Yes, I know. Sorry to be so late. I got hung up in traffic coming from Helena's.'

'How is she?'

'Fine, I think. This new bloke of hers seems to be doing her well. Have you met him?'

'No, not yet. She's keeping him firmly under wraps; I'm not sure why. What makes you think it's working?'

'She was looking prettier than usual,' he said with a dryness that was unlike him. He laughed. 'Almost sleek, actually. But she'll be here in no time and you can judge for yourself. I'll look in on Father on my way up, see how he is.'

Irene smiled at Ivo and patted his lean, golden cheek. He bounded off upstairs and she went into the kitchen to make sure her two catering friends were happy with all the arrangements. Later the front door bell rang and she went to open it herself.

Helena was standing on the step, looking surprisingly glamorous in a stunning skirt of baroque-looking damask and a clinging smooth black top. Irene thought she saw what Ivo had meant and held out her arms.

'You look lovely,' she said and was pleased to see Helena's thin, serious face lighten into one of her best smiles.

'Really?'

'Yes.'

'So do you,' Helena answered, coming into the house. 'Glowing and glorious, Irene. Oh, it is good to see you.'

Mindful of her makeup, Irene hugged her stepdaughter instead of kissing her and felt all the usual pleasure when Helena leaned against her and squeezed.

'You feel lovely, too.'

'What, soft and squidgy?' suggested Irene in amusement.

'Just that,' said Helena, with a laugh. 'Heavenly. I don't know how you do it, but you can always make a girl feel safe and wonderful.'

'Not all girls,' said Irene, less cheerfully. She thought of the angrily demanding letter Fin was probably re-reading upstairs. 'I seem to make Jane feel quite the opposite. Come on in and have a drink.'

As they walked together into the big, dark green and gold drawing room, Helena stroked her stepmother's arm and said: 'It's probably just Jane's age. She'll get over it.'

'I hope so, but it's been going on a long time now. And you never went through a stage like that, even though if anyone had the right to be difficult it was you.'

'Wasn't I?'

'You know you weren't.' Irene did ignore her makeup then and kissed Helena, carefully wiping away the lipstick smear afterwards. 'You've been nothing but ease, delight and joy ever since I first saw you. It was the biggest surprise of my life, and one of the most satisfying.'

As Irene smiled at her, Helena looked back with all the passionate gratitude that had been with her for so long. She had been just three when Irene had first picked her up and surrounded her with safety. Until then she had been subject to the frightening ministrations of a variety of disapproving relations and the temporary nannies who had been employed after her mother's disappearance. Her father had been kind in an irritable, preoccupied fashion, but he had never played with her or read to her, still less touched her except when he was inexpertly and impatiently trying to button up her coat or tie her shoelaces. There had been days at a time when he had never smiled and hardly spoken. Helena had been frightened of him then, and, absurd though it was, she knew that she was frightened of him still.

When Irene had appeared in the house, she had changed him almost overnight into a laughing, cheerful, happy man, just as she had transformed Helena herself. From that first day, Helena had been hugged even before she knew she needed it, and all her fears had been taken seriously. Food, which had always been the subject of threatening battles, had become delicious; outings had been planned with full consultation, books bought, games played, and endless stories read.

She could never quite pinpoint the moment when things had

changed between Fin and Irene, but as a child she had feared that it must have been her fault. Irene had certainly not done anything to deserve it.

'How are you?' Helena asked. 'You look a bit tired under all the magnificence. Is everything all right?'

'Pretty much. I'm battling on, you know.' She saw that Helena was looking doubtful and then gave in to honesty: 'To tell you the truth, I'm more than a little scared of meeting Richard Orleton tomorrow.'

'You shouldn't be,' said Helena, deeply relieved that for once it was not Fin who had upset Irene. 'He's the most important director working in London at the moment, and the only one who could possibly take a new playwright's work straight to the West End.'

'Precisely! Although West End is stretching it a bit.'

'Well, London anyway. He chose your play, Irene. It must be good. He never picks a loser. It's the most enormous compliment. But you know all that. You don't need me to reassure you.'

'Yes, I do know that, but . . . Damn, there's the door. Here we go. Be nice to your father when he comes down, won't you? He's in a state about all sorts of things just now, not least Jane's latest debts, and he's tetchy.'

'I'll try,' said Helena, hearing the sound of voices approaching the top of the stairs. She smiled. 'But actually, I'm not sure it's going to be necessary. I think Ivo may already have sorted him.'

While one of the caterers' waitresses was opening the front door and taking the first guest's coat, Irene and Helena both listened to Ivo and his father. Fin's voice was entirely different from the pinched, angry tones in which he had been talking earlier. It almost sounded as though he was enjoying himself. The two women looked at each other in satisfaction.

'Ivo is wonderful,' said Helena so that Irene did not have to say it and could preserve her pretence of maternal detachment.

The dinner went reasonably well. The food was good, if richer than Irene liked and much too conventional for her, and the conversation unbroken. Elizabeth Duxford and Helena both worked hard to support her and make sure that any taciturn guests within reach were stimulated into doing their share of the talking. Geoffrey was becomingly restrained in his self-satisfaction, and he and Fin had a lovely time reminiscing about their early days in chambers when they vied for dreary briefs that hardly paid their train fares to court.

It was half past twelve by the time the last guests had gone and Ivo had disappeared to his own room at the top of the house. Irene was longing for her bed, but it was at that moment that Fin chose to show her Jane's letter and announce that this time, whatever Irene said, he was going to stand firm. Jane was incorrigible and she had to learn the value of money. He was not going to increase her allowance or pay any of her debts. He added in quite unnecessary provocation that if he found that Irene was sending Jane extra money behind his back he would be seriously displeased.

'How can you even say that?' she asked, stung by the injustice. 'I am not deceitful, in spite of all your attempts to make me so.'

'You've always done everything you could to undermine my authority with the children, haven't you?' he said as though she had not spoken. 'I sometimes think that for some bizarre and twisted reason of your own you want them to grow up as feckless and spendthrift as you are yourself.'

She considered holding her tongue, but the implications of his accusation were so outrageous that she had to answer it.

'If you had any idea how hard I've always worked to stop them complaining about you, you wouldn't dare say that. You are a shit, you know, Fin. All it would take to free Jane is a thousand pounds. That's nothing to you and it means the whole world to her at the moment. If I had it, I'd send it straight away, but as you very well know, until I get paid the next tranche of play money, I haven't got anything except the housekeeping.'

'Thank God for that,' he said nastily. 'Jane needs to be shocked into seeing what it is she's risking by this stupidity. She needs the fear to cure her extravagance before it's too late.'

'No-one needs fear,' said Irene passionately, thinking of the completely destructive terror that Fin could still induce in his elder

24

daughter. Jane had inherited enough of her mother's character to ensure that she tended to anger rather than terror, but there was no guarantee that she could not be made to feel afraid.

'On the contrary. It's the only thing that keeps most people in line,' Fin said in a voice that brooked no argument.

Irene shook her head, almost giving up. After a moment she realized she could not leave it there or he would think he had won.

'You're wrong,' she said. 'I know you can't bear to admit that, but you should. Being afraid is foul, and it does nothing but harm. It makes people stupid and irrational. We mustn't do that to Jane. I want her to have some money, but please don't let's argue about it now. We can deal with it tomorrow.'

'You simply will not discuss anything in a reasonable manner, will you?' thundered Fin, glaring at her. 'You throw out these statements about what you think we should do and if I show any sign of disagreement you sulk and refuse to listen. We have to—'

'Yes, I know we do,' said Irene quickly, 'but tomorrow, Fin, please. I've got my first meeting with Richard Orleton about the play in the morning. I must sleep or I'll be stupid and not operate properly and waste this opportunity.' She did her best to keep any hint of victimhood out of her face and voice as she added: 'It's seriously important to me. Please let me sleep.'

They were still arguing at a quarter to two.

# Chapter Three

At half past three that morning Helena woke with a headache and a queasy feeling in the pit of her stomach. Neither was the result of a hangover. She rarely drank enough to have any effect at all and never in her father's company. One and a half glasses of wine could not have made even a teetotaller tight.

She lay for a moment, wondering what had woken her. It could, she supposed, have been either the heat or indigestion from all the rich food. There was certainly an uncomfortable tightness in her gut. Rolling over on to her front to ease it and turning her head to the left, she decided it was not so much what she had eaten as the tension that gripped her whenever she saw that her father and Irene were on the brink of one of their battles.

Ivo had worked wonders, but the way Fin had looked at Irene throughout the evening, and the coldness with which he had spoken to her after the guests had left, had made it all too clear that he was furiously angry about something. When Helena had tried to sympathize with Irene as they said good night, Irene had shrugged and said something about his complete unreasonableness, adding: 'I sometimes think it's impossible to believe that he managed to produce a daughter as kind as you. No two people could be less alike.'

Giving up hope of a quick return to sleep, Helena pushed back the light duvet, intending to fetch a glass of water. Just as she swung her legs to the ground, she heard the sound of angry sobbing through the thin party wall and then a loud male voice, shouting: 'Oh, stop snivelling, you maggot-faced bitch.'

Franny and Jack Thompson, who had lived next door for the

past two years, had once been the best of good neighbours. Helena liked both of them. She had always fed their two fat tabby cats whenever the Thompsons were away and watched their house for damage or burglars, and they did the same for her. Franny was a potter and Jack a teacher, and until recently they had seemed entirely happy with their life and with each other.

All that had changed in the last few months, and the sound of their rows was becoming an almost daily occurrence. Ordinary conversation came through the wall as a kind of low buzzing sound with indistinguishable words, but raised voices were easily audible. Helena tried never to listen to what they were shouting at each other, but it was not always possible to avoid it. That night, without even any traffic noise to compete, their argument might have been taking place in her bedroom.

Helena had always detested loud voices even when they were not angry, and real arguments, laced as the Thompsons' usually were with tears and the sound of a fist crashing into the wall, filled her with a mixture of irrational fear and a flooding anger of her own. If she had been able to do anything to help them it might not have been so bad, but she knew perfectly well that there was nothing she could do. She went downstairs to drink a glass of water in the kitchen.

It should have been possible for her to ring the Thompsons up and tell them that she could hear everything they were yelling at each other, to knock on the front door and ask whichever of them appeared to keep a little quieter, or even to bang on the wall to remind them how thin it was, but she could not bring herself to do any of it. Ashamed of her ludicrous over-sensitivity to something that was no threat to her, and of her cowardice in not telling her neighbours how much their noise disturbed her, she fetched her duvet and wax earplugs and lay down on the drawing room sofa. From there she could still just hear them, but once she put in the earplugs she had peace again.

Even so, she could not get back to sleep until well after five and then she was disturbed by wildly tangled dreams, in most of which she was trying to grab hold of Franny to save her from some agonizing fate but unable to make her hear or catch up with her. Eventually, some time after eight, Helena gave up trying to sleep and made herself some coffee. There was complete silence from next door.

Her tongue felt furry and her eyes were burning, but she thought that strong coffee might set her to rights. The first sip tasted so unpleasant that she poured the coffee down the sink and drank some apple juice instead.

Later, as she read the newspaper in her bath, she realized that she was not going to be able to do any of the delicate work on the girandole for some time. Her hands were steady enough, but her mind felt fogged and she doubted that she would achieve the concentration she needed to ensure that she did not damage the gold leaf.

Dropping the paper on the floor, she sank down under the water, sluicing it through her fine hair and letting it smooth over her hot, painful eyelids. At least working for herself meant that she could decide to take a morning off without exploiting colleagues or causing trouble to anyone. She sat up and washed her hair, rubbing vigorously at her scalp.

Later, wrapped in a towel, she went downstairs to see whether a fresh pot of coffee would taste any better than the first. Half ashamed of the self-indulgence of her life, she took the coffee back to bed. There she lay, with her wet hair spread out on a towel over the pillow, drinking, reading, and only gradually understanding that the suppressed guilt at lazing in bed instead of working was making her feel even worse than she had before. Inertia kept her lying down, even though by then she knew she would feel better if she got up and did something useful.

Only the telephone made her move when it rang soon after half past ten.

'Hello?' she said, using her customary unhelpful response.

'Helena, it's Mike. How are you?'

'Fine,' she said as usual, instead of: lazy, badly slept, ashamed of myself and jangled. But the sound of his deep, unurgent voice made her smile. 'What about you?'

'Not bad at all. Look, I've had an unexpected escape today. I was supposed to be lunching with some clients who were due in on the Red Eye this morning, but they've been held up in New York. Fog apparently. I don't want to interrupt you if you're working, but I did just wonder whether we might have lunch together. Is there any chance?'

'Oh, what a heavenly idea! I haven't been feeling at all like work, but not-work hasn't been doing what I wanted either. Would you like to come here?'

'That was rather what I had in mind,' he said with an appealing mixture of hesitancy and suggestiveness in his slow voice. As usual it was tinged with laughter, as though he found the whole of life a pleasant entertainment. Helena loved his lighthearted confidence.

'Good. I'll expect you about one, then,' she said, remembering the previous Saturday when he had come to lunch and they had spent three glorious hours together in bed before picnicking on fruit and cheese.

Their affair was quite new and they were still learning each other's codes and discovering the unexpected vulnerabilities that lay hidden behind the masks they showed to the rest of the world, but so far it was going really rather well. They had known each other casually for some time, having several friends in common, but neither had taken much notice of the other until they had been to stay in the same house one weekend at the end of February.

It had been a lugubrious couple of days, damned by cold grey skies and unremitting rain, and the only diversion had been provided by their hosts' horribly obvious dislike of one another. Helena and Mike had been the only guests. She had arrived first and by the time she had been in the house for an hour she had realized that she had been invited so that Harriet and George Bromyard need not speak to each other or be alone together. Helena had been tempted to invent a reason to flee back to London at once. Something about the desperate pleading in Harriet's face had made it impossible to go, and Helena had done her best to chatter away merrily and appear to be enjoying herself.

Mike's arrival two hours after hers had given all three of them some much-needed relief, and Helena had watched in silent admiration as he single-handedly started to change the laborious conversation into real talk. She still did not know how he had done it, but she had followed his lead, agreed to play every game he had suggested throughout the weekend, helped Harriet cook and gone out for walks with George, listening to them both and doing her best not to side with either. By the end of the weekend, she had been exhausted and had driven back to London noticing almost nothing in her longing to be in her own empty, quarrel-less house, where she could nearly always sleep.

The following day Mike had telephoned, told her how much he had admired the way she had dealt with the Bromyards and invited her to have dinner with him in a well-regarded restaurant in Chelsea.

Helena had liked him even more on his own and they had seen each other two or three times each week since then. It had not been long before she began to think they might end up as lovers and to realize how much she wanted that. Her last relationship had collapsed nearly eighteen months earlier, and she had not been tempted to surrender her safe solitude until she had got to know Mike. It was beginning to seem less satisfactory, but she had enjoyed the interval of celibacy so much that she wanted to surrender her solitude freely and not have it wheedled out of her after a series of well-used courtship rituals.

When Mike sent her a large but informal bunch of garden flowers with a carefully judged – and quite amusing – amorous note, she had rung him up to thank him and, to her own surprise as much as his, added: 'But don't let's go through all that performance. I should very much like to go to bed with you and it seems silly at my age to start pretending that I wouldn't in order to inflame your passions or persuade you that I'm not what my stepmother still calls an easy lay.'

She had heard him laugh and added more confidently: 'If you feel the same, would you like to come round to supper tonight?'

That had been the beginning and she had quickly discovered that Mike was as responsive and amusing in bed as out of it. She still felt that she knew about him only what he was prepared to let her know, but she was almost always content in his company and often felt very nearly safe with him. She had never yet been to his house, although he had invited her there more than once.

Each time they had arranged to meet it had seemed easier for them both if he came to Clerkenwell, and she thought she had detected a hint of relief whenever she said as much. Mike had certainly never pressed any of his invitations and had recently fallen into the habit of ringing up to ask whether he could come and visit her, without even mentioning his own house.

The prospect of seeing him unexpectedly in the middle of the day was so cheering that she ignored her still-uneasy stomach and aching head and quickly got dressed in clean shorts and T-shirt. She changed the sheets and tidied her already impeccable bedroom before nipping over to the workshed to inspect the gilding on the girandole.

Having checked the patch and seen that it really was as unobtrusive as she had thought the previous evening, she moved to the far end of the shed to have another look at Ivo's desk. As her close examination of the dowels, the patination, the rust marks left by the screws and all the other signs of authenticity began to make her think that against all the odds the desk might be genuine, she became so engrossed that she forgot Mike's imminent arrival. Her hair kept falling into her eyes and so she bundled it up in a new rubber band and began to jot down notes, describing the piece in full and outlining every flaw, whether or not she thought it should be corrected.

To Helena's taste, there was little worse than furniture so heavily restored that it looked like a reproduction, but she always made a careful list of even the slightest marks and chips in the veneer before deciding how much she wanted to do to a piece. Even then she would discuss the whole project with her client to make absolutely certain that they were in complete agreement about the repairs she planned to make and the flaws she intended to leave as they were.

She was soon so absorbed that she completely forgot her headache, the fight between Franny and Jack that had woken her, and her dislike of the barely suppressed aggression between her father and Irene. At one moment, when she dropped her pencil and had to grovel on the floor for it, she remembered how reluctant she had been to get down to work and laughed at herself. It had happened so often before that she could not understand why she never remembered that work was the only thing that invariably made her feel better.

When Mike rang her buzzer, she was still there, squatting down between the desk and the wall, checking the backboards. It took her a moment to lever herself out and, when she saw on the monitor that he was dressed in full City fig and realized how grubby she must look, she laughed.

'What's so funny?' he said over the intercom. 'Have I gone green?'

'Nothing of the sort,' she said, pressing the buzzer. 'At least not as far as I can see, but the screen's only black and white. Come on in. I'll meet you in the hall.'

He was standing, peering at his face in the long, triptych-like mirror she had hanging over the hall radiator. As so often when she saw him after an interval apart, she was struck by the unlikeliness of his looks.

Taller than Ivo, he was more substantial too, with big shoulders and strong thighs. He dressed with all the expensive conventionality expected of successful City men, but his amusing face and the coarse, mousy hair that would never lie tidily flat saved him from sleekness. He had a big, almost spreading nose and a flat, wide smile, which always made her think of a duck; the nicest kind of duck, as she would remind herself whenever she felt it might be an unfair comparison. His brown eyes were usually narrowed in amusement and his dark lashes were considerably longer and thicker than hers. He looked kind, aware, intelligent and fun. So far, to her surprise, he had lived up to his appearance.

'I can't see anything odd at all,' he said, still examining his reflection, 'except for my dreadful nose.'

'It isn't and, anyway, I told you there was nothing wrong,' she said, waiting for him to kiss her. 'You just didn't believe me.'

Mike straightened up to smile at her. Almost at once his face changed. The amusement left his eyes. Realizing with dismay that he was frowning at her clothes, Helena glanced down at her sweaty, dusty legs. For an uncomfortable moment she wondered whether he could have expected her to dress up for him in black lace suspenders or something even worse. The knowledge that he had never even hinted at such a thing did not help.

'What is it?' she said almost as coldly as her father might have spoken.

'I thought you weren't working this morning,' Mike said, sounding accusatory. Helena took a step backwards. 'I'd never have come if I'd known I was disturbing you.'

'You're not,' she said, sighing in relief. She brushed some of the cobwebs off her shorts and moved closer to him again. 'And this wasn't really work anyway. Yesterday my brother brought me a desk he's just acquired, and I was having a look at it to see how much restoration it needs. It's such a lovely piece that I got carried away. Don't worry about it.'

'But I do. I know that nothing would make you clam up so quickly as my assuming rights over your time – or you.'

'I won't hug you,' she said, 'because I'm so grubby, but will you consider yourself hugged and stop talking nonsense?'

His face lightened then and he kissed her at last, keeping his suit well away from the dust.

'Good,' she said when he let her go. 'Now would you like some food while I clean up or . . . ?'

'Why don't we just go up and have a bath together?' he suggested and was enchanted when he saw her blush.

When he had first met her some years earlier, he had thought she was one of the most guarded women he had ever seen, and he had always assumed that she would turn out to be dreary if he bothered to get to know her. Her heroic attempts to deal with the unspeakable weekend that had been imposed on them both by the miserable Bromyards had interested him because they seemed so unexpected in the woman he had thought she was. Later, as he had seen more of her, she had revealed glimpses of a character he found unexpectedly appealing.

Since then, he had discovered that when she was at ease and happy she could be the best companion he had ever known. Aware of aspects of him that no-one else had ever understood, terrifically affectionate – and often very funny – she had got past all his defences. He longed to make her feel safe enough to show her real self all the time. So far he thought he was doing pretty well, but there was still a long way to go.

He had come to think of her as one of those sea creatures that inhabit discarded empty shells and only occasionally ease out of them in the sea itself. There were times when he wished he could think of a more attractive image, for the creatures were, as far as he could remember from some old natural history films, disgustingly sluglike or unpleasantly scuttly; but there was nothing else that quite expressed Helena's forays out of her shell and the inevitable quick retreats as she remembered her fear of dangers that he suspected would turn out to be wholly imaginary if he could ever discover what they were.

If the extent of her need for protection surprised him, then so did her unexpected flashes of bravado. It had appalled him to discover that she had no anxiety about walking alone, after dark, through the streets of London. Whenever he challenged her, she just laughed and reminded him that she had been doing it for years, that Clerkenwell was her home, and that she was not going to give way to the fear whipped up by media stories of the relatively few serious assaults that were actually suffered by Londoners.

'Listen,' she had said to him once. 'I don't carry a handbag, I never wear jewellery, I'm always in jeans or trousers of some sort when I'm walking home. Why should anyone attack me? They never have.'

Surprised by her easy dismissal of physical danger when she had confessed that in the past she had been made almost ill by fantastic fears of all sorts, he had stopped trying to persuade her to change her ways.

He had also come to see that the idiosyncratic working life she had created for herself was peculiarly suited to her. The thought of her tackling any of the worlds, like the financial one in which he worked, where aggression was a prerequisite and at least an appearance of unassailable self-confidence vital made him shudder. There were times when even he found it tough, and he had spent fifteen years at it and knew well enough what was expected of him and how to provide it.

Leaving the noisy world of his work for the quiet of Helena's house was often hard. Sometimes he did not manage to adjust quickly enough and would see her shrivel in front of him as he spoke in the voice he would have used to a colleague: impatient, pulling no punches, insisting on his own way. With Helena it was crucial to pull all punches if he wanted her to feel safe.

She was looking up at him with the best of her smiles, almost confident, slightly naughty, wholly affectionate.

'Come on, Mike,' she said. 'Let's bath. There should be plenty of hot water.'

By the time he had wrapped her in soft towels and, in spite of her ludicrous protests that she was too heavy for him, carried her to her bed, they were both laughing. He laid her down on the dark blue duvet and unfolded the white towels from her thin body.

Later, when Mike was lying slumped against her, Helena stroked his hair and kissed him and forgot about having to worry about anything at all. Whatever happened in the future, they had what they had and were able to give to each other, and that was all that mattered.

After a while she realized that he was asleep and, feeling restless as she nearly always did when he went away from her into unconsciousness, she slid out of bed and went downstairs to see what food there might be for lunch.

She rarely ate elaborate meals and did not like cooking anything much except vegetables, eggs or pasta. There were some red onions left and so she cut two of them almost into quarters and put them into the oven to roast in olive oil with some halved red peppers, before opening a tin of anchovies, and washing a bag of watercress.

She often worried about Mike's heart since he worked so ferociously hard and appeared to live on the worst possible kind of food when he was alone – butter, cheese, bacon, and take-away meals that were full of salt and fat – and she liked to feed him on all the foods that were currently supposed to prevent heart disease. He did not much like walnuts, but she sneaked them into her simple cooking whenever possible, along with broccoli, olive oil, other approved vegetables, lots of garlic and as much red wine as possible.

Mike usually slept for nearly an hour after they made love and even the onions should be cooked by then. She poured herself a glass of mineral water mixed with elderflower cordial, smiling at the memories of Ivo that the scent evoked, and went to lie on the sofa in the drawing room to read until Mike should happen to wake. Serenely happy, she had no need of the previous night's comforting novel and took up a new book about fakes and art-market scandals she had been reading with a mixture of interest and alarm.

When the telephone rang she was furious, both with the unknown caller, who should have known that someone might be sleeping in the middle of a sunny May afternoon and with herself for forgetting to switch on the answering machine.

'Yes?' she said crossly when she had grabbed the receiver.

'Ms Webton? Helena Webton?' said a fruity male voice that she did not recognize.

'Yes.'

'Ah, excellent. I have just acquired some eighteenth-century chairs – Chippendale – that need restoration and you've been recommended to me by several people recently. They're a trifle wormy, one or two of the legs wobble, the arm of one of the carvers is split, and all the C scrolls need tidying up. Would you be prepared to have a look at them for me and give me a price?'

'Who are you?' she said much less politely than she would normally have spoken, and she held her dressing gown more tightly across her chest.

'My name is Dean Swift.'

'And who exactly was it who told you that I might do some

work for you?' she asked, suppressing a laugh as she thought about the names he might produce next. John Dryden would probably fit best with Swift, or even Elkanah Settle. She wondered what his real name might be.

'You sound remarkably suspicious, my dear,' he said in the most patronizing voice she had heard for some time. 'I hear your name all over the place, sale rooms, other dealers, that sort of thing.'

'I see,' she said, trying to sound reasonably civil.

'So, when will you come to look at my chairs?'

'I'm afraid that I am very busy just now, and I really don't think that I could take on any more work for at least six months.' Helena gritted her teeth and added: 'But it was kind of you to think of me.'

The politeness seemed wasted since he did not bother to say anything else at all. When he had put down his receiver she thought of dialling 1471 to find out where he was ringing from in an attempt to identify him, but then decided that she would prefer not to know.

'What was all that about?'

Helena turned and, seeing Mike tying the cord of the dressing gown she had bought him a couple of weeks earlier, went to hug him.

'Lunch?' she said after a moment and was relieved when he did not repeat his question about the telephone call. She wanted to forget it.

'Lovely,' he said, pushing both hands through his untidy hair and shrugging his big shoulders until the silk of the dressing gown sat more comfortably on them. He turned to look at the clock over the fireplace.

Helena waited to hear that he was going to have to get back to the office and told herself that she would not mind if he did since she had plenty of things to do and they had had a pleasant time together and nothing else mattered. He was always busy, but, even if he had not been, she would have done her best to avoid seeming clingy. From the beginning she had schooled herself to smile and encourage him to go whenever he showed the first signs of thinking about leaving.

'Although tea would be more accurate,' he said.

The powerful rush of delight that flooded through Helena surprised her. She told herself that she could not possibly mind that much about whether Mike stayed or left.

'Except that tea would have to be cucumber sandwiches and little pink cakes,' she said, trying to sound relaxed. 'Let's eat in the kitchen – if you don't mind?'

'Not at all. Best place. Was your telephone call very private? You sounded quite unlike yourself, hard and rather angry.'

'Did I?' she said, realizing that she would have to say something to explain why she was reluctant to talk about it. 'No, it wasn't private at all; just a man wanting me to do some work, but he seemed more than a bit shifty.'

'In what way?'

Helena shrugged and added reluctantly: 'Well . . . the name he used must have been false. But, worse than that, he refused to tell me who had recommended me. I may be neurotic, but I won't work for people I know nothing about.'

Mike, who had been smiling at her unabashed admission of neurosis, quickly said: 'Quite right. None of us can these days. KYC is crucial. We din it into all our new recruits before almost anything else.'

'KYC?'

'Know your customer. In these days of money-laundering it's absolutely vital. When you can get fourteen years for assisting a money-launderer and five for just not reporting your suspicions, you can't take any chances. We screen all our new clients these days as carefully as though we were MI6.'

'I'm glad to hear it,' said Helena, marvelling once again that anyone could survive in the world in which Mike apparently felt so at home. 'Thank heavens I don't have to worry about that.'

'Don't you?' Mike wondered whether Helena could really be as ignorant as she sounded of the use money-launderers made of the art market. As he knew better than most, transactions in antiques and paintings were among the simplest ways of disguising the origins of dirty money. Remembering how easily spooked she could be, he thought it might be better not to enlighten her for the moment at least.

'No, I don't. I never deal in furniture. I just restore the stuff. All I have to worry about is whether I'm working on stolen property or having any contact with the sort of iffy dealers who ask restorers to produce fakes or made-up pieces.'

'And that's what this man was?'

'I thought he might have been, not least because he talked of the C scrolls needing to be tidied up.'

'What's the problem with that?'

'"Tidying up" is the kind of code some bent dealers use to ask restorers to add something like the C scrolls that prove a piece was made by Chippendale. It's much the same as a picture restorer being asked to ink in a signature that's said to have been washed away in the cleaning of a watercolour.'

'But you haven't any actual proof that's what this man was after, have you?'

'No. But even if he were legit, there'd be no point my risking it. I have quite enough honest work these days from people I know are trustworthy without having to take on dubious strangers who come without an introduction.'

'Bully for you,' Mike said, trying to sound casual. He yawned and sat down in the chair furthest from the cooker. 'Something smells wonderful. I hope you weren't slaving while I was asleep?'

'Certainly not.' Helena was surprised by the abrupt change of subject but accepted it without comment. 'You'll see how simple it is in a moment. Wine? There's some nice red in the rack.'

Mike shook his head. 'I'll have to go back and work this evening. My clients are due in at dawn tomorrow.' He paused, and then, apparently unaware that he might be revealing an anxiety of his own, added: 'Do you mind that I came round now rather than tonight?'

'I don't know how you knew, but it was the most perfect thing you could possibly have done,' she said, touching his hand, more worried about his anxiety than any feeling of her own.

She told him a little about her noisy neighbours, adding: 'And in any case, I was feeling pretty ghastly after a dinner at my father's last night and knew I wouldn't be able to work. When you rang, it all changed. Bliss, as my stepmother would say.'

'Would she?' Mike's face had lost some of its humour again. 'Helena, when are you going to let me meet the family?'

She stiffened and turned away to arrange the food on a long, white plate. Knowing that her movements were jerky, she deliberately made them smoother, hating the thought that he might misinterpret her reluctance as criticism. Since she detested being criticized herself, she did everything she could to agree with people she liked, and expressing any real complaint or anger could make her feel like a murderer. It took a great deal to push her into saying anything negative and when she did she worried about the consequences for days.

'Don't try to change it,' she said, biting her lip. She felt Mike's hand on her back through the thin cotton of her dressing gown. 'Please.'

'I'm not trying to change anything,' he said with careful gentleness. 'But I want to know more of you, to feel more included in your life. Is that so odd? You say that your parents' dinner was ghastly, but . . .'

'You wouldn't have liked it,' she said hastily. 'And anyway, my father doesn't know anything about you, and even if he did he'd have made a fuss if I'd tried to get you invited. He's . . .'

'That sounds as though your stepmother at least does know about me.'

'Well, yes, in fact she does.'

Mike turned her around so that she was leaning back against the worktop. Trying not to let the impatience make him sound angry or critical, he said lightly: 'And does she approve of what she knows?'

He was rewarded for his patience when Helena smiled. 'Yes, and she's told me she envies us the freedom that we have.'

'Freedom?' He frowned and then his face relaxed as he provided his own answer. 'You mean to meet and frolic in the middle of a working day like this? It is pretty amazing, although I don't often get the chance to skive off like this.'

'It's partly that, but probably more that we're free to see each other when we want and not see each other if we don't. It's heaven to me to be sure that you see me only because you want to. I couldn't bear it if you – if either of us – felt some kind of obligation or had to pretend about anything.'

Mike took his hands away from her narrow hips and went to sit down again.

'Don't you see?' Helena said urgently, wanting him to understand and, if possible, agree with her. 'That's what makes this so safe. We have our own houses; we don't owe each other anything . . .'

'Don't we?' He sounded almost harsh, quite unlike himself. She blinked.

'I was going to say: anything except honesty and love while we feel it,' she said with as much calm dignity as she could manage.

'That suggests you envisage the love stopping.' Mike was sounding more and more distant.

She shook her head, hoping that he was not about to get angry. The soft fair hair had slipped across her eyes so that she could hardly see him. He had never shown any anger, but she was sure that there was some in him somewhere and she dreaded finding it.

'It would be silly to pretend it could never happen,' she said, hoping to placate him. 'And like this we don't have to keep wondering if it already has. This way we can just enjoy it. If it ends tomorrow then it ends, but today isn't spoiled, whatever happens, unless we get to the point where we have to watch each other to see if tomorrow might have come today. Don't you understand?'

'Yes,' he said. Knowing how much reassurance she needed to make her feel even fairly secure, he suppressed his irritation and smiled. Helena brushed the hair away from her face but she did not smile back.

'I understand,' he said, 'and I almost sympathize, even though I don't agree with it at all.'

'Lunch,' she said decisively, filling his plate and putting it down in front of him.

What she had never felt able to explain to him was that while they were visitors in each other's lives, they were not at risk of what had happened to Franny and Jack, the Bromyards, Fin and Irene, and in fact to most of the couples she knew well. The thought of finding herself trapped in an angry relationship like any of those filled her with horror. She would rather have lived entirely alone than at war with someone she loved.

She had grown up subject to disabling panic attacks, which she had more or less conquered by learning to avoid the stresses that triggered them. Feeling herself at fault had always been one of the worst, and there was nothing like being the target of someone else's anger to make her feel in the wrong.

The attacks had always seemed to her to be like savage animals, leaping on her from nowhere, sinking their teeth into the back of her neck and then worrying her from side to side until she had lost all ability to think sensibly or do anything to help herself. She had been free of them for some time but she was not cocky enough to believe that she had overcome them for good and, dreading them so much, she would have done anything she could to prevent them.

# Chapter Four

Irene lay awake for more than an hour after Fin had finally stopped yelling at her about Jane's debts. She was bitterly angry with him, not only for his lack of generosity to the daughter who had always adored him and taken his part in everything, but also because he had forced Irene to tell him how much she dreaded her meeting with Richard Orleton. Her one comfort was that Fin could have had no idea why she was concerned.

She had not spoken to Richard for nearly thirty years and she did not know whether he remembered her at all. They had met during her first year at drama school, when he was a star – *the* star, really – of the third year. Everyone had admired him, in spite of his sarcastic tongue and dangerous reputation. Looking back, she tried to work out why he had seemed quite so desirable when he was known to be untrustworthy and often foul to people.

It was partly, of course, because he was thought to be brilliant and destined for the top. He was also attractive, and in a rather unlikely way for an actor, with a long thin body and a surprising face with delicate features under soft, gleaming blond hair. In fact he looked more like a scholar than an actor, but there was an aura of power around him that few scholars could boast.

Irene had never been able to work out just where Richard's power had come from, and she still could not decide. His reputation for rejecting people who adored him too obviously did him no harm; nor did his angry restlessness and his cutting tongue. And when he chose to bestow himself on someone he could make them feel almost godlike for a while.

For a time, a short time, he had chosen Irene. She had been at the Theatre School for only a few weeks when he first came near her. By then she had had to face the fact that her triumphs in school plays had nothing at all to do with whatever it was her new tutors were trying to teach her. Every day, she had to struggle to understand what they wanted her to do, let alone actually do any of it. She was alone in London for the first time in her life, aware that her family disapproved of the whole idea of the stage, lonely and frighteningly incompetent about the practicalities of living with three other girls in a rented flat.

Then one morning Richard had strolled in to one of her classes and everything had changed. Leaning against the wall he had watched the efforts of the ten nervous beginners, who had all recognized him instantly and become even more fumblingly inefficient than usual. Afterwards he had spoken to Irene and told her that she really had something, and that none of the other girls in her year had it.

The other students who had overheard him teased Irene for days afterwards, telling her that Richard just wanted to get into her knickers. That was a phrase she had not heard until then, but it was easily understood. Furiously angry, she had done her best to ignore them, and Richard too.

For the next few weeks he would often appear during her classes, but he showed no sign of wanting to seduce her. After a while, he casually suggested taking her to have a cup of coffee after class. She declined. He tried again a few days later. Eventually she accepted and found that she enjoyed herself. Thereafter it became a fixture of the day. Richard would pick her up at the end of the morning's classes and take her across the road to the little café opposite the school. They would sit at either side of one of the red formica-topped tables and talk about acting. Irene had sometimes thought that the little she learned of the craft had come from Richard and not from the terrifying tutors with their incomprehensible Stanislavskian instructions.

Slowly she had begun to feel more at ease with him and had even, privately at first, begun to fantasize about how they might one day act together. The dreams had grown wilder and less and less confined to work, especially after he had taken her out to dinner in a tiny restaurant with a dance floor on which they had swayed, plastered against each other, for a delirious two hours one night. So happy had she become, and so nearly confident, that she had idiotically confided some of her hopes to one of her flatmates that night.

Irene had never discovered whether the flatmate had passed on the luscious bit of gossip so that it had reached Richard's ears and made him drop her or whether the timing of his dismissal had been coincidental. Apart from one or two encounters at the local swimming pool, he had hardly ever spoken to her again and there had been no more shared dinners or even cups of coffee.

The combination of that humiliation, and the much greater loneliness that threatened to submerge her after Richard had stopped talking to her, had made Irene loathe everything about the Theatre School. But she had never been a quitter and had been determined to stick with it and let no-one guess how awful she felt. Thinking of ways to show how little she cared about the malicious amusement her predicament had caused, she planned to appear at the beginning of the second term in devastatingly glamorous new clothes. Her allowance would not stretch to the sort of things she wanted to buy and so she looked for a temporary and well-paid job to do during the Christmas vacation.

The first position she was offered was as nanny to three-year-old Helena Webton. Accepting it without a second's thought, Irene had written to her parents to say that she would not be home for the holidays. They had remonstrated with her, but she had stuck to her decision.

Almost before she had unpacked and learned her way about Fin's gloomy house, she had discovered the balm of Helena's uncritical and apparently unalterable devotion. It was not long before Fin himself had come to seem almost as needy as his daughter and very nearly as appealing.

Handsome, tormented by the loss of his wife, working ferociously hard and obviously being brilliantly successful at what he did, he had seemed even more glamorous than Richard. Fin had also been much older and infinitely more sophisticated. The result was probably inevitable. Irene had never gone back to the Theatre School.

Life with Fin could probably never have remained on the plateau of bliss she had found at first, but after Ivo's birth it had for a time become so bleak that she had begun to recast her memories of her brief time at drama school, concentrating on the few happy ones and persuading herself that the confusion and humiliation had not been so bad after all. Slowly she had rediscovered her old fantasies of acting with Richard and finding transcendental happiness in his arms before they took theatrical London by storm together.

With the familiar sound of imaginary applause in her ears she drifted off to sleep at last. It seemed only an instant before the alarm clock woke her at half past seven and she dragged herself out of bed in a fury of resentment to make Fin's breakfast.

As she automatically boiled the kettle and the eggs and put bread in the toaster, Irene tried to forget her own rage and think sensibly of how best to persuade Fin to send Jane some money. It crossed Irene's mind that one way might be to urge him not to send Jane anything at all and force her to face up to her debts herself. But, as Irene had told him, she was not deceitful and she hated the thought of resorting to that kind of manipulation. Besides, she did not see why she should stoop so low just to make him feel more comfortable about what he ought to be doing.

She heard him coming into the kitchen and turned to open fire. He smiled at her, which was so unusual first thing in the morning that it made her pause before saying anything.

'I'm sure that it will go well today, Irene,' he said as he sat down at the table. He did not even pick up the newspaper. In amazed silence she poured his coffee.

'Orleton's judgement is known to be sound and he has chosen *The House on the Canal*. You really do not need to be so nervous about it. It is undoubtedly a good piece of work. You should remember that.'

'Perhaps,' she said, pouring her own coffee. 'Although it's hard not to worry.' Recognizing his gesture for what it was, she added as pleasantly as she could: 'Thank you, Fin.'

'That's all right,' he said as he picked up his newspaper and folded it open at the Law Reports as usual.

Irene felt cowardly as she fetched his boiled egg and toast and sat down opposite him in silence, but there was nothing she could do about it. After his almost unprecedented kindness, she could not bring herself to restart the battle over Jane's debts. She hated the thought of her daughter's being left in a noose of anxiety any longer than was absolutely necessary and hoped that the tension would not drive her into doing something stupid.

As she acknowledged that fear, Irene corrected herself at once. She knew that whatever Jane might do it would never be stupid. Irene promised herself and her absent daughter that she would tackle Fin properly and force him to do the right thing when they both got back to the house that evening. One more day would not make all that much difference to Jane and it might make quite a large difference to her parents.

Fin left for court at his usual time without saying anything else at all, and Irene went upstairs to get ready for her meeting. Wishing that her brain were sharper and her face less ragged-looking, she dressed with care, wanting to make it plain to Richard (if by any chance he should have remembered her) that she was no longer the ingenuous, manipulable girl he had known, but a confident, well-off, talented and sophisticated woman.

A suit seemed much too formal and middle-aged, but most of her good clothes were suits, chosen for occasions on which she had to play up to her role as a judge's wife.

In the end, after an hour of dressing and undressing and a brief foray into the garden to check the temperature, she settled on a baggy peacock-blue jacket over a shocking pink shirt tucked into a pair of very dark purple coarse linen trousers. She was tempted to wrap a bright yellow silk belt around her non-existent waist, but she thought that might be going too far.

Looking at herself in the mirror, glad that she had managed to recreate most of the effect the hairdresser had produced the previous day, she thought of Fin's likely comments about her choice of clothes. Parrots would, she was sure, have figured somewhere in his insults.

'Well, Fin can go stuff himself,' she said aloud and with great satisfaction.

By the time she got to the building where Richard had his permanent office, much of her confidence had dissolved. She felt her heart banging in her chest. Her hands were sweating disgustingly, too, and she had to find a cloakroom so that she could wash and dry them before she had to risk shaking his. It was absurd at her age to be nervous, but, absurd or not, that was what she was.

She was deeply relieved she had washed her hands when she was shown into his office five minutes later. He was sitting at a big polished wooden desk, reading a file when his secretary opened the door and announced Irene. She thought he looked like any middle-aged man at work. The blond hair had gone completely grey and he was wearing tortoiseshell spectacles.

Then he looked up, and she almost took a step backwards. His long face with the finely marked, arched eyebrows, thin skin and beautiful mouth was instantly recognizable. There were many more lines on his face, marking the creases made by both smiles and frowns, and he looked much older than his forty-eight years. As he smiled, she saw that his firing enthusiasm was unchanged.

He took off his glasses as though to see her better, flung them down on the desk on top of the file he had been reading, shoved back his chair with a huge crash, and stood up with both arms outstretched.

'Irene! My God! I'd have known you anywhere.'

She had not heard that voice for nearly thirty years and would not have been able to describe it to anyone, but it was instantly familiar: light but edged with all the old exciting, dangerous ambivalence. As he came round the desk to where she was standing she remembered the frequent and always useless efforts her fellow-students had made to copy it.

He seized both her hands and kissed them.

'But you're far more gorgeous than I ever thought you'd become. Isn't this fun? Come and sit down. I couldn't believe it at first. I read your stunning play and thought, "Lumme! I've stumbled on something here." And then I found that you were you and it was yours. Amazing! Not many playwrights come up with something so good at first go, you know.'

'It wasn't exactly my first,' said Irene, finding her voice at last and taking her hands out of his. 'More like seventh in fact.'

'Was it? Well, that just shows you've got all the grit I always thought you must have. Coffee?'

'What?' she said as that single word whisked her back to his first ever invitation and her own astonishment that he might want to have anything to do with her. 'Oh, coffee? Yes, please. Thank you.'

He yelled instructions to his secretary and then shut the door so that they were alone.

'Come and sit down,' he said, taking Irene's hands again and pulling her towards a large sofa covered in oatmeal tweed that stood between two potted rubber plants. She was rather surprised that the Richard she had known, who had always been aware of what was in fashion, should have chosen such passé decorations.

'Isn't this place too ghastly?' he said, laughing at her expression. 'Journalists always comment and designer friends try to make me have something better, but what's the point? The building's so fearfully convenient that I'd put up with much worse, and it's never seemed worth spending any money on it since I'm hardly ever here once the play's on the go, whichever one it is.'

'What do you really  ...?' Irene began, but she got no further.

'We'll talk about yours soon, but I don't want to start until we can be sure of being uninterrupted. But there's lots else to be said, isn't there? Thirty years to catch up on, nearly. You'd better start.'

'When did you realize it was me?' Irene regretted asking that almost as soon as she had said the words, but it was too late to take them back.

Richard pushed his feet forwards and leaned expansively against the sofa with his hands behind his head. She saw that he was wearing the scruffiest of ancient carpet slippers beneath his expensive-looking corduroy trousers and eccentrically cut black suede jacket.

'Pretty soon,' he said, grinning at her with a teasing affection that showed it had not mattered in the least that she had given him the power to fire the first shot. 'I know,' he went on, although he could not possibly have known what she was thinking. 'Here we are again, and I never thought we would be. It's . . . oh, I can't tell you what a treat it is.'

Irene smiled and did not bother to speak. Richard was saying everything that needed to be expressed. There was no war to be fought with him; she could just be herself and not worry about anything she might say or leave unsaid. It was the most liberating feeling she had had in years.

'Why Webton, by the way?' he asked out of the blue. 'It's not a name that suits you and it sounds deadly. Spindlebury was much more you.'

'Only because you knew me then. Webton's been my name for the past quarter century and it's how I think of myself,' she said, amused to realize through the singing pleasure in her mind that Richard had shown no sign of concern that she might not have remembered him. That was typical. And yet what did it matter if he was pleased with himself, even arrogant? What did anything matter any more?

'Have you been happy in those years?' he asked quietly. The amusement had gone from his voice, and he sounded as though he cared.

Irene looked at him, determined to make sure that there was no sign of malice in his face. He had always been an entertaining raconteur and if he were planning to describe their encounter to his current friends and admirers, she did not want him talking wittily about her private feelings.

'Why do you ask?'

He took his hands from behind his head. Looking down at his hands and picking at one of his nails, he said: 'Not for any prurient reason, believe me. I suppose it's partly because the play doesn't read as though it was written by someone happy.'

Irene flinched. Richard stopped concentrating on his nails and looked up. After a moment he seemed to realize that she needed some reassurance for which she would never ask and added seriously: 'Not least because very few good plays are written by entirely happy people and, believe me, yours is definitely good.'

Even though she knew that Richard had not always told the truth when he had set out to charm someone, she believed him then.

'And partly because there was an air about it that I recognized,' he added, looking almost self-conscious. 'At first, after I'd realized that it was yours, I thought that must have been why. I mean that there must have been a lot of you in it and that was what I'd seen. But I've come to think that just as we shared so much in the old days we must have been sharing this, too.'

'What's this "this" we're talking about here?' Irene did not trust herself to say any more. The idea that he remembered them as having shared 'so much' was very different from all her dawn fears of the contempt with which he might have been thinking about her.

'Oh.' He pursed his lips and then laughed derisively. She was not sure which of them he found absurd. 'A loss. A disappointment. A sadness that life hasn't turned out as one had a right to expect. You were always so tough that I was surprised when I realized you'd been hit by much the same as me.' He broke off as they both heard the door opening. 'Ah, good: coffee. Thanks, Patsy.'

Irene was glad of the distraction. In those five or six minutes Richard had given her a great deal to think about and she had no idea how to respond to any of it. Almost the oddest was that he should have thought her tough. It was what she wanted to be, more than almost anything else, but she had always thought she had a long way to go.

'Here you are,' he said, handing her a cup from which rose the powerful scent of strong Italian coffee. Irene drank and almost gasped.

'Too strong?' asked Richard, clearly amused.

'No,' said Irene with unnecessary passion. 'Absolutely wonderful. I haven't had coffee like this for years.'

'Well, take it carefully then. We don't want you having palpitations – at least not over the coffee.'

They both laughed at that and Irene felt as though her skin and eyes were growing more luminous as her brain started to work effectively again. Her fears about Richard's not remembering her, or taking the opportunity to humiliate her for her presumptuous designs on him all those years earlier, had gone completely. She realized that if they had been meeting for the first time she would have liked him at once.

'And do you really like the play?' she asked. 'I mean really?'

'You sound as though you don't think I should.' He looked into her face and then, as though seeing something vulnerable there behind the mask of gaiety and confidence, added with absolutely direct seriousness: 'You ought to know that it's good.'

She shrugged, not in the least minding that she was revealing a severe weakness.

'I've lost all confidence in my judgement. I didn't think the first play I ever wrote was up to much but it won a prize and got some amazing reviews when it was done on the radio. Then among the five in between were some I did think had something, but no-one else liked any of them – except for dear Michael Vestry, who was trying to so hard to keep me going. And now this one, which quite frankly I've had my doubts about from the beginning, is thought by people who matter to be quite good. You can see why I don't know any more.'

'Well, try to believe one of the people who matter. It's great. Much as I've wanted to see you again for years, I'd never have done it like this if I hadn't thought the play worthwhile.' He looked at her with all the old arrogant confidence and then his face broke into a wickedly mocking smile. She would have felt outraged if the mockery had been directed at her, but it was so clearly at himself that she could only laugh. 'After all, I do have my reputation to consider.'

'Yes, you always were aware of how important that was. But I'm glad.' She finished her coffee. 'So, where do we go from here, Richard? I've never had a play put on live. I don't know anything about what's expected of me.'

'Don't worry. I'll teach you. It'll be fun – and it'll let us pick up where we left off.' Richard got bored with holding his coffee cup and dumped it clumsily down on the floor beside his sofa.

Irene saw that the cup had tipped up in the saucer, and was delighted to think that it was not her responsibility if any of the dregs spilled over onto the beige carpet. She was free of all such deadening, time-wasting, boring preoccupations for the time being at least.

'First thing we must discuss is the casting. I'm sure you've got some ideas about that.'

'Well yes, actually I have,' Irene said, feeling shyer than she had for some time, 'but the names I've been thinking about may be a bit above my station.'

'Always aim high,' said Richard, smiling. 'Didn't we agree that in the coffee bar that day?'

Irene nodded and felt one of the hairpins spring out of her hair. That was the problem – one of the problems – with such thick hair. Very few pins were strong enough to hold it up. She bent down to pick up the pin and thrust it furiously back into place, grazing her scalp.

'Oh, that wonderful, Medusa-like head of yours!' said Richard, watching her in amusement. 'Even if there'd been nothing else, we'd all have been mesmerized by your hair. Do you still wear it loose?'

'Only in bed.' Absurdly she felt herself blushing. 'I'm a bit embarrassed,' she said hastily, trying to cover her silliness, 'because the actor I've always had in mind for Major Blackson is Peter Callfield.'

'Brilliant! He's exactly the man I want, too, and the wonderfully satisfactory thing is that he thinks it might suit him to do it. He's read the piece, likes it, and we're negotiating with his agent at the moment.'

Irene had a sudden doubt. She wondered if the whole of this miraculous business were an enormous tease. No-one could be given so much luck, particularly not her. She was not – and never had been – a lucky person. Perhaps this was Richard's revenge for her fantasies after all.

'It's true,' he said, seeing the doubt distorting her magnificent face. 'His face and voice, in fact the whole character, leaped off the page the first time I read the play and I got on to his agent at once. In fact, if we hadn't managed to get him interested, I'd have had much less chance of raising the cash to do the play at all. Don't think I'm putting you down or criticizing your work, Irene, but it's tricky to get a no-name play staged at all these days.'

'Good God, I know that,' said Irene. 'That's why I'm finding all this so hard to believe. Who else have you been talking to? I mean for the other parts.'

As Richard told her his proposed cast for her play she was plunged into a mess of feelings that surprised her. The names he recited were much starrier than she could ever have expected, but even as she was wallowing in gratitude and amazement at them she had the feeling that Richard had taken control of something that belonged to her. He had said that he wanted to discuss the casting with her, and yet it was perfectly clear that he had already decided whom he wanted and was going to have.

When she thought about it, Irene realized that he would have had to have negotiated the actors' contracts by then if the play were about to go into rehearsal. She assumed that better-known playwrights were involved at a much earlier stage and thought quite humbly about the time when she might be treated like them.

'And the girl?' she said, trying not to sound too aggressive. 'Whom have you got for her?'

'That's the tricky one.' Richard got up and went to stand looking out of one of the huge windows. He turned back and smiled reassuringly. 'Don't look so worried. It may be tricky, but it's not impossible. In fact I have got my eye on someone, but I'm not absolutely sure about her yet. Whoever we use has got to be intelligent and yet vulnerable, mesmerizingly good but wholly unknown. She mustn't appear carrying baggage from other parts in other plays.'

'That makes sense.'

'You'd have been perfect in the old days,' he said, making Irene smile again and hang on to her common sense with difficulty. 'And once I'd realized that, I started to have a word with some of my mates in the schools to see whether any of them had a girl we might use.'

'And had they?' asked Irene, who had no use for dramatic pauses in life, however useful they might be in the theatre.

Richard nodded. 'She's called Bella Hawkins, and I want to take you round to the Theatre School to have a look at her this afternoon,' he said. 'I've been a couple of times to sit in on her classes, and I think she's perfect. She auditioned for me last week and was terrific, but I want to make sure you agree. It's such an important part, and we'll be taking a risk with someone quite so young. I thought we'd nip out for some lunch first and then take a cab to the school in time for her afternoon session.'

'What year is she?'

'Second.'

'Oh, dear.'

'Why? I assure you she's perfectly competent.' The arrogance was back in Richard's voice and stance, for once undiluted by humour. 'I would not even have considered her otherwise.'

'It isn't that, and I'm not questioning your judgement of her ability,' said Irene in a hurry. 'I just don't like the idea of taking her out of school before she's finished her course.'

'I'm sure they'll have her back if necessary. But I shouldn't think she'll need it. She's a stunning actress already and she'll do better working on plays like yours than enduring any more of old Ben's Method madness. Come on. Lunch.'

They ate in a very small, very good restaurant, talking with so little constraint or self-consciousness that Irene felt as though she were outside time. She could not afterwards remember what they had eaten or what either of them had actually said, but she had felt known and liked for what she really was by someone who had shed all his own disguises. None of Richard's capriciousness was in evidence, or his vanity, and when he talked briefly about his own just-contained marital disaster he seemed remarkably ungrudging in his acceptance of at least half the blame. Irene found herself wanting to ask his advice about her own dealings with Fin, but she controlled the impulse, trying instead to learn all she could from what Richard told her about his wife.

Eventually he called for the bill and Irene watched him drop his gold credit card on it, thinking of the day when she might be successful enough to have her own. Her teeth clamped together as she silently vowed to do anything, absolutely anything, to ensure the success of the play. It was her last chance to earn her own money and a place in the world and she was going to make the most of it.

The determination was still with her as they took a taxi to the Theatre School, but then it left her. In its place was a quite different feeling that made her stop on the steps of the building, unable to move.

'What's wrong?' asked Richard impatiently with one hand on the front door, turning back to look at her. She thought that if he had had car keys in his other hand he would have been rattling them at her.

'Nothing,' she said, shaking her head, unwilling to tell him quite how uncertain and pathetic her humiliating memories were making her feel. 'It's just so odd coming back like this.'

'D'you mean you've never seen the old place since you ran away that term?'

'That's right. I occasionally used to fantasize . . .' Irene broke off for a moment to command herself not to look self-conscious. 'I used to fantasize about turning into a brilliant actress and coming back like a conqueror to lecture the students and having Ben falling on his face in amazed admiration.' She laughed. 'But even in the middle of the daydreams, I never believed them. Not one of them.'

'Well, you are coming back as a conqueror,' said Richard more pleasantly. 'Come on and stop looking so scared. It doesn't suit you and there's no need. There are a great many more successful actors than there are good playwrights. And the actors are no use without the writers.'

Irene took that compliment with a bigger pinch of salt than usual. In spite of Richard's admiration, she found it surprisingly difficult to feel anything but a creeping failure as the smell of the school hit her. It was exactly the same as it had always been: musty, slightly rotten, greasy, sweaty and full of intimations of inadequate plumbing.

Thinking of it as the very smell of anxiety, she followed Richard along the narrow passages to the main rehearsal stage, recognizing the expressions on the faces of some of the students they passed. Seeing their exhaustion and despairing fear, Irene could not suppress a shudder.

'My dear, how delightful to see you,' said a middle-European voice she would have known anywhere. 'This is such a good outcome to an unpleasant moment of disillusion.'

'Hello, Ben,' said Irene, trying not to sound like the eighteen-year-old student she had been the last time they met.

He, too, looked almost exactly the same: whiter and more craggy, but just as predatory as ever. She was determined to show that he no longer had any power to tear chunks of emotional flesh out of her.

'I don't think I was disillusioned exactly; more frustrated,' she said lightly, smiling at him with an assumption of exactly the kind of pitying superiority she disliked in other judges' wives.

'I'm not talking about you,' he said with a ferocity that did not seem to be as artificial as she thought it ought to have been. '*I* was disillusioned when you let me down. I'd fought so hard to have you offered a place here that when you ran away to marry your lawyer you made a fool of me. That is something I find hard to forgive.'

'Oh, dear.' About to apologize, Irene reminded herself of the hell of Ben's first few classes, told herself that she owed him nothing and that a little disillusion for him was the tiniest possible revenge for what he had done to her. She produced what she hoped was a convincing smile. 'Still, there's nothing so educational as feeling a fool. Perhaps my defection will have taught you something.'

'Not to back my hunches over rich girls who are not hungry enough to put up with a little emotional discomfort,' he said drily, 'or intelligent enough to understand what is happening to them and why, or what the consequences may be.'

'Most people,' said Irene, hearing an echo of what she had already said to Fin, 'give of their best when they feel secure, not when they are mocked into believing themselves stupid and useless.'

'But then you have no experience of training students for the stage, have you, my dear? Anyone who finds my classes too hard has no hope of surviving long enough to become a professional.'

'Now, now, you two,' said Richard, who had been watching them both with amusement that was undoubtedly malicious. 'You're fighting ancient battles here, and I don't believe for one moment, Ben, that you remember Irene at all.'

'But of course I do. The most stubborn student I ever had here. Even worse than you. I had to take a chisel to her – metaphorically speaking – to get her to do anything and I'd just made my first crack in her surface when she escaped.'

At last Irene began to feel more comfortable. Stubbornness seemed an admirable trait to have in one's character, much better than the simple failure to understand that she had believed to be her worst fault.

'Now, you want to see my other stubborn girl, do you?'

'That's right, you old tyrant,' said Richard cheerfully. 'Bring her on.'

He and Irene took seats behind Ben and the other tutors and waited in silence for the afternoon's class to begin.

As soon as the young actor they had come to see appeared, Irene knew that Richard's instinct had not let her down. Bella Hawkins was vulnerable and yet wickedly funny, attractive without being at all pretty, and enviably confident on stage. Even when Ben stopped her and savaged her with quite unnecessarily cruel criticism, she merely listened, returned to her place, smiled at her fellow actors and replayed the passage he had disliked.

Afterwards, Richard summoned her to be introduced to Irene. For a moment or two, the three of them talked politely about the class and then Richard slouched off to talk to Ben at the far side of the big room.

'Are you quite happy about this?' asked Irene as soon as she was alone with Bella.

'Ecstatic,' she said, clasping both hands under her square chin. 'Mrs Webton, you cannot possibly imagine how wonderful I feel at the prospect of getting out of here.'

Irene laughed.

'And,' added Bella demurely, 'from what Richard Orleton has told me about your play, it sounds extremely interesting. He said he wouldn't let me read the whole of it until you had decided whether or not you wanted me for the part, but that if you agreed I could have a copy today, so that I have time to get to grips with it before the first read-through.'

'I certainly do want you.' Irene was still laughing, but she stopped as she added seriously: 'But, Bella, are you sure you want to leap out of your course like this? I know how easy it is to get out of here and ... I'd hate you to lose something important. I mean, I think you're a terrific actress already and I'm sure you'll make a success of the part, but it may be a dead end for you and you might do better staying on here to do your last year.'

'Ben has said he'll have me back,' she said, sounding perfectly sensible and rather more aware of the consequences of her actions than Irene had been at her age. 'So if it all collapses or there's no sign of an agent or another part, I'll do my last year, I promise. It's all right, Mrs Webton. Really it is. Don't stop him giving me the part, please.'

Irene wished she could believe that it really would turn out all right and that her presentiment of disaster was nothing more than a reflection of what had happened to her after she left the school.

'I am over the age of consent, you know,' said Bella, looking both intelligent and sophisticated.

Oh, toughen up, Irene, she said to herself. You'll be getting as bad as Helena if you go on like this. You are not responsible for other people, even people as young, attractive, and exploitable as this one. Bella will survive whatever happens; and if she doesn't it won't be your fault.

# Chapter Five

Helena could hardly bear to see Mike leave. It was not that she felt any sense of desertion. She was just reluctant to admit that the evening had arrived. Mockingly reminding herself of the dangers of self-delusion, she waved him off as cheerfully as possible and went upstairs to change. Then, dressed in a pair of straight black silk trousers and a loose, silver-grey silk and cotton sweater, she locked up the house and set off westwards towards Gray's Inn Road and on to John Street.

The walk took her twenty minutes and carried her from the lively scruffiness of Clerkenwell to the much more rarified atmosphere of Bloomsbury. John Street itself was an admirable example of Georgian town architecture with elegantly austere brick houses on either side of the broad road. Plane trees grew at intervals along the pavement and many of the buildings had neatly planted window boxes in the ground-floor windows. Most of the houses were used by lawyers or as the head offices of commercial companies, but a few were still privately owned.

Helena stopped outside one of them, noticing that the window boxes had been replanted since she was last there. They had stiff little miniature standard rose trees rising out of a sea of grey-green ivy, which she thought suited the straight lines of the building and added an unusual gaiety.

Even though she despised herself for bothering about how she looked, she smoothed her hair back with both hands and brushed some street dust off the knees of her trousers. When she could not put it off any longer, she went up to the front door and knocked. There was a longish pause, which she understood easily. It meant:

I do not mind that you are half an hour later than you said you would be; I have not been watching out for you; I have plenty of other things to do; I do not depend on you. Nor am I angry. I do not expect anything and will make no demands.

The door opened at last and her mother stood there, politely smiling.

'Hello,' Helena said, throwing back her head as though she were facing a threat of some kind.

Miranda Webton nodded, still smiling, but she did not lean forward to be kissed or even hold out her hand.

'Hello, Helena,' she said calmly. 'Do come on in.'

'Thank you.'

'It's so hot,' Miranda said, standing aside so that Helena could walk past her into the shadowed hall, 'that I thought we might have a glass of wine in the garden. Would that be all right for you?'

'Yes, thank you. I'd like that.' Helena smiled then, too, relieved not to be faced with the drawing room again.

She had been shocked the first time she had visited the house – only a few months earlier – to see how like her own it was. Somehow the pale-walled room, which was sparsely furnished with exactly the sort of chairs, tables and paintings that she herself most liked, had been even worse than the familiarity of her mother's looks. The shape of their small-boned, freckled faces, the unruly fineness of their hair and the soft greeny-blue colour of their eyes had clearly been dictated by their genes, and that did not seem either odd or difficult to accept; but Helena had still not properly come to terms with the fact that her tastes and character might also be like Miranda's.

They walked through the house into the small garden. That, at least, was not at all like Helena's, which, apart from the clematis near the iron steps, was a relatively hard-edged affair of paving and shrubs in large terracotta pots. Miranda's was much more romantic, with small fruit trees and drifts of late-flowering narcissi naturalized in the long grass, climbers winding through the trees and the painted trellis that topped the low walls. Scents of a whole range of aromatic herbs reached Helena as she stood on the threshold.

There was an expensive-looking teak table and comfortably cushioned chairs near the house with a bottle of white wine waiting in a terracotta cooler beside some glasses and a plate under a stiffened muslin cover.

'Do sit down, Helena,' said Miranda, who had never yet used any kind of endearment. 'And tell me how you've been.'

'Quite well, thank you.'

'Busy?'

'Yes, I am quite.' Helena made a greater effort. 'Which is nice and reassuring, too. Being self-employed can be so worrying when one's clients go quiet.'

Miranda looked as though she might laugh. Helena, who loved laughter and would usually do anything to bring it out of anyone, nodded stiffly.

'Of course,' she said. 'I always forget that barristers are self-employed, too.'

'And we often don't get paid for years, which makes it all the more frightening. I'm glad you're doing all right.'

'What about you?'

'Oh, there's plenty of work these days, but it wasn't always like that,' said Miranda, picking up the tall, brown bottle. 'Is this all right for you? It's a hock, dryish.'

'Lovely.' Helena could not think what to say next. It seemed absurd.

'I know,' said Miranda, pouring the wine before taking the cover off the plate, which proved to contain some highly professional-looking canapés. 'Have one of these.'

'What do you know?'

'How difficult it is. There's so much to say and yet none of it can be said at all easily. We're complete strangers to each other and yet we're not strangers at all. I look at you and see myself at your age. I want to know all sorts of things and yet I couldn't possibly ask them.'

'What sort of things? If I can, of course I'll tell you whatever you want to know. Answering questions is somehow easier than . . .' Helena could not finish the thought even in the privacy of her mind. It occurred to her worryingly that she was already older than Miranda had been when she ran away. She wondered yet again why Miranda had got in touch with her after so many years' silence and what – exactly – she wanted.

'I couldn't possibly ask.' There was a pause. Then Miranda said: 'Why not tell me something about whatever you're working on at the moment?'

Helena took a deep breath and described the girandole, which belonged to her oldest and most faithful client, Katharine Lidstone, who had recently suffered an appalling burglary. Helena spoke more easily as they got further away from the brink of the emotional chasm that lay between them. Miranda asked a series of sensible questions about the gilding technique Helena was using and the materials it involved and whether the restoration would enhance the value of the girandole or not, but eventually even they ran out.

'And Ivo, my brother, has asked me to work on the most glorious desk he's just acquired,' Helena went on in order to prevent a difficult silence.

'Ah, Ivo,' said Miranda. 'What a charmer!'

Helena put down her glass with extreme care and looked at her mother in surprise.

'I didn't know that you knew him,' she said, remembering Irene's dry comment that she could always tell when Fin had encountered his first wife in court – or outside it – because he was more than usually prickly and difficult when he came home afterwards. If Miranda were moving in on Ivo as well, Irene might be seriously hurt. That could not be allowed.

'Did I never tell you? He came to see me a day or two after last Christmas,' said Miranda. 'He rang the bell one Sunday morning and introduced himself, saying that he thought it was time he met the person whose ghost was so strongly alive in his home.'

Helena breathed in so deeply and so fast that her chest hurt. She put a hand to her breastbone.

'You mind that, don't you?' Miranda showed no emotion at all in spite of having just made the most personal comment of their short acquaintance. 'Why?'

'No, of course I don't mind. It just seemed strange, that was all. I mean a strange phrase for Ivo to have used.' Helena tried to pull herself together. At least Ivo was a relatively easy topic for conversation. 'And it's odd that he's never told me he'd met you.'

'Perhaps,' said Miranda, not looking at Helena. 'Anyway, it's thanks to him that we're here now.'

'Really? Why? I mean, how?'

'The way he talked about you undid all my good resolutions about not bothering you, and I realized I had to get to know you.'

'Oh,' said Helena, feeling even more at a loss than usual. She could not think what to say and after a moment went back to Miranda's first comment about Ivo and said: 'You're right, though. He does have charm.'

'He certainly does; and he knows exactly how best to use it to get what he wants and how to hide behind it.'

'I don't think that's fair,' said Helena at once. 'He doesn't hide. Why should he? He doesn't have any reason to hide.'

'Are you quite sure of that?'

'Absolutely.'

Helena hoped that her tone would make it clear to her mother that there was no more to be said on the subject of Ivo, but it could not have done, for Miranda went on: 'He seemed to me to be one of those people who is capable of projecting an air of openness and generosity that is quite at odds with his real character.'

'That's outrageous,' said Helena, completely forgetting that she disliked criticizing people or finding herself in conflict. 'I've known Ivo all my life and you've hardly met him. You can't possibly know anything about him, and you've got no right to say things like that. What kind of axe can you have to grind that you have to slander someone who's done you no harm?'

'I'm sorry if I sounded critical,' said Miranda in a completely passionless voice. Helena noticed that all the character had disappeared from her eyes. There was no expression in them at all and very little light. 'I know you're fond of him. And he certainly cares about you. That was very clear.'

Helena, who was already regretting her outburst, did not consciously decide to punish Miranda, but before she could stop herself she said: 'I'm not surprised. He's never been afraid to show his feelings. He must get that from Irene. After all, no-one could pretend that Fin was demonstrative – or had the sort of feelings one might want to have demonstrated.'

Miranda frowned and Helena wished that she had thought before she spoke. It looked as though she had hurt Miranda and she did not want that; she did not want to hurt anyone.

'Fin can be remarkably charming too, and kind.'

'When he bothers to think about it and when it isn't inconvenient to him or in danger of giving encouragement to someone or something of which he disapproves.'

Miranda laughed then, sounding almost normal again. 'He's right when he says you're not stupid.'

'And what does he say after that?' As she spoke, Helena recognized the expression in Miranda's face and guessed that she was about to come in for a little punishment herself. That was fair enough.

'Merely that it's odd that with your brains and all the genes you must've inherited from us both, you should have chosen to become a glorified carpenter.'

Helena laughed. It had not been nearly as bad as she had expected – or deserved; and it was something she had heard often enough before. She picked up her glass again and raised it in a small toast to her mother. Miranda watched her with an enigmatic expression in her eyes.

'Of course I didn't point out to him why you might have chosen to spend your life mending things,' she said at last in an unusually gentle voice.

Helena shook her head. It was much easier to take verbal punishment from Miranda than kindness. They did not know each other well enough for anything so personal. Helena swallowed some wine and leaned forward to take a canape off the plate so that she could hide her face. When she had eaten it, she said:

'What's your current brief? There hasn't been anything about you in the Law Reports for a while.'

She saw Miranda register the fact that she bothered to read the Law Reports for news and wished she had not given herself away so clearly.

'I wasn't in court today. I spent the afternoon in a conference, working out the best defence for a young man alleged to have broken into a house in Kent last year and beaten ...'

'Not one of the ones who nearly killed that couple by trying to get them to say that they had a safe?' Helena was too appalled to wait for her mother to finish. 'Tied them up and tortured them and then left them for dead? Those two?'

'Yes.'

'And you're going to defend them?'

'One of them, yes.' Miranda's expression had not changed, but her voice was quite cold as she added: 'And please don't ask me how I can bring myself to side with people you consider to be so vilely beneath contempt. Brought up in a legal household, you ought to know better than that.'

'Yes, I suppose so. But don't you mind having to deal with people like that?'

'Sometimes. But there's no option. It's one of the costs of the job.'

Thinking of what Katharine Lidstone had suffered – and was still suffering – as a result of the burglary that had taken place when she was not even in the house, Helena could hardly bear to think what the couple in Kent must have endured.

'I know it is. I'm sorry. I'm not rational on the subject of burglars – any burglars, not just the violent ones.'

'I can understand that,' said Miranda. She looked up at the clouds. 'I think it's going to rain. We'd better go in. Would you like to stay for supper? There's plenty of food.'

'Actually, I think I ought to get back,' said Helena quickly, trying to sound just as casual and not managing it as well.

'Fine,' said Miranda before Helena could embark on any kind of excuse. 'It was sweet of you to come this evening.'

'I've enjoyed it,' said Helena with a tight smile. 'Thank you very much. Shall I give you a hand in with the cushions and things?'

'No, don't worry about that. I'll ring you in due course, next week, perhaps, or the one after. Good luck with Ivo's desk.'

'And you with your case.'

At the front door, Helena turned back to look at her mother. She wanted to make some kind of gesture that might express all the things that she did not know how to say: I'm sorry it's so cold and difficult; I'm sorry I'm going; I want very much to find some way of communicating with you, but I don't know how. There are a million things I want to know, but it's impossible to ask the questions. I know that we should be able to like each other, but I don't know how. I want, very much, for you to touch me.

Miranda stood courteously waiting. Helena took a deep breath and leaned forward. For an instant her cheek brushed Miranda's and then they both pulled back.

'Goodbye,' said Helena, wrestling with the front door latch.

'Goodbye,' said Miranda from behind her, sounding almost as shaken as Helena felt.

Helena walked slowly towards Doughty Street, feeling as though she had just run a marathon. She wondered whether it would ever be possible to ask the crucial question that had been in her mind ever since she had been old enough to understand what had happened in her family.

She had been home for only ten minutes, pottering about the house to re-establish herself in it and deal with what she considered was the melodramatic silliness of her emotions, when the buzzer went. Since there was no monitor in the drawing room, she looked out of the window.

'Irene!' she called, knocking on the glass, and saw her stepmother look up and wave.

Helena ran into the hall and flung open the door. 'Come on in. How lovely!'

Irene, whose mind had been full of her own affairs, stepped over the threshold, took one look at Helena and said quickly: 'You're all of a dooh-dah, Helena. What is it?'

'Nothing important now.'

Without any difficulty at all, she stepped forward into Irene's soft, safe embrace.

'But what was it?'

'Nothing important.' Helena stepped back. 'It was all nonsense. I'm perfectly all right. Come in and have something to eat or drink. You're looking pretty wild yourself. What have you been doing?'

'Sure you're OK?' said Irene, not wanting to pour out her news if Helena were as distressed as she had seemed. Irene owed her far too much for such selfishness.

'Positive. Come on. What's been going on?' Helena concentrated on Irene's life instead of her own. 'You had your meeting with Richard Orleton today, didn't you? How was it? Was he terrifying, or glamorous – or both?'

'Much as I remembered him actually,' said Irene, childishly screwing up her face.

Helena laughed and felt as though she were slotting back into her real self instead of the idiotic, shamingly agitated person she had let herself become again after John Street.

'I didn't realize you'd ever met. You'd better tell me all about it,' she said. 'D'you want a drink?'

Irene shook her head. The coils of black hair were beginning to collapse down the back of her neck. She looked gloriously happy.

'I'm so high on excitement that drink might make me do something really weird,' said Irene. 'D'you really want to know all about it?'

'Of course I do. But perhaps not in the hall. Come into the drawing room, put up your sore feet and disgorge.'

Obediently Irene followed her into the long room, which still looked light, in spite of the increasingly dingy-looking evening. Irene kicked off her shoes, which were indeed tight, and thought that it was typical of Helena's practical kindness to have noticed that through whatever it was that had been upsetting her. Irene lay on the chaise longue and poured out everything she had been feeling all afternoon.

Helena was the most marvellous listener, Irene thought as she described her first few encounters with Richard at the Theatre

School, and all the fears that had turned out to have been unnecessary.

'It was a tremendous day. I sort of feel as though I've put myself right with my own past,' she said at last, 'if you see what I mean?'

'Yes, I do,' said Helena with feeling. 'I'm really glad.'

'And you?' Irene said, remembering the trembling body she had held only half an hour earlier. 'What was the matter?'

'Perhaps not having put myself right with my past,' said Helena reluctantly.

'I don't understand,' said Irene, looking less confidently happy than she had. 'Am I being extra thick?'

Knowing how much Irene hated it when Fin saw Miranda, Helena did not want to mention her mother's name or admit that over the past five months they had been meeting at least once every fortnight.

'You're never thick,' she said quickly, deciding to sacrifice Mike in the interest of not upsetting Irene. 'You couldn't be. And it's lovely to see you so happy. You deserve it. No, I was just a bit stirred up because I had a smashing afternoon with my ... my paramour until he started talking about wanting to meet the family and things like that, and it went a bit sour.'

'And you still don't want him to meet us?'

'Not terribly.'

'Ashamed of him or of us?' asked Irene lightly. Her black eyes were glittering with interest.

'Neither.' Helena laughed with difficulty. 'It's just something separate. I don't want to muddle the two. It's too new. It may never ... It might stop tomorrow, and then I wouldn't want everyone else to have had a piece of it. D'you see what I mean?'

'Not really, but don't worry about it. I'm just glad that it's going well in whatever way it is.'

'Thank you, Irene,' Helena said, determined to get quickly away from the subject of her own emotions. 'Now, when are you going to let me read the play?'

She was amused to see her confident stepmother looking almost nervous. After a moment Irene shook her head decisively.

'I don't think that I'm ever going to let you read it. I'd much rather you saw it on a stage with actors. Honestly, as it stands on the page, you might not . . . It's not. . .'

'You're not really worried about what I might think, are you?' asked Helena in amazement.

'Of course I am. Your good opinion is crucial,' said Irene in surprise. 'You must know that by now.'

'Well, I . . . Goodness! I've come over all unnecessary, as Mrs Clark-the-Char used to say. If it is important, I'm glad, but I do want to know about the play, you know. It's such a big part of you that I hate being kept out of it.'

Irene's expression of surprise was taken over by pleasure.

'Really? I never meant to exclude you. I just thought it would be tempting fate to let anyone read it before I was sure it was going to be staged.' More hair slipped out of its pins and down her back as she laughed. 'I see what you mean about your young man. It's the same sort of thing, isn't it?'

'Sounds like it. But come on: tell me a bit about it.'

'It's a sort of crossover kind of a thing,' said Irene as self-consciousness made her unusually inarticulate. 'About this girl, Maria, who'd been incredibly happy in the house where she grew up. Then, because of outside circumstances, she became less happy, but she couldn't do anything about it because she was trapped. When a possibility of escape appeared, she took it without understanding what it would cost her. Later she discovered that it meant she had to be exiled from the only place where she might have been all right if she'd been let alone. So half the play is about her, leading up to the moment when she left the house on the canal, and the other half is her thirty-odd years later, trying to get back there and being stopped by all sorts of things. So, you get the two sorts of tensions leading up to the two crunchpoints at the crossover at the end. D'you see?'

'Not altogether,' said Helena truthfully, 'but I think I get the drift. It sounds interesting. Where is the house on the canal?'

'Well, I'd thought Venice because I love it so much and so does almost everybody else, and it would look so nice, but Richard and the set designer want it to be Amsterdam. In fact . . .' To Helena's amusement, Irene was blushing. 'In fact, Richard wants us all to go there next weekend to see it and talk about the play and work out some of the bits of staging that he says my directions are too fuzzy about.'

'What a brilliant idea! And it should be fun, too.'

'D'you think so, Helena? That's what I wanted to ask you about. Is it decent for me to go? I never have taken a private holiday; I mean without Fin, and I can't see him enjoying a weekend like this even if Richard were prepared to have him tagging along.'

'Of course it's decent and it isn't a holiday at all. It's like the old days when he was on circuit. It's your work. You don't think he'd object or try to stop you, do you?'

Irene shook her head and yet more hair collapsed. 'He's always been good about my writing. It's the one thing he's never narked at me about. You know that. It's just that going off with Richard . . . I suppose I feel a bit nervous because I like the idea of it so much.'

'Then go ahead and do it – not that you need my permission.' Helena was amused and felt fully restored to adulthood and confidence. Irene had always managed to do that for her, too. 'You deserve a treat and if it's going to make the play better then go for it.'

Irene kissed her.

# Chapter Six

Irene flew to Amsterdam with Richard and his designer, Adam Fernhill, on the last flight the following Friday evening. At first, driving in from the airport in the dusk, she thought that they had made a serious mistake in planning to shift her play to Amsterdam. The evening arrival at Venice had always been completely mesmerizing, and it was part of the whole atmosphere of the place that had made her choose it as her setting.

The airport, Mestre and the rest of the mainland were hardly beautiful but the pulsating rush of a small motorboat tearing across the lagoon, surging forward between the old, dark brown stakes that marked the channel, making for the smudge on the horizon that grew slowly into Venice, had a romance about it that the traffic-clogged drive through the ordinary streets of Amsterdam's suburbs entirely lacked. But as they turned at last into Prinsengraacht, where they were to stay, Irene began to understand.

They were deposited beside the canal and, while their luggage was carried into the hotel, the three of them stood at the edge of the water, looking at the reflected lights and what they could see of the tall, thin, gabled houses through the trees on the far side.

'I think I'm going to like this,' said Irene, turning in pleasure to Richard.

He touched her face briefly and said: 'Good. Let's go in. It's late and you're beginning to look stretched with tiredness.'

She stood in front of him, speechless with gratitude that he should have noticed her state and produced exactly the right word for it. Although it was not tiredness that had done it to her, stretched was just how she felt, like a piece of elastic that has no spring left in it and might snap at any moment.

Yes, she thought, stretched out by fury with Fin, anxiety about Jane, fear for the play, and the constant effort of not surrendering to anyone.

It would be so much easier to give in to Fin, let him take all the decisions about their joint life and responsibilities and order her about as he wanted, and yet if she did that she would have no hope for her work or herself for the rest of her life. However hard it was to keep up the struggle, she had to fight back.

Richard smiled encouragingly at her. There was no need to say anything. If he had understood so easily how she was feeling, then he would know what his perception had done for her.

'Breakfast at nine all right for you, Irene?' he said casually as he and Adam left her at the door of her bedroom ten minutes later. 'There's no point getting up any earlier than we have to, and they're comfortably late starters here.'

'Sure,' she said. 'I'll meet you in the breakfast room, shall I?'

Richard nodded and raised a hand. Irene shut the door on them both and unpacked the few clothes she had brought. Moving about in the large twin-bedded room on her own seemed to be the extreme of luxury, and, having had a long, scented bath, she ordered some cold white wine from room service, and drank it in bed watching television. It was an extra boon that she could get BBC programmes as well as the usual international news and shopping channels that were available in other European countries. She lay back, taking a private pleasure in the fact that Fin would have disapproved of it all so much. Eating and drinking in bed were anathema to him; the television hardly figured in his life at all, and he would have been horrified by the idea that she was lolling in bed watching it when she should have been either looking at Amsterdam or reading up the guide books in preparation for serious sightseeing the following day.

'This is the life I like,' she said aloud in supreme satisfaction. 'And his views suck.'

She had not quite got to the stage of using phrases like 'this sucks' in public, but she took a good deal of pleasure in saying them aloud to herself.

The satisfaction lasted through a more comfortable night's sleep than she had had in weeks and she woke feeling not only healthy and clear-headed, but also full of energy. She could hardly wait until twenty to nine when she thought it was just about decent to find the breakfast room and get started on the day. Richard appeared ten minutes later, but Adam was very late.

She and Richard sat in easy companionship, eating a huge breakfast of sausages, eggs, onions and tomatoes, followed by cheese and pumpernickel, fruit and cakes, while she read *The Times* and he the *Independent*. Their coffee cups were refilled whenever they were empty. No one interrupted or bothered them until Adam appeared, looking rumpled and wet-haired at half past nine.

'Sorry,' he said with a charming smile. 'My alarm clock failed me.'

'It couldn't matter less. We've plenty of time,' said Richard. 'All we've got to do is let Irene see what we mean about the place and show her the particular stretch of the canal you want as the basis for your sets. Get yourself some food and we can plan the morning. I think we might lunch on the Brouwersgraacht.'

'Lunch?' said Irene in almost genuine horror as she looked at the remains of the food on her plate. 'I won't be able to eat again for a week.'

The two men laughed and Adam went off to the buffet to load his plate even higher than she had done. When he came back and started to eat, Richard began to talk to her about Amsterdam and its history, revealing a much less arrogant side of himself than she had yet seen. He clearly knew a lot about the place and cared for it, too. When Irene asked why he liked it so much, he paused and after a while said thoughtfully: 'I think because it's so at ease with itself. Once hugely powerful . . .'

'Like Venice,' she said and nodded.

'Yes, but it's not a museum like Venice,' he said, his eyes almost disappearing as his face wrinkled into a cheerful smile. 'Amsterdam's a real place with real people. There are far too many of them really, and yet they deal with the overcrowding by extra civility rather than the aggression of somewhere like New York. You'll see. I've never felt ripped off here or a target for anything. There's no show or having to stand up for yourself. It's a great place, the acme of civilization.'

'It sounds as though my stepdaughter would love it,' said Irene, forgetting Richard for the moment. 'I must bring her one day.'

'I didn't know you had one. How old is she?'

'Thirty-one.' Watching Richard's face, Irene wondered how much – if anything – he knew of her life since they had parted twenty-eight years earlier. 'I know she's far too old to be brought anywhere. It's just . . . Oh, well: I don't want to bore you with stepmaternal chat.'

'You couldn't bore me,' said Richard, 'and Adam's far too interested in his food to mind what we talk about.'

The designer looked up with his extraordinarily sweet smile and said nothing.

'I expect you'll meet her soon and then you'll see what I mean,' said Irene. 'She's my greatest friend, I suppose, what's made life bearable during some pretty tricky moments, and so I like to share my pleasures with her.'

'Yes,' said Richard, 'I remember that about you.'

'What d'you remember?'

'Your generosity. It was always obvious and quite different from other people's careful weighing up of what they could afford to give.'

Irene felt as though her real self had suddenly become visible again for the first time in years.

The two men took her to places they particularly liked, clearly wanting to know what she thought and felt, instead of wanting to make sure that she was not feeling – or about to say – something that would need containing or altering to make it acceptable. The effect of that combined with the slowly revealed charm of the small city until she felt peculiarly at ease.

The scale of the place pleased her enormously as did the domestic elegance of the grey houses. Richard had been right. Except on the grander parts of the Kaisergraacht and Heerengraacht, which she did not much like, none of the houses was pompous or showy. Their scale was comfortable, and they looked thoroughly civilized. Some were purple-grey, others nearly black, others again pale grey. With the dark grey-brown water of the canals, the green of the trees, the cream paint of the window frames and the pinkish-grey of the bridges, the whole scene was relaxed. Irene had rarely felt less angry or impatient.

She had a sensation of coming home, too, although she had never been to Amsterdam before in her life. Increasingly as the morning went on she saw how perceptive Adam and Richard had been in choosing the place for her play. That, after all, was partly about getting oneself to the point at which one could go home and be at ease with oneself and one's surroundings.

In deference to her appetite, they did not eat a proper lunch, but stopped in a smoky, brown-walled café for beer and sandwiches. The comfortably informal place was staffed by a slender couple, both dressed in jeans and open-necked shirts, who seemed untroubled by the numbers of people milling around ordering food and drinks. Irene, thinking of similiar establishments in London filled with a mixture of students, adult inhabitants, and tourists, was bemused by their good humour. She sat at the old, scarred wooden table, resting her feet, which were beginning to swell after the morning's walk, and watching the people around her.

As she and the two men waited for their drinks, they looked through the Polaroids Adam had been taking of each particularly appealing bit of canal and argued amicably about exactly what the play's house should look like. Irene had strong views and was once or twice tempted to expostulate that it was her play and she had imagined the house and so she should choose, but she slowly began to admit that both Richard and Adam had read the play with such sympathetic understanding that they, too, had some rights over it.

When they had eventually agreed on the house Adam had always wanted to use, a smallish, dark-grey and cream one on the corner of Prinsengraacht and one of the streets that ran north from it, they paid the bill and went back to double-check the reality.

'Sure?' said Adam when they had walked across the bridge to view it from the far side of the canal and walked up the side street to check it from there, too. 'This is really the one?'

Richard looked at Irene, apparently deferring to her.

'Yes,' she said, smiling at first one and then the other. 'This is it. This is where my girl really could have been happy. You're brilliant, the pair of you. I'd never have known if it hadn't been for you.'

'We've always been a good team,' said Richard cheerfully, 'and you're an honorary member too now. OK, Adam?'

'Sure. Look, I'll stay and take some more photographs and check my measurements and things, and then I think I'll leg it straight back on the last flight out tonight – unless you need me for anything else?'

'No,' said Richard definitely. 'Irene and I have to sort out one or two things in the text now that we know we're here for sure, but all the rest of the visual stuff – lighting and so on – can wait until we're back in London. All right with you, Irene?'

'Absolutely fine,' she said. 'But are you going to have time, Adam? I've only just realized that if rehearsals are about to start, your set needs . . .'

'That's OK,' said Adam with an air of unshakeable confidence. 'The basic design works for both here and Venice. A bridge over a canal, a house, and either a *straat* running down between it and the next or a *calle*. Easy. It's only the detail and the colours that are different. I'll adjust the model as soon as I get back and then the workroom can get on with painting the flats.'

'You mean you've already made the model?'

'Sure. You're looking very worried. I don't think you need, do you, Richard?'

'No. But she's new to all this. She still thinks she has to be responsible for everything.' He turned to Irene. 'Doesn't she?'

'In a way. But it isn't that. There are so many things to ask. I've never been sure how much scene changing . . .'

'Ssh,' said Adam, holding up his hand as though he were directing the traffic. 'It's all under control. Look, there's a bench over there under the plane trees. Why don't we sit down and I'll tell you what we're doing?'

'All right.'

The two of them sat at either end of the bench, while Richard leaned against one of the tree trunks, looking detached and wildly romantic. Bicyclists whizzed past at the most dangerous-looking speeds, sometimes loaded with parcels or passengers, but Irene did her best to concentrate on what Adam was telling her.

'The scenes with the older version of Maria in the airport will all be at the front of the stage. There will be two sets of back-to-back seats and lots of silent extras coming and going with prams and babies . . .'

'And luggage,' said Irene urgently. 'It really is important that Maria has lots of luggage.'

'Yes, I know. I grasped that: by the time we reach her age we all have a great deal of accumulated baggage to carry about with us, which trips us up and causes trouble.'

'Exactly.' Irene looked at his sensitive bony face and wanted to take it between her hands and kiss it.

'Then high up, hanging against the plain black cloth will be one of those announcement boards they have at mainline stations. The sort with all the black flaps that clatter up and down. D'you know what I mean?'

'Yes. But airports don't have them.'

'No, I know. This is a bit of artistic licence, but I want to have it. Have you ever seen a station crowd on a night when all the trains are delayed? Every time one of those columns of clattering bits starts moving, the whole crowd shifts; and then when it becomes clear that no new information is coming up, they subside again. The fogbound airport will be very like that. It really is justified. And it'll work.'

Richard moved away from his tree as though he could not bear not to be centre-stage for very long.

'Budge up, you two,' he said. 'And then, you see, Irene, as Maria's talking about her past, the announcement board will disappear up into the flies and the black cloth will be revealed as a gauze as the

78

lights come on and we see the house behind it. I know, I know,' he added, as though Irene had protested, which she had not even thought of doing, 'gauzes are fantastically old-fashioned, but Adam thinks it's the best way of getting over what we need to express.'

'We thought,' said Adam, deciding to grab the initiative again, 'that we'd divide the stage for all the non-airport scenes so that both the house and the canal and its bridge are visible all the time. We'll fly the front of the house so that for the interior scenes there just won't be a front and for the exterior ones all the audience will see is the façade.'

'I'm impressed,' said Irene. 'I can't wait to see the model. But what are you going to do about the canal itself?'

Adam looked at Richard. They were both boiling over with satisfaction.

'You say,' said Richard. 'It's your coup.'

'OK. You see, Irene, we think we've worked out how we can have real water. Obviously it can't be deep, not least because the stage has to be raked, but it will be wet – and Blackson will produce a noticeable splash when he flings the books into it from the upstairs window. The audience will see passers-by getting wet.'

'The same silent extras, I take it, from the airport scenes. It sounds wonderful,' said Irene. Then, looking down at the water, which was a good five foot lower than the edge of the canal, she frowned.

'All right, it's true we will have to cheat,' said Adam with the first hint of petulance. 'That's inevitable.'

'And it doesn't matter,' said Richard. 'The whole of theatre is an illusion. We'll make the audience believe in it. Don't you worry your pretty little head, Irene.'

For once she did not automatically rebel at the sound of a patronizing instruction coming at her in a confident male voice. Instead she smiled at the cliché and bowed her thoroughly large – and not at all pretty – head, feeling unusually glad of her bulbous nose and wide mouth.

They left Adam on his own with his cameras and sketch books soon after that and wandered back through the warm streets, stopping here and there, leafing through old prints in a gallery, examining antique Delft tiles, and eyeing a window full of the most lavish-looking cakes and wishing that they were hungry enough to want to eat again. They talked about everything except the play and did not get down to serious work on it until they had reached the hotel again. Then, sitting either side of a small table in Richard's room, they went through a long list of questions he had prepared.

Irene began to understand that part of the reason he had wanted her to come to Amsterdam must have been to soften her up, to get her believing in his pleasure in what she had written so that his various comments and criticisms were not too wounding. It was unexpectedly sensitive of him, but even so there were times when she did feel wounded.

The work was also wearing; surprisingly so. She had to concentrate hard to see the point he was making, work out an accurate response, and then find acceptable words for it, pushing the ensuing argument to the limit of what she could bear.

By six, Irene was genuinely tired and snapped a thoughtless answer to something Richard said. Before she could apologize or make a joke to dilute her anger, he had put down his pencil, taken off his glasses and looked at her with unexpected benevolence.

'Done enough for the moment?'

'Yes, I think I must have,' she said, rubbing her forehead. 'I'm aching and cross and almost . . .'

'Tearful?' suggested Richard with a hint of a smile.

'Certainly not,' said Irene. 'I am never – *ever* – tearful.'

'It wouldn't be surprising if you were. Big strong men get weepy when their words are misunderstood or misapplied or criticized.'

'Do they? Well, perhaps that explains my tetchiness, then.' She frowned as though that might make the feelings go away. 'It's all so new to me – first having my play taken at all seriously and now savaged like this. It makes me wonder what you really think about it, whether I can trust those first compliments, or . . . Perhaps I just need a bit of a break.'

'Probably,' said Richard. 'And a drink and some more food in due course. Why don't you go and have a bath and change? Then we'll go out to supper. They eat early here, so I've booked us a table at seven-thirty. Is that all right?'

Almost beyond the stage of being able to say anything coherent, Irene just nodded and went back to her own room. Once she had had her bath, she wrapped herself in one of the hotel's comfortingly large towels and telephoned Fin, telling herself that all she wanted was to make sure that he was managing without her.

He sounded quite untroubled by her absence, politely interested in the work she had been doing, and sympathetic to her brief, supposedly funny description of her dislike of Richard's attempts to change some of what she had written.

'How have you been?' she asked eventually, remembering why she had called him.

'Irritable. Partly because I made a nonsense of cooking my lunch and partly because I've had another letter from Jane.'

Ignoring the question of his lunch, which had entailed nothing more complicated than grilling two lamb chops she had bought him and cooking a few vegetables, she asked about the letter. Fin gave her a crisp précis and then said outrageously: 'I've decided that we must pay her a greater allowance in spite of your reservations about her extravagance. She really should not be put through so much anxiety while she is working for her degree.'

Irene opened her mouth to protest, but then said nothing. There seemed no point when Fin had at last agreed with what she had always wanted him to do. And if she needed extra ammunition at any later stage in their war, she could always use it then.

'I've sent her a cheque and a letter suggesting that she learns a little of Ivo's self-discipline. You could do with it, too, Irene. Your telephone bill will be huge if we speak any longer.'

'Have you any idea how humiliating it is to be criticized for what I'm spending, even when it's not you who has to pay?'

'Irene,' he said, sounding tired. 'What are you talking about now?'

'I'm perfectly well aware that the money I spend on the house, food and children was originally yours, but the cost of this trip is nothing to do with you. This is to do with *my* work and you have no right to criticize me for anything that I do in connection with it or for anything I spend while I am being funded by it.'

'Irene, I'm perfectly well aware that you are trying to manufacture a quarrel, but it is quite absurd. I passed an idle remark about the cost of international telephone calls, which is huge, particularly when a hotel's profits have to be added. You must admit that there are times when you, quite as much as your daughter, need reminding of the value of money and its limited supply.'

'Oh, no, I do not, Fin. If I were ever to get into debt, you could, I suppose, have some reason to talk like that, or if I were to feed you on lentils when you had given me enough to buy fillet steak you could ask why – ask, mind you, not assume I've embezzled it. Oh, there are times when you make me so unutterably furious that I . . . What's the use in talking?'

'None, as I said, but then you never listen to me. Good night, Irene.'

She banged down the receiver, telling herself that everything would be different once the play was actually staged. If it should have even a moderate success she would earn some more money. Once she had some money of her own, she would be fine. She would be able to put Fin in his place once and for all, even leave him if she wanted.

'He's such a cantankerous old bugger,' she said aloud. 'What a blissful word that is! Bugger off, you old bugger.'

In a spirit of renewed, furious rebellion, she dressed in black and scarlet and stormed out to meet Richard, who was waiting for her in the big, white lobby.

'You look devastating,' he said, brushing her silken shoulder with his hand as he bent down to kiss her cheek. It struck her that he really was remarkably tall. At five foot eleven, she was almost the same height as Fin, but Richard was a good three inches taller. She liked that, just as she liked his easy, unembarrassed stroking. Fin had never been much of a toucher except when they were making love, and Jane had shrunk from her mother's hugs and kisses from a very early age. Ivo let her pat his arm or shoulder sometimes, and had recently taken to kissing her forehead in an almost avuncular fashion whenever they met. Only Helena was unequivocally glad to be hugged, and that left Irene seriously short of physical contact.

'Are you on for another walk or are you too tired?' Richard asked, looking at her with friendly concern. 'We could easily whistle up a taxi.'

'No, I'd like to walk – whip up a bit of an appetite.'

He laughed and took her off to a small, wonderfully camp restaurant with antiqued gold walls and very pretty waiters, who brought them delectable food and kept out of the way when they were not wanted.

'So tell me what happened to you after you ran away to your lawyer,' said Richard as he shared out the last of the wine between their glasses.

'In fact or emotionally?' she said, knowing that she could tell him anything but determined not to bore him with anything he did not want to know.

'Emotionally.'

'I fell in love, I thought, with the glamour of Fin's sadness and all his need,' she said, looking down at her smeared plate with a kind of self-disgust she had not recognized before. 'And all too quickly I discovered that neither was quite what it seemed – or at all glamorous.'

'Fin?'

'That's what everyone calls him. His mother, who suffered from serious *folie de grandeur*, had him christened Godolphin and he shortened it as soon as he realized what she'd done to him.'

'Poor blighter.'

'Perhaps.' The rekindled anger was too hot in her to be concealed. 'I must say I've occasionally wondered why he didn't shorten it to God, which is how he appears to see himself.'

'Aha,' said Richard, grinning at her. 'Bossy, is he?'

'You could say so.' Suddenly ashamed of moaning about her husband to someone who had never even met him, Irene quickly added: 'What about you? You didn't go into any great detail about your wife when you were talking about your marriage at lunch last week.'

'No, I don't suppose I did. She's gorgeous to look at, even now, and very clever. But she's got a tongue like razor and she uses it.'

'Why?'

'That's the question I often ask when she's being particularly cutting. Personally I think she regrets having refused to have children in order to pursue her career. But she's always denied it and pretends that it's a colleague, friend, or – more often – me who's making her angry.'

He looked at Irene for a second, letting her have a glimpse of the hurting human behind the mask of success and superiority he usually wore. Then he laughed and the mask slid back into place.

'As you know, I've never minded paying for sins I have committed, but I'm damned if I'm going to take the blame for things that aren't my fault. When she lams into me unjustly, I let her have it all back with interest. That, of course, makes her even more vituperative, and so it goes on.'

'But you are still together, aren't you?'

'After a fashion,' said Richard, turning down the comers of his mouth in disgust. 'I don't always go home. Don't let's talk about that now. It's too depressing. You and I have left them both behind for the moment, and for now it's the two of us again as it always should have been. Let's just enjoy that while we can.'

Irene sat with her chin in her hands, watching him and wondering if he could have altered as much as he seemed to have done.

'Did you ever think about me in between?' she asked at last and saw him smile, not the usual mocking or polite widening of the lips, but with a kind of half-private, self-conscious pleasure that reminded her vividly of her own feelings whenever she had let herself indulge in fantasies of the life they might have led together.

'Yes. When things got particularly lurid with Clottie, I'd half comfort and half torment myself with how life might have been if I hadn't accepted your dismissal that day.'

'My what?' Irene sat up and spoke much less languorously.

'Your dismissal.' He raised his fine eyebrows. 'Don't pretend you don't know what I'm talking about: the time when you turned me down in those astonishingly disdainful tones that still make me shudder whenever I think of them.'

'But you never asked me for anything. What on earth are you talking about, Richard?'

'Of course I did. I invited you to come to Dartmoor with me. Don't you remember that? You can't have forgotten something so important.'

'No, I haven't forgotten, but it was just a try-on, wasn't it? A kind of joke?'

'I told you some friends had offered me the loan of a cottage on Dartmoor for the week before Christmas and asked you to go there with me. I described the log fire in the sitting room and the sheepskin rug in front of it and told you how amazing it would be to make love to you there. A bloke could hardly have been any clearer, Irene, if he'd written a placard six feet high and paraded it up Oxford Street shouting through a meagaphone: I want Irene; I want Irene.'

She could not say anything, just looked at him, her mind back in the dank, smelly corridor outside the changing rooms of the little local authority swimming pool most of the students had used at the time in an effort to keep fit and slim. It struck her that it had been an odd choice of place in which to proposition anyone, both of them dripping with chlorine-smelling pool water and clutching inadequate, hard, greyish-white towels around their shivering bodies. Perhaps he really had been in earnest. It was an extraordinary thought.

'Don't you remember what you said then?' he asked.

She shook her head, although she did remember perfectly well, just as she remembered trying so hard to look and sound as sophisticated as she possibly could.

'You said that you had better things to do than let me use you to enhance my reputation as a stud,' he said, sounding more acerbic than at any time since they had met again in his rubber-planted office. 'And then you added that if you'd fancied me it might have been different, but since you didn't there wouldn't be much in it for you.'

'You minded, didn't you?' said Irene slowly, surprised by her breathlessness. She took a moment to make sure it would not sound in her voice. 'My God, you were serious. It never crossed my mind or I wouldn't have . . .'

'You didn't know?'

She shook her head and felt a coil of hair bursting its pins apart. Putting up a hand to stuff the pins back, ramming the ends against her skull, she said: 'I thought you were teasing me, sort of setting me up to make a fool of myself. I am sorry, Richard.'

'So you should be. It took me months to get over it. And then I heard – far too late, after you'd buggered off for ever – that you'd told that friend of yours – Maggie, was it? – that you were half dead of unrequited love and doing your best to make sure it didn't show and put me off. I could have slaughtered you. If I'd got my hands on you I probably would have. You made me hellishly unhappy, you know.'

'Oh, Richard, I can't tell you . . . Hell! No, I won't let you make me feel guilty, especially not after all this time.' She smiled. 'After all, you were known as a stud and you did trail your conquests about. Everyone warned me, and they teased me too. "He'll drop you like a hot potato as soon as you've given in. He won't want you if he thinks he can have you too easily." That's what they all said and since I knew nothing whatever about anything I believed them and acted accordingly.' More of Irene's hair came down and she put up both hands to repin it.

'Do that here and I won't answer for myself,' Richard said with mock savagery and called for the bill.

'What do you mean? It's so heavy it will push the pins out. I'm just pushing them back.'

He laughed. 'I thought you were about to let down your hair and shake it at me. We'll save that, shall we? Until we get back to the hotel at least.'

'Yes,' she said after a silent conversation with her irritatingly obtrusive conscience, 'I suppose we'd better.'

'Good.' He stood up and thrust his credit card at their waiter, standing over him in obvious impatience throughout the production of the slip. He signed in the flamboyant writing she remembered well and ushered her out of the restaurant.

It had taken them twenty minutes to walk there from the hotel, but they could have been back in much less time. Irene felt his hand under her elbow, urging her on as they walked faster and faster. She was not sure how they were going to make themselves wait to say or do anything else until they reached the hotel. In the end they did not. As they were passing the end of a dark street that led deep into the Jordaan, Richard pulled her into the shadow of a house, stood her up against the wall and kissed her, pushing her face up with his thumbs hard under her chin.

'God! I've waited for this.'

She felt her whole body soften, longing to be gathered up and taken over and made to forget the bitter, wasted years. Clinging to what was left of her self-control, she touched his face and, when he withdrew, said breathlessly: 'All this caveman stuff, Richard. We don't need it. We're far too old.'

'Need has nothing to do with it, and I don't feel old at all,' he said before kissing her again more lightly. 'You're making me feel about eighteen again. I haven't wanted anyone this ferociously for years, decades. It's wonderful.' He moved away, grabbing her hand. 'Come on.'

By the time they were in his room at the hotel, Irene had stopped thinking about trying to be self-controlled, amused and middle-aged. As he kissed her again, standing just inside the door and trailing his fingertips up and down her back, she found herself in a state she had entirely forgotten. It struck her that if they did not get their clothes off and start touching each other she would probably scream. She said as much and heard him laugh.

'Come on then,' he said and started to unbutton his shirt.

As she saw one of the buttons fly off as he tugged impatiently at it, she had a sudden, horrible memory of a passage about 'three-button love' in *Madame Bovary*. She pushed the thought away and concentrated on taking her own clothes off as gracefully as possible.

Relieved to be under the bedclothes, hiding her stretch-marks and dimples, she realized that she had lost most of the impetus that had sent her there. But she smiled for Richard and reached up to kiss him as he leaned over her.

She soon recognized his technique as masterly as he began to repair the damage her inconvenient memory had done, stroking her, kissing her, talking to her and asking no questions. For a moment she thought that it was going to work and relaxed under his hands. He smiled and let them move more insistently, telling her she was wonderful, talking about the times they had shared in the past when they had understood each other, about his memories of her, about the longing that had resurfaced as soon as he read her play and recognized so much of her in it.

She could not concentrate. All sorts of other memories and ideas kept occurring to her. The excitement had gone completely, although her body was responding to what he was doing. She could not forget herself even when she felt him begin to make love to her.

It was then that all her muscles began to stiffen. She bit her lip. Richard stopped moving and, propping himself up on his hands as though he were doing press-ups, looked down at her.

'What is it?'

'I'm awfully sorry,' she said, mortified by her lack of desire. 'I know this is awful and I'm not doing it to tease. God forbid! It's just that I've sort of gone off the boil and now I can't get it back. But don't mind me. You go ahead. You know, enjoy yourself.'

He pulled away at once, saying impatiently: 'Don't be idiotic. I want to make love with you – you – not entertain myself with a dummy.' He laughed. 'You can buy them here, you know.'

'What?'

'Inflatable women, designed for all sorts of nefarious purposes.'

'You're joking.'

'No, I'm not actually,' he said, smiling in a friendly way that she thought was remarkably generous in the circumstances. He pushed a strand of her long hair away from her face with surprising gentleness. 'They're part of the other Amsterdam, which is quite different from ours.'

'You mean you're not angry?' said Irene, despising herself for the childish question as much as her lack of sexual sophistication.

'Of course I'm not. It's not an unknown phenomenon, you know.'

'What isn't?'

'Arousal at the thought of making love and de-arousal at the reality. Don't worry about it. I rather think that you're a good bit less experienced than I'd realized. Am I right?'

'I don't know why that should make me feel that I ought to apologize,' said Irene, feeling more like herself and sounding tougher too. 'Yes, I suppose I am. There hasn't been anyone but Fin and it's some time since ...' She saw that she did not need to finish the sentence.

'Well, there you are then. That explains it. And there are no bones broken. It was all a bit precipitate. Silly of me, really; I should have thought. But since the tension was starting to split all the atoms in the air between us, I couldn't stop myself. D'you want a drink? The minibar's got most things.'

'Actually, if you don't mind, I think I might nip straight back to my own room.'

'I hope you brought a teddy bear to cuddle.'

When she saw that he was laughing at her, she pulled a pillow from behind her head and hit him with it.

'I may be inexperienced, but I'm not eight,' she said indignantly.

'Or even eighteen any longer. I shouldn't have let you brush me off then. It's all quite as much my fault as yours. The great seducer getting his timing completely wrong all over again. Would you like me to switch off the light while you get dressed?'

She produced a laugh of her own then to show her appreciation of his friendly voice and hoped that she had not damaged the chances for her play. At least he did not sound at all humiliated by what she had done. It came to her that the one thing Richard might not be able to forgive was humiliation. It also occurred to her, surprisingly in view of what she thought she had felt for him, that he would not be above taking revenge for that in any way he could.

Producing a series of furious, silent instructions to herself, Irene collected her clothes from the tumbled heap on the floor, got them back on, thanked him for dinner with as much dignity as she could manage, and found her way back to her own bedroom. There she leaned against the locked door and breathed deeply, covering her face with her hands.

'You fool,' she said into them. 'You unutterable fool. What on earth were you thinking of?'

Sex, answered her conscience drily. Or quite possibly lust.

'No, I wasn't. It's what I said to Helena. I wanted to put myself right with my own past. No wonder it didn't work. It wasn't Richard I wanted at all, or love or even just sex; it was an idea of myself.'

What she did want, very much indeed, at that moment was to talk to Helena, but it seemed unfairly late to ring her.

# Chapter Seven

Helena was asleep in the crook of Mike's arm. It did not last long but for a time it was real sleep, and that was worth a lot to her. She longed to feel safe with him, not just with her conscious, willed mind but with all the uncontrollable, only half-understood parts of her subconscious. If she could have done it by wanting and trying, it would already have happened. When she knew that she was not going to sleep again, she got up, collected the novel she was reading and went to bed again alone in the spare room.

She was up and dressed, sipping coffee and reading the arts section of her Sunday paper by the time Mike emerged, looking enticingly rumpled. He wandered into the kitchen in his bare feet, rubbing his big hands over his face.

'Sleep all right?' he asked, blinking at her and smiling sleepily.

'Yes,' she said, not wanting to bore him with her oddities. 'Coffee?'

'Mm. That would be nice.'

'And what to eat? I can't offer you kidneys and bacon or anything like that, but there's toast, muesli, eggs, fruit. That's about it, I think. Oh, no, there are some sausages in the freezer, if you'd like.'

He laughed. 'No thanks. Toast would be great, especially if you've got any butter for once.'

'As it happens, I have,' she said. 'In an access of sentimentality, I bought you some in case you should happen to be here for breakfast ever. It'll be a bit cold, but it's there.'

He blew her a kiss. 'Greater love hath no woman.'

'What? Than to buy her lover food she knows is bad for him?'

'That's it. But in any case you don't "know" it's bad. You only think it is because of what you've read other people writing, and they don't know either. They're just spoilsports. I listen to my body and *know* that butter is good for me.'

'You are a shocker, you know. And a wheedler, which is probably worse.'

He kissed the top of her head and then pulled her into his arms and hugged her.

'I never thought I could be grateful for that hellish weekend we spent with Harriet and George,' he said. 'And yet it's led to this.'

'Who'd have thought it?' agreed Helena. She tried to look up at him, but she could see little more than his broad chest and bristly chin. 'You look quite bizarre from this angle.' She stepped back and saw his friendly duck-like smile. 'That's better. Now what am I supposed to be doing? Oh, yes, your toast. Sit down and I'll bring it. D'you want some of the paper? Help yourself.'

'Thanks,' he said, leafing about among the innumerable sections that were spread all over the kitchen table. 'What would you like to do today?'

'I hadn't thought much beyond breakfast and the newspaper,' she said, looking at him over her shoulder. 'Why? Have you got plans?'

'There's an auction at Beamie's next week and the stuff's available for viewing today. I did wonder whether you'd like to come with me.'

'I'd love to,' said Helena. 'I like Beamie's, although most of their things are way beyond my price range. But I'm surprised you know about the sale. You're not a collector, are you?'

'Only in a very small way, but I happen to have a bit of spare cash at the moment and what with the index being so toppy and interest rates so pathetic, I thought I might put a bit into some really good furniture.'

'Antiques hardly ever represent a good investment in purely financial terms, you know,' Helena warned him, surprised that he had never mentioned any interest in old furniture before. 'Particularly in the short term.'

'No, I am aware of that,' he said, looking even more amused than usual. She wondered if he were about to tell her not to teach her grandmother to suck eggs. 'But it gives you nice things to use and look at in the meantime, and who knows? There may be another boom in eighteenth-century English furniture, and then I can flog it all and make a decent return. Quite as good as I'd get putting it in equities before the market crashes again. I must do something with it. One can't leave money hanging about doing nothing, you know.'

'No, I suppose one can't,' she said, trying not to laugh. She herself never had much more than was necessary to service the mortgage, pay the bills, and buy herself the odd treat, so she had never had to worry about investments.

'Will you come? I don't want to exploit your expertise, but I'd like to persuade you to have a quick look at a chair that sounds rather good in the catalogue. I'll pay you a fee, if you like.'

'Certainly not,' she said in genuine outrage. 'I'd love to look at it for you, but I'd be appalled if you paid me.'

'Why? I'd be using your professional knowledge.'

'Yes. But it would be the greatest possible pleasure for me to be able to give it to you,' she said with a formality that she hoped would persuade him that she meant what she said.

'Good. It's a deal then. We'll have a real London Sunday jaunt.'

'We always used to go to the zoo when I was a child,' said Helena irrelevantly. The coffee rose into the top half of the espresso pot and she poured him a cupful. 'Or one of the parks. At least, Irene and I did. Fin was usually working. Once or twice she even took me to Battersea funfair. That was the best.'

Helena could remember the experience with astonishing clarity, almost able to feel the wholly exciting and half-frightening swooping sensation as the various machines swirled her about and turned her upside down. Lost in memories of the probably tawdry, but to a child thrilling, pleasures of the funfair, she did not notice Mike taking the cup from her.

'Thanks,' he said, stroking her hand and making her jump.

'For what?'

'The coffee.'

'You're laughing at me again,' she said, returning to the present.

'Yes, I am. You don't mind, though, do you?'

'To tell you the truth, I love it. But why this time?'

'I was just amused to think that on all the occasions I've sat wondering how to make you happy, I'd never realized that the easiest way would be to take you to a funfair. For some weird reason it hadn't even struck me as a possibility. I can't think why not.'

By then she was laughing too and pretended to aim a punch at his head.

'I don't suppose I'd like it these days,' she said. 'It's probably like candyfloss and thumb-sucking.'

'Have you been trying those recently?' asked Mike in deep amusement.

'Idiot. No, of course I haven't, but I can well remember the miserable disillusion of finding that they had lost their appeal.'

'On your last birthday, you mean?'

'Just a trifle earlier than that,' Helena said. 'You do me good, Mike. I haven't laughed as much as this in years and years. Oh, lord! The toast.'

The acrid smell of burning made her run to the toaster, which seemed to have jammed. She could not think why neither of them had noticed it before or seen the smoke that was billowing along the worktop under the cupboards. She unlocked the window and flung it open to clear the air.

They took their time over breakfast and a shared bath, and it was nearly twelve by the time they were both dressed.

'We'll miss Beamie's if we hang about any longer,' Helena said lightly as she buttoned up her loose turquoise dress, revelling in the warmth that seemed to be going to last for ever. The endless rainy summers of her past seemed almost impossible to believe in as day succeeded day with hardly a cloud to be seen. She pulled a wide straw hat off a peg on the back of the door and picked up her dark glasses. 'We'd better get going.'

Mike nodded, zipped up his trousers and pulled on his socks. It amused him that Helena was not going to dress up for Beamie's. True it was a Sunday and most people dressed informally for

Sunday viewings, but even so her bare legs and scooped-neck dress seemed remarkably casual for St James's.

When they walked into the sale rooms in Bury Street half an hour later, Helena was immediately hailed by a young man dressed in the sort of cream-coloured trousers and blazer that a young farmer might wear when tidied up for Sunday lunch. He nodded to Mike and then kissed Helena. Mike stood aside and watched them talk until Helena remembered him and introduced the young man as Jonathan Beamie, the director in charge of furniture at the auction rooms.

'And this is Michael Alfrick,' she said, urging him forward.

'How do you do?' said young Mr Beamie, shaking hands and looking at Mike properly for the first time. 'But we've met before, haven't we?'

'Once or twice,' he said shortly. Then he caught sight of Helena's look of surprise and added in a more relaxed voice: 'I've been in here several times. You were the auctioneer one evening last year when I bought a breakfast table – oval on a single shaft with four particularly elegant splayed legs.'

'That must be it. I remember that table well. Rather gorgeous, wasn't it? Although the condition could have been better. Regency; satinwood with kingwood stringing?'

'That's the one.'

Helena was looking at Mike and wondering why she had never noticed him at any of the sales she had attended, and whether he had seen her.

'Have you still got it?' Jonathan Beamie was asking.

'Sure. I eat off it. Had I known Helena in those days I'd have got her to restore it rather than the firm I did get, who did an immensely expensive and rather obtrusive job on it.'

As Mike was talking, Helena suddenly realized why he might have hidden his interest in antiques from her. If he had been so afraid of exploiting her knowledge that he had offered to pay her to look at the chair he was thinking of buying that day, he might well have thought that she would interpret any earlier questions as attempts to get free professional advice out of her and resent them. She almost blushed as she thought of how her wariness could have been misconstrued.

'Oh, Helena's undoubtedly one of the best in London these days,' Jonathan Beamie was saying, 'but very hard to get. Which reminds me, Helena, my father was saying only the other day that he would like you to have a go at a set of Chippendale chairs he's found. Would you consider it?'

'Really Chippendale?' she asked, remembering the unpleasant telephone call and hoping that this was not another attempt to get her to increase the saleability of the same 'naughty' chairs.

'Possibly, although there are no C scrolls.'

Helena sighed in relief. They might still be the same chairs, but at least the brief was going to be different and she would not be asked to fake anything. That could make it possible to accept the work, and she would if she could. The Beamies were a good source of clients and she did not want to antagonize them if she could possibly avoid it.

'The date's about right, though,' Jonathan went on, 'which comes to much the same thing in the end. Shall I get my father to ring you?'

'Thanks, Jonathan. He's got my number and if I'm out or working the machine will be on.'

'Great stuff.' Jonathan Beamie waved at someone over her head, thanked her again, and left them.

Mike took her arm and they strolled upstairs to the main auction rooms.

'You do hide your light under a bushel, don't you?' he said as they paused before a games table, most beautifully made and inlaid with several different exotic woods. 'I hadn't realized quite how distinguished you were. Old Mr Beamie . . .' He stopped talking when he saw that Helena was not listening. She had bent down to look under the surface of the table.

'Well?' he said when she re-emerged, red in the face from stooping.

'Naughty,' she said. 'What were you saying?'

'Nothing. My chair's over there. Will you give it the once-over for me?'

'Of course I will. I told you I would.'

They went off to inspect it and after a minute search, during which she took a lens out of her capacious pocket to examine a particular joint, she pronounced herself satisfied. The upper estimate was, she told him, a little high, but it was worth putting in a lowball and seeing how the bidding went.

Amused by her carefully limited enthusiasm, he left her to wander around the rest of the lots while he went to arrange a commission bid with one of the receptionists. Helena was stopped by Jonathan Beamie again when she had returned to look sadly at the games table.

'Don't you approve?' he said. She looked round and shook her head, smiling politely.

'You know as well as I do that it's been made up. They were never built like that. This has one table's legs with a quite different table's folding top bunged on them. The hinges are all wrong, and so's the stringing down the legs.'

'Nicely done, though, don't you think?'

'Yes, quite. The inlay is certainly pretty clean. But I think your cataloguing's on the optimistic side to say the least. There's no way that this is a nineteenth-century games table, even if its legs might have been made before 1900.'

'And many of the other parts I imagine, although, not being responsible for the valuations or the catalogue descriptions, I haven't examined it closely myself. There's no need to look like that. As you know perfectly well, we're merely agents for the seller here. We carry no liability. *Caveat emptor.*'

'Doesn't it worry you that the ignorant might think this table really was made just as it is in the nineteenth century?'

'Why should it? After all, everyone knows the basis on which we work and it's printed in all our catalogues. We'd never knowingly authenticate a fake. God forbid! But if our valuer's view of something is different from someone else's . . .'

'Who put it together?' she asked suddenly, looking up at him again. 'You're right. It is good work.'

'I have absolutely no idea,' he said coldly. 'Why?'

'I just thought that it's been remarkably well done, and I was trying to think which of the really good cabinet makers could have done it. But perhaps it isn't English work. Who brought it in?'

'I don't know and you're beginning to sound like a policewoman. You want to watch that. What's your friend up to?'

'He's leaving a commission bid on that nice little elbow chair over there. He obviously doesn't trust me to bid for him.'

'You passed the chair then, did you?' Jonathan was obviously trying to sound pleasant, but Helena knew that he was seriously annoyed about her strictures on the games table. As he led her back to re-examine the elbow chair, she wondered whether he was staying beside her to ensure that she did not repeat her observations on the table to any possible buyer.

'Yes, I did pass it,' she said, looking at it again. 'It's been mended more than once and obviously re-upholstered, but in a perfectly respectable way.'

'You'd much prefer the Chinese system, wouldn't you?' Jonathan was still smiling, but it was clear that he was not remotely amused.

'Yes, I would. It's so much more honest to keep all repairs deliberately visible. You know exactly where you are, and you'd know that no-one you were working for could be using your work to mislead other people.'

'But it's not so pretty. I hope your friend gets the chair. He probably will; he's bought several things for quite good prices over the past six months or so.'

Helena stood up straight and looked at Beamie in surprise. 'But I thought you only just managed to recognize him after I'd introduced you.'

Jonathan Beamie looked faintly embarrassed. He coughed and ran his stubby fingers through his short, sleek, dark hair.

'I thought he was familiar when I spotted the pair of you coming in,' he said, not meeting her eyes, 'but I couldn't remember his name and didn't want to seem rude by getting it wrong since he's becoming a good customer. It seemed politic to wait for you to introduce us.'

Helena was about to ask what else Mike had bought when she saw him returning from the front desk and so she said nothing.

'Don't look so worried,' Jonathan whispered in her ear. 'Chaps as rich as he must be are used to keeping their assets hidden. Have a look round next time you go to his place and see what you can see. I'd have said he's a pretty good catch. You'll be doing quite well for yourself if you manage to nab him on a permanent basis.'

'Are you all right?' asked Mike as he reached her side. Jonathan had already gone, but Helena could feel the heat in her cheeks and hoped that they were not as red as she thought they might be.

'Yes,' she said. 'But the atmosphere in here always gets a bit stuffy. D'you want to see any more? Would you mind if I go and sit on the steps outside and wait for you there?'

'No. I've seen all I need. I'll come with you. We could sit in Green Park for a bit if that would help.'

'I like St James's better,' she said, reminding herself that it was she who had always refused to go to Mike's house and insisted that he come to hers. There was no need to suspect a conspiracy just because he had never talked about the antiques he owned or told her that he had attended many of the same sales as she had done. She still wondered whether he had noticed her at any of them and did not like the idea that he might have been watching her and said nothing about it. She told herself sharply to stop being so silly; if she had not seen him, there was no reason in the world why he should have noticed her. 'Let's go.'

They sat in the grass like office workers in their lunch break, soaking up the sun and watching the waterbirds on the lake until the ground began to seem much too hard. Mike shifted position for the fourth time in as many minutes and asked her what she would like to do next and whether he could take her out for lunch.

'Could we go to your house? I'd love to see it. I realize I've never been.'

She was surprised when he looked pleased and put an arm around her shoulders. 'Of course. Come back to the car and we'll go straight away. I hope you won't be disappointed. It's not actually a house – just a flat. I'd love you to see it. You've always turned up your nose at the prospect before.'

Driving towards Regent's Park, Mike laughed. When Helena asked what was so amusing, he said: 'It's the breakfast table, isn't it? The one I bought from Beamie's. You want to know what it looks like. Collector's curiosity, eh?'

'No, no, no! Nothing like that. I just suddenly realized that there's an enormous amount I don't know about you, even though we know each other as well as we possibly could in some ways. I thought it might help if I were to see where you live. D'you mind?'

'I have to say that I'm delighted. But there's nothing there to feed you on and you haven't had any lunch yet. It's no wonder you came over a bit faint.'

'I don't need any food. It was just the stuffiness.'

Mike pulled up outside a large white house on the edge of Regent's Park.

'It looks a bit pompous from the outside, I'm afraid,' he said, 'but the room's are such good sizes and I like the view.'

He let her in and escorted her into a tall, gloomy hall with an unyielding floor of black and white stone. Helena was relieved to discover much more light and space upstairs, even though it was all very grand. The main room was huge, much more elaborately decorated than anything in her house. She stood in the doorway, taking it all in and trying to connect what she could see with the man she had learned to know in her own much simpler surroundings.

There were shelves on either side of the fireplace, stretching from floor to ceiling and full of books that he had obviously bought to read, rather than for their bindings or because they were valuable first editions. More books were stored in a glass-fronted secretaire-bookcase between the two long windows that looked out over the park.

A large, absolutely plain looking-glass filled the space above the chimneypiece on which stood a low rectangular black vase stuffed with terracotta-coloured roses cut very short. Matching sofas covered in terracotta linen piped in black were arranged on either side of the fire with a low table between them. From where she was standing the table seemed to be made of a slab of polished, fossil-filled beige stone resting on a single pedestal. There was a heap of books at one end and a small bronze bust in the far corner.

The curtains were heavy cream linen naively printed in gold, terracotta and black, the floor was ebonized wood, and there were several old and probably valuable rugs. The breakfast table from Beamie's gleamed with its newly restored polish, and a variety of beautiful, but not matching, chairs stood around it. A card table, which looked much more authentic than the one Jonathan Beamie had tried to defend, was folded against the wall.

'Is something the matter?' Mike said from behind her. Helena turned.

'You live on such a grand scale,' she said, opening her eyes very wide. 'You must have felt you were slumming it in Clerkenwell. I had no idea you were so . . .' There was no tactful way of putting it, and so she finished frankly: 'So rich.'

He laughed and put his arms round her. 'I love Clerkenwell. And it isn't slumming anyway. But I do earn quite a lot, you know, bonuses, profit-shares and all that, and there's no point working hard if you don't ever do anything with the money.'

'You must have been working exceedingly hard,' she said, looking again at the secretaire, which was one of the most desirable pieces she had seen in a long time.

'Yes. But I've had some luck, too. You need it in venture capital,' he said seriously. 'You can find really good people with seriously good ideas and adequate know-how, give them the money they need, ensure that there are plenty of safeguards, and yet the whole thing still goes belly up. Luckily that hasn't happened to me for a while, hence the bonuses. Now, would you like a drink, or tea, or something to eat if I can find anything?'

'A cup of tea would be lovely.'

'Good. Sit down. Make yourself comfortable. I won't be long.'

While he disappeared into the kitchen, she walked around the big room, wondering how she could have had so little curiosity about a man she liked so much and with whom she was prepared to make love. Looking along the rows of his bookshelves, she realized that he was a serious reader of much more than newspapers. Many of the novels and biographies were ones she recognized from her own reading or from book reviews, but there were plenty of others that were completely strange to her. There were even some in French and Italian. Picking one out, she turned the pages and saw his name written on the flyleaf in a strange hand above a message in Italian and a date two years old. Not wanting to pry into his past, she quickly replaced the book and went to look more closely at the breakfast table.

It looked right and was beautifully proportioned, but she could not help running her fingers over the joins between the inlay and the crossbanding. Sadly she felt the smoothness and knew that Mike had paid for a table that was a great deal more modern than he thought. If it had been made during the Regency, the timbers would have shrunk and forced the inlay up, higher than the rest.

As she ran her fingers once more over the smoothness where there should have been a ridge, she wished it was as easy to tell whether people were real or fake.

Hearing Mike returning from the kitchen, she moved away from the table and went to look at the pictures. She was not sure she shared his eclectic taste in paintings; there was a Schiele, which she definitely did not like, and a pair of rather dull watercolours, which she was fairly sure were by Peter de Wint, over the games table on the wall opposite the fireplace. On the other hand, a drawing of ruins that looked remarkably like one of Ben Nicholson's was very much to her taste, if surprising in a room as sombrely rich as Mike's.

Helena remembered his suggestion that he would sell the elbow chair if the price of English furniture ever rose steeply again and wondered whether he had bought the pictures purely for their investment value. The idea was not pleasant.

'You look worried,' he said. She turned and saw that he was putting a tray down on the fossil table. 'Don't you like Schiele?'

'Not a lot, but I was really just remembering that business of the over-restored painting that was auctioned in London.'

Mike frowned and then nodded. 'I remember. There was a court case, wasn't there? And the auctioneers had to repay everything. I think this one's all right, though. I'm particularly proud of it because it came from a lucky bet that I should never have made.'

'I didn't know you gambled,' said Helena, trying not to sound censorious. It was not the idea of his betting that she minded so much as the thought that he had never told her he did it, just as he had never told her that he collected antiques. She wondered unhappily how much more there was to discover and was surprised to see that he was laughing at her.

'Darling heart, it's what I do all the time. It's what venture capitalism is all about.'

'Oh, I see what you mean. Silly of me. Sorry. You mean you backed a winner in one of your clients?'

'Yup. I had a hunch about one young man my colleagues insisted on turning down a few years back. Since I couldn't persuade my then boss to go for the project, I put most of what I'd accumulated myself into the client's business and reaped very handsome rewards. In retrospect I can hardly believe I did anything so risky. I sometimes wake in the night sweating about it, but it came out all right.'

Helena admired the courage that could let anyone take such a risk.

'Did I mention that I was off to New York again tomorrow?' said Mike before she could tell him so. She nodded. He stroked her hair away from her face with both hands, looking down into her eyes much more seriously than usual.

'I fly out tomorrow, but I'll be back on Friday evening. May I come straight to Clerkenwell? For the weekend, I mean?'

She smiled as she shook her head. 'I've got to go down to Worcestershire to see a client first thing on Saturday morning. I can't postpone it. It's too important.'

'Couldn't I come too? I could give you a lift. Wouldn't you be more comfortable in my car than that rattly old van of yours?'

'Much. But even so I can't take you with me. The client's elderly and hates changes to arrangements or having to worry about new people. I've promised to drive down in the morning and have lunch with her. I can't take another person, honestly. I'm sorry, Mike.'

'All right,' he said, looking less kind. 'Then what about Sunday? You'll be back by then, won't you?'

'Yes, probably. But I'm not quite sure exactly when I'll get home. Why don't I ring you then? Would that be all right?'

'Why shouldn't it be?' he asked coolly.

# Chapter Eight

Waking soon after eight, after a surprisingly undisturbed sleep, Irene lay in the huge empty bed thinking about her next encounter with Richard. It was not a scene she felt confident of playing. She considered a dignified apology the best way to start and set about preparing suitable dialogue. After a while she became aware that she was speaking both parts aloud and wondered what the people in the next room must be thinking. With luck, she thought, they might know that she was a dramatist and assume that she was working on a play.

In sudden amusement at her arrogance in believing that any stranger would know who she was – or care – Irene changed her mind about the forthcoming scene. The only reason to apologize would be to winkle yet more reassurance out of Richard. That would not only make her look silly; it would also suggest that he had power over her – or rights of some kind. Much more genuine dignity would come from ignoring the whole fiasco. Irene was not sure that she had the technique to carry that off, but she was determined to try.

Dressed in her dark purple trousers, but with a cream shirt and black jacket instead of the jaunty parrot colours she had chosen for their first encounter, she walked through the art-filled glass corridors of the hotel towards the breakfast room. It seemed important to look neither shifty nor swaggering, and she practised as she went. One or two people she passed looked at her oddly and one very young man in a dark suit had difficulty suppressing laughter. She did not mind that; it gave her useful feedback. By the time she reached the breakfast room, she had just about got her stride and her expression right.

Her efforts were quite unnecessary as it turned out, for Richard was reading the newspaper he held in one hand while raising his coffee cup to his mouth with the other. As Irene saw him miss his aim and slop coffee down his chin, she almost laughed. Muttering an imprecation about the unkindness of *Schadenfreude*, which did nothing to reduce her satisfaction, she chose a newspaper from the stack for herself, carried it over to Richard's table and dropped it in the place opposite his.

'Sorry to be late,' she said lightly. 'If they come with the pots while I'm getting my food, could you ask for coffee – black – please?'

'Sure,' he said, looking up briefly to smile at her.

She did not look at him and took her time choosing what to eat. It all looked so alluring that her usual delight in food overtook her embarrassment and her fears of what he might think of her behaviour the previous evening. By the time she returned to the table with a plate loaded with cumin-flavoured cheese, pumpernickel and fruit, she felt that she ought to be able to cope with anything he might do.

'That looks modest,' said Richard, looking up briefly from his newspaper. He said nothing else.

Relieved to have got off so lightly, Irene shook out her paper and opened it at the theatre reviews, reading them carefully as she ate and drank. One critic so enraged her that, with her mouth full of pumpernickel, she muttered: 'It's so bloody unfair.'

'What?'

'The way reviewers take this kind of godlike tone with playwrights.' She swallowed and said more clearly: 'Instead of just saying they don't like something – or more likely can't see the point of it – they lean down from their great height and announce that it is not good enough, often not even bothering to explain why. It's just a question of taste and expectation after all, theirs versus the writer's. The arrogance of it!'

Richard let his newspaper drop onto the table and picked up

his cup, holding it lightly between both hands. He watched her. Determined not to let her eyelids flutter or her colour rise, she looked straight back at him.

'You don't like arrogance, do you?' he said.

'Who does?'

'Lots of people, believe me. It gives them confidence.'

Irene smiled but decided it would be politic not to comment.

'Don't worry too much about the critics,' he said. 'Are you bothered about what they'll write about *The House on the Canal*?'

'Of course. Aren't you?'

'I'd be lying if I said I didn't care,' Richard said with a smile that was much lighter and more attractive than the seductive version he had used before. 'But I am not anxious. It is such a good play that I'm sure between us all we can make it work. And I'm not entirely without influence, you know.'

'No,' she agreed, laughing and feeling some of her own confidence and strength of character returning, 'I know you're not. But you can't mean that you'll tell the critics what to write, or that if you tried they'd obey.'

'No, they wouldn't. The good ones are much too cussed for that. But there are things one can do to help them towards the right conclusion. I can't guarantee good reviews, but I know we'll get enough useful quotes out of them at least to hang up outside the theatre.'

'What, you mean things like "Go and see this play" taken out of a review that says, "If you want to have the most boring and uncomfortable evening of your life, go and see this play"?'

'That's right.' Richard drank some more coffee. 'You really don't need to worry so much. You've written the thing; it's over to us now.'

'But you said you'd want me there at rehearsals.'

'Yes. There will probably be bits and pieces of rewriting that need doing, and it helps the actors if the writer can be there to answer questions. But the responsibility isn't yours any more. You can let go.' His eyebrows rose and he looked half wary, half mischievous. 'Even though I realize that's something you find quite hard to do.'

'Oh, you rotter,' she said before she could stop herself. 'That's not fair.'

He laughed and after a moment she joined in.

'Yes, but we can't pretend last night didn't happen or that it is of any significance at all. It's not. And we need to laugh about it or it'll fester and cause trouble with the play.'

'That sounds sensible. I am sorry, you know, Richard.'

'Don't be. You were honest and that counts for a great deal.' He took off his reading glasses and let them drop against his chest, suspended from what looked like two old bootlaces knotted together. 'A lot of women would have gone in for a spot of faking, and I can't tell you how grateful I am that you didn't. That took guts.'

'Oh, Richard!' His generosity made her regret both her own reluctance to apologize to him and her pleasure in the moment when he had made himself look only slightly foolish with the spilt coffee.

'Well, come on then,' he said a few moments later in a tone that made it clear he was enjoying a private joke. Irene could not make her brain work fast enough to understand it.

'Come on, what?' she said eventually, trying not to sound stupid or irritable.

'I think the full quotation you're looking for is, "O, Richard, o, mon roi." Shakespeare.' He sat up and looked down his long nose as though he were performing one of Ben's acting exercises in regality.

'You're quite pleased enough with yourself without my addressing you as my liege lord,' she said with asperity. She was so grateful to him for giving her back her sense of herself as an admirable human being that she could have kissed him.

'That's all you know,' he said, looking pleased with her, too. 'Now, have you had enough to eat? If so, we need to get back to work. I want to finish my notes while we're here. We can always have more coffee sent in later.'

'Great.' Most of her pleasure in the play had been regained. The thought of working with Richard seemed possible again, and, more than that, exciting. The muddle they had made between them might even prove useful. They had got something important out of the way and now they could throw away all the baggage from the past that they had been lugging around with them for years and concentrate on the present.

Or at least, she said silently as she corrected herself, I can.

'What will I have to do at the rehearsals?' she said aloud.

'Not a lot to start with. As you know I want you there for the first read-through, in case the actors have any questions, and then I'll want you to disappear for a good week after that.'

At the sight of her face, losing all its amusement in the anxiety that made it look pinched instead of magnificent, Richard added: 'We need time for blocking in the entrances and exits, which I think you'd find very dull. Then the actors need to find their way into the play and suck out the meaning and the ways in which they can bring it out for the audience. I think you might find that process disturbing. Anything and everything is allowed. It has to be. Actors say and do some thoroughly peculiar things then. I don't want you to have to be involved at that stage; it might hurt.' He paused and then smiled in reassurance. 'And I don't want you hurt, Irene; not any more and not for anything.'

'Oh, Richard,' she said again, trying to put all her gratitude and her affection into her voice. He looked at her and, recognizing a sly glint in his pale eyes, she quickly corrected her own expression.

'Because that would undoubtedly affect the actors and I don't want them to have to worry about you as well as their proper job,' he said, making her scowl at him.

'You are hard.'

'Like you,' he said lightly. 'And to me that's a compliment. Come on. We must get down to work if we're to finish my notes before the last flight.'

They spent the rest of the day working. Irene often found herself infuriated by something Richard said about what she had written and, in trying to explain why he had so badly misread it, would stumble on a better way of putting what she had actually meant. Occasionally either he or she would play a bit of dialogue as though they were on stage to show the other what they meant and they slowly worked themselves into complete agreement. By the end of the day, tired though they both were, they were finishing each other's sentences and answering their own questions as soon as they had articulated them, as though they were almost the same person.

They caught the seven o'clock plane back to Heathrow in a mood of satisfaction with each other that could hardly have been bettered even if they had been lovers. The flight seemed to take less time than a tube journey across London and as they walked into the baggage-reclaim hall, they looked at each other. At Irene's expression, Richard laughed, sounding resigned rather than amused.

'You, too?' she said.

'Yes. There's nothing like a weekend with a kindred spirit to make going back to an angry house and an unfriendly spouse seem . . . dull.'

'As perfect an example of understatement as I've ever heard,' she said. 'Still, there's always tomorrow.'

He hugged her. They seemed to have covered an immense amount of emotional ground and to have emerged onto a plateau of friendship that stretched ahead without any apparent hazards at all.

'And tomorrow and tomorrow and tomorrow.'

'I thought it was bad luck to quote from *Macbeth*,' said Irene, crossing her fingers behind her back.

'Only inside the theatre. And anyway, it's a silly superstition. I don't hold with that sort of thing. Isn't that your bag?'

'Oh, yes,' she said, as she saw the red and black parachute bag twitch past.

They got it off the rollers the next time it came round and had to wait for another three whole revolutions before Richard's expensive canvas and brown leather grip appeared. Then, carrying a bag in each hand, disdaining the trolleys, he walked ahead of her through the blue channel in the Customs hall. She hurried to catch up with his stride and they were nearly at the end of the broad white passage when an unimpassioned female voice said: 'Just a moment, sir, madam.'

Irene looked round. A young woman in the sub-naval uniform of the Customs and Excise had appeared through a concealed door in the white wall, between two wide mirrors.

'What is it now?' asked Richard irritably.

Irene said nothing at all. She was appalled at the possibilty that there might be a tabloid journalist or a stray photographer passing by who recognized her. However dreary she found the prospect of going back to Herbert Crescent to play the part of Fin's decorous wife again, she did not want to embarrass him with headlines about being arrested by Customs after a weekend in Amsterdam with a man to whom she was not married.

Casting a quick look at the luggage suspended from Richard's large hands, she noticed that there were about four unlockable, zipped pockets in the outside of her bag. It dawned on her that it would have been exceedingly easy for someone to have planted drugs there. She felt the blood leaving her face and put a hand on Richard's shoulder to stop herself keeling over.

After a moment the faintness receded and she let him go, telling herself to stop behaving as neurotically as Helena, who could hardly be restrained from going through the red channel and begging for her luggage to be opened just in case she might have forgotten that she had acquired something that she was not allowed to bring into the country. Noticing that there was a bulge in the biggest of the zipped pockets, Irene was about to say something when she heard Richard's voice, as arrogant as it had ever been: 'Don't you think this is a little ridiculous? I know that this is one of your favourite flights. Everyone who goes to Amsterdam knows that. Do you not think that if I were criminal enough to want to use or import drugs I might have the intelligence not to choose a flight like this to bring them in on?'

'Now, now, sir, please calm down. I am just doing my job. Would you please put the bags on this table?'

With a heavy sigh and a shrug, Richard swung the two bags

onto the white table. He looked over his shoulder at Irene and saw several of the other passengers on their flight waltzing past with expressions of excited satisfaction at his predicament.

'Sorry about this,' he said to Irene. For a moment, she thought that he was confessing to something. 'It tends to happen to me. It's something to do with the way I look or dress. It makes me so angry that I can't be rational about it.'

'Are you aware of the regulations governing what you may and may not bring into this country?' asked the officer with her hand on Richard's khaki-canvas bag.

'Yes, yes. Get a move on and get this farce over with. We're tired and we want to get home.'

'And you, madam?'

'I know about the duty-free limits,' said Irene with a smile, determined not to antagonize the woman and more in sympathy with her than Richard seemed to be.

Irene had always detested the thought of drugs and was deeply thankful that both her children had been sensible enough – and successful enough – to avoid them. When three boys from Ivo's class at school had been expelled for smoking cannabis when they were sixteen, she had been worried enough to talk to him about it. His vast contempt for what he called their stupidity had reassured her. Ivo was very rarely contemptuous of anyone, but at that moment he might have been Fin at his most disdainful. In the circumstances, Irene had found it reassuring.

'And I can assure you that I have never had anything to do with drugs,' she went on. 'I loathe the very thought of them.'

'Satisfied now?' said Richard rudely.

'Do you know that it is an offence to import pornography?' asked the Customs officer.

'Oh, for God's sake!' Richard sounded like a man at the end of his tether. 'Do either of us look as though we're likely to have brought pornography with us? Have you any idea who you are talking to?'

'Richard, please don't. Pornography is a red herring. This must be about drugs and that's important. If we're ever going to get rid of them from the country, this sort of thing has to be done.' Irene turned to smile once more at the young officer. 'Yes, we both know that. Would you like me to open my bag?'

'Thank you, madam.'

Irene leaned forward to unzip the parachute bag and felt Richard's hand on her wrist.

'I don't think you should,' he said. 'This is outrageous. They have to have some reason to search us and there isn't any. It's an infringement of our civil liberties. You mustn't encourage them.'

'It isn't a problem, Richard,' said Irene, trying to make him see sense. 'I'm all for being searched, and searched quickly, so that we can get home. They have the right to do it. Get it over with. It's not important.'

'I disagree.'

'Richard,' she said firmly. 'Stop behaving like a child and get a move on.'

Surprised by her tone, he stared at her.

'You're winding everyone up and making a completely unnecessary fuss,' Irene went on, a little more calmly. 'We'd practically be home by now if you hadn't been so obstructive.'

'Oh, all right then. But I think you're making a serious mistake.'

Hoping that he had not been mad enough to buy anything illegal or cruel enough to plant it in her luggage, Irene unzipped her bag and stood back, watching Richard as he undid the buckles of the heavy leather straps and then the zip of his bag.

The Customs officer took out every single thing from both bags and felt in all the pockets. Irene was almost sick with relief when she saw that the lump she had noticed in one of the outer pockets was simply the outline of the bottom of her shampoo bottle, which had slipped down among her clothes. The Customs officer took the tops off all the bottles and smelled their contents, before trying to unscrew the bottom of a can of shaving foam that Richard had with him. He raised his eyes to heaven and sighed melodramatically. Irene was almost certain that if he had not been so unpleasant the search would have been infinitely less thorough.

Eventually the officer appeared to be satisfied and told them that they could repack. When Richard was about to swing the two bags off the table, she said:

'Would you please come with me?'

'What on earth now?'

'Richard,' said Irene, again in the tones of an exasperated nanny. 'Co-operate.'

By the time she discovered that she was to be strip-searched, Irene herself was seething with annoyance. Because of her unchangeable belief in the necessity of keeping imported drugs out of the country, she could not let herself be angry with the Customs officers and had transferred all her fury to Richard. She privately admitted that it would serve him right if he were found to be carrying a minute amount of something like cannabis that would cause him embarrassment and a fine but not real trouble.

When the young officer had gained a senior's permission to carry out a full search, she then informed Richard and Irene that they had the right to appeal to an independent senior officer or a magistrate. Richard was all for causing the maximum inconvenience and demanding a magistrate, but Irene eventually persuaded him that co-operation was the more sensible option.

Alone in a brightly lit, cream-painted room with two women officers, Irene was first frisked and then asked to take off her clothes. Humiliated and, in spite of her innocence, anxious, she did as she was told, folding her clothes neatly on the grey-topped table.

Remembering all the dimples and unattractive sagging flesh, she stood very straight, facing the two women and trying to pretend that she was no more than part of a scene she had invented. To her surprise neither officer touched her; they merely looked, asked her to move, looked again, made notes, thanked her for her co-operation and told her that she could dress and leave.

More upset by the whole episode than she wanted to believe, Irene pulled on her clothes as quickly as she could, trying not to remember the similar scene she had enacted in Richard's hotel bedroom on Saturday night. The memories were so sharp that she could not wait to be gone and left half her buttons undone and one of the shirt tails hanging out over the back of her trousers. Without looking at the officers again, she pulled on her jacket. It caught in her hair, dragging out some of the pins. There was a mirror on the wall of the interview room beside the door, but she hardly glanced at herself. All she wanted was to be out of the place.

By the time she had put on her shoes again, determined to have all her clothes cleaned or washed before she wore any of them again, she was even more furious with Richard than she had been before the search. The whole vile incident was his fault. If he had not annoyed the Customs officer in the first place, they could have answered her questions politely and been on their way. Planning exactly what she would say to Richard as she walked back towards the outside world, Irene suddenly stopped and thought about the powers he had.

Without Richard's good will her play had no chance of success at all. Much though she wanted to get to the point where she could say everything she thought to anyone without fear of the consequences, she had to admit that she had not reached it yet. If she were to tell Richard quite how stupid, childish, destructive, infuriating and generally objectionable he had been, she might be jeopardizing the future for which she had worked so hard and of which she had dreamed for so long. She despised herself for what she saw as her cowardice, and hated the way it reminded her of the almost sycophantic way she had treated Fin in the early days of their marriage, but she could not see that she had any option.

Richard was waiting for her in the Customs hall when she stumbled out. He looked thoroughly impatient, but at the sight of her his expression changed. When she reached his side he put out both hands to touch the loose masses of hair that were falling about her neck.

'Did they really rip out your hairpins?' he asked. 'I never meant our weekend to end like this. All in all it's been a pretty good failure, hasn't it?'

'No,' she said, sounding more definite than she felt because he looked so guilty. 'It's been a trifle odd, but no worse than that. And we got a lot of work done.'

'So we did.' His long face had relaxed and he was smiling much more naturally. 'What a fighter you are! Thank you, my dear.'

'Thank goodness there don't seem to have been any journalists around to see us,' said Irene as they eventually reached the taxi rank.

Richard laughed as he opened the door of the leading cab for her.

'Good for you, Pollyanna. And there's no queue here, either. We're positively lucky, aren't we?'

'No,' she said, trying not to sound at all sycophantic. 'But I like to look on the bright side when I can.'

'I know you do. You always did, even when you were finding Ben's bullying just that bit too much.' Richard slung her parachute bag into the cab at her feet and looked at her. 'I suppose I ought to apologize to you for all that. It probably wouldn't have happened in the first place if I hadn't let that woman see that she'd got up my nose so badly.'

'Don't worry about it,' said Irene, almost completely disarmed. She had never expected Richard to admit that he might have been at fault.

He put his hand through the open window of the cab and tucked some of the hair behind her ear.

'You are . . .' he said and then shook his head as though he could not find the right words.

'It was a fairly educational weekend, taken all in all, Richard. Thank you for being so . . . friendly about Saturday night.'

'That was nothing.' He smiled as though he meant it and added, sighing: 'I wish I could take you home with me; or rather not home but somewhere else. But I don't think we can. I'll see you tomorrow week at the read-through. You know where to come, don't you?'

Irene nodded and gave the driver her address, surprised to find that she was almost looking forward to being back with Fin. Trying to work out why her brief taste of freedom should not have left her wanting more, she decided that she must want to tell him about the unpleasant experience with the Customs officers in order to get it right out of her system. He, at least, shared her revulsion where drugs were concerned and the effect they had on some of the children who used them, and he would have understood exactly why she had urged Richard to co-operate with the searching of their luggage.

When she got home she found a note on the hall chest, written in Fin's aggressively heavy, black italic hand: 'Irene, you're very late. I have an early start tomorrow and too much to do to wait up for you any longer. I shall sleep in the spare room. Have the goodness to try not to make your customary noise going to bed. I shall see you tomorrow evening. Fin.'

Outraged by the wholly unnecessary provocation of the note, and his assumption that the delay was her fault, Irene stumped angrily upstairs to her bedroom. She had only one comfort: at least Fin could have had no idea of her sentimental wish to tell him about what had happened to her.

It might have been only an accident that the handle of her bedroom door slipped out of her grasp so that the door slammed noisily enough to wake the heaviest of sleepers.

# Chapter Nine

On Friday evening Helena dictated an affectionate message to Mike's answering machine, saying among other things that she hoped his week in New York had gone well. She then went to have dinner in a local Italian restaurant with Franny and Jack, who seemed to have made peace for the moment. When Helena got back home she ignored her own answering machine and went to bed.

The next morning she played her messages to make sure that Katharine Lidstone had not rung asking her to postpone her visit and heard Mike's voice thanking her for her message, sending his love, and saying he hoped they would be able to meet on Sunday. Helena decided that she did not have time to ring him before she left for Worcestershire.

It was a glorious day and as soon as she was clear of the London suburbs she enjoyed the journey. The traffic was not too bad and the banks of the smaller roads she chose were starred with wild flowers. The orchards in the Vale of Evesham were a mass of blossom, and the grey stone and cream stucco villages looked prettily satisfied in the sun. The new bypasses and motorways might be damaging untouched fields and woods, she thought, but there was no doubt at all that they had released the ancient villages from the horror of standing traffic jams, fumes, and noise.

She reached Katharine Lidstone's village just after noon, which left her with half an hour to kill. At eighty-three, Mrs Lidstone did not like shocks, unexpected visitors or anxiety-inducing lateness. She had asked Helena for twelve-thirty, and Helena would always rather waste time after an early arrival than rush and fret her way to a late one. There was almost always something to look at or buy in most places where she found herself with time to spare.

She parked her car in the small market square, bought a ticket from the 'Pay and Display' machine and pottered happily about the shops. In a small grocer's she found freshly made local pork pies and bought two, which she took back to the car before going into the antique shop she knew quite well. The proprietor recognized her, although he obviously could not remember her name, and they had a polite conversation about the dreariness of the trade generally and his hopes for plenty of American visitors in the holiday season. Helena sympathized and asked what he had bought recently. He showed her a nice enough folding tea table, for which she thought he was asking much too much, probably because of its recent varnishing, and then her eye was caught by a set of brightly coloured porcelain plates.

'Those are nice.'

'Aren't they? China's not one of my specialities, but I liked them.'

'It's not mine either. What are they?'

'Nothing very special. Nineteenth-century European chinoiserie. There's no maker's mark, but that's not particularly surprising. It was so popular that a lot of it was made. These are quite pretty, but, as I say, nothing very distinguished.'

'Where did you find them?'

He raised his eyebrows at the question, but it was a reasonable one for a prospective purchaser to ask. After a moment he said casually: 'A young woman brought them in a while ago. They'd been left to her by her grandmother.'

Helena nodded. 'What are you asking for them?'

The dealer looked at her, rather too obviously trying to decide whether she might be a serious buyer or not, and then said with an expression of sympathetic apology: 'A hundred and fifty, I'm afraid.'

Helena looked at them again. It was true that she knew very little about nineteenth-century porcelain, but there were ten plates; none of them had been repaired and there were only two little chips and three cracks in the whole set. They were attractive and, at fifteen pounds a plate, a good deal cheaper than most modern chain-store equivalents.

'If you can do a little on the price,' she said automatically, 'I'll have them.'

The dealer went through the usual performance of checking the stock number on the ticket, looking up the price he had paid, pretending to make all sorts of calculations on the back of an envelope and then said he could take off fifteen pounds. Helena, trying hard not to smile as she recognized a straight 10 per cent discount, nodded.

'All right. Do you take Access or would you rather have a cheque?'

'Any chance of cash? It's just that with the banks shut for the weekend, it would be much easier.'

'I'm sorry. I don't carry that much. I could give you thirty-five in cash and a cheque for a hundred. Would that help?'

'That would be fine,' he said.

She thought: yes, you'll put a hundred through the books, showing only a tiny profit, and pocket the rest tax-free. I wonder how much you did pay the 'young woman' and whether you checked that she had ever had a grandmother who owned the plates. I wonder whose they really were.

Then she castigated herself for her suspicions and remembered Mike telling her once that the world was not as dishonest a place as she seemed to think. While the owner of the shop was packing up the plates, she took three ten-pound notes and a fiver out of her wallet and wrote out her cheque.

'Could you put your address on the back?' he called from the back shop, re-awakening all Helena's suspicions.

Rather than have an argument about it, or explain why she did not particularly want strange antique dealers knowing where she lived, she wrote her name on the back and then the address of her bank. She saw him register what she had done when he came to write the number of her card on the back of the cheque and felt a mixture of relief and suspicion when he did not comment.

'Thank you,' he said, handing over the untidy parcel. 'I hope you enjoy them.'

'I'm sure I shall,' she said. 'Could I have a receipt, please?'

Looking furious, he pulled a duplicate book from a shelf above his till and scribbled a receipt on one of the numbered pages, stamping the address of his shop at the top of the sheet.

'Thank you,' she said, reading what he had written: Set of ten nineteenth-century porcelain fruit plates, one hundred and thirty-five pounds. 'That's lovely. Next time I'm in the area I'll call back. I hope you have a good summer season. Goodbye.'

She reached Mrs Lidstone's house at exactly twelve thirty and found her hostess bending stiffly over her bushy lavender hedge, pulling up weeds even though she was dressed for lunch rather than gardening. She straightened up at the sound of the gate and brushed some dry soil off her hands.

'My dear, how kind of you to come! And such a long way. It's very good of you to pander to my fears like this.'

'It's a pleasure,' said Helena, shaking her hand with extreme care of the arthritic finger joints. 'And the drive was nice. I avoided the motorway completely and had a good time. And I've just bought some nice Chinesey plates in the antique shop in the village.'

'Hmm,' said old Mrs Lidstone. 'I hope he didn't do you down. Some of his prices are exorbitant.'

'In fact, I don't think he did. Now, shall I fetch your girandole and get it safely into the house before we relax?'

'Would you? And perhaps you could help me hang it, too.'

Helena carried it into the house, wincing as she saw all the gaps where the valuable furniture and paintings had once been. The walls had all been painted in a soft, bluish pink that had made a good background to both the mahogany and the satinwood furniture, but with nothing in front of it the colour looked thoroughly depressing, and the dust marks around the empty picture hooks made it even worse. She wished that she had thought to buy some flowers for her hostess. A vase or two of roses would have done a lot to cheer up the dismal room.

The old Persian and Chinese rugs had worn patches where the legs of the chests and tables had stood, and the darns in them showed up much more than they had when the rooms were full of furniture. Seeing the full devastation for the first time, Helena felt a mixture of deep sympathy for her hostess and powerful rage at what had been done to her. She would probably get the monetary equivalent of her possessions from her insurance company, and she could buy new furniture to replace the old as soon as she felt strong enough, but that would never make up for everything she was suffering. It seemed horribly unfair. Helena said as much.

'I know,' said Katharine Lidstone. 'But I'm beginning to find that it's possible not to think about it for hours at a time.'

'I'm sorry,' said Helena, turning to smile at her. 'I shouldn't have reminded you, but it makes me so angry to see what they did to you. I'm not surprised you can't bear to leave the house.'

'And yet I don't like being here alone either,' she said, suddenly sitting down in one of the few chairs the burglars had left. It was one of a pair of thickly upholstered Edwardian armchairs covered in flowered cretonne, very comfortable but of no value. 'I try not to be so silly, but, d'you know, when it gets dark I can hardly bear it here on my own. I suppose . . .'

Her face looked grey and the lines that ran from her nose to her chin, dragging down the corners of her lips, seemed very deep. Helena waited.

'I suppose I ought to move into some kind of bungalow full of ramps and grab handles, with a warden and a batch of other dotty widows for neighbours,' she said, trying to make it into a joke and failing. Both her voice and her hands were shaking.

'Why not get an alarm here?' suggested Helena. 'If it were tied into the local police station, you'd feel safer, wouldn't you?'

'I've already got one. I did it straight away,' said Mrs Lidstone, waving a brown-spotted hand at the infra-red detectors over the doors, which Helena had not noticed in her shock at the denuded state of the room. 'And I have a panic button beside my bed and another by the front door in case someone calls and demands money with menaces, but I'm still stupidly frightened. I sometimes think I ought to have a dog, but at my age I'm not sure I could cope with one that was big enough to be useful.'

She breathed carefully and then smiled. Helena felt so proud of her courage and so sympathetic that she could not think of anything to say.

'But it's nice that Aunt Juliana's girandole survived. I think I'd like it to hang where the Constable used to be. Could you manage that, Helena?'

'Over the chimneypiece? What a good idea! It'll add light to the room, too.'

'That's what I thought. Although, they do say that you should never hang a glass above a fire because ladies will stand in front of it preening themselves and never notice when their skirts catch light.'

Helena laughed. 'But so few of us wear those sorts of skirts nowadays.'

Katharine Lidstone nodded and looked down at her own sensible straight greenish tweed skirt, which came to just below her knees.

'True. That must have been in the days of frothing muslins. Now, can I help? Would you like me to hold the steps?'

'I'll manage. Thank you. I've got hooks and hammers in the van. I'll just go and fetch them.'

'Excellent. I'll pour out some sherry for us to have when you're done.'

Together they decided exactly where the girandole was to hang and then Helena banged in the hooks, adjusted the wire at the back of the girandole and carefully hung it up.

'How's that?'

'Lovely. Much better than the gap. Now, let's take our sherry into the garden.'

They walked slowly along the old stone paths, sipping their wine and discussing roses and butterflies. Helena noticed that her old friend was walking more slowly than she had done even six weeks earlier, and there were many more weeds in the flower beds than there had been the last time she had visited the house. It was increasingly obvious that Katharine, who had always been astonishingly capable and fit for her age, was becoming less and less able to cope. Helena was wondering how she might phrase a sympathetic comment about hoping she had plenty of help in the house, when the old lady herself said: 'I want to ask another favour, my dear, but I'm not sure whether it's quite fair. I don't want to take advantage of your good nature.'

'Please ask,' said Helena warmly. 'I owe you so much that if there is anything I can possibly do, I'd love to. How can I help?'

'Well, as you know, I told my insurance company about the burglary and sent them the list you helped me with on the telephone with photographs of the important things like the clock and the Constable, but now they're sending me a loss adjustor and he telephoned yesterday to say that he wants more detail about some of the furniture, and I feel really rather helpless. I've told them everything I can remember. If he starts asking me questions, I shall only get muddled and sound silly. I do so hate getting old, you know.'

'I'll do anything I can,' said Helena quickly. 'Although I only know about the pieces you've sent me for mending over the years.'

'I know. But that'll help, and at least proper details about those things will show the young man that I'm not making it all up. I mean, if you can give practical descriptions of things like my bureau and explain where you mended it and what with. Things like that. Then, you see, perhaps he won't think that I'm a batty old lady and dismiss everything I say.'

'Of course I will.' Helena was smiling. 'Although I don't for one moment believe that the loss adjustor would think any such thing, or that you were making any of it up. When I get home, I'll copy all the survey sheets I have of your furniture and send them to you with prints of the before-and-after photographs I took. How would that be? The survey sheets have full descriptions, as accurate as I could make them, of the furniture with details of all the marks and flaws and an account of the repairs I carried out, and the photographs are pretty detailed, too.'

'That would be marvellous. Have you really got all that?'

'Yes. I always take photographs and draw up surveys before I start work and so far I've kept them all. Anything you've sent me will still have a file.'

'Helena, my dear child, you have taken a load off my mind. The adjustor-man is coming next Thursday.'

'Well, that gives us plenty of time. I'll look out the files as soon as I get home and send you copies on Monday. Has your insurance company said anything about putting an advertisement in *Find*?'

'Find, my dear? I'm afraid I don't know what that is.'

They had reached the end of the lime walk and Katharine stumbled as she turned back towards the house. Helena put out a hand to steady her and, afraid that she might fall, gripped her wrist too tightly. As she saw Katharine wince in obviously serious pain, Helena quickly apologized.

'Not your fault,' said the old lady, breathing fast. She looked very pale and there was sweat on her upper lip. Once again Helena thought that she really should not be living alone. It was much too dangerous. What if she fell in the garden and could not get up?

'I am going to have to think seriously about sheltered housing of some kind,' Katharine said, struggling to sound casual. 'But I do hate the idea. What if there were a bullying matron? Or unpleasant staff? Or horrid residents?'

Helena answered with all the sympathy she felt, wishing that she could do something useful to help and quite unwilling to offer spuriously comforting platitudes. Katharine Lidstone was far too intelligent and clear-sighted to want any such thing.

'I beg your pardon, my dear. What a subject for a lovely day like this!'

'Any subject as important as this is suitable for any kind of day,' said Helena. 'Have you started to look at places for if and when the time does come?'

'Not yet. I am thinking about it and I have sent for some catalogues, but I haven't been able to bear to open them yet. Friends have been telling me for years that one has to put oneself on a waiting list in good time, and pay a deposit, too. That's rather large for the better places and I have not been able to afford it until now. The insurance company's cheque will make all the difference. It is ironic, isn't it? Perhaps it was fate that sent the burglars, both to show me how helpless I have become and at the same time to provide the capital with which to book myself into a comfortable nursing home.' She shuddered and then said more cheerfully: 'Let's forget about it and have some lunch. It's just a picnic, I'm afraid.'

'That's the best kind.'

'There's some smoked salmon, my dear. Could you open the packet for me? The cellophane is rather tough for my fingers.'

They ate smoked salmon and quails' eggs and salad, followed by bottled raspberries and whipped cream with shortbread.

It was only as they were finishing the shortbread that Mrs Lidstone remembered Helena's mention of *Find* and again asked her what it was.

'It's a magazine,' said Helena, 'run from York. You can advertise in it when you have had things stolen so that if they're offered to a dealer, he or she can identify them and alert the police so that you get your possessions back.'

'Oh. I'm not sure whether … My insurance company said something about the Art Loss Register, which sounds much the same. I shouldn't like to duplicate their work or tread on their toes or anything.'

'It isn't quite the same,' said Helena. 'Look, why don't I send you some old copies of *Find* with the survey sheets so that you can see the sort of thing it is and decide whether you want to go to the expense of putting in an advertisement. You could always clear it with the insurers first if you do think you might like to do it. You might not want to bother since they'll definitely pay you the value of what's been stolen in any case.'

'Eventually. What would happen if my claim was paid and then I got my possessions back?'

'I think you'd simply explain and return the money they'd paid you. I'm not sure exactly what the law is. I mean, presumably, they would actually own your things by then, but I'm sure they'd rather have the money than your furniture and jewellery.'

'Yes, I'm sure they would.' Katharine Lidstone laughed shakily. 'You've a very clear head, Helena, my dear. Now, we must stop talking about my sad affairs. Tell me how you are. Are you happy? You're looking better than you have for some time. Is that because of the young man you told me about?'

Helena felt herself smile and, rather surprised at herself, nodded.

'I suppose it is him. Did I really tell you about him?'

'A little,' said Mrs Lidstone, pushing herself up out of her chair and reaching for her stick. 'Come and help me make the coffee and tell me more. I think you said that he was tall and good looking.'

Helena followed her into the kitchen and said: 'I suppose he is in a way, but what I especially like about him is that he takes life so lightly. I don't mean that he's silly about it or irresponsible, but he can almost always find a way to laugh about the awful things that happen; he tells very good jokes, too; and even when he's actually giving me a wigging of some sort, he usually manages to do it in an amusing way.'

Katharine, who had been carefully scooping coffee grounds into a cafetière, put down her spoon and turned to look at Helena with an expression of great severity on her soft, lined face.

'I'm not sure that I like the idea of his giving you what you call a wigging about anything at all. What right has he to tell you what you should be doing?'

Helena brushed Katharine's wrist in a gesture of reassurance, remembering the arthritis in time to take care to touch very lightly.

'It isn't like that,' she said, realizing from her instinctive internal protest that she must feel even more loyalty to Mike than she had suspected.

'Well, so long as it's making you happy.' Katharine turned back to make the coffee and Helena knew that she had been reprimanded in the gentlest possible way.

'I'd like you to think of him with affection,' she said at last. 'He is making my life much better – happier – than it was without him.'

'I'm glad. Can you manage the tray?'

'Of course,' said Helena, holding out her hands. 'I think that you and Mike might have quite a lot in common,' she said. 'Next time you come to London, would you let me introduce you to him?'

'I'd like that,' said Katharine, looking surprised. 'But I cannot see myself coming up for a while. I can't even make myself go shopping just now, you know. I have everything delivered. And my dear GP is good enough to come and see me nearly once a week at the moment, and he brings me the pills I need for my heart. I hope I'll brace up again soon, but . . .' Her voice trailed into nothing and yet again Helena felt an anger against the burglars that was almost violent.

She left the old lady soon after three o'clock, promising to come back again soon. She would have stayed longer if Katharine had shown any signs of wanting her, but she had begun to look tired and when Helena had asked directly whether she usually had a sleep in the afternoons, she had admitted that she liked to go to bed for an hour or two. Having helped to stack the washing up in the sink, which was all Katharine would allow, Helena drove away.

Reluctant to thunder boringly down the motorway all the way back to London, she took one of the smaller roads, planning to dawdle through some of the prettier villages and perhaps stop for tea somewhere. It was not until she was halfway to Oxford that it occurred to her to drop in on Ivo instead. She kept a lookout for a telephone box so that she could find out whether he was at home or not, but when she did not pass one in the first few miles she decided to take a chance. His farmhouse was not much out of her way and she would be amused to see it even if he were not there.

He had found it the previous summer in a typical example of the sort of luck that followed him everywhere. While Jane paid a large proportion of her allowance for an ill-furnished bed-sitting room in a dilapidated house in Durham, Ivo lived rent-free in three rooms of an attractive Cotswold farmhouse in return for light caretaking duties. The owner had apparently been posted to Hong Kong for a year with his company's Far Eastern office and, rather than let the house, with all the attendant problems of agents, inventories and possible damage to his possessions, he had imported Ivo to monitor its alarms and guard against leaks and fires and other sorts of damage.

Helena had often written to him there and had letters back from him, but she had never seen it. She found the place without much difficulty, driving the last two miles down a rutted, unsurfaced private road between fields full of calm, fat Jersey cows, and thought she had rarely seen such a perfect example of England in early summer.

The wild roses were already flowering palely pink in the hedges while the last of the may was still out. The grass was green and succulent, the rutted chalk path brightly white and the cows the colour of half-crystallized honey. She caught sight of what must be Ivo's house on the far side of a gate and pulled up so that she could get out to open it. Discovering that it was heavily padlocked, she assumed that must be part of the terms of his agreement with the real owner of the house and got back in the car to manoeuvre it up onto the shallow bank so that there would be room for another vehicle to pass, picked her handbag off the back seat, locked the car and climbed the gate, pulling up her short skirt so that she could swing her leg over it.

'Cor!' came a hoarse, admiring shout.

Standing insecurely astride the top of the gate, she looked around and saw an unfamiliar young man with a dog at heel, leaning against the flank of one of the honey-coloured cows in the field to the right of the house. He was dressed in baggy corduroys, boots, and a shirt in an even worse state than Ivo's usually were and there was unmistakable lust in his eyes. Helena hastily pulled down her skirt.

'Do you know whether the man who lives here is in?' she asked. 'Ivo Webton.'

'Doubt it,' said the young man in a strong Oxfordshire accent. 'There's no sign of his car. It's an old Mini, you know.'

'Yes, I do know.' She smiled politely. 'I'm his sister.'

'Ah. Know you were coming, did he?'

She shook her head. 'But it doesn't matter. I'll leave him a note. Thank you very much.'

The young man nodded and turned away, slapping the cow's rump, calling to his dog and beginning to chivvy the rest of the herd up to the far end of the field. It dawned on Helena belatedly that he must be taking them for milking. For the first time she wondered how Ivo, as fully town-bred as she was herself, had taken to living in the middle of a working farm.

She rang the bell beside the back door of the house in case he was in after all and when there was no answer walked all round the house, peering in through the windows. She could see very little since most of them were firmly shuttered, but one gave her a good view of the kitchen, which looked pleasant, if in a typically Ivo-like state of mess with heaps of newspapers, books, bottles, socks, and shirts waiting to be ironed. She wondered whether the owner had any idea of the sort of man he had chosen to look after his house and saw her own affectionate smile reflected back at her from the window pane between the bars.

Eventually admitting that Ivo genuinely was not at home and that she was not going to be able to see him, Helena sat down on an old mounting block beside the door and took out her notebook and pen so that she could leave him a message. Thinking he might find it odd that she should have driven to see him without bothering to find out whether he would be there or not, she explained about her trip to Katharine Lidstone, described the sadness of her house stripped of almost everything, and ended:

*And so not surprisingly she was both sad and fragile – although terrifically brave about it all – and I thought I'd like to see you to cheer myself up. Silly of me not to ring from her house. One of these days I really will buy a mobile.*

*A lecherous cowman whistled at my legs and told me you weren't in, but I thought I'd check and prowled about a bit. Your employer is keen on security, isn't he? It's like a fortress here, even down to the bars in the kitchen window.*

*I thought I was neurotic about security, but this place makes me seem thoroughly casual. Terrifically therapeutic! Not as good as seeing you, but great nonetheless. I hope you're all right. I'm about to start work on your desk.*

*All my love, Helena.*

She ripped the pages out of the notebook, folded them in two, wrote Ivo's full name on the outside and posted it through the door, noticing as she did so that there was a basket on the other side of the slot to catch anything that was pushed through.

More disappointed than she had admitted to herself, Helena drove back towards the motorway and London, feeling unusually lonely. Her own house seemed very empty, too, and much less of a sanctuary than she had expected. The sight of a winking light on her answering machine was welcome for once and she listened eagerly to the messages. There was another from Mike hoping that her day had gone well and adding that it would be good to see her on Sunday. It was so friendly and unthreatening that she immediately rang him back.

He reached the house an hour later and stood in the hall, hugging her as warmly and undemandingly as Irene might have done.

'That was exceedingly nice,' she said, pulling away. 'Thank you, Mike. I must say you're looking very well.'

'Jet lag,' he said casually. 'Paradoxically it always gees me up. Takes me days to get calm again.'

'I thought it might be some amazing coup you'd pulled off in New York.'

'Well, there is that, too, but I didn't want to boast about the fantastic deal I've just done. At least I hope I have. It's not finalized yet and I'm probably going to have to go back again next week. But it's looking good.' He laughed and kissed her again. 'And then there's you. I must admit that your ringing me this evening has given me quite a kick.'

'Has it?'

'Yes. You must have really wanted to see me.'

'Did you doubt it?'

He nodded. 'You seemed so distant and so anxious to get away from me last weekend that I thought I might not hear from you again.'

She felt her eyebrows tightening over the top of her nose.

'How could you possibly have thought that? You must have known . . .'

'Now, now,' he said, putting his hands on her shoulders and pushing against them. 'That's a bloke's line. And I'm damned if I'm going to play the girl's part.' In a horrible, peevish falsetto, he added: 'How *can* I know if you won't tell me?'

'I'm not sure of my lines here,' Helena said, trying not to smile at his all-too convincing performance. 'What do blokes usually say next?'

'Say? Say?' Mike's voice of theatrical astonishment made her cheeks ache with the effort of keeping a straight face. 'They don't say anything. They grunt and shake the newspaper. You don't know much, do you, Helena?'

She shook her head, allowing the smile out at last.

'I've always refused to go in for that sort of thing – which I suppose could be why my affairs have tended to be rather short-lived,' she said, adding less lightly, 'I am as I am and if what I am is not wanted I don't stay to hear about it. What's the point?'

He nodded and let the muscles in his arms slacken so that she automatically moved closer to him. He lifted his right hand from her shoulder and drew a line from her chin down her neck and between her breasts.

'How did you decide that they didn't want you any more?' he asked, looking at his hand rather than her face. He felt her responding to his touch and repeated it.

She picked his other hand off her shoulder and, holding it in hers, led him towards the stairs, saying over her shoulder: 'When they stopped talking to me, or contradicted me too often, or put out that repelling miasma that people do when they're bad-tempered, or used me as a target for all the rage they'd accumulated throughout the day.'

They reached her bedroom and she opened the door with her free hand. Mike stopped and held her back.

'In other words,' he said more seriously, 'you decided that you didn't want them. That's rather what I'd assumed all along.'

'I'm not sure which came first. After all, they couldn't have behaved like that if they had wanted me.' At the sight of his expression, she added: 'Could they?'

'A lot of people do behave like that for all sorts of reasons.'

'Well, they shouldn't,' said Helena with unusual energy. She pulled her hand out of his and went to shut her bedroom curtains. 'If they can't be pleasant to people they care about they deserve to be thrown out.'

Mike had still not commented by the time she had drawn both pairs of curtains and turned to face him again.

'Don't you think that?' She looked worried and as though she had sucked the whole of her body back into the shell again.

'On the other hand,' he said carefully, 'there might be a school of thought that said that the other half of such a pair ought to be understanding enough to absorb some surly behaviour. It isn't always possible to be charming and attentive, particularly if one is having a very bad time, say in the office.'

Helena knew perfectly well that they were exchanging notes about past relationships that had foundered. She also understood for the first time that the rocks on which hers had been wrecked might have been similar to the ones that had ruined his, even if they had been approached from opposite sides.

'Not charming and attentive, perhaps,' she said, watching him, 'but do they have to be cruel or sullen? Is it too much to ask that they avoid active nastiness? Isn't it possible to say: "I'm feeling like shit at the moment because of a, b, and c. I haven't anything much to spare for you. I love you (or like, or am fond, or whatever) as much as I always have done, but I won't be able to show it for a bit. Can you give me time to get myself straight again?" Wouldn't that be fairer than just stomping about being disagreeable without any explanation and inviting retaliation?'

'Much fairer,' said Mike, walking towards her, 'but awfully difficult to do when one is in the kind of state that too much stress causes. At times like that people one loves sometimes do seem to be part of the problem and, with the best will in the world, they *do* sometimes get blamed for it.'

'Well, they shouldn't,' she said, thinking more of Fin and Irene than any of her own failed relationships. 'It's grossly unjust and I for one won't have it. I warn you, Mike. It's not conceit or anything. But I am not tough enough to take being treated like that. Perhaps I ought to be, but I'm not. That's exactly why I go on about keeping what we have as we have it. If you get into a state like that, I'd much rather you stayed away in your flat until it was over.'

'And if I needed you then, your support or your comfort? I'm not saying I'd have any right to it; I'm just saying I might need it. What would happen then?'

'Then you'd have to ask for it. And if you asked, it would be all right and I'd put up with anything. Anything. It's the unprovoked, unexplained aggression I can't stand.'

'If I were able to ask, I probably shouldn't need it,' he said, looking almost as though he was about to laugh, which bothered her. 'It's a real catch-22.'

'If I understand you correctly,' said Helena after she had had time to consider what he had said, 'you're suggesting that the more revoltingly you behave towards me, the more you might need from me. Have I got that right?'

'Pretty much. It might never happen, but it would be silly to pretend that it never could.'

'It has happened to you before, then?' Since they were having what amounted to a serious contractual negotiation, Helena wanted to get everything absolutely clear between them.

'Oh, yes,' he said, sitting down on the edge of her bed and taking off his shoes. 'Just as it seems to have happened to you.'

'To me and to other people I care about, which is why I'm so wary of getting myself into that sort of thing again.' She did not want to betray Irene's difficulties with Fin to someone who had not met either of them.

'I know it is, but that wasn't exactly what I meant. I expect you've done much the same as the men you've chucked out.'

'Of course I haven't,' Helena said in outrage and then almost immediately added: 'Have I been doing something like that to you?'

'No, not yet,' he said, 'but I suspect you have to other people. It's human nature, Helena; you must have understood that much by now, watcher that you are. Unmet needs do make people disagreeable to those nearest to them.'

'That's not fair,' she said, coming to sit beside him.

'What isn't? My suggesting that you're not always perfect?'

'Lunatic! Of course not. No, I meant that it isn't fair to be disagreeable about your unmet needs if you've never told anyone what they are.'

He smiled and lay back so that he was looking up at her. He blew her a kiss and said: 'Most of us assume that if people say they care about us they will know what it is we need.'

'Well, that's completely barmy. Much sillier than anything I've ever said or felt. How can anyone know? That assumption is exactly how the trouble starts. And if you're going to . . .'

'I'm not. Don't worry so much, Helena. It seems to me that while you and I can talk like this, we're well on the way to being able to sort out most things.'

She leaned over him, searching his face. There was nothing in it to scare her, no coldness, no half-hidden dislike, no anger. Knowing that she was on the verge of committing herself to something, she took a breath and nodded, but she could not make herself say anything at all.

# Chapter Ten

They got on so well together that night and for most of Sunday that it was not until Mike had gone home to sort himself out for the week that Helena remembered her promises to Katharine Lidstone. Full of compunction she went across the tiny garden to her workshed, stopping for a moment to pick a deadhead off the climbing rose by the steps.

The withered petals felt like loose clammy skin between her fingers and she shook them off irritably, disliking the way they clung to her. When she had got rid of them at last, she saw that there was a minute black beetle under one of her nails and picked it out. Then she stood for a moment longer, breathing in the scent of the still-living flowers. Smelling a different, even richer, scent than the roses', she realized that the honeysuckle growing against the far fence must have come into flower as well.

Who, she asked herself, could possibly want to live like Ivo in the middle of messy fields when they could have a neat, protected little garden with no cowpats or agricultural machinery clanking away in the background, or even leering countrymen attended by dogs of unknown savagery.

She unlocked the workshed and went up the creaking stairs to the top floor, where she kept all her archives and the back numbers of sale room catalogues and trade magazines. The filing cabinets were neatly labelled, and she found the photographs and survey sheets for Katharine's various pieces of furniture without difficulty and laid them in a heap on the top stair. The copies of *Find* were in a tall stack that leaned precariously against the wall.

Tempted simply to take a few copies off the top, Helena decided that they were too recent to send away. If she were given something to restore by an unknown client, she might well need to check through the previous few seasons' copies to make sure that the piece was not one that had been advertised as having been stolen.

Bending down, she put her fingers around a bunch of about eight magazines three-quarters of the way down the stack and pulled. The ink on the glossy paper must have melted or amalgamated with the paper or something because the magazines were stuck to each other. As she pulled, the whole stack teetered and then fell on top of her.

The pile of paper was nothing like heavy enough to do her any damage, but it was uncomfortable and clouds of dust came down with the magazines. Choking, she pulled herself away from the slippery heap of glossy paper and set about sorting the copies into date order again and repiling them. It was surprisingly tiring work, bending and stretching uncomfortably.

By the time it was finished she was both irritated with herself and stiff. She took the copies she had set aside for Katharine out of the shed, shook the dust off them, and carried them into the house with the survey sheets and photographs.

She poured herself a glass of fruit juice and took it upstairs to drink in the bath. When she had finished washing off all the dust and anointed her various scrapes and bruises with TCP and witch hazel, she had got over her rage at having been so lazy and hamfisted. Wrapped in a dark blue towelling dressing gown, she went back downstairs, refilled her glass and leafed through the magazines, planning to point Katharine in the direction of the most suitable advertisements to copy.

Half an hour later, Helena was still sitting there, reading and re-reading a displayed paragraph put in by an anonymous owner who had listed only a box number for replies. The pieces that had been stolen from him or her included a Queen Anne walnut kneehole desk with three drawers on each side, and three across the top.

The more often Helena re-read the description, the more it sounded like Ivo's desk. She had listed the marks and flaws so scrupulously and so recently that she could not help matching every one in the advertisement to those she herself had assessed. The lists were almost identical. She could not persuade herself that Ivo was not in possession of stolen property.

Racking her brains to think of ways to protect him from the possible consequences, Helena went to her bookshelves in search of something that might tell her exactly where he stood in law. Her various layman's guides did not help much. There was one that explained in detail the principle of *nemo dat quod non habet*, that a buyer cannot acquire a better title to something than the seller has, which she knew already and which was precisely what had been worrying her. The book also included a chapter on the old markets overt, in which a purchaser, providing he was acting in good faith, could acquire clean title to something even if it had just been stolen. Having existed for centuries, such markets had been outlawed only in 1994.

Helena had always hated them since they meant that stolen antiques could be quickly passed on into the legitimate trade without the real owners having any right to get them back even if they appeared in a respectable shop as little as twenty-four hours after the burglary, but for once the idea was comforting.

The sound of the telephone ringing broke into her thoughts. Reluctantly, walking sideways, she went to pick up the receiver, telling herself it was absurd to imagine that the caller would be someone in authority demanding to know what she was doing with stolen antiques on her property.

Trying to laugh at her silly fear, she could not help wondering where she would stand in law. Someone had once told her that a householder whose guests consumed illicit drugs on her premises would be breaking the law, even if she had no idea what they were doing. She had never known whether that was true or not, but even the possibility that it might have been meant that there were people she would not allow through her front door because they occasionally smoked cannabis. Once or twice she had thought of asking Fin what the law really was so that she could stop worrying, but she knew that he would start asking questions and probably demand the names and addresses of her drug-taking friends. She did not want to risk that either.

'Hello?' she said warily into the telephone.

'Helena? It's Miranda here.'

'Oh, how wonderful!' she said on a long, deep breath. 'Thank you very much for ringing.'

There was a short pause before Miranda said: 'Is there something the matter?'

Helena realized that she had never sounded so pleased to hear her mother's voice before.

'I'm fine. I've had a curious couple of days one way and another and the prospect of talking to you is – appealing.'

'Well, how very nice, Helena. Thank you. I was in fact simply telephoning to ask whether you might like to come and have supper with me one night next week, bringing your friend if you'd like or coming on your own if you'd prefer that.'

'I think I would rather come on my own,' said Helena without stopping to think about it at all, 'but, look, are you very busy at the moment or might you feel like coming to have some scrambled eggs or something this evening?'

'In your house?'

'Yes, would you mind that? We could always go out if you'd prefer. There are lots of places round here where one can eat reasonably well and quite quickly even on a Sunday.'

'I'd love to see your house. How very kind! When shall I come?'

'Why not straight away? There is in fact something I'd like to ask you. Not that I'm trying to get free legal advice or anything; well, not really.'

Miranda laughed and said easily enough: 'You'd be surprised how many people think they have a right to that. But if anyone does, it's you, Helena. I'll help in any way I can. It'll take me about twenty minutes to sort things out here and drive over.'

Gathering up all the copies of *Find*, Helena bundled them into the cupboard under the stairs with the survey sheets clipped together on top of the pile. Then she ran for the Hoover to pick up any dust that might have sullied the polished wooden floor. Plumping up the cushions took only a moment and she thought she would have plenty of time to dress when she caught sight of a vase of dead flowers. They had to be flung onto the compost heap behind the workshed, the vase washed out and refilled with fresh roses and two of the loose heads of yellow and white honeysuckle, which left her only four minutes to stuff a very expensive bottle of white wine in between the packets of food in the freezer and then run upstairs to rip off her dressing gown and pull on the first thing that came to hand in her wardrobe: an unyielding denim dress she had bought in a sale and never worn. She might have changed it for something she liked more had she not heard the front door bell ring. Barefoot, she ran down to let her mother into the house for the first time.

'Come in,' she said, still breathless from dashing about.

Miranda walked across the threshold without fuss and took off the loose beige linen jacket she was wearing over her charcoal linen culottes and striped shirt. Helena took the jacket from her and hung it over the end of the banister.

'This way,' she said, sounding irritatingly young to herself, as she pushed open the drawing room door. She watched her mother's face registering the similarity of their rooms. For once it did not seem threatening.

'What would you like to drink?'

'Whatever you're having.'

Helena went to retrieve the expensive white burgundy from the freezer, held the bottle against her cheek for a second to check that it was cold enough and decided that it would just do. Having opened it in the kitchen and poured some wine into two glasses, she rammed the cork back and stood the bottle upright in the milk rack of the fridge.

'I hope this is all right,' she said, handing a glass to Miranda.

'Thank you.' She sipped it, looked at Helena over the rim and then laughed.

'What is it?'

'You didn't have to bribe me with a Montrachet, you know. I

told you, if anyone has a right to free legal advice from me, it's you.'

'It wasn't that,' said Helena, hoping that she did not look as pouty as she felt.

She was also intrigued to learn that her mother could so quickly identify the wine. Irene drank whatever she was given, enjoyed some wines more than others, but was not interested enough to distinguish between them.

'I wanted to give you something that would mark the occasion. You see, it is quite an occasion, for me anyway.'

'And for me,' said Miranda. 'That was kind. I shouldn't have teased you. What's the problem?'

'I so much didn't want to sound as though I . . .'

'. . . was only asking me here because you needed help? I know that. Don't worry about it.' Miranda saw that Helena was finding it hard to begin and put her glass down. 'Listen: whether you realize it or not, it is a source of satisfaction that you thought of turning to me.'

'Really?'

Miranda nodded.

'That's generous,' said Helena. 'All right. Let me tell you and then we can forget it and just talk about ordinary things afterwards.'

'Fine.'

When Helena still did not say anything, Miranda picked up her glass again, took another sip, and leaned back against the carefully plumped sofa cushions.

'Is it that you've done something that's bothering you?' she asked, not looking at her daughter.

'Me? Good heavens! No. Nothing like that.'

'Well, then,' said Miranda, showing distinct signs of relief. 'There's no need to be so coy about it. Out with it.'

'A client has left a piece of furniture with me that they bought recently. I have discovered quite by chance that a piece which sounds exactly like it was stolen some time ago. I wanted to find out, if it is the same piece, what position – legally, I mean – my client is in.'

Miranda had been listening carefully, as though well aware that she was hearing only a small part of the story. She nodded as Helena finished speaking and sat up to say: 'I'm no specialist in the law of title, but I probably know enough. Is there any possibility that your client bought the piece at a market overt before 1994?'

'No. I thought of that, too. But I'm fairly sure that he – they – acquired it only in the last month or so. It's obviously possible that at least one previous owner got it in a market overt, which would make it all right, wouldn't it?'

'Yes. How long ago was it stolen?'

'I'm not sure. But I can find out. Hang on.' Helena put her own glass down on the table beside the sofa and went to fetch the relevant copy of *Find* from under the stairs. 'At least six years and two months,' she said as she came back, having checked the date on the front of the magazine.

'Then I think your client probably is in the clear as far as the law is concerned. If he bought it in good faith, and it sounds as though he did, then six years is probably enough to give him reasonable security. As far as I can remember the wording of the Act is quite tricky, and whether it's six years from the theft or six years from the first sale to a real purchaser, I'm not sure. But your client's probably safe enough if he has only just acquired it.'

There was a strange expression in Miranda's eyes, which for once Helena could not interpret at all. She frowned, trying to understand it.

'I take it,' Miranda said after a while, 'that this is the desk Ivo bought, the eighteenth-century one that you told me about before?'

'What? Well, yes, actually it is. That's why I mind so much. I mean, I'd be concerned for anyone who might have taken on a stolen piece by mistake, but this is family. That makes it much more important.'

'I can see that. But from everything you've told me, I think Ivo's in the clear. On this at least. Anyway, none of it's your responsibility. Do you really need to worry so much about it?'

Wanting to say, 'Of course I do', Helena wondered whether she could be reverting to the panicky self she thought she had outgrown.

'I think so,' she said reasonably calmly. 'He's my brother, my younger brother. He might find himself in serious trouble over this. Having discovered that, surely it's my responsibility to do anything I can to protect him? Isn't it? Am I being completely neurotic?'

Miranda laughed.

'What's so funny?'

'Nothing. Except that I'm the last person to ask that sort of question.'

'Why?'

'Because I'm like you, Helena: always on the lookout for the next disaster and convinced either that I've caused it or that I ought to have done something to prevent it. I knew you'd inherited my freckles and my taste in interior decoration, but I'm sorry you should have got the angst as well.'

Helena stared at her. Miranda looked back with eyes that seemed to hold an almost equal measure of amusement and pain.

'Hasn't Fin ever told you that? It used to drive him mad.'

Reluctant to say that Fin had rarely mentioned Miranda's name, Helena shook her head.

'I've sometimes wondered whether Irene's attraction for him was her amazing insouciance. It makes his teeth ache these days, but I can see that it could have been very appealing in contrast to my endless twitters.'

'I don't understand,' said Helena, frowning. 'What insouciance, and why does it make him ache, and how do you know anyway?'

Miranda stood up.

'Didn't you say something about eggs? Should we go and cook them? It's getting quite late, Helena.'

'In a minute. This is important. What did you mean about Irene?'

'It was silly of me to say it. I know you don't like discussing her with me.'

'Unlike my father, it seems.'

Miranda sighed. 'He needs somewhere to blow off steam, Helena. Don't grudge him that. He has quite a hard time with her, you know.'

'I don't think you can have any idea how he treats her. If you'd heard the sort of things he says to her, the endless bickering she has to put up with, you wouldn't . . .' Helena turned away, unable to be fair to both women and reluctant to be unfair to either.

'It takes two to bicker,' said Miranda gently from behind her.

Helena looked round. 'You mean that she's not doing her duty by him unless she takes everything he says with a simpering smile and lets him do exactly as he pleases?'

She did not add the other words in her mind, which were: how can you criticize her for the way she behaves to him? She puts up with it and you weren't prepared to do that. You have no right to judge her.

Miranda shook her head. Her face was full of pity, which seemed even harder to take than her criticism of Irene.

'No, that's not what I meant. One of the many things I've learned is that if you choose to, you can always fight your corner without bickering. Come on: eggs. Or shall I take you out to eat?'

Helena shook her head. 'No. I'll go and cook. Which do you like: omelette, scrambled, fried, poached, boiled, coddled?'

'Omelette, since you ask.'

'OK. There are some chives and parsley in the garden beyond the compost heap behind the shed. Could you bear to go and pick some?'

Without a word, Miranda went down the iron staircase between the roses to fetch the herbs. Helena was left to assemble the things she needed to make the omelette and sort out her reactions to what had just been said.

'What a gorgeous garden!' Miranda was standing in the doorway with a bunch of greenery in her hands. She seemed to be signalling a return to their usual civilized chat.

'I'm glad you like it.' Helena smiled as she started breaking eggs. 'I don't have much time to deal with it – or, frankly, much tolerance for upending myself and stuffing my fingers into what passes for soil in London – hence the pots.'

'They're nice. If I couldn't have afforded a gardener once a week, I don't know that I would have gone for the labour-intensive sort of garden I have. Where did you find that big, garlanded pot?'

Grateful for the unemotional subject, Helena talked easily about all the terracotta tubs she had bought and where she had found them and what she had planted in them. Later, halfway through answering a question of Miranda's about the climbing roses, she suddenly stopped talking and rested her hands on the worktop for a moment.

'None of this is at all important,' she went on as she picked up the fork to whisk up the eggs. 'I'm sorry. I . . .'

'It may not be important, but it's a way of getting round the difficult things. As I said, I know that you don't like talking about your stepmother,' said Miranda. 'I'm not sure that I do either, but sometimes I can't help it; just as I can't help defending Fin when you automatically take her part. He isn't happy either.'

'Well, he could be. If he wasn't so horrible to her, she would be fun and good company, and . . . He must have loved her once. He must have.'

'Yes.' For a moment Miranda looked as Helena imagined someone might after being shot. Then she smiled again. 'I think that pan is hot enough.'

Helene belatedly became aware of a burning smell. Cursing herself she took the omelette pan off the gas and ran it under cold water before wiping it out with a cloth and starting again.

The omelettes were good and went well enough with the Montrachet. They had finished the bottle before Helena took away the empty plates. Having put a bowl of grapes on the table and an old Delft dish of dried apricots and sweet almonds, she squatted down in front of her wine rack to choose another bottle. Looking round, she said: 'What would you like now? More of the Montrachet or something red or some pudding wine? I've got some Barsac here, which is quite nice.'

'I'm not too keen,' said Miranda frankly. 'I find them all a bit sickly. But, you know, I'm not sure we need any more wine at all.'

'No. Perhaps not. But it would be nice, wouldn't it?' Helena put another bottle of the Montrachet in the freezer and took from the fridge below it the half-drunk bottle of fruity Australian white that she had had there for several days. 'But we can have this while the other's getting cold.'

Miranda looked at her for a moment and then smiled and pushed her glass forward. 'That's lovely, Helena. You are very generous.'

They picked at the grapes and apricots and drank the rest of the bottle, talking all the time. They avoided the contentious subjects, but both knew that they were all still there and that at some stage they would have to be thrashed out.

'Tell me about Mike,' said Miranda when Helena poured the last of the Australian wine into her glass.

Helena wondered whether her mother was feeling as weird as she was herself. It was not just the drink, although her head was swimming in a way she had not felt for years. It was also the sensation of several different conversations taking place at once. There was the one they were conducting in words, but there seemed to be several others too, silent communications in which the two of them were suggesting that the past was important but that it might be over, that all sorts of uncharitable things they had felt were no longer quite the same. It was all most peculiar.

'Mike's a banker,' Helena said aloud, hearing the s sounding very sloppy. She articulated more clearly as she added: 'He's four years older than me; tall; good company; I like him.'

'Has he ever been married?'

'I don't think so. But there are all sorts of things I keep discovering that he's never told me, so I suppose it's possible.' She frowned and wondered if it really was possible. Shaking her head, she got up to fetch the Montrachet from the freezer, looked at her mother, and then opened the bottle and poured some wine into their glasses.

'I don't think he can have been. He's talked about relationships that went wrong, and I'm sure he'd have said if any of them had included a marriage. I'm sure he would.'

Helena drank and noticed that the wine tasted almost metallic. She had had far too much already, but it seemed important to go on. She was not sure why. As she settled herself, one elbow slipped off the table and she almost fell into her lap. She straightened up with as much dignity as she could achieve.

Miranda sipped her wine. 'I can't think of any reason why he wouldn't tell you something like that.'

'Nor can I. What about you? I mean, are you in the middle of something – you know, a relationship – at the moment?'

Looking amused, Miranda said: 'I'm practically sixty. It's been a good year or two since I had the energy or the desire to be romantically involved with anyone.'

'But you've got lots of friends, haven't you?'

'Plenty.' Miranda looked at her daughter for a while. 'That's not why I wanted to get to know you, Helena.'

'Would you like some coffee or anything?' Helena got to her feet, kicked the leg of the table and steadied herself with difficulty.

'That would be nice. But not coffee or I'll never sleep. Some tea, if you've got some.'

'OK.' Helena filled the kettle, feeling dizzy but not caring about it. That seemed the least of her problems. She sloshed some water onto the worktop as she plugged in the kettle and looked very carefully to make sure that the lid was properly on. She had once burned her hand quite badly when the lid slipped off the kettle and she was not prepared to risk that again, however tight she was. Fumbling in the china cupboard, she took out two bone china mugs and put a tea bag in each.

'Then why?' she asked, quite without meaning to. 'I mean, why did you suddenly want to get to know me after all this time?'

'Because of something Ivo said.'

'Ivo?' Helena frowned. 'What did he say? Anyway, I thought you didn't trust him.'

'Not exactly, although ...' Miranda broke off, took another small sip of wine, smiled and said more firmly: 'He talked about you in a way that made me realize how much you and I might have in common and how much I might like you.'

Helena risked a glance at her. Miranda was looking gravely back, slowly tilting her wine glass this way and that.

'And he also made it quite clear that you were a thoroughly effective, well-rooted person, about whom I might not have to feel as devastatingly guilty as I had been feeling.'

'Guilty?' said Helena quietly while her mind was yelling with a fury of which she had not known herself capable: of course you ought to feel guilty: you dumped me; you left me; you abandoned me; you made me terrified of caring about anyone else in case it happened again; if it hadn't been for Irene, what you did to me would have made it impossible for me to have any kind of normal life at all. And then you wonder why I always defend her and try to make me feel ashamed of it.

'You must have known I'd feel guilty,' said Miranda.

The crucial question was almost askable, but in spite of the untying of several of her mental knots, Helena found she still could not quite do it.

'Are you feeling all right, Helena?'

'I think that I must be rather drunk.' She smiled and felt her lips slacken more than she had meant. Trying to look and sound sternly in control, she added: 'D'you mind?'

'Not at all. Tell me: are you happy with your Mike?'

'Yes. Most of the time it's wonderful. Goodn't – no, couldn't, sorry, couldn't be better. Are you sure you don't mind?'

'Not at all, but you're beginning to look very tired.'

'Tactful.'

'I think I'd better get out of your hair and let you get to bed. Shall we wash up before I ring for a taxi?'

'Didn't you come in a car?'

'Yes. But I can hardly drive like this. I'll pick the car up tomorrow, if that's all right with you?'

Helena nodded and got up to dial the number of the local minicab firm. For the first time, she could not remember it and had to scuffle around for the telephone book. She found the number at last, dialled, got through and ordered a cab for Miranda.

'Now, let's wash up before he comes.'

'No. Don't let's bother.' Helena tried to think of a reason. 'I'd only drop something.'

She needed space and time to think on her own. Even the prospect of having someone else – anyone else – in her kitchen doing anything at all was agony.

'I'll be fine. I'll just stack them in the dishwasher, the plates, I mean, and deal with it all tomorrow. Thank you for coming and telling me about the desk. I'm sorry I got so drunk.' Helena swayed and had to hold on to the wall.

'It's fine. You're well within the bounds of decency. But you ought to go bed soon. Drink plenty of water first and then you won't have too bad a head in the morning. Will you be all right?'

'Yes.'

Hearing the peremptory sound of a car's horn outside, Miranda collected her jacket and handbag from the hall and reminded Helena to come for dinner on Wednesday. Miranda put her hand on the latch. Helena looked at her, longing to say something to show she had understood the silent talk. Miranda looked back at her and then, as the car horn sounded again, dropped her bag and jacket on the floor and held out her arms. Helena walked forward without a word and felt herself tightly held.

The embrace could not have been more different from Irene's. There was no softness, no comfort. As Miranda held her, Helena could feel only bone, but the tightness of her mother's arms was extraordinarily important. It told Helena that she was not the only one to have dropped her guard, to have been unable to say aloud the things that really mattered. It also told her, as her earlier words had not, that Miranda might not need to be told what her daughter had thought of her desertion.

The car's horn sounded again, longer and more angrily than before. Miranda let Helena go, collected her things and left the house without a word.

Helena stood in the empty hall, leaning against the door and beginning to feel very unwell. She could not distinguish between the effects of the wine and her emotions. With great care, she walked back into the kitchen, ran cold water over the plates and pans, put away the bread and butter, checked that she had turned off the gas and the lights and went upstairs.

Later she had to go back to the kitchen to make absolutely certain that the gas was off and stood in the darkness, holding on to the cooker and saying aloud: 'There's nothing clever, or interesting, or in any way admirable about being anxious. It's silly and wasteful and crippling. You knew you had turned it off. You've grown out of obsessive panics. You're not like that any more. Get back to bed and control yourself.'

She went and lay down again, hardly noticing that Franny and Jack had started up another crashing row next door. The pillow swung beneath her head like a hammock in a storm-tossed boat. She tried to pretend that it was an exhilarating sensation and, later, that she was back at the funfair with Irene on a Saturday afternoon in summer, revelling in being whirled around and upside down and back again.

# Chapter Eleven

Irene set off for the first read-through of *The House on the Canal* in a conquering mood, ready for anything, but when she reached the rehearsal room she was disconcerted to find that it was a bleak, dusty church hall without even a proper stage. Boxes of what looked like jumble were stacked at one end. At the other, half a dozen people were standing, all holding thick mugs in their hands and talking excitedly. They had wonderful, huge smiles on their faces.

Irene stood just inside the door, wondering whether she had gone to the wrong address until she saw Richard. He was standing at the far end of the room, looking graciously down at Bella Hawkins, who was gazing up at him with an expression that made Irene want to spit. Good company he might be, a splendid director he certainly was, but he was definitely not the kind of perfect, god-like being that Bella's awed adoration suggested.

He looked away from her enraptured face, saw Irene and nodded. Having said something to Bella, he left her and crossed the long room to the front door. There, with a nicely judged air of excessive delight, he kissed Irene on both cheeks.

'You are a pig, you know, Richard,' she said by way of greeting.

'Charming. What have I done to deserve that?'

'The way you're letting that child worship you. It's indecent.'

'Nonsense. It's good for her; it'll make her listen properly and do as she's told. Will you?'

'Will I what?'

'Do as you're told?'

'Richard, don't go all tyrannical on me. I get enough of that at home. I warn you, I'm not prepared to take it from you, too.'

He laughed. 'Surely you know that all directors are tyrants. We have to be. Seriously though, it's important for the actors that you and I are seen to be working happily together. It'll panic them if they think we disagree. Will your residual acting skills be up to pretending you think I'm wonderful, too?'

'I suppose they might be stretched that far if it's really important,' she said, hugely enjoying the fact that it was possible to trade insults without any kind of anger or intent to hurt. 'Will yours?'

He took her face between both hands and kissed her. Straightening up, he said: 'Yes, but I shan't need them. You must know I think you're brilliant.'

'Yeah, yeah,' said Irene, which made him laugh again.

Taking her by the arm, he introduced her to the actors, each of whom said something charming about the play. In spite of their bright smiles, she saw that they all had frightened eyes and she began to understand why Richard wanted to make them all feel safe. They reminded her a little of Helena, which gave her own smiles an extra warmth. For herself safety was the last thing she wanted. Her need was for excitement and danger, as much of it and as soon as possible.

A young stage manager brought her a mug of tea just as Richard said: 'And this, of course, is Peter Callfield.'

Irene took the mug and flashed a grateful smile at the stage manager before holding out her free hand to Callfield.

'This is such an honour,' she said, hoping that she was hitting the right note of confidence-building enthusiasm without sounding too much like a gushing fan. 'I've seen virtually everything you've been in for the past ten years.'

'How frightfully nice of you,' he said in the famous broken-glass-and-concrete voice that she had had in her mind as she wrote every word of his part. 'I can't think why we haven't met before except that Richard's always tended to be selfish about keeping his friends to himself.'

'To tell you the truth,' said Irene, shuddering at the taste of a mouthful of ferociously strong tea, 'I've only just met him again after more than quarter of a century. It's very odd: in some ways I feel I know him better than almost anyone else in my life, and yet we're complete strangers.'

'Really? What fun! Mysterious disappearances and surprising reunions are just my bag. Do tell me how it happened.'

'It's not all that thrilling,' Irene said, knowing perfectly well that he was merely making conversation and could not have cared less about her relationship with Richard. 'We were at the Theatre School together and then lost touch when I left to get married. I had no idea my agent was going to send him this play and was amazed when I heard.'

'Well . . .' Callfield began just as Richard interrupted: 'Stop flirting, you two. There's work to be done. Irene, I want you to meet Carrie Fletsham, who's to play the elder Maria, and Annette Brimfield.'

Irene shook hands with them both, saw how nervous they were and wished that she could make their anxiety less. Almost as soon as she had told them both how much she had admired their work in the past, Richard took her to the far end of the room, where Adam was standing beside his model of the set. He kissed her, too, and stood back so that she could see the model. He seemed to have done an enormous amount since he had left them in Amsterdam, and showed her exactly how the different scenes would work, pulling up the various flats that would be stored in the fly-tower and letting them down again. She looked at everything with great care and heart-lifting excitement. For the first time she felt that she could truly envisage her play in performance.

'It's brilliant,' she said at last. 'So economical and yet so beautiful; realistic, too. I can't tell you how pleased I am. It's much better than my ideas of Venice could ever have been. Thank you.'

'Good,' said Richard from behind her. 'Come along, Irene. We must get going.'

He led her away from the models and the costume sketches that she had not been allowed time to see and put her into a chair at the end of a horseshoe-shaped row. The actors, all moving with enviable grace, took the rest of the chairs and looked expectantly at Richard.

'I'm not going to go into any detail about *The House on the Canal*,' he said, looking round impartially at all of them. 'I want you to read it straight through without stopping for questions or comments. We will then discuss it and sort out any immediate problems. I know that Irene will answer any questions you may have. All right with you, Irene?'

'Of course,' she said, surprised to find herself quite without anxiety. There was so much that could still go wrong that she ought to have been worried at the very least, but all she could feel was curiosity about the way the actors would bring out the parts she had written for them.

'Whenever you're ready, Annette,' said Richard.

They set off, while Irene listened in a mixture of fascination and frustration. She kept wanting to interrupt to say, 'No, no, *not* like that,' but Richard's icily forbidding expression stopped her making any sound at all. By the time they reached the end she felt as though she might pop. Bella Hawkins said the last line and they let their scripts flutter down into their laps.

'That's wonderful,' said Callfield, sighing as though in an ecstasy of relief. 'It's got everything: tragedy, excitement, love, loss, and wit too. It's going to be a humdinger.'

'Oh, thank you,' Irene said, reminding herself that he was a brilliant actor and might not be quite as sincere as he sounded.

'Now, some of you must have some questions,' suggested Richard.

Later, when Helena asked how the rehearsal had gone, Irene could not remember a single thing she had been asked or said, but the discussion went on for nearly an hour and her throat was aching by the time she got home and so she must have been speaking. The only thing that stuck in her mind was Bella's saying: 'I'm not sure about the very end. This confrontation between the woman and the girl. Will the audience believe in it since they've known from the beginning that the two of them are the same person?'

Irene was about to say, well, if they don't they're stupid or insensitive, when Richard took it upon himself to answer for her.

'We won't know that, Bellissima, until we've got there. It's the kind of resolution that can only come out of the work that we'll be doing. If it seems false, I'm sure Irene will modify it for us.' He turned to look at her, raising his eyebrows.

Irene, who was appalled at the prospect of changing anything else in the play or doing any more rewriting, did her best to look enthusiastically confident as she nodded.

'Oh, yes,' she said. 'Anything that needs changing . . .' She could not make herself finish the sentence and saw Callfield looking at her with so much sympathy that she thought he must understand exactly how she was feeling.

Eventually the actors drifted away and Irene was left alone with Richard, who put a hand on her shoulder.

'You're looking pretty sick. Don't let it get you down. This is all very preliminary stuff and it always hurts. If it didn't there would be something to worry about. The actors are terrified and no-one knows where we're going with it yet. It isn't only you.'

'No,' she agreed, frowning. 'But there were moments when it sounded so banal, so empty. There seemed to be nothing there at all. No point. It's like this beastly great room.' She shivered.

Richard put both arms around her and hugged her in a completely sexless embrace.

'There's plenty there,' he said. 'But we've got to dig it out ourselves now. That's why I don't want you with us for the next week while we start chipping away.'

'At the play?'

'No, at our obstructions to it.'

'I don't understand.'

'Don't you? No, I suppose not. Look here, the play is real in itself, but it cannot be made to seem real in performance until the actors have found it in themselves and themselves in it. Don't worry too much. The words don't exist to explain the process they have to go through – and I with them. You'll see when you come back to us that we're beginning to get there. Don't be afraid. Have you got something nice to do this week?'

'No.'

Richard laughed at her obstinate refusal to be comforted. 'Well, find yourself something. Have a massage. Go to a health farm. Have a scene with your wretched husband. Take your stepdaughter to Amsterdam. Anything. Just don't brood or you'll lose what's left of your courage. If that happened, you wouldn't be you at all, and that would be a disaster. D'you see what I mean?'

'No,' she said again, adding: 'But I'll do my best.'

'Good girl. Now, off with you. I need to talk to the cast. I'll ring you up at intervals to tell you how it's going. Goodbye.'

Dismissed, Irene left and tried to believe that it would be fair to drop in on Helena. She decided that it would not and took the tube back to Herbert Crescent, which seemed gloomier and more oppressive even than usual. Her study was her own again now that the dining room table had been reassembled in its proper place and she retreated there.

She knew she ought to be thinking about a new play in order to build on the success she still hoped would come from *The House on the Canal*, but she felt as though she would never have another fruitful idea in her life.

The telephone rang and she went out to answer it and found her daughter on the line.

'Jane!' she said, working to put enthusiasm into her voice. 'How are you?'

'So so. Is Dad there?'

'No.' Irene looked down at her watch. 'He's sitting today. I shouldn't think he'll be back for another hour at least. Anything I can do?'

'Not really. He sent me a cheque, you know.'

'Yes, he told me when I rang him from Amsterdam. I'm very glad, darling.'

'Are you? He said in his letter that you disapproved,' said Jane, clearly not the least interested in what her mother might have been doing in Holland.

Irene did not mind that, but she was furious with Fin. Trying to keep the rage out of her voice, she said: 'That's not exactly true, but we'd better not go into it now. Did it settle all the bills?'

'Most of them, but not quite all. There's one other I must pay, which is why I need to talk to him.'

'Is it a big one, Jane?' asked Irene, thinking about her latest bank statement and the bills she would have to settle before Fin paid the next tranche of housekeeping into her account.

'That depends on how realistic you are,' her daughter said tartly. 'It's seventy-five pounds for the electricity. They're threatening to cut it off and the hot water runs off it as well as the lights. I can't do without either of them. I thought I'd have enough, but, having pacified the bank manager, I haven't.'

'Don't worry about it any more. I can cover that much. I'll send you a cheque straight away.'

'You?'

Irene grimaced at the astonishment in Jane's voice. 'Yes. Don't bother Fin with this one. I can cover it from the housekeeping, and I couldn't bear the thought of you having to have cold baths.'

'Thanks,' said Jane, still sounding as though she could not believe her ears.

'Heard anything from Ivo?' asked Irene, wanting to prolong the contact between them.

'Not a lot. He seems pretty busy at the moment. I thought he rang you all the time.'

'Not these days. I imagine he must have a lot of work.'

'He's not the only one,' said Jane drily. 'I must go. The bill's urgent. It's a red one and there's only another day.'

'I'll go the post office now and express it to you.'

'That's great, Mum. I mean . . . really. Anyway, thanks.'

'It's a pleasure,' said Irene, but she was saying it to a blank receiver. Jane had gone.

Having reached the post office just in time, Irene returned to the house more slowly and then decided to allow herself the rare treat of ringing Ivo. She did not often do that, not wanting to cluck over him or bore him, but she was sure he would be interested in her weekend, much more interested than either Jane or Fin. She listened to his telephone ringing and then heard the clicks and recorded message of his answering machine. Disappointed, but making herself sound cheerful, she said: 'It's me, Ivo. I hope things are going well. I had a good weekend in Amsterdam and a fairly dramatic time on the way back. I was stopped going through Customs and searched for drugs. Me! It was seriously undignified. I can't think why they should have picked on a respectable middle-aged woman like me. Can you? Anyway, do give me a ring when you've got a minute. I've got lots to tell you and it would be nice to hear what you've been up to. 'Bye.'

Putting the receiver back on the telephone, she realized that she had nothing else to do but cook dinner for herself and Fin. As she peeled and chopped she began to think about all the other meals she had cooked and the number of times Fin had returned to the house in a bad mood, unappreciative of her efforts and unaware of her as anything but his housekeeper, and his unpaid housekeeper at that. She found herself rehearsing old arguments and thinking up new ones, getting angrier and angrier until by the time she heard his key in the lock she was almost ready to hit him.

As it turned out, she did not need to do any such thing. He, too, was in fighting mood and unknowingly obliged her by saying as he put his briefcase on the floor by the kitchen table in the most inconvenient possible place, where she was bound to trip over it: 'I suppose it was necessary to make all that noise last night?'

'What noise?'

Fin just looked at her, his thin nostrils distending and his lips lengthening. 'You know perfectly well. You were very late back from the airport, weren't you?'

'Yes.' Irene waited for him to ask why so that she could tell him everything and watch his resentful irritation turn to apology and support. She really wanted him to be on her side for once.

He turned his back, leaving his briefcase where it was, and walked into the cloakroom beside the front door to change his shoes. It was all she could do not to follow him, shouting out her need. Instead she kicked the briefcase to push it under the table out of her way and went back to her pans.

'Could you lay the table?' she called as she heard Fin emerging in his house shoes. 'I haven't had time. Three courses. We'll be ready in about ten minutes.'

She waited for a comment. Anything would have been welcome, particularly something on the lines of: three courses! You are amazing to have gone to so much trouble for me, especially after all the work you've been doing all day. How did it go? Are you pleased with your play? Do you like the actors?

Even an angry refusal to help would have been bearable, not least because it would have allowed her to be angry back, but Fin could not be bothered to give her even that.

# Chapter Twelve

Helena had got rid of the last of her cataclysmic hangover by Tuesday morning, and she woke with a clear head and a determination to get on with Ivo's desk as soon as she could. She had talked to three of the clients who should have taken precedence of him; two of them had been quite prepared to wait a little longer, but one was adamant that he needed his chair back within the time she had originally given him. He was well within his rights and she set about the work without resentment and as methodically as usual.

She had just removed the last tarnished brass-topped screw from the cracked green leather seat and was about to lift the cover away when she heard the front door buzzer. Having put the screw in the pocket of her carpenter's apron, she brushed some flyaway hair away from her eyes with the back of her right hand and looked up at the monitor. The unexpected sight of Ivo on the screen made her smile as she reached up to press the button on the intercom.

Having locked the shed, she ran up the iron stairs and got into the drawing room just as he did, ready to cry out her delight at seeing him. But at the sight of his face she stopped, framed in the french windows with the dying roses behind her.

'What is it? What's the matter?' Helena was not certain whether Ivo was ill, hurt or angry, but she realized that there was something very wrong indeed.

His face was much paler than usual and the skin looked tight over his bones. His lips were thinned and tucked back, which made him look so like Fin that Helena felt quite sick and her heart started to bang within her ribs.

'What is it?' she said again, hating the breathlessness in her voice. She tried to keep calm.

'What do you think you're doing?' Ivo's voice was quiet, but no less threatening for that.

Trying to control her automatic fear of anger, which in the case of Ivo was ludicrous, Helena looked away from his taut face.

'I don't understand,' she said. 'What's the matter? What do *you* think I'm doing?'

'Spying. And I want to know why. What's happened? Is it this man of yours? Has he been saying something to you?'

'Ivo, stop.' Helena walked across the polished floor, hearing the slap of her espadrilles at each step.

He did not move even one pace towards her. When she got to him, she put a placatory hand on his arm.

'There's no need to be in such a state,' she said gently, hoping to soothe him out of the anger as quickly as possible. 'What d'you mean, spying? Are you talking about Saturday, when I dropped in to see you on my way back to London?'

'Just exactly that.'

'But I had no idea you'd mind. Why on earth did you never say you didn't want visitors? You must know that I'd never have gone anywhere near the place if I'd known you didn't want me there.'

Helena tried to think that Ivo's face had relaxed but there was little evidence for that. He did not speak. She tried again, watching him carefully.

'I don't understand what you're so cross about. Come on, Ivo. I only dropped in.'

'And took full advantage of the fact that I wasn't there, didn't you? One of the cowmen told me you spent hours poking around. Just what was it that you expected to find?'

'Only you. Ivo, come and sit down and stop being so silly.' Helena was breathing more easily again. 'You scared me, you know; I thought there was something seriously wrong.'

'But the cowman had already told you I wasn't there.'

'Yes, but I had no way of knowing whether he was right. Look, it's no big deal. I was near your house as I was driving back from

Worcestershire and I thought I'd like to see you. While I was climbing over the gate to get to the door, I was hailed by this complete stranger, who said you weren't there. I decided to leave you a note, and before writing it I thought I'd just see what the place is like. It may have been cheek on my part, but it certainly wasn't spying. It was sisterly curiosity.'

'Dan said you peered through all the windows – and even the letter box. What did you think you'd see? Murdered bodies or something?'

'Oh, don't be so silly,' she said, laughing because he was being so melodramatic. 'Come on. All I saw was piles of dirty socks and crockery, which was exactly what I'd expected. Typical graduate's digs. You're not ashamed of the mess, are you?'

Ivo was still looking at her with fierce anger in his dark eyes, but there were a few signs of relaxation in him at last.

'Sit down while I make some coffee and tell me why you're in such a rage,' said Helena, taking encouragement from them.

'I'll come with you,' he said and followed her down the passage.

He perched on the edge of the kitchen table while she filled the kettle and ground some beans. He had often done that before, but the atmosphere between them had never been so odd. She became aware, as she had not been previously, of the physical power he represented. The sleeves of his cream shirt were rolled up to the elbow and the muscles in his tanned arms were impressively taut.

'And what about this letter of yours that I got this morning?' he said. 'About my desk.'

Helena turned so sharply that the water from the tap missed the kettle and splashed over her hand.

'Is that it?'

'What?'

'What brought you up here in such a bad mood. But, Ivo, didn't you read the letter properly? I checked with my mother – Miranda, I mean – and she told me that even though she's no specialist in that sort of law she doesn't think your title to the desk is in any doubt. I just thought you'd be interested that I'd seen it in *Find*. No, actually that's not quite true. I thought you ought to know that it might once have been stolen. It didn't seem fair to have the knowledge myself and not pass it on to you. But that's all. It's nothing to get so hot under the collar about.'

Ivo slipped off the edge of the table, took the kettle from her, plugged it in and came back to stand with his hand under her chin, turning her face to the light so that he could see it properly. For a moment she was not only puzzled but almost frightened. A thought flashed into her mind: perhaps this unpleasant confrontation with Ivo was the price she had to pay for the new relationship she was building with Miranda. She pushed his hand away.

'You mean it's coincidence?' he said, frowning.

'What's coincidence? Ivo, you're being mysterious and worrying again, and it's upsetting me. I wish you'd tell me what all this is really about.'

He pushed back his smooth dark hair in an unusually irritable gesture. 'Make the coffee.'

Raising her eyebrows at his unusual bossiness, Helena did as she was told. She could not help remembering Miranda's casual remarks about Ivo hiding behind his charm.

He carried the tray back into the drawing room for her and poured them both mugs of coffee, adding milk to hers and milk and sugar to his own without saying anything. Then, when he had drunk some coffee, he looked at her and with an attractive, rueful smile said: 'I'm sorry. I think I must've been doing you an injustice.'

'Yes, I think you probably have been. What I still don't know is what it is you suspected me of doing – or why.'

He shrugged, smiled again, and looked more like his usual affectionate self.

'I suppose it really is coincidence. It's just that I had a letter from Jane making all sorts of outrageous accusations, and then I heard that you'd been spying around at the farmhouse. Then your letter arrived this morning, practically accusing me of fencing stolen property, and I got a bit antsy. I thought perhaps Jane had been tickling you up and you'd decided to come poking around the house to see whether there was any more stolen property there. You must see why I got angry.'

'I think you must have gone completely mad,' Helena said frankly, for once not responding to his appeal. In fact she had hardly noticed it. 'For one thing I don't understand what Jane's letter has got to do with me. I didn't even know she'd written to you. For another, there was absolutely nothing in my letter to suggest that I thought *you* had done anything wrong about the desk. I went out of my way to tell you I didn't.' She paused to disentangle her various thoughts and emotions and then took a risk because it seemed so important. 'Why are you so defensive? You're behaving like someone with a guilty conscience. What have you been up to, Ivo?'

He laughed and wriggled a little, looking exactly as he always had when he had had to own up to some minor infraction of house rules or some more important nursery crime. He had done it when she had accused him of drawing in indelible ink on the frill of her best party dress when she was nearly eleven and he three. He had wriggled in just the same way a year or two later when he had admitted to eating the large and lavish Easter egg she had bought for Irene with weeks' worth of saved-up pocket money.

'You've definitely been doing something, Ivo. What was it Jane accused you of?'

'You're sounding like an older sister again.'

'I am your older sister. Come on; out with it.'

Ivo shrugged. 'She's in debt again and she's had a ferocious wigging from Dad, which has made her come over all resentful. She wrote to me for the first time in months in a complete rage and said that if I can really live without borrowing I must have a great deal more money than she gets, which must mean – according to her – that I'm either on the game or blackmailing someone. Neither of which is true, I may say.'

'Of course it isn't. But what is true? Something's going on or you wouldn't be behaving like this. I've never known you so weird.'

'Nothing very serious.' Ivo laughed and wriggled again. 'I'd have told you ages ago except that it's so trivial and if Dad ever found out I didn't want him thinking you should have told him about it.'

'Told him about what? Ivo, come on. I can't bear this teasing.'

'It's only that I've been playing cards. You know what Dad's like about that.'

'You mean you've been gambling? Is that all? You are a loon. You must have known that he'd go berserk if he found out, and he's bound to one day.'

'Which is precisely why I've kept it quiet and not involved you. *I* can cope with berserker rage, but I know you can't.'

Helena leaned towards him in a mixture of gratitude and apology.

'I'm sorry, Ivo. That never occurred to me, and it's sweet of you. But how did you ever get involved in gambling?'

'The grateful father of one of the A level pupils I've been tutoring took me to a casino a while ago,' he said lightly. 'He staked me one evening, as a kind of thank you for getting his thick boy through. Having won rather a lot under his aegis, I couldn't resist going back alone to see if I could do it for myself. It turns out it wasn't just beginner's luck. I seem to have a kind of golden touch. It's been augmenting my pathetic allowance for some time now, which has made life considerably more pleasant, and it hasn't done any harm to anyone else.'

Helena got to her feet, no longer as comfortable – or as apologetic – as she had been.

'Except Jane,' she said.

'It hasn't done anything to her at all.'

'Of course it has. Ivo, think. Pretending you can survive on the allowance that she finds so inadequate means that you've made her look feckless. Less than you. Worse than you. That's not fair.'

He shrugged, looking as though he did not mind that in the least. Helena left him and went to sit at the top of the iron steps down into the garden, nursing her coffee mug between her bare knees. After a moment, she felt his hand on her bare neck and heard his voice, soft and seductive: 'Are you really angry with me? I hadn't bargained on that at all. I would have told you ages ago if I thought you could have coped with the fallout if Dad heard what I'd been doing.'

She turned, feeling his hand slipping round to her throat.

'And I never claimed to be an angel,' he went on, sitting down beside her. 'Isn't it unfair of you to have expected it?'

'It would be if I had, but I haven't.' She thought of Miranda's coded warning. 'But I have always trusted you, and now I see that I shouldn't have. That hurts. I thought I knew you, Ivo.'

'You do know me, and of course you should trust me.' He took the coffee mug from her, impatiently flung the dregs into the roses, dumped the mug on the step and put his arms round her.

Feeling most uncomfortable, she withdrew at once, saying: 'What are you going to do about Jane? I do think you ought to tell Fin what you've been up to, you know.'

'I couldn't possibly. You know how badly he'd take it. He thinks gambling is almost as heinous as theft. More, probably. He'd go ballistic and that's unfair on my mother. Remember what the house was like when you were fighting your battle to go to furniture school or whatever it was instead of Somerville?' Seeing Helena frown, he added as a clincher: 'You must remember what that did to my mother. D'you think it would be fair to her, especially now of all times when she's half addled with anxiety about her play, to make her go through it all again?'

Helena shook her head. Her sympathy for Jane was immense, but she could not risk hurting Irene even for that.

'I'm not pleased with you,' she said as she stood up. 'You'll have to do something to sort it out soon; as soon as you can after the first night.'

He leaned sideways so that his smooth head stroked her bare legs.

'That's my Helena,' he said with satisfaction. 'I knew you'd understand. You mind about her as much as I do. I'll sort it out once the play's up and running and a success. I promise I will. But I can't do anything before then.'

She smiled down at him then, almost ready to forgive him. He smiled back. 'Now can I take you out to lunch on some of my ill-gotten winnings? Come on. Let me do that at least. I'll take you somewhere really nice to make up.'

'No,' she said sadly. 'Much as I'd like to have lunch with you, I don't think I can.'

He did not try to persuade her and they said goodbye more coolly than usual, but Ivo looked quite at ease as he sauntered away down the road. Helena watched him from the drawing room window. When he was out of sight, she turned away from the window and filled out a cheque for five hundred pounds in her half-sister's name. Sitting down at her desk, she wrote:

*My dear Jane, Having heard on the family jungle drums that you're having a few money worries, I thought the enclosed might help. I'm sorry I didn't do it in time to stop you having any of the worries in the first place, but cash flow was tight until a client paid a big bill.*

*I hope your work is going well and that the worries haven't completely spoiled the term for you. I know how hellishly distracting anxiety can be. But things are looking quite rosy on my financial front at the moment and so I'm free of it for once, which is lovely. If you need more money will you let me know?*

Helena paused there and re-read what she had written. She wanted to apologize for having been swayed by Fin's Ivo-induced criticism of Jane's extravagance, but there seemed no way of putting it that would not make the offence even greater. She also wanted to stop Jane feeling aggrieved, and to tell her what Ivo had been doing, but neither seemed possible. After a while she picked up her pen again.

*Irene's play is well and truly in production now and seems to be absorbing most of her energies – or all those that are left after Fin's had his daily pound of flesh. Be nice to her if you can. I get the feeling that she's having rather a rough time herself just now.*

*When are you coming back to London? Let's make a plan*

*to do something together. It would be good to have some time to talk. Love, Helena.*

Poor Jane, she thought, as she licked the envelope and stuck it down. Exiled, admittedly by her own choice, to the far north, living in depressing digs without enough money to buy food and clothes, let alone the books she needed, always contrasted unfavourably with Ivo, she deserved a break.

# Chapter Thirteen

Irene set off for the first full-length rehearsal of *The House on the Canal* at the beginning of the following week, feeling as though she were on her way at last. Short of an earthquake or the outbreak of civil war, the play was going to be performed. It might yet fail, but it would be seen. Her name would be on the programme. Her words would be spoken; her ideas heard. Some people at least would take her seriously. At forty-six, she was making a very late start, but it was a real start, and no-one could take that away from her.

She arrived at the church hall in good time, just as Richard swept up in his Audi soft-top. He had Bella Hawkins in the passenger seat beside him. She opened the car door as soon as he had pulled up the brake and smiled up at Irene, who thought that she looked remarkably pleased with herself.

'Hello,' Irene said as casually as though she had expected to see Bella in Richard's car.

Bella put one long bare brown leg out of the car and stood up with enviable ease. She was wearing an impossibly short orange skirt, which looked as though it had been made from deckchair canvas, and a cobweb-thin white muslin shirt with tactfully placed double-thickness pockets over her small breasts. Her long hair fell down her back almost to her waist, and it looked much blonder than it had done at the read-through. She had an entirely new aura of sleek confidence.

Irene, who was feeling distinctly glad of her loose black linen trousers and the expensive Italian jacket that skimmed past all her bulges, hoped that the confidence had come only from Bella's success in rehearsals.

'Good morning, Mrs Webton,' she said politely, shaking hands.

Irene, feeling every one of her twenty-seven years' seniority, could not for the moment think of anything to say to her and stood in silence until Richard walked round the long bonnet of his car and kissed her casually on the cheek.

'Hello, Richard.'

'It's good to see you, Irene. Things have been going reasonably well, as you'll see in a minute or two. Especially as far as our sparkling new star is concerned.' He patted Bella on the head and she twisted round so that she could smile up at him. 'I hope you'll be pleased with what you see, Irene. Coming?'

He strode off towards the hall without waiting for either of them to agree or precede him. Irene raised her eyebrows at the patronizing tone he had taken towards Bella and turned to smile sympathetically at her. Bella looked momentarily confused, but then she fell back on one of the brilliant smiles Irene had begun to recognize as the typical actor's mask to hide nervousness. She began to feel more warmly towards Bella and urged her to go ahead into the church hall.

Some of the others had already arrived, but Peter Callfield was still to come. The stage managers had made tea as usual and Irene took a mug herself and perched on the edge of a chair, sipping the raw-tasting liquid. Rather to her surprise, Bella came to sit beside her and said: 'Mrs Webton, can I ask you something?'

'Yes, of course, Bella.'

'It's just that all last week Richard was telling me to make Maria fluttery and fragile, and somehow that doesn't feel right to me. I'm not sure if it's simply that I can't do what he wants because I'm not at all fragile myself, or if he's . . . well, you know, sort of wrong about the character.'

Irene put her cup down on the floor and swivelled in her chair to look directly at the girl.

'Good,' she said after a while. 'I'm glad you're not so much under his spell that you can't question his judgement.'

To Irene's distress Bella blushed, but she did not say anything. Trying to ignore all her reawakened suspicions and concentrate on the play, Irene went on: 'And in this case I think you're right. Maria is certainly ignorant but she's not remotely fragile. In fact she has a dangerous kind of confidence. That's really what the play's all about.'

'Ignorant of what?' asked Bella, giving Irene a chance to offer at least a veiled warning.

'Herself, other people, what she wants of them and of life – everything really. It's what makes her both so strong and so vulnerable. But her vulnerability is anything but fragile. It's dangerous, not pathetic. D'you see the difference?'

'Absolutely,' said Bella. Her smile had changed completely. It was not as glamorous as the professional version, but it offered hints of all sorts of interesting and difficult emotions. 'And so the house is a kind of metaphor, is it, for her unthinking certainties? Once she leaves it – is forced to leave it – she can't get back in because she knows too much to have that kind of dangerous over-confidence ever again? Is that right?'

Irene put her hand on Bella's knee. 'I knew you'd be right for the character,' she said. 'That is certainly part of it, although I'm not sure I've ever thought it out as clearly as that myself. Good for you. Play the girl like that and all should be well.'

Bella's face lit with pleasure and she dropped her hand over Irene's for a second.

'Thank you for that confidence-boost,' she said as she stood up. 'It'll help me stand up to Richard when he starts bullying me.'

'Yes, you need to stand up for yourself,' said Irene slowly enough to make it sound important, but she did not look at Bella. She did not want to see her blush again.

They both started as they heard the sound of short, sharp clapping and then Richard's voice: 'Come on, come on. Settle down. We've a lot to get through. I want to take it from scene two, getting as far as we can, although I will stop you whenever I have to.' He turned to say over his shoulder to Irene: 'If there are things you want to say, I'd like you to keep them until the end of each scene unless someone stops to ask you something. Can you do that?'

'I expect so.'

'Take notes as we go or you'll forget what you want to say. There's a pad and pen here if you haven't thought to bring any of your own.'

There was no scenery, but tapes had been pinned to the floor to represent the various doors and walls, the canal and the bridge. A shabby old formica-topped table stood in for the darkly polished oak version Irene had imagined and a row of chairs represented the deep window seat on which Bella was leaning as the scene opened. Her back was to the audience. Irene remembered her own stage directions: 'Almost all the light is on the canal outside so that the audience does not know how old the woman is or what she looks like. They must simply get an impression of stillness, of satisfaction and yet of an underlying, only half-recognized yearning to escape.'

Even at the moment when she was writing the words, she had understood that she might be asking too much. After all how could any silent, still woman persuade an audience that she was both satisfied and trapped? But she had left it in as a clue to the actors. As far as she could see, Bella was merely still and silent, but it would have been hard to establish anything else with no scenery and a glaring, even light falling directly on her. But there was something in her stillness and in her pose that was arresting. As they waited, Irene began to feel part of what she had hoped the girl would express.

Then an older woman's voice called from off-stage. In the real play light would flood the front of the stage at that moment. As Bella half turned her head towards both the audience and the sound, the back of Irene's neck felt cold. It was an extraordinary sensation, and quite unexpected. In that moment Bella's short skirt, the lack of scenery, subtle light and everything else no longer mattered. She had become the girl who had lived in Irene's head for so long.

Bella's face had something of the incommunicable feeling of

Vermeer's Girl with a Pearl Earring. She could have been sad or sympathetic, greeting or saying farewell, on the point of speech, or never to speak again. At last she moved once more and began to say her first lines.

The moment was over, but Irene was so shaken by it that she could not quite distinguish her gratitude to Bella from a feeling that something she should have kept private had been betrayed.

Richard let Bella and Annette Brimfield, the actress playing her mother, perform the whole scene without interruption. At the end, he said simply: 'It's really coming now. Well done. Irene?'

'Yes?'

'Any problems for you?'

'None at all. Bella, I ... You did that first movement extraordinarily well. Thank you.'

'Good,' said Richard, not bothering to hide his impatience to get on. He did not even look at Irene. The moment that had meant so much to her seemed to have barely registered with him. 'Then, Peter, when you're ready.'

The play proceeded with many interruptions. There were no more moments of chilling emotion for Irene, but as the morning went on she began to feel increasingly uncomfortable. Watching the actors, she realized that they had peeled a masking layer off her play and revealed something she had not known was there.

She had always admitted to herself that there were echoes of her own story in the play, but she had thought that they were quite distant and would not be heard by anyone else. Sitting in the silence that Richard had ordered, she was shocked into admitting that they were not so much echoes as deafening trumpet blasts.

Neither the actors nor Richard could have known what they had done, because none of them knew enough about her or her history to understand what she had used in the play, but the thought of Fin and the children, even Helena, seeing it as it was turning out to be was worrying. And what Fin's friends like Geoffrey and Elizabeth Duxford would make of it, Irene did not want to think.

It was not so much Bella's character that worried her; the girl Irene had been was strange enough to everyone likely to see the play for her revelations not to matter. And in any case, there were a great many things about the girl that had nothing to do with Irene, even as she had been before Fin had taken her away from the Theatre School into the exile that her marriage had become. But the older version, the woman who was trying to get back into the house, played by Carrie Fletsham seemed frighteningly familiar and, which was worse, almost completely unsympathetic. Irene sat watching Carrie's performance and absorbing a whole series of unpleasant revelations.

The great pile of luggage that Irene had imagined as part of the elder Maria's burden was represented by an unstable-looking pile of boxes beside the chairs that were standing in for the airport benches. As she spoke her lines, she was forever fiddling with the boxes, obsessively checking that they were all there and that their fastenings were tightly shut. Instead of the bravely enduring character Irene had thought she was creating, she was faced with a grudging, self-absorbed woman, on whom she herself would not have wasted any affection whatsoever.

At one moment, when Richard was preparing Bella for her big scene, Peter Callfield came to sit beside Irene.

'How are you enjoying it?' he asked as gently as his trademark voice would allow.

'I'm not entirely sure that enjoyment plays any part in what I'm feeling,' she said, watching Richard and the girl arguing. 'But I think you're all amazing, and the things you've done to the play are stirring me up summink chronick.'

He laughed at her outdated cod-cockney expression.

'Why is it agitating you? Because a lot of it is rather personal?'

'What makes you say that?'

'Because the whole play has the feeling of something pretty real,' he said without any suggestion of criticism or mockery. If anything he sounded admiring, which gave Irene enough confidence to say: 'If you'd asked me yesterday, I'd have said that very little of substance had anything to do with me at all, but sitting here this morning, I've been seeing that I've put into it all sorts of things that are – well, fairly personal.'

'And that's worrying you?' Callfield sounded surprised as he said that.

'Wouldn't it you?'

'Not exactly.' He frowned as though he was finding it difficult to choose exactly what words to use, which seemed unlike the little she knew of him. 'Perhaps because it's something we actors have to do all the time: find a way to reveal ourselves on stage, in public. Is it the act of revelation that's a problem for you or what people will think?'

'You see too much.'

Irene had had to turn away from him and was surprised when he said: 'Did you say "see" or "say"?'

'I'm not sure. But I meant "see".'

'That's all right then. You mustn't let me say any more than you can take. What worries you most?'

Irene was quite unable to tell one of the truths, which she had only just seen for herself: that in revealing herself in all her unattractive self-indulgence she would be giving Fin a whole new range of weapons to use against her, along with the equivalent of an instruction manual with precise descriptions of the best way to operate them to inflict maximum damage.

'Is Richard sleeping with that girl?' she said instead.

'I'm afraid so,' answered Callfield without even trying to keep Irene to the point. 'But don't worry about it too much. I suspect that it'll give her a great thrill for a while, a little pain when he moves on, as he will, and some charming memories of her own naivety to recapture when she's become cynical and famous. In a way, it's not much more than a rite of passage. A lot of other young actresses have been through it before her and come out the other end none the worse. And it helps Richard cope with a fairly tricky situation at home.'

'I wonder.'

'I can assure you it does help him.'

'That's not quite what I meant.' For once Irene stopped to think before rushing into speech and then said slowly as she tried to separate her memories of her own life from her fears for Bella: 'It's the lack of damage I was questioning. Whatever he did or didn't do to the others, this one's so young, so unaware. I do think he might damage her.'

'I don't think you need worry so much. Truly,' said Callfield, just as Richard yelled: 'Peter, where the hell are you? You've missed your cue.'

Richard had never sounded so abrasive and Irene was impressed when Callfield did not retaliate, but merely raised his remarkable voice to say clearly but peaceably: 'Coming. I was having a word about the character with Irene. A very necessary word. I'll be with you in a second.' He stood up but waited long enough to say privately to Irene: 'Try not to worry about it quite so much. I know it must feel like hell, watching us work on what you've written, but it'll all come out right in the end. You'll see.'

He moved away towards the improvised stage, shambling slightly and looking not at all attractive, until he reached Bella's side. There he slotted into his part without apparently doing anything at all.

The wise, experienced comforter who had been talking to Irene had gone, and in his place was a tempting Mephistopheles, all charm and a need that only the girl on stage could not see was spurious. She was doing remarkably well, wide-eyed but not stupid, tempted but no pushover. Her attraction for the man was absolutely clear and his for her. For a second Irene found herself longing to call out to Bella and say: 'See! That's exactly what you're risking with Richard. Don't let him use you. Get out while you can before you give up too much.'

Richard himself was lounging against the wall, his spectacles perched on the end of his nose so that he could both look over them at his actors and down at the crumpled, annotated script he held in his hands. He stopped the actors and issued a terse instruction to Bella, who clearly could not understand what he wanted. She asked him what he meant.

His voice sharpened so much that Irene had difficulty not wincing at the sound. Bella seemed to be growing tenser as he criticized her acting. After a moment Callfield intervened, moving her three steps towards the back wall, where he whispered something to her. No-one else, even Richard, could possibly have heard what he said.

Bella wiped the back of her hand across her eyes, nodded, and returned to her original position. They replayed the last three lines with only the subtlest of differences.

'That's a bit better,' said Richard, nodding his head in the rhythm of their speech. 'But you must try harder, Bella. It's the part you always get wrong. On you go. Yes!'

In the end it was that tiny scene that remained longer with Irene than any of her own fictional ones. Bella's small failure reminded her so vividly of her own inability to understand what Ben had tried to teach her of acting that she was forced to confront it directly. For years she had blamed Fin for stealing her chance of a career when all he had really done was present her with the opportunity to give up something she had found humiliatingly difficult. He had not forced her to leave the Theatre School; he had merely opened the door for her and she gone through it without a moment's thought for what she might meet on the other side. Callfield's remarkable voice broke into her thoughts: 'It's very easy,' he said at his most seductive.

Bella gazed up at him, the personification of yearning. Her hands were clasped beneath her chin and the very tightness of her grip on herself told the small audience that it was he whom she wanted to touch.

'All you have to do is say "yes". Once you've said it, you won't have anything more to worry about ever again. I've never found anyone else like you and I thought I never would. Come with me and save us both.'

He had put so much sly menace into the apparently flattering words that Irene decided she might have been a little too harsh with herself. After all, even if Fin had not forced her to abandon the life she had originally chosen, he had undoubtedly played a part in what had happened to her after she had left it. She might have gone to war with him out of unfair resentment at what she herself had given up, but he had fought her, too, and with a harshness that could not have come only from self-defence. Beginning to feel better as soon as she regained her sense of justified anger, Irene was able to think about the actors rather than her own memories once more.

By the end of the afternoon everyone in the hall was tired and most of them were irritable. So many mugs of tea had been drunk that Irene feared a mass outbreak of tannin poisoning. When Richard announced that they had done enough for the day there was a distinct air of relaxation in the gloomy great room. The actors began to collect their scattered belongings and talked about having a drink in the local pub on the way home.

'Bella? What about you?' said Carrie Fletsham.

Looking drained and red-eyed, Bella shook her head.

'Oh, come on,' said Carrie, rubbing her shoulder. 'It'll do you good. I know you feel as though you haven't got enough energy even to get yourself home, but a drink and laugh will do you more good than anything else just now, even sleep.'

Bella smiled, half turned towards Richard as though she were about to ask his permission, and then shrugged.

'Thank you,' she said, looking towards Carrie again. 'I'd like that.' With no more hesitation, she hurried across the room to the far wall, where she had left her sloppy canvas bag.

Irene watched Richard with interest. He was ostensibly talking to Peter Callfield, but she knew that he had absorbed every nuance of the counter-seduction of Bella. He looked furious.

When Callfield had left, blowing a kiss to Irene, she strolled over to where Richard was still standing, glaring after the departed Bella.

'Don't have a row with her about it,' she said. 'She needs to play with people nearer her own age.'

'Just what are you talking about?' Richard took off his spectacles and let them drop against his chest. He rubbed his eyes.

'Bella. You look as though you've got a headache. D'you want a pill? I've got some in my bag.'

'No.'

Richard's tone was so obstructive that Irene was tempted to say no more, but she was no coward, and it had to be said.

'When you see her again, don't bawl her out for going for a drink with the others. I don't know whether you'd arranged something with her or whether you just assumed she'd wait for you to decide what to do this evening, but . . .'

'You're taking rather a lot on yourself, aren't you?' Richard's voice was not friendly. The idea that she had been passionately kissing him only a few weeks earlier seemed impossible to believe.

'I don't think so. She's so young, Richard. You . . .'

'Ah, I see what it is: a spot of the old jealousy, eh? Really, Irene, isn't that a bit undignified? What is it you mind so much? That I turned to her so soon after our little fiasco? Or that she's young and pretty – and able to satisfy me when you couldn't?'

Irene stared at him, finding it hard to believe that he was the same man who had been so generous to her in Amsterdam, so far-seeing and aware of the things that mattered to her. She was not sure whether it was her criticism of the way he was behaving that had aroused his unpleasant anger or whether it had something to do with his domestic situation. Peter Callfield had suggested that Richard was having a particularly bad time at home and so it might have been that.

Furious with herself for wasting so long daydreaming about how happy she could have been – and how kind – if she had spent her life with Richard rather than Fin, Irene said coolly: 'Neither. What I mind so much is that you're exploiting your age, glamour and power over her without a single thought about what your selfish pleasure will do to her, probably for the rest of her life.'

'Oh, don't be so prissy – or so melodramatic. You've no idea what you're talking about. I don't see that it's any of your business, but if you must know, what I am doing is helping Bella produce what is going to be a spectacularly good performance in *your* play, provided that you don't interfere.'

'Oh, that's a masterpiece, Richard.' Irene's anger was momentarily displaced by amusement.

'I don't know what you're talking about and I don't think I particularly want to continue this conversation. I'm tired and I want to go home.'

'You can stay a moment longer and listen,' she said firmly. 'Here's a translation of what you've just said: You're not interested in your own gratification at all; your seduction of Bella has been almost entirely for her own good; the only other person likely to benefit from it is me because it'll help my play. Have I got that right so far?'

Richard did not answer, but his face gave him away.

'Yes, I thought so,' said Irene with considerable satisfaction. 'And there was a veiled threat in there, too, wasn't there? If I criticize you for taking advantage of her naivety, you'll make sure that my play is a failure.'

Richard laughed, great rolling gusts of unconvincing sound that reminded Irene that he, too, had once been an actor.

'What a woman will do when she feels that she has failed as a woman! You mustn't mind so much about your frigidity, Irene. It's pretty common in a woman of your age with so little experience. If I'd had more time and energy in Amsterdam, I could have made you respond to me. But don't worry, you will find someone who can make you come eventually. And then you'll feel better about it all.'

He patted her cheek. 'You're still attractive enough. It'll probably happen for you before it's too late.'

Irene felt as though she had only two options. She could hit him or she could pretend not to have understood his various insults. Deciding that a blow would only add to his conceit, she smiled with all the saccharine sweetness at her disposal and thanked him.

'Think nothing of it,' said Richard ambiguously. She nodded and turned to go. 'By the way,' he said in a quite different voice, 'there is one thing I need to talk to you about. Rather more important than all that. Sorry I lost my temper.'

His apology made her stop halfway to the door and she looked back, raising her eyebrows in a silent question.

'Come back and sit down. This really is important, Irene. I should have said it first.'

Shrugging, she went back to the row of chairs and sat down. 'Well?'

'Bella told me that you gave her an alternative interpretation of her part.'

'Yes, I did,' said Irene in surprise. 'She'd had an interesting idea about it and was finding your obstructiveness upsetting. I told her that I thought her idea was a good one and that she mustn't let you bully her.'

She was even more surprised when Richard neither raised his eyes to the ceiling in exasperation nor shouted at her. Instead he came to stand beside her, put one foot on the stretcher of the chair next to hers, and spoke in a voice almost as familiar and friendly as the one he had used in Amsterdam: 'I don't mind your answering questions from any of the actors about what you have written, obviously, but I can't let you question my interpretation of the piece or my instructions to them.'

'But Richard, it's my play. I wrote it. I know what it means and what the characters are like better than anyone. How can I possibly pretend to know less about them than you?'

'It's not exactly your play any longer.' When Irene leaned away from him, Richard took her by the shoulders. 'No, listen to me. This is important, Irene. It's nothing to do with you and me or me and Bella or anything like that. As I said, I ought to have made sure we talked about it before we had our little spat, but you caught me on the raw.'

'Did I really?'

'Yes. But that's over and this is work, so you must listen: not just to the sounds, but to what I'm saying. I'm not trying to score any points now. Can you accept that?'

'I suppose so.'

'Good. You wrote *The House on the Canal*, but I am the director, and for the moment I have to run things. Of course if you think I'm going wrong, you must say. But you must say it in private. In a way our partnership has to be like a good marriage. If you don't trust me to play my part in the collaboration, we're lost. D'you understand?'

'Oh, I understand,' she said bitterly. 'And you're right: it sounds precisely like a marriage, though perhaps not a good one. You've grabbed the high ground; you feel that you have some kind of authority over me; and I'm to keep my mouth shut and not challenge you. I know all about that, and I am not prepared to take it in my professional life, even if I've had to do it at home.'

Richard let her go and swung away from her to walk fast to the row of chairs that had stood in for Bella's window seat. He sighed.

'I hadn't meant to tickle up your private resentments, Irene. Perhaps marriage was the wrong analogy. I keep forgetting that this is all new to you. Let me put it like this: the actors are afraid. All of them, even Peter. They have got to go through a painful and difficult process before we get to the first night. As I said, if they lose confidence in the play they won't be able to give what we both want of them. And they will lose confidence if they see that you and I are not pulling in the same direction. D'you see that?'

'Yes,' she said reluctantly. 'So far so understandable.'

'Privately we can fight about anything you like, but it has to be private. They must be utterly convinced that we both know where we're going together and are happy with it. OK?'

Irene took a moment to think through the implications and then nodded, feeling her lips stretch into a humourless sort of smile. Richard came back and held out his right hand.

'Deal?' he asked.

'Yes.' Irene took his hand. 'It's a deal. I do see what you mean.'

'Good. Then we'll get somewhere after all. And look here, you don't have to worry about Bella. Honestly. She may be playing your part, but she's not you, you know. She's a tough little cookie.'

Irene laughed. It was only after she had declined a lift and seen Richard accelerate away down the road with quite unnecessary force that she remembered he had claimed to have remembered her as 'tough'.

When she found a taxi, she asked the driver to take her up to Clerkenwell. She knew she could not go straight back to Herbert Crescent, and she wanted the comfort of Helena's unemotional good sense and constant benevolence. But she found that she was not going to get it. There was no answer when she rang the front door bell.

As Irene was walking back down the front path, deliberately straightening her shoulders to counteract any tendency to a defeated stoop, she heard a car door bang and looked up in hope.

There was still no sign of Helena; only a tall man in his mid-thirties dressed in an impeccable suit made of dark bird's-eye worsted. To her surprise he smiled as he came towards her.

'This is probably going to sound impertinent,' he said in a deep, affectionate kind of voice, 'but could you possibly be Irene?'

'Yes,' she said, smiling herself. 'Mike?'

'The same. And I take it we're here on the same mission.'

'In search of Helena? Yes. But she doesn't seem to be here. I dropped in on the off chance and assumed she must be with you. Was she expecting you?'

'Not specifically this evening, no,' he answered. 'I've been in New York and I didn't know when I was going to get back. I arrived on her doorstep about ten minutes ago and thought I'd hang around in case she'd just gone shopping or something.'

Irene hardly heard him. She felt unusually confused and could not think what to do. The idea of discovering something about Helena's mysterious lover was intriguing and yet she did not like the thought of going behind her back.

'This is the most tremendous luck,' Mike said. 'I've been longing to meet you, but Helena's been reluctant to let it happen. I'm not sure why.'

'I know, which makes me feel as though I shouldn't be talking to you without her knowledge. It seems sneaky.'

'I think it's all right,' said Mike with such an affectionate expression that Irene was almost reassured. 'After all, this way, if we discover we can't stand each other, we'll be forewarned when she does eventually introduce us and so we can save her from one anxiety at least.'

'If you want to do that,' said Irene, smiling more naturally, 'then I think we'll probably like each other quite a lot. But I still think we ought to part now. I hope she lets us meet soon.'

'Won't you come and have a drink with me?'

'No, I think I'd better not.'

'Don't you want to check me out?' Mike asked, looking amused again.

'What? To see if you're a suitable companion for my stepdaughter?'

'Just that.'

'She's a grown woman,' said Irene, laughing. 'And wholly capable of doing everything she needs. Any checking is up to her. I've enjoyed meeting you, and I'm glad to be able to put a face to your name, but I'll say goodbye now.' Irene held out her hand. Mike shook it.

'Then could I give you a lift? I noticed that you didn't come by car.'

'No. Really, we must keep to what she wants us to do.'

Irene walked away, wishing that her scruples had let her take him up on his offer. She did in fact very much want to know what he was like and what he really felt about Helena, and whether he was likely to be good for her, but it would have been a betrayal. And Helena was far too valuable – and vulnerable – to betray.

# Chapter Fourteen

Earlier that evening, as Helena was working on the chair she had to finish before tackling Ivo's desk, she had been distracted by the sound of the telephone. Wanting to finish what she was doing, she had left it to ring until the answering machine cut in. By seven both her concentration and her hands had started to wobble, and she packed up for the day. When she had cleaned her tools and locked the shed, she went across to the house to listen to all the messages. The last was from her mother, who had said: 'Hello, Helena. This is Miranda. My case has just finished, and I feel like a treat. I know you don't approve of what I've been doing, but I wondered whether you would be prepared to celebrate with me? I'd very much like to take you out to dinner. If you are around and would like to come, could you give me a ring? I was thinking about Ferrato's in Old Gloucester Street. It's new but said to be very good.'

Helena quickly tapped in her mother's number and thanked her for the invitation, agreeing to meet at the restaurant at eight o'clock. Catching sight of herself in the bathroom mirror a moment later and seeing what a mess she looked, she wished that she had asked for an extra half hour. She wrenched off her clothes and turned on the shower to maximum force, letting the jets sluice the dust out of her hair and off her skin before rubbing in shampoo and soap. She got some of both in her eyes and eventually emerged from the shower clean but uncomfortable.

Later, when she had dried her hair, she dressed in the black silk trousers and a taupe shirt. As she stroked on some mascara to disguise the redness of her eyes, she noticed that her clean hair was looking particularly lank. She rummaged in one of the cupboards for some mousse that Mike's predecessor had given her in an attempt to endow her with the sort of hair he thought his girlfriend should have.

When she had smoothed in the small spreading ball of sticky white foam and attempted to put her hair into some kind of shape, the whole effect was worse than before, stiff and most unlike her. Irritated and despising herself for minding so much about how she looked, she rushed back into the bathroom to wash her hair all over again. Then she had to change her shirt because she had splashed so much water on it.

The whole silly process left her no time to walk to Ferrato's, which she had wanted to do to loosen her muscles after bending over her work all day. Instead she took the van to Old Gloucester Street and found a parking space easily enough, but she was ten minutes late when she walked, breathless, into the restaurant.

To her surprise Miranda stood up and said: 'Oh, you do look well. How lovely!'

'Really? Ratstaily hair and all?'

'Definitely. You've got more colour than usual and a wonderful light in your eyes. Come and sit down and tell me why. What would you like to drink?'

Helena tried to think of something to order that would not make it seem as though she were either alcoholic or ashamed of the amount she had drunk when Miranda came to Clerkenwell. After a moment Miranda said: 'I'm having a glass of the house claret. How would that be?'

'That would be fine,' said Helena. 'Look, I don't want you to think . . .' She could not work out how to finish the sentence. Her mother laughed.

'I don't. And I have assumed that you don't think that's the amount I normally drink either.'

'No, of course not.'

'There you are, then. That's your answer. As we now know, we're enough alike for you to have had similar reactions to mine.'

'Yes, I suppose that's true. I did feel bad about it though, when I realized how much I'd got through.'

'You shouldn't have worried. *I* enjoyed the evening very much indeed, and I was glad that you could let go of that much control with me. I hoped the same might be true for you.'

Helena could not think of a neat enough phrase to return the compliment and so she merely smiled.

'And I'm also relieved to see,' said Miranda with a more impish look than usual, 'that nothing dreadful came of it.'

At that Helena laughed and said quite easily: 'My hangover could certainly have been described as dreadful, but I do know what you mean.'

'That's better,' said her mother with an entirely new smile, warm and almost trustful.

'Isn't it? Now tell me about the case. Presumably you won it if you're in a mood to celebrate.'

'I did, which is why I was in two minds about whether to involve you this evening. I know that the idea of those two out on the streets again worries you.'

'And it doesn't worry you? Really?' As Miranda hesitated, Helena added with deliberate wickedness: 'After all, we are very alike.'

'I deserved that. Yes, all right; it does bother me. But that's all you're getting on that subject. By the way, I've brought you a kind of present. I'm not sure that you're going to like it much, but . . .'

'A present? I'm sure I will,' said Helena with unusual emphasis. 'How frightfully kind of you!'

Miranda leaned down to get something out of her handbag. When she sat up again she was holding an ordinary white envelope, which she passed across the table. As Helena accepted it, wondering why she suddenly felt unsafe, a waitress appeared to take their order. Miranda waved her away.

'I've been in two minds about this as well, but since we shared that evening I've been wanting to clear something up and this seemed the best way.'

'I don't understand.' Helena held on to the envelope but could not bring herself to open it. She reminded herself that there were innumerable occasions in the past on which she had felt just as much at risk for no reason whatsoever.

Miranda licked her lips as though they had become suddenly dry. She looked directly at Helena and said formally: 'I know I upset you that evening last month when you came to my house and I suggested that Ivo might be hiding something. I found that I couldn't bear you to think I'd said it out of malice.'

Helena frowned, remembering her own discovery that Ivo had not been as open with her as she had once assumed.

'I'm not sure I thought it was malice exactly,' she said, 'but I suppose I was a bit troubled that you should say those sorts of things about someone you hardly know. After all, you've no reason to slander him. It did seem unfair.'

'I know. That's why I wanted to show you what I meant.'

'Oh.'

'The easiest way seemed to be to find out who it is he's working for at that farmhouse he lives in,' said Miranda.

'And have you?'

'Not exactly. Have a look.'

Helena knew that she did not want the 'present' her mother was offering her. She also knew that she would never be able to refuse it. If she did not look at whatever document Miranda had produced, she would end up tormenting herself with wild imaginings of what it might have been. Eventually, knowing that she would have to do something, she tore open the envelope.

It contained a copy of the Land Registry certificate for Ivo's farmhouse. Helena read it twice and looked up, frowning.

'But I don't understand,' she said, feeling as obstructive as she used to feel whenever Fin had tried to explain anything legal to her. 'I thought they had to put the freeholder's name in, not the caretaker or the tenant.'

'They have to put the name of the registered proprietor and that of any mortgage holder.' Miranda sounded as though she were controlling impatience with difficulty. 'And that's exactly what they've done.'

'You mean you're telling me that the whole house is Ivo's?' said Helena, still staring at her mother. 'And without a mortgage?'

'Either that or he's someone's nominee, yes,' said Miranda. She raised her hand and then let it drop onto the tablecloth again as though she had wanted to reach across to touch Helena and then thought better of it. 'Shall we order some food? You look as though you need it. You've gone a bit pale. Here, have a look at the menu.'

Helena stared down at the stiff card, not feeling hungry, and chose the lightest things she could see, which were melon and grilled sole. Miranda waved to the waitress and gave the order, herself choosing an artichoke and calves' liver with sage. She also asked for a litre of sparkling mineral water.

Helena noticed the gleam of amusement in Miranda's eyes as she talked of water, but could not respond to it. All her energies were involved in dealing with what she had just learned. She was no expert in property prices, but the house she had seen had been a large one and appealing, set as it was in countryside that was probably very attractive to those who liked that sort of thing. She imagined that Ivo must have paid something like two hundred thousand for it, possibly even more. He could hardly have made that much from tutoring and gambling, however successful he might have been.

'What is it?' asked Miranda quietly.

Helena looked up to see that the waitress had gone. She shook her head, finding the sympathy in her mother's eyes almost harder to bear than the coldness that had preceded it or the incipient contempt she thought she had seen.

'I don't understand,' Helena said. 'He told me that he had an understanding bank manager when I asked how on earth he had managed to buy that desk, which is worth a small fortune itself. But this . . . Do *you* know how he paid for it?'

Miranda shook her head. 'There's probably a perfectly simple explanation, merely one he hasn't chosen to give the people who care about him.'

Helena looked away, trying not to think about all the implications of that. The waitress brought their first courses. Still in silence

Helena picked up her spoon and ate some melon, which was ripe and highly scented but she could hardly taste at all. Miranda pulled off the leaves of her artichoke one by one and scraped off the glaucous flesh between her small, sharp-looking teeth.

'What sort of explanation?' Helena asked when her mother was about halfway to the choke itself.

'I've no idea.' Miranda glanced up, a scraped leaf between her fingers, looking surprised. 'You know him so much better than I that you must be in a much better position to guess. What do you think?'

Helena did not want to answer what had sounded like a taunt, and yet she had to say something.

'His sister suggested that he might be on the game.' She tried to sound frivolous and as though she were enjoying a trivial joke that could have no connection to anything in real life. 'Perhaps he's got a rich admirer who bought it and bestowed it on him.'

'Well, he's certainly pretty enough,' said her mother just as lightly. 'And good enough company to be very expensive.'

'Yes, but it's a stupid idea. I don't believe it.'

'I know you don't. Nor do I.'

'Why did you do it?' asked Helena after a long, uncomfortable silence.

'I told you: to show you that I wasn't being unfair when I suggested he might not be quite the simple, charming young man he pretends to be.' Miranda paused, looking at her daughter, and then added casually, as though it didn't matter very much: 'You see, I mind what you think of me, Helena.'

'I wish I could believe that.'

'You can.'

Helena shook her head. She was surprised to find that there was a paradoxical reassurance mixed in with all the other emotions that were making it so difficult to eat, but it did not take her long to understand it. For months she had been wrestling with the knowledge that the cruel, unfeeling deserter of her childhood was in fact an intelligent, sympathetic woman, whom she would have had no difficulty in liking if they had met as strangers. To discover that Miranda was indeed ruthless – perhaps even malicious and certainly conscienceless – made the old anger seem more acceptable to Helena than it had for some time.

'In that case, what possible motive do you imagine I might have had?' asked Miranda as coolly as though she were cross-examining a hostile witness.

Helena looked at the familiar face in front of her and felt an equally familiar misery.

'I don't know. Perhaps to make trouble between me and Ivo in order to hurt Irene. After all, you hate her, don't you?'

Miranda had stopped tearing the leaves off her artichoke. Helena noticed the waitress coming back towards their table as though to remove their plates and then, having seen their faces, backing away.

'You don't know me very well,' said Miranda, looking at the floor.

'I haven't exactly had much chance,' snapped Helena before she could stop herself. She moderated her voice and added quietly: 'And you do hate her, don't you?'

'I suppose in a way I do. I think we'd better stop this conversation here. It's not going anywhere useful. I'm sorry the information has been so unwelcome.'

After a short silence, which Helena could not find a way to break, Miranda launched into an account of some of the more entertaining cases of her career. As she talked, Helena managed to bury her difficult feelings and retrieve most of her manners.

'You enjoy your work, don't you?' she said politely as she finished a respectable amount of the fish and was relieved to hear that her voice had returned to normal.

'Yes, I do now. It was hard to begin with; so hard that I can't imagine how I stuck to it. And I still get so nervous sometimes that I can hardly force myself to walk into court.'

'Although you win mostly these days, don't you?'

'Often enough, but not mostly. All barristers have to lose sometimes. After all, fifty per cent of all cases are lost.'

It took Helena a moment to work that out but then she smiled.

'Yes, I suppose so, but not, I imagine, fifty per cent of each individual barrister's cases. Some must lose an awful lot more than others.'

'Naturally. Now, pudding?'

'No, thank you. It's been a good dinner, and I'm glad . . . well, you know, that in a way we've got back on track. But I think I ought to be getting home now.'

'Won't you even have coffee with me?'

'No, thank you. Really. But it's been . . .'

'Not exactly fun, I know. But at least *I'm* not hiding anything from you. That seemed important.'

Helena flinched and tried to disguise the movement by laying her napkin on the table. Miranda, apparently unaware of her daughter's turmoil, signalled for the bill, paid by credit card and got up. When they reached the door, she said: 'Thank you for coming this evening. It's meant a lot to me. I'm sorry about the bad bits.'

'It was kind of you to bring me here,' said Helena as they went out on to the warm, dusty pavement to walk to her van. 'Can I give you a lift home?'

'No, thank you. It's only a short walk and it'll do me good.' Miranda waited on the pavement as Helena unlocked the van and got into the driving seat, winding down the window. Miranda bent down, smiled and said casually: 'The only reason I have ever had for hating Irene is that she made you love her so much. Good night.'

She straightened up and walked away without giving Helena a chance to say anything at all, which was perhaps just as well since she had no idea what she would have said.

When she got back home, having tried to think of nothing but the traffic and the way the van's gears were sticking, she found a note from Mike pushed through her letter box.

*Dearest Helena, Just back from New York – the deal was done and they signed! – I whizzed round, but there you weren't. Alas. I found your stepmother and thought I was going to be consoled by her company, but she refused even to have a drink*

*with me on the grounds that you haven't introduced us yet.
I thought that was rather a pity. She looked both interesting
and ... nice is the only word I can think of and it's pretty
pathetic. Anyway, I wasn't surprised that you like her so much.
And she clearly feels just the same. You're very lucky.*

*It would be good if you felt like ringing when you get in.
I hope you had a good evening. All love, Mike.*

Touched both by his choice of words and by Irene's loyalty,
Helena walked over to the answering machine. Sure enough, the
light was winking. She pressed the various buttons and soon heard
Irene's voice, saying: 'I think your Mike is thoroughly attractive.
I'm not surprised you don't want to share him. We ran into each
other outside your front door, both wanting the solace of your
company. I hope he got his. I'll settle for a chat in due course when
you have time to ring.'

The world is good and there are good people in it, and I don't
have to think about anything or anyone except them, thought
Helena as she pressed the automatic dialling button for Irene's
number. Then she realized that she could not talk to Irene until
she had sorted out what, if anything, she was going to do with
the knowledge Miranda had given her. She cancelled the call just
in time and instead rang Mike, who for once seemed safer than
anyone else in her life.

'Helena! You're back,' he said before she had opened her mouth.
It was only later that she thought it odd that he had known it was
she who was calling him.

'Yes. Sorry I wasn't here when you came round.'

'No need for that. You're allowed a life of your own.'

'Yes. Perhaps. Anyway, how was your trip?'

'Oh, all right. Look, it's not very late. Would you ... How would
you feel if I popped round and told you all about it?'

'I'd love it. Have you eaten? I'm not sure there's much food
here.'

'I'm not after food.' He laughed. 'Just you.'

Helena laughed too and hoped that the sound was convincing.

She had been feeling the first signs of panic and was determined to stop them before they grew into a full-blown attack. Her breathing was faster and shallower than usual, her forehead felt tight, nausea gripped her stomach, and she wanted more than anything else for someone to hold on to her physically and tell her that everything would be all right.

'I don't have panic attacks any more,' she said as soon as she had put down the telephone receiver. 'I've grown out of them. This is something else. I can stop it.'

If she could have wiped out the knowledge Miranda had given her, she would have done so at once, but it was there in her mind and nothing she could do would take it away or calm the wild fears it was whipping up. No matter how often she told herself that Ivo could not possibly be storing stolen antiques in the farmhouse, or acting as a front for a money launderer, or, as Jane had already suggested, blackmailing someone, Helena could not persuade herself that he was not involved in something illegal.

Mike arrived before she could work herself into a complete frenzy and she ran out of the drawing room to open the front door. Even the sight of his cheerful duck-like face was reassuring. As he stepped across the threshold, she laid her head against his broad chest and felt his arms close around her.

Kissing the top of her head, he kicked the door shut behind him and said nothing. He just stood there, stroking her back until she moved away.

'Hello,' she said, leaning away to smile up at him. 'Sorry about that. Come and tell me all about New York. It must have been very tiring having to go back so soon like that.'

'I'm used to it,' he said, following her into the drawing room, where the remains of the day's light had drawn warm lines on the polished wooden floor. 'The worst was the weather. Manhattan was still revoltingly hot. Coming out of those air-conditioned buildings into the street was like walking into a wall of wringing wet, hot towels. But they did finally sign and that was all that mattered. I saw some old friends, too, who sent you a message.'

'Me? Do I know them?'

'No. But they said to tell you that you were doing a great job. They said they'd never seen my stress levels so low and that since that must be down to you they'd like to make your acquaintance next time I go over.'

Helena smiled. 'How lovely! I'm not sure I could ever take the credit for relaxing anyone, but it's a jolly nice compliment.'

'Would you come?' he asked casually, watching her over the rims of his glasses. 'To New York I mean?'

'Yes,' she said at once, before she remembered how much she detested travelling. Then she decided that Mike's offer to include her in his life was worth much more than any of her old phobias and said again: 'Yes. I'd like that, very much.'

'Good. That's settled then. So what have you been doing while I was away?'

'Nothing half as interesting as you. Finishing a chair I've been restoring for a faithful but impatient client is really all.'

'And this evening?' As her face closed in, Mike quickly added: 'You don't need to look like that. I was only asking. I'm not trying to keep tabs on you.'

'No, I know,' she said quickly. 'It's only that I was dining with my mother and finding it even harder than usual. Let's talk about something different. I . . . I'll tell you all about her in the end, but I can't quite yet. It's still too kind of raw.'

'I liked your stepmother,' he said obediently.

'Good.' Helena relaxed and let herself lean against him on the sofa. 'Ah, that's better. She's good-looking, isn't she?'

Mike frowned. 'I suppose so, in a magnificent sort of way.'

'Don't you like magnificence?'

'Not all that much in people. She'd make a striking statue, but . . .' He smiled suddenly. 'Come on, Helena. You know that you're my ideal of feminine whatsit; am I likely to be taken with someone almost your exact opposite?'

She blinked. 'I am?'

'You must know that.'

Amused, taken aback, and very pleased, she was tempted to use his own question back to him: how can I possibly know if you don't tell me?

'Would I be this besotted with you if you weren't?'

'I don't know. Are you?'

He raised his eyes to the ceiling. Then he looked at her again, shaking his head.

'I think I'd better take you up to bed, hadn't I? Physical communication seems to be a lot easier than words.'

Later, as they were unromantically drinking large mugs of tea-bag tea in bed, Helena said as casually as possible: 'Mike, you know how you said that people with money to launder use businesses like yours?'

'I'm not sure I ever said anything quite like that.' He turned his head sleepily to watch her face. 'I imagine it was more that money-launderers would *like* to use businesses like mine.'

'Yes, probably. It comes to much the same.'

'No, it doesn't: not the same at all,' he said with a note of mock outrage in his voice. 'Come on, Helena. Don't insult me or my company.'

'No, sorry,' she said, trying to look as though she shared his amusement. 'I've just been wondering ever since you told me that: what other sorts of businesses do money launderers use?'

'Why have you been wondering that? What are money launderers to you, Helena?'

'Or me to Hecuba?' she said without thinking.

'I'm sorry?' Mike looked so puzzled that she realized what she had said and tried to explain, repeating: '"What's Hecuba to him or he to Hecuba?" *Hamlet*, you know. It's just one of those quotations that pop up like toast whenever a phrase pushes the right button.'

Mike looked at her as though she was talking nonsense and she reached out to touch his bare shoulder.

'It's not important, Mike. Nor are money-launderers. I was just curious and you seemed to know such a lot about them that I thought I'd ask what it is they actually do when they suborn a business.'

196

As she watched his face change, Helena knew that his New York friends would have changed their minds about her effect on his stress levels.

'As far as I know,' he said, sounding bored, 'the usual thing is to try to find a cash-based retail concern: garage, restaurant, hairdresser or casino; something like that. Anyone who regularly takes large amounts of cash to a bank is useful. The people with the funds to launder will add them to the legitimate takings and then be repaid, perhaps on spurious invoices in the case of garages and the like or with a casino's note. Any form of gambling is particularly useful because the amounts can be so large and as they're tax-free I imagine the records can be more flexible than in other sorts of business.'

Helena listened with only half her mind as Mike went on to describe the three stages of money-laundering: placement, layering and integration. The rest was obsessed with the words 'gambling', 'casinos', and 'flexible records', which seemed to lead her straight back to Ivo's reluctant – and in retrospect wholly unconvincing – explanation of his wealth. She wished that she had never started the conversation.

'And, as you know perfectly well, art and antiques are exceedingly useful because of the secrecy your sort of business uses,' Mike added, making Helena's mind switch to the present again with an almost visible jolt.

'Yes, I do know,' she said bleakly. 'Not least because no-one has to prove title to an antique or work of art before they sell it.'

'Helena, what's the matter?' he said in a quite different voice.

'Nothing. I must be tired.' She pretended to yawn.

Mike did not look convinced, but after a long look at her defended face he nodded as though he had seen something there. Having put his mug down on the bedside table, he took her head between his hands and stroked the hair away from her face.

'Try not to worry too much,' he said gently.

'Worry? I'm not worrying.'

'You're a dreadful liar, Helena, which is admirable from my point of view if not from yours. If you've persuaded yourself that someone is trying to use you to launder money, I honestly think you're off your trolley. Without wanting to be rude, your business just isn't big enough to interest a money-launderer.'

She managed to laugh. 'That's not rude at all. It's lovely and reassuring.'

'Good. Now, I know you fret about all sorts of things, but thinking you might become unknowingly involved in a money-laundering scam is pretty far-fetched even for you. I take it that is what the problem is?'

'In a way.'

'Well, it's idiotic. I'm sorry if that sounds unsympathetic, but it's a completely irrational fear. Now, I'm going to have to go because I've got a hellishly early start tomorrow and meetings stacked up all day. If the last one finishes at a civilized hour, I'll ring you. Can you control your terrors until then?'

'I'll do my best,' she said, surprised and touched that he wanted to help. 'I'm sorry to be so silly.'

'No need. Just don't torment yourself with weird fantasies about things that are never going to happen. No, don't get up. I'll let myself out.'

'I'll have to,' she said, reaching for her dressing gown. 'I've got to lock up after you.'

# Chapter Fifteen

Irene dressed for breakfast. She had known for years that Fin disliked her habit of coming down in one of her many flamboyant dressing gowns, particularly when she left the sash trailing behind her and the dressing gown itself hanging open over her nightdress, but until she had understood something of her part in the war they had been fighting, she had never been prepared to change her habits to placate him.

She put on black trousers and a well-ironed natural linen overshirt, did up her hair, and went downstairs to lay the kitchen table, feeling remarkably pleased with her own generosity. In the time it took Fin to get up and follow her to the kitchen, she had made coffee and toast and boiled his egg. He registered her unusual tidiness with raised eyebrows, but he said nothing, which was disappointing if not altogether unexpected.

She watched as he began to perform his usual morning rituals, folding *The Times* open at the Law Reports and placing it to his left. Then he tapped around the shell of his egg with the blade of his knife as he always did before lifting off the top in a neat hemisphere and laying it upturned on his plate to the right of the egg cup. He straightened the handle of his coffee cup so that it was precisely at right angles to his knife and waited for her to pour his coffee.

Irene knew every move he would make and in what order, but instead of the usual boiling irritation at his predictability, his ludicrous routines, his prissy, pernickety movements, she felt something like pleasure in the familiarity of it all.

Leaving him to his chosen silence, she fetched the post from the hall and sorted it into two piles. In hers was an envelope addressed in Jane's writing, which she opened as soon as she had sat down again.

*Hi, Mum, Thanks for your letter and the cheque. It saved the day. I'm glad to know that the play's going well. My tutor is starting to talk optimistically about the chances for my degree, but we'll have to see. I'd quite like to wipe Ivo's eye with one as good as his, I must say.*

*On which score, I think I'd better work through the summer instead of trying to get a job or go abroad. Would you mind if I bummed around in Herbert Crescent? Tell me some time. If you would mind I can make other arrangements, but I'd need notice for that, so the sooner I know the better.*

She had signed the letter 'J' without any mention of love or anything else. Even so Irene felt warmed by it. The tone was offhand in Jane's usual way, even rather graceless, but the whole letter was quite different from her usual sharply phrased notes. Still looking down at it, Irene reached for the coffee pot and accidentally spilled a little on Fin's newspaper as she refilled her cup.

'Really, Irene.' He might have been talking to a boisterous puppy, she thought in a surge of familiar fury that she could not prevent. 'Must you always make such a mess?'

'Sorry,' she said with all the casualness she knew he hated. Looking up to see what it was she had done, she added: 'I wasn't looking. I've had a letter from Jane.'

'So I see.' Fin was removing the last of the springy-looking white from the bottom of the eggshell.

'She seems happier now and much friendlier than usual.'

'Well, that's hardly surprising since you've been sending her money behind my back.' Fin's voice had cooled and hardened like cracking, overcooked toffee. 'I thought I had specifically asked you to refrain from that.'

'You know you did,' said Irene. She felt as though she might have to hold on to her throat in order to stop hotly furious words from erupting all over him, and she was determined not to let that happen again. Her own kinder feelings towards him had pleased her so much that she wanted to hang on to them for as long as possible. 'And I sent her only enough to pay a single electricity bill to stop it being cut off.'

'I sometimes wonder whether you deliberately set about trying to do the very things that will cause me most distress or whether it happens by accident because you're too insensitive to understand.'

Irene forced herself to wait before speaking. She drank some coffee and then she smiled slowly and she hoped pleasantly.

'Didn't you hear what I said?' demanded Fin, crunching his spoon through the empty eggshell that he had been protecting so carefully as he ate.

'Yes. But I don't think you can have heard what *I* said. I told you that I sent her only enough to pay that one bill. It was an important one and your cheque hadn't covered it. She telephoned one afternoon wanting to speak to you. You were not here and so she told me what she needed and that she needed it by the following day. I therefore sent her seventy-five pounds.'

'Then where has she suddenly got five hundred from? Don't lie to me, Irene.' He closed his eyes for a moment, sighed, and added: 'That, at least, is something you've never sunk to before.'

'No,' she agreed, working hard to remember the pleasure her own benevolence had brought her. It was hard to keep any of it in the face of Fin's unreasonable refusal ever to listen to anything she said to him or take it seriously, but she had to try. 'I don't lie,' she went on. 'And I'm not lying about this. I have wanted to send Jane a substantial amount of cash because, although I agree with you that she must learn to control money and not be controlled by it, I don't think you're giving her enough; but I said I wouldn't and I didn't.'

Irene paused and wondered how long she could hold her fire if Fin started sniping at her again. At the sight of his derisive, disbelieving expression, she laughed unpleasantly and gave in to temptation at last.

'You of all people ought to know that I haven't got anything like five hundred pounds that I wouldn't have to account for to you.'

Fin glared at her.

'How do you know she's got that much anyway?' Irene asked, looking back at him and seeing no signs of affection at all. All her own gentler feelings, all her plans to achieve peace seemed like weakness again.

Fin opened his mouth to speak and she thought he looked remarkably like a snake as his head swayed on his thin wrinkled neck.

'She told me so in the letter I got yesterday, taunting me in exactly the tones you've just used. When I saw that she had written separately to you, I assumed . . .'

'And you thought it fair to make assumptions about my truthfulness on no evidence whatsoever?' Irene laughed. 'With all your training in weighing up the merits of a disputed case? You surprise me, Fin.'

Seeing hurt in his eyes, which suddenly looked very like Helena's, Irene felt a lurch of unexpected but unmistakable distress.

'You sometimes make it exceedingly hard to be fair, Irene. But I wish . . .'

He did not tell her what it was he wished. She leaned forward to refill his coffee cup and then pushed the toast rack nearer to him.

'Fin?'

'Yes?' He was not looking at her and the expression on his face told her that he wanted her to think he was bored with the conversation and wished to be left alone with the newspaper.

'This is all getting very silly. D'you think there is any way in which we could call a truce so that we might perhaps negotiate some kind of permanent peace?'

Fin sighed and assembled one of his other familiar expressions, the one that said: you are so stupid, feckless, untidy and careless, that my life with you is like carrying around bags of lead on my back. His mouth produced rather different words.

'Irene, what *are* you talking about?'

'We've been battling with each other for years over the stupidest, most trivial of things. Why don't we just stop for once and talk about the big ones, the ones that matter, and find out what it is that's really wrong between us? It would be so much better for the children – not to speak of being less unpleasant for the two of us.'

'I don't know what you're talking about, and there are much more important things to think about than your childish resentment. For one thing, if Jane's been importuning people outside the family to lend her money we must find out who they are and what she's said to them, and put a stop to it at once. I shall have to make some discreet enquiries.'

'Why not just ask her?' The effort Irene was making to contain the fury Fin's insult had provoked made her voice sound more contemptuous than she had intended. She added more moderately: 'Or if you don't want to, I'll do it. You have to trust people sometimes, you know, Fin. If you don't, they will never become trustworthy.'

He wiped his lips fastidiously and dropped his napkin on the table as though it were filthy.

'I must go,' he said.

Half wishing that she were saintly enough to ignore the provocation, Irene shrugged and turned away. She had done her best and he had offered nothing in return. She was not prepared to give any more ground.

Almost as soon as he had gone and she was sitting alone amid the wreckage of their breakfast, the telephone rang. She picked up the receiver and heard Helena's voice, sounding unusually tentative.

'Oh, I can't tell you how good it is to hear you,' Irene said at once. 'I'd have rung you myself if I hadn't been afraid of disturbing your work.'

'Are you all right, Irene?' said Helena. 'You don't sound it.'

'Not exactly. I got up this morning full of compunction about what I've been doing to your father and determined to make up for it. But I made one gigantic mistake. I assumed that if I stopped needling him he'd stop needling me. But it didn't work. I don't think he even noticed. He just savaged me for going behind his back to send Jane five hundred pounds. When I said that I hadn't, he even accused me of lying. Considering that I'd gone out of my way to suppress my maternal instinct to send her everything she wanted because he was so *fucking* sure he knew best, I feel unutterably furious.'

'Oh, Irene, I am sorry.'

'Why? It's hardly your fault that Fin is so unreasonable.'

'No,' said Helena, drawing out the vowel. 'At least I hope not. But it is my fault that Jane has suddenly got five hundred pounds. It was me who sent it to her.'

'You? Why? I mean it's kind of you, but . . .'

'I sort of felt guilty in a way. A client had just paid a huge bill and I was feeling flush and thinking about poor Jane being so worried about her bills and probably cold alone up there in the north. So I sent her a cheque. It never occurred to me that I ought to brief you or that Fin would use it as yet another stick to beat you with. It's almost as though one can't do anything at all – take any kind of action – without causing trouble.'

'Helena, calm down,' said Irene, alarmed by the note of hysteria. 'It was tiresome to have Fin banging on at me this morning, but it's not serious.'

'No? Good. Oh, thank you.'

At the sound of Helena's jumpy voice, Irene suspected that some new panic was in the making. Past experience told her that it was probably better not to ask questions but to be ready with reassurance if and when it was invited.

'I suppose my perennial sympathy for you made it all seem worse,' said Helena, still obviously upset. 'I'd do anything to stop Fin causing you such trouble, you know.'

'It's not your responsibility,' said Irene at once.

'What isn't?'

'Our war. You shouldn't feel any obligation to join one side or the other. In fact, you shouldn't join in at all. It's not your problem – or your business. Now, what is it I can do for you?'

'Oh, nothing,' Helena said unconvincingly. 'I just wanted to find out how you were and to thank you for your message, the one I found when I got in last night. I was sorry I wasn't here when you came round. Did you need …? I mean, was there a problem?'

'Oh, yes, I did come to Clerkenwell, didn't I?' Irene laughed. 'Sorry. Rather a lot seems to be happening to me just at the moment, but Fin's idiocy this morning has made me forget nearly everything else. You know, I did take to your Mike.'

'Did you? I'm glad. He liked you, too, although he said he was surprised by your scruples about talking to him unchaperoned.'

Irene laughed again and felt more like herself.

'I know you mind about your privacy, Helena, and I didn't want to be responsible for invading it. But when you feel like letting us meet properly, I'd love to have a chance to get to know him. He looked just the sort of confident, funny, intelligent, generous person we all dream of finding.' Thinking of the unbridgeable chasm between such a dream and the reality of Fin, she wanted to swear. Instead, she asked at random: 'What were you up to last night if you weren't with him?'

'I was having dinner with my m—with Miranda.'

'Oh. I didn't know. I mean, how absurd of me! And how nice for you. I hope you enjoyed it?' Irene's voice had become clipped.

'Not entirely. I find it difficult being with her,' said Helena frankly. 'And we hardly ever talk about anything real. We tried yesterday, but the realest thing that got said was when she told me that …' Helena paused for a moment and then because it was so important added in a rush: 'That the only hostility she has ever felt towards you was because I love you so much. I've never told her that I do, but she can apparently see it written all over me. Look, I'd better get on. I hope today's rehearsal goes well. 'Bye.'

'Helena,' said Irene urgently, but there was no answer. She sat looking into the silent mouthpiece of the telephone, wishing that she had never grudged Helena either her freedom or her apparently almost perfect lover. Then she remembered the last thing Helena had said and looked at the kitchen clock.

'Oh, shit!'

If she did not hurry she would be late and that might make

Richard think she had been upset by the row they had had. Irene was damned if she was going to let him think his insults had even registered in her brain, let alone troubled her.

Running upstairs for the jacket that went with her canvas trousers, she seized her makeup, banged all the doors shut, shot back down to the kitchen to fling the uneaten toast and Fin's eggshells into the waste disposal unit, piled the plates in the dishwasher and ran for the front door. Then she thought of something else and took a minute or two more to scribble Fin a note about Helena's generosity to Jane in case he got home from work first and started making embarrassing telephone calls to friends and relations who might have lent her money. Then, having turned on the burglar alarm, Irene fled the house.

There was a taxi coming from the Knightsbridge Crown Court as she double-locked the front door behind her and she yelled over her shoulder to the driver. He stopped with a shrieking of brakes and waited for her. She gave the address of the church hall, asking him to hurry, and collapsed onto the seat as he drove off. Putting on her makeup in the swaying vehicle was more difficult than she had imagined, but there were enough traffic jams and red lights to let her get most of it on before she arrived at the hall.

Rehearsals that day were something of an anticlimax. Richard greeted her unemotionally and got down to work as soon as the last of the actors had arrived. He spent most of the morning going over and over the same minute parts of a few scenes without achieving any new effects. Irene was surprised to find herself becoming bored as she watched. After lunch, he moved on to the second part of the play, and the atmosphere grew more intense. He showed less and less patience and everyone else became thoroughly tetchy. Actors, even those with the smallest parts, began to question their lines, saying that they were unplayable or sounded false.

Irene found herself having to defend some that she particularly valued and detested the feeling of being unfairly criticized. Eventually she did agree to change a few small passages and sat at the back of the hall writing and rewriting them until the actors were prepared to accept them.

It was not only hard work but also dispiriting. By the time Richard sent the cast home, Irene had an excruciating headache. Even the thought of spending the next few hours with Fin seemed preferable to another moment with the people she had once found so sympathetic, who had turned on her and almost destroyed her faith in the work she had done. She sat in her chair, listening to them all clomping across the hard floor to fetch their bags and calling farewells to each other in voices that sounded shrill with malice. Eventually there was silence again and she leaned down to pick up her own bag.

'Don't worry about it so much,' said Richard. She looked up and saw in his face the first kindness she had been offered all day.

'I didn't realize you were still here.'

'You didn't really think I was going to leave you feeling like this, did you? I just had to wait until they'd all gone.'

'Even Bella?' said Irene before she could stop herself.

'Even Bella. At this moment your needs are rather more important than any of hers, so I sent her home. Try not to let today get to you, Irene. Everything's going to be fine, you know.'

'Today was horrible. I don't see how . . .'

'Just teething troubles,' Richard said, looking at her with sympathy in the eyes that had seemed hard and critical all day. 'A new play is always tricky at this stage.'

'Then how can you bear to go through it so often?'

'One gets used to it,' he said, plumping down on a chair and putting his hand over hers. 'It's always difficult and depressing, and one begins to think that there will never be a happy resolution, but there nearly always is. It's just a question of hanging on, and doing all the necessary work, and not letting anything anyone says hurt you.'

'That's going to be quite hard,' said Irene, who would have denied feeling anything but anger if it had not been for his surprising gentleness. She never let Fin know when he had hurt her. 'After the actors had all been so sweet to me at the beginning, they seemed beastly today, cruel.'

'I know. But you just have to let it wash over you and not take it personally.'

'I don't see why I should,' said Irene. Then laughed at herself. 'Sorry to sound like a petulant three-year-old. It's probably only my headache that makes it all seem so vile.'

'You sound like a woman who needs to relax,' he said gently, rubbing her hand. As she swayed a little towards him, he smiled with the same smile she had seen in the restaurant in Amsterdam. His hand moved further up her arm. 'D'you want to come and have a joint at the office with me?'

Irene quickly took her hand from under his and drew her whole body away from him, leaning uncomfortably sideways.

'Do you mean what I think you mean?' she demanded.

'That you look like a woman who needs to relax? Yes. That I think the best way of relaxing is smoking a joint? Yes. What are you looking like an outraged virgin for? Have you got so bogged down in your wretched husband's stuffy legality that you take the nonsensical drug laws seriously? You must be mad.'

'I take all laws seriously. I have to while I'm married to Fin. Anyway I don't approve of drugs.'

'What? Not even alcohol? That does far more damage than cannabis, you know.'

'Perhaps, but alcohol's not illegal. I'd never have thought you'd ...' She paused, looking at him, and then slowly shook her head. 'Is that why we were searched at the airport? Did you have something with you then?'

'Certainly not. I never carry anything through Customs. That's just stupid, and there's no need,' said Richard, who seemed amused by her reaction. 'There's no reason why it should have been anything to do with me. It could just as easily have been something about you or your luggage that set off their suspicions. One never can tell with that mob.'

'Don't be childish. Of course there wasn't anything about me.

If you'd been buying hash in Amsterdam, which I take it you had, someone must have seen and shopped you.'

'As it happens I did nip out to a smoking café after you ran out on me that night. A man needs to do something, you know, when he's in that state. But there's no reason for anyone to have spotted me. The place was chock-a-block, and with plenty of Brits, too. They can't all have been searched on the way back. Must I get rid of my stash now? Are you going to shop me for possession?'

Irene looked at him with what she hoped was a withering expression and stood up, saying merely: 'I think you're absurdly irresponsible to risk being caught breaking the law, but it's nothing to do with me. I must go. Will you need me tomorrow?'

'Absolutely. Nine-thirty sharp. Don't be late. We've got a lot to get through.'

She left him without another word.

# Chapter Sixteen

Helena forced herself to work, breaking off only when it was a respectable time for lunch. She could not eat much, but it was a relief to be out of sight of Ivo's desk for a while. After she had put the uneaten food back in the fridge, she went for a long walk and tried to forget the increasingly lurid suspicions that were fomenting her panic.

Back in the shed, she got down to work and eventually completed the restoration of the chair. By then not only her head but also her neck, back and arms were aching and she longed to lie down and sleep, but there were still things to be done. It had occurred to her that only by rigidly following her own routines would she be able to keep any sense of control over the stupid terror that she could not stop.

She fetched her camera and recorded the day's work as she always did, filled in the last section of the survey form, filed it, switched on the word processor, composed a letter to the client and printed it out with a carefully itemized bill.

Having switched off the machine and put away her tools, she swept the shed, keeping her eyes averted from Ivo's desk, locked up and went back to the house for a bath. Halfway across the garden, she stopped to pick some sprays from the rosemary tree that grew, covered in small blue flowers, against the fence.

She took the sprays up to the bathroom and put them in the bath, running cool water over them and smiling at the memory of an ancient herbalist's instruction she had once read, that 'if thou be feeble, boyle the leaves in cleane water and washe theyself and thou shalt wax shiny'.

Well, I'm definitely feeble, she thought, breathing in the half-medicinal, half-churchy smell with pleasure.

For a while she just lay in the scented water, letting herself relax, and felt all her muscles begin to soften. She realized that she must have been grinding her teeth all day and let her jaw go slack. The pain in her neck began to ease almost at once.

It was then that the questions started again: why had Miranda shown her the Land Registry certificate? What else did she know or suspect? Was Ivo the real owner of the house or a nominee? What was hidden behind its shutters? Was there, could there be, an innocent explanation of it all? If so, why had he been so angry when he thought Helena had been spying?

Sitting up and scrubbing at her dirty nails with a stiff brush, she told herself to stop it. She reminded herself, as she had done so often, that none of her previous panics had had any basis in fact at all. Her powers of judgement were suspended as soon as her heart began to race. There were hardly any facts holding up the teetering edifice of suspicion she had been building ever since she had seen the certificate. The fear was stupid and she had to get rid of it.

There was no reason whatsoever to believe that Ivo was in the pay of money-launderers or that he, or someone else, had bought the farmhouse as a store for stolen antiques that needed keeping for several years before they could be fed into the market, perhaps through her restoring business. She had invented both fears and neither was anything except a product of her own neurosis.

'What makes you so sure?' she asked herself aloud as she stood up and reached for her towel.

Hearing her voice echoing in the tiled bathroom, Helena savagely told herself to shut up. Having wrapped herself in the towel, she leaned forward to rest her aching forehead against the mirror for a moment. When she straightened up again, she could see her face reflected in the smeared, dripping patch she had wiped on the glass. Her eyes were surrounded by shadows. Her upper lip was tucked between her teeth.

'You're going dotty,' she said to her reflection. 'To be mistrusting

Ivo, whom you've known and loved all your life, is mad. This is just a panic attack. It's not real. For heaven's sake get a grip on yourself.'

She rubbed her body violently with the towel and when she was dry bent down to pick up some spiky rosemary leaves that were stuck between her toes. They had not done much good, she thought, feeling just as feeble as she had before the bath.

Only a little later a possible explanation of the panic occurred to her. The advent of Miranda had upset all kinds of laboriously constructed certainties and probably put Helena under greater stress than she had understood. It was more than possible that her ludicrous suspicions of Ivo were no more than a displacement of the suppressed anxiety that had been generated by Miranda's reappearance in her life.

Helena had known for a long time that her mother's desertion had left her terrified of trusting anyone's affection or relying on them in any way. It was all too likely that her return had created an emotional upheaval that could make even the safest people seem alarming.

Once more almost within reach of self-control, Helena dressed in clean shorts and a loose shirt and went downstairs to the kitchen to see what she had left that she could eat for supper. Mike had said he might ring her, but she knew from experience that there was no point waiting until then before eating. If he did arrive hungry later, she could always assemble a salad or cook him some eggs. She poured herself a glass of elderflower-flavoured mineral water.

There was not much fresh food left apart from the salad and so she cooked some fettuccine with a sauce made from scraps of smoked salmon and half an onion sautéed in butter whizzed into a couple of tablespoons of crème fraiche. She took her supper into the drawing room and, since she did not want to risk letting her mind free to re-create the terrors she had only just managed to stop, she turned on the BBC nine o'clock news.

With the glass of elderflower water beside her on the floor and the plate of pasta on her knee, Helena watched the real disasters that were happening around the world. The news ended before she had finished the fettuccine and so she watched the weather forecast and then the local news. After those came a sitcom and then *Crimewatch*.

Helena was soon watching films of armed robbers caught on security video cameras and police officers describing various unsolved crimes for which they needed public help and information. Her own anxieties seemed even sillier than before. She finished her supper with much greater enjoyment, put the empty plate on the floor beside the glass and slid further down her chair, relaxing into comfort.

She watched the whole programme through, wondering what it must feel like to be faced with someone you knew on a security film replayed on television, and whether it would be possible to ring up a police incident room and say: 'I've just seen a friend of mine on your programme. His name is such and such and he lives at so and so.'

What kind of person would you have to be to betray someone you cared about?

And what kind of person could you possibly be, she asked herself, still silently but more tartly, to let someone capable of a serious crime go free? You would have to report them, however important they might be to you.

The woman on the screen was reciting the last of the incident room numbers and then she invited anyone watching to ring Crimestoppers with information about any crime that had not been mentioned in the programme. When her picture faded, Helena stood up to switch off the television and pottered across to the bookshelves to choose something to read in bed. The telephone rang before she had found a book that looked alluring enough.

She smiled when she heard Mike's voice and they had a long, silly, and tremendously reassuring conversation about nothing very much. Half an hour later they said good night to each other and Helena went up to bed, hoping to sleep.

That night was not too bad, but her hard-won peace did not last. During the next few days whole new waves of panic washed over her without warning, each one more powerful than its predecessor. However often and however forcibly she tried to tell herself that it was nonsensical to imagine that Ivo might be involved in anything criminal, she could not believe it. Her theories about displacement anxieties seemed less and less convincing every day and she hung on to them only with the greatest difficulty.

Trying to mock herself back into rationality, she often sang 'Sweet Polly Oliver' to herself, repeating the line about 'sudden strange fancies came into her head' over and over again. Mike caught her at it one evening when she was washing sawdust out of her hair in the bath and he was supposed to be making a late supper for them both.

He had rung up after nine and, when he had discovered that she was still working and had not eaten anything all day, he had told her that he would come round and bring food with him.

'What's that you keep singing?' he asked, looking round the bathroom door to smile at her.

'Sorry,' she said at once. 'Is it driving you mad?'

'No. It's a pretty enough tune. But I can't identify it.'

She told him the name of the song.

'And why that line?'

She tried to smile and, finding she could not, proceeded to lather soap all over her face, muttering something about the rasp of the sawdust against her skin. Getting soap in her eyes and on her tongue, she thought it a suitable punishment for someone who told as many lies as she was beginning to tell both herself and Mike.

Blinded and with the disgusting taste in her mouth, she felt his hands on her slippery shoulders, pressing her backwards. Obediently, she lay against the end of the bath and felt a cool flannel wiping the soap from her face.

'Open your eyes,' he said firmly. When she did so, the remaining soap stung so much that involuntary tears spurted out of her eyes. Even so, she could see that Mike was holding out a towel.

'Mop,' he said brusquely.

She did as he told her and then accepted a glass of cold water from him to wash the soap out of her mouth. He took the glass back from her, but he did not go away.

'Now, tell me what's going on,' he said at last, sitting down on the closed lavatory.

'Nothing's going on.'

'Helena, I'm neither stupid nor insensitive. You've been behaving in the most bizarre way for the past week. If you're trying to get rid of me, just say so. I'll go without any sort of fuss. You ought to know that. But if that's not what you want, for God's sake tell me what is going on.'

'Bizarre? What d'you mean?'

He laughed, but it was not the usual, enticing gurgling sound that had always made her smile. Instead it was a short angry bark.

'Where shall I start? You talk to yourself when you think I'm not attending. You toss and turn in bed, where you used to be able to lie peacefully for nearly quarter of an hour at a time. Sometimes you look at me as though you hate me and then a few minutes later you fling yourself at me and cling more tightly than you ever have before. You don't initiate any conversations and you answer questions in the most perfunctory way I can imagine. You used to be relatively interested in me and apparently liked me. I am not aware of having done anything particularly dreadful, but if I have, I'd prefer it if you told me directly instead of playing games and sending me messages in this impenetrable code of yours.'

Disliking his increasingly angry voice, shocked that her private terrors should have been making her behave with visible oddity when she thought they had been well enough controlled to be hidden from everyone but herself, she could not say anything.

'Is it something your stepmother said after I met her that evening when you were out? Did she take against me and warn you off?'

Helena shook her head. 'It's not like that at all. You don't understand, Mike.'

'You're telling me. Then has someone else been talking about me? Who? And what have they been saying?'

Helena covered her mouth with her hand, once more shaking her head.

'No,' she said before she could stop herself. The sound did not reach beyond her hand.

'I can't hear you. What did you say? Take your hand away from your mouth. Who's been talking to you? What have you been told?'

'No-one,' she said and was glad both that it was the truth and that she sounded reasonably sane. 'No-one's been talking about you. I'm just worried at the moment. Family matters. I'm sorry if it's been making me weird. I hadn't realized that it showed. Since it does, I think perhaps I ... erm ... perhaps I ought to have a little time to myself to sort it out. Look, why don't I ring you in a day or two when I've ...?'

'Helena, for fuck's sake!' roared Mike.

She cowered against the back of the bath, appalled by his temper. She had always known that it must be there, but he had never shown it to her before. Her nakedness and smallness put her at such a disadvantage that she would have said anything to get him out of the room.

'I can't talk like this. Let me get out and get dressed.'

'I'm not stopping you,' he said disagreeably.

'I can't get out while you're here.'

'You always have before. We've had innumerable baths together. What on earth is going on, Helena?'

'You're frightening me. I can't get out while you're angry like this.'

'I? I? My God, but you take some beating. It's not I who's behaving abnormally. But I've never been one to outstay my welcome. I'll go with pleasure. I only hope it makes you happier.'

She lay in the bath, shivering in spite of the heat of the evening, and heard the front door bang. Then she sank down under the surface. When she had rinsed the soapy water out of her hair and off her body under the shower, she found the biggest of her clean towels, wrapped it around herself, put an enormous dressing gown over that and got into bed to lie with the duvet pulled up around her until she was dry and warm again.

She remembered later that Mike had been cooking and went

down to make sure that he had not left on any burners in the kitchen. He had not.

For the first time since he had slammed out of the house she felt guilty rather than scared. But she knew that she could never have told him about her fears. If they were as irrational as she hoped, then Mike would think her completely mad, madder even than he already thought; if they were real, she would have betrayed Ivo, and she could not do that.

Having eaten some of the food Mike had made, she washed her hands and telephoned him to apologize. He did not answer and she was faced with the dilemma of whether to ring off or leave a message that he might be hearing over the speaker as she was giving it.

'Mike, it's me, Helena,' she said eventually. 'All I can say is that I'm very sorry to have been so weird. I think it was partly hunger. I've been working so hard that I forgot to stop for lunch and didn't have any breakfast either; that sort of thing. I've just eaten and I feel a lot less light-headed: just silly and apologetic. I wasn't pretending when I told you that I'm bothered about various family matters or that I needed a bit of time to sort them out. Look, can you give me a couple of days? Perhaps even one would be enough. I'll get to grips with the situation and then be normal again. Could I come round and see you the day after tomorrow? Leave a message on my machine, will you, to say yes or no and if yes what time? Thank you. I . . . well, you know how I feel. 'Bye.'

She tidied up the kitchen, thought about eating some more and then decided to leave it while she did something to sort herself out. Having tried to write a letter to Irene and then one to Ivo himself and eventually one to her father, she re-read the drafts and threw them all away. She did not know how to get herself free of the turmoil Miranda had wished on her, but she knew she had to do something quickly, and not only for herself.

She had already harmed Mike, without even realizing it, and there was no saying what she might do to other people if she let herself carry on. Eventually the idea that had been nagging at the edges of her mind for days returned. It had been more insistent each time she had thought of it and it was gradually coming to seem less silly and perhaps even less cowardly.

If she were to ring the Crimestoppers telephone number, anonymously, and say that she was afraid there was something going on at Ivo's farmhouse, then it could be investigated. No-one would need to know that she had had anything to do with it. If her fears were as stupid as she hoped they were, and Ivo was entirely innocent, no one would be hurt. The police would have wasted some time, it was true, but they must waste time on false leads often enough. And if she told the Crimestoppers only that she was afraid something might be happening at the farmhouse, it would not be her fault that they had wasted time. Something must be happening; whether or not it was against the law was a different matter.

The thought of what her action might do if it were ever discovered to have been hers was frightening, but it was less frightening than the possible consequences for her and for Ivo, and for Mike and the rest of the family, too, if she did nothing.

It was such a dramatic step that she decided she would have to sleep on it before doing anything, but she did not sleep very much, and by the morning it no longer seemed melodramatic or even absurd.

Dressed in jeans and a polo shirt, she locked the house carefully and drove the van miles away to the other side of London, where she knew of a large shopping centre. She parked, bought some food for cash in Marks & Spencer as cover in case anyone who might have recognized her had seen her in the area, and then found a telephone box. There, feeling a fool but determined never to be identified as the caller, she put on her gloves and tapped in the Crimestoppers number.

When her call was answered, she gave the man her prepared speech, told him the address of the farmhouse and when he asked what she suspected gently put down the telephone receiver.

She drove carefully back to Clerkenwell, anxious not to arouse any police interest by going through any red lights or breaking the Highway Code.

'Please let them not find anything,' she said over and over again as she drove, not minding that she was saying it aloud. 'Please let it just be my neurotic silliness. Please let Ivo be all right. Please let there not be anything to find.'

# Chapter Seventeen

Helena was never able to pinpoint the moment when she became convinced that it was safe to be happy again, but it must have been some time during August. It turned out to be a wonderful month for her: the sun shone every day; she was working well; Mike was his old self again and came to Clerkenwell as often as he had ever done; best of all, nothing dreadful had come of her hysterical report to Crimestoppers. In fact nothing had come of it at all.

The police had obviously investigated Ivo and the farmhouse and found that both were innocent. No-one knew what Helena had done, and her panic had gone completely. She was beginning to allow herself to believe that, having conquered that one, she really had conquered them all for ever.

Miranda had come several times to the house in Clerkenwell, and they usually managed the whole evening without quarrelling or going cold on each other. Helena had persuaded herself that Miranda's presentation of the Land Registry certificate had not been made in malice. They had never spoken of it since.

Helena had not yet let her mother meet Mike, but he and Irene had been formally introduced. Since they obviously liked each other so much, Helena invited Irene to join her and Mike for dinner whenever Fin and Jane were otherwise engaged. Occasionally Franny and Jack joined them from next door.

They all seemed to belong to the same generation as Irene sat in the garden, swapping jokes with Mike and revelling in the City-slang he was teaching her. He had seemed a little surprised at first when Irene had asked whether he knew of any particularly salty insults and swear words she might not have come across, but her infectious enjoyment of them made him laugh, and he went out of his way to collect new ones for her.

When evenings alone with Mike had become something of a rarity, Helena began to treat them as special occasions. One evening when only he was expected she made a favourite salad of cold lamb and spinach in a sweet, garlic-flavoured dressing and laid the garden table with extra care. The night-scented stocks she had planted in the terracotta pots were smelling wonderful and the air was soft and warm. There were candles ready in the glass storm lanterns, but they would not be needed for hours. A bottle of Beaujolais was waiting in the fridge, and she put some yearny violin music on the CD player.

Mike arrived soon after nine, just as she was telling herself that he must be stuck in a meeting that might last the whole night, and she hugged him in delighted relief. When they had carried the food and wine out into the garden, Mike stripped off the jacket of his suit and, having asked if Helena minded, took off his shoes and socks as well.

'Ah, that's better,' he said, wriggling his toes against the relatively cool flagstones. 'I can't wait for the autumn. This heat is killing me.'

'I'm rather enjoying it for once.'

'No doubt. But then you practically live in this garden and you don't have to sweat in a suit all day.'

'True,' she said, spooning salad onto his plate and then her own. Mike filled their glasses with wine.

'This smells glorious. Lots of garlic for my clogged-up arteries?'

'Exactly that,' she said, laughing. 'You don't mind, do you?'

The long buzz of the front door bell made her sigh and put down her fork.

'Damn,' she said, getting up. 'Just when we were settled.'

'Must you answer? You don't always when you're working.'

'No, I know. But it might be Irene in a state about the play or Fin.' Helena frowned.

'Much more likely to be Jehovah's Witnesses or someone trying to sell you something.'

'Would you mind terribly if I see who it is, Mike? I know it's not fair when you've had a hellish day, and we've hardly had any time on our own for weeks, but it might be someone in real need.'

He reached across the table to touch her hand. 'Go on and answer it. I know you won't be able to relax if you don't. I don't mind.'

'Sure?'

'Get on with it,' he said with intimations of real impatience.

When she found her half-sister on the doorstep, gripping the handlebars of her bicycle and glowering, Helena unfairly wished that she had resisted her urge to answer the summons, but she pushed the door wide open and smiled.

'Come on in and have some supper with us. There's masses of food.'

Jane looked down at her watch. 'Sorry, I thought you would have eaten ages ago. I don't want to get in your way; I just had to get out of Herbert Crescent for a bit, and I thought . . .'

'You won't be in the way at all,' said Helena, realizing that there was a real need to be answered and consequently feeling genuinely welcoming. 'Chain up the bike and come on through to the garden. A friend of mine's here. Mike. You'll like him.'

When Helena had taken Jane out to be introduced to Mike, she fetched another plate and glass from the kitchen and a loaf of olive bread. Jane gruffly apologized again for interrupting them.

'Don't worry about it,' said Mike kindly, pulling out the third chair for her. 'Glass of wine or are you driving?'

'God, no. My finances only just stretch to a bike. I'd love some wine.'

'You can be done for being drunk in charge of a bicycle, too, you know,' he said, sloshing the wine into her glass.

'You sound nearly as neurotic as Helena,' said Jane irritably. Looking at him, she caught the mockery in his eyes and laughed. 'Sorry. I've been in the thick of a parental row and it's clobbered my sense of humour.'

'What were they fighting about?' asked Helena.

'All the usual things. I hope to heaven Ma's play is a success.'

'Why?' asked Mike. 'I mean we all do, obviously; why in particular?'

'Because she'll be free then, which may stop her indulging in these endless trivial rows. Tonight's blew up out of almost nothing. I can't even remember what he said; something to do with the food she'd cooked, I think. It was just a bit of tetchiness to begin with, but she couldn't let it drop. Not that it's only her. He's just as bad. As soon as she accused him of being a skinflint, he yelled at her for wanton extravagance. One of them brought up my debts, and he yelled at me, and she yelled at him, and then they started talking about sainted Ivo, and the whole circus started up.' Jane looked round the small peaceful garden and sighed. 'So I came here. I must say, it's lovely. So peaceful. You are lucky not to live at home any more, Hella.'

'Your chance will come,' said Helena, loading up a plate for her. 'Tuck in and forget it.'

'Thanks,' said Jane as she began to eat hungrily. 'This is great.'

Helena suddenly noticed that when Jane smiled she looked quite as attractive as Ivo. As the evening progressed, she smiled more often and more easily. Mike drew her out with enormous skill, never flattering her but showing apparently real interest in her work, her ideas, and her ambitions. As she talked, she grew less spiky and most of her sulky anger seemed to drop away. Helena watched them both with surprise and pleasure.

When Mike went into the house to make coffee, Jane turned to her.

'He's cool. You are lucky.'

'I know. And he clearly likes you, too. It's nice to see what good taste you've both got. How are you? Apart from tonight's spat in Herbert Crescent, I mean.'

'Oh, not so bad. Working quite hard, which at least gets me out of the way most of the time. It's only meals that are so grim, and if I weren't so greedy – or so poor – I could avoid them. I say, Helena, I ought to have come ages ago to thank you properly for that cheque, but I didn't quite . . . which is why . . . But, look, it was incredibly generous of you.'

'It was a pleasure and you've thanked me more than properly in your letters.'

'Oh, well, look. Anyway. I haven't spent any of it yet. Would you like it back? It's an awful lot of money to hand out like that.'

'Why not hang on to it until you've got your degree?' said Helena, intrigued that none of it had been spent. 'Even if you've managed without it so far, you might need it later. If you don't, you can always give it me back then.'

'Helena, I . . .'

'What?'

'I always used to think you were a stuck-up, Ivo-worshipping . . .' She hesitated, a little of Irene's mischief showing in her big dark eyes.

'Cow?' suggested Helena.

Unnoticed by either of them Mike stood at the top of the iron steps with the coffee pot in his hand, watching them both.

'Bitch? Swine?' Helena went on.

'That sort of thing,' said Jane as a blush stained her sallow skin. 'But then we never have really talked, have we?'

'No. Never.' Reminding herself of her nine years' seniority, Helena resisted the temptation to express some of the things she had thought about Jane in the past, in particular her quite unnecessarily harsh treatment of Irene. 'I wonder what's happened to Mike.'

'I'm up here. I thought I'd let you get your wallowing in sisterly devotion done with before I joined in again. I've never liked an excess of sentimentality, as you know.'

Both of them started laughing and their shared genetic inheritance was visible for once, in spite of their very different looks. Mike watched them both, amused to see a new side of Helena. It made him wonder even more what the family crisis had been and why it had made her behave so oddly. But he forgot it as soon as Jane left and he could take Helena upstairs to make love.

Jane bicycled round to the house after lunch the following day to leave a small bunch of anemones for Helena with a note thanking her for both the cheque and the impromptu supper. Helena, who had been out shopping, arrived home in time to stop her leaving and persuaded her to take some more time away from her books and cool off in the garden.

They spent the afternoon talking with unprecedented intimacy. They had never known each other particularly well, mainly because of the big gap in their ages, but also because of their very different relationships with Irene. As Jane talked about her memories of their shared past, Helena began to understand how difficult some of it must have been for Jane and to understand why she had often seemed so sulky and uncooperative.

When she eventually got up to leave, Helena asked her to come again whenever she felt like it. She took up the invitation several times in the following weeks, always telephoning first to make sure of her welcome and then arriving on her bicycle. Helena was concerned that it was too far to ride, but Jane assured her that she was quite fit enough to do it and was not going to waste any of her scarce resources paying for transport.

Mike was often sitting jacketless and barefoot in the garden when Jane arrived and would get up to give her a huge hug the moment he saw her. She, who had never let anyone touch her at home, seemed to revel in his boisterous affection. Helena watched the flowering of their friendship with almost as much pleasure as she felt about her own new relationship with Jane, but she was surprised to discover that Mike had such a high opinion of Jane's brains that he had promised to give her a job during the Christmas vacation.

He was back in New York when Jane told Helena about the offer, and she did not see him to thank him until the evening before Irene's first night. He appeared in Clerkenwell much earlier than usual, only just after seven, carrying a large bunch of pale green and white flowers.

'You look lovely,' he said, laying them down on the kitchen table. 'How've you been?'

'Fine.' She kissed him. 'Although I've missed you. What about you, though? You look worn out.'

'I suppose I am. New York's hell at this time of the summer, and we had an all-night meeting the night before last.'

'And then jet lag on top of that. You ought to be in bed.'

'I wanted to see you more than I wanted sleep,' he said as he wrapped his arms round her and hugged her. 'Are we on our own tonight?'

'Yup. I've put out the word that we don't want any interruptions from anyone, however important.'

'Great. I like them both such a lot, but I need just you tonight,' he said, laying his head on her hair and tightening his arms round her thin body.

'Supper in the garden?' she said when he eventually let her go. 'It's cooling off a bit now, but I think it's still warm enough.'

'Perfect,' he said.

When she bent down to take the food out of the fridge, he stroked her shorts. Straightening up, she brushed his face with a hand made cold by its contact with the fridge. He shuddered pleasurably.

'By the way, it is beyond the call of duty for you to have offered Jane a job. She's over the moon about it.'

'Is she? Good. It was pure self-interest, though,' said Mike. 'She's got a lot about her and we're always busy before Christmas. I'll get my money's worth out of her, don't you worry.'

'I won't.' Helena put everything on the tray and picked it up. 'Come on. Let's take this lot out and relax.'

Later, as she was sitting with her elbows on the table picking at a bunch of grapes, she noticed that Mike was looking very carefully at her, almost as though he were suspicious of something or had something difficult to tell her. Surprised, but not yet really worried, she raised her eyebrows in a silent question. He did not answer it and so she said: 'What is it, Mike?'

'Nothing really,' he said and then quickly added: 'Actually, there is something. You're looking so easy and happy at the moment, quite different from how you were a month or two back, that I've been wondering whether something's happened.'

'In a way.' Remembering the transforming relief that the knowledge that nothing was going to come of her telephone call to Crimestoppers had brought her, she stretched expansively, reaching up to push her hair away from her head and then letting it fountain back out of her hands. 'But it isn't anything you need to worry about. I was fantastically – and I mean it was like a fantasy – worried about something that never existed. Now that I know it was only fantasy, I feel unbelievably wonderful.'

'So what was it that was bothering you so much?'

'Oh, I couldn't possibly tell you that.' Helena felt herself blushing and laughed in an attempt to distract him, letting her arms drop to her sides again. 'It's too silly to admit.'

'I'd like to know.'

'No. Honestly, Mike, I can't expose my stupid panics to anyone whose good opinion I value as much as I do yours.'

As he looked at her in silence, Helena thought that she could see a hint of anger in his eyes. She hoped that they were not going to have a repetition of the agonizing scene in her bathroom and felt herself tensing up to prepare for it.

'Please, Mike,' she said more urgently. 'When we're further away from it I'll tell you if you seriously want to know, but bits of me still feel too raw to expose, even to you.'

He was silent for a while and her teeth clamped together and her neck began to stiffen as she waited. No longer looking at her, he said: 'I don't mean to sound vain or anything, but was it something to do with me? If it was, I think I have a right to know.'

'No. I don't mean you wouldn't have a right, but no, it wasn't anything to do with you. I promise you that.'

'Helena,' he said seriously.

'Yes?'

There was a pause while she waited for him to tell her that if she couldn't bring herself to trust him, he was going to leave her.

'Will you come to bed?'

In her relief she laughed and reached both hands across the table to him, knocking one of the glasses onto the flagstones where it smashed into hundreds of pieces.

'Yes, please, Mike.'

'What about the glass? Hadn't we better do something about it first?'

'No. Let's leave it. We have more important things to do. I'll deal with it in the morning. But be careful of your bare feet.'

He stepped carefully over the glass splinters to take her in his arms, saying: 'Wonderful!'

'Why? I mean, what's wonderful?' she asked as they went through the french doors into the drawing room.

'The ease in you. When we first met you'd never have left sharp bits of glass lying around. After all, what if a prowling burglar were to hurt himself?'

'Tough,' she said, knowing that he was laughing at her and positively enjoying it.

He stopped on the stairs and kissed her, running his big hands up and down her neck. She felt free and safe, and luxuriously sexy. Later that night she slept at his side almost as well as she would have alone. She woke only three times in the entire night and was heavily asleep when Mike got out of bed at six in the morning and stood looking down at her for a long time.

# Chapter Eighteen

For once Irene had a bad night. She longed to be able to sleep in order to be at her best for the first night of *The House on the Canal*, but she could not do it. So much hung on the play that she could not help worrying about how it would be received.

She and Richard had re-established friendly relations, although she knew perfectly well that they had discovered too many fundamental differences of opinion ever to feel the almost delirious affection that they had shared in Amsterdam. It was clear that he was still sleeping with Bella, but Irene had learned to accept that, not least because there was nothing she could do about it.

So far Bella seemed happy enough, and her grasp of the character she was playing had grown much surer under Richard's tutelage. Irene knew that all she could do was hope that the break would come before Richard had done too much damage and that it would happen at a time when Bella was confident enough to cope with it.

Irene had always known that she could not go to Bella and explain what she thought Richard was up to or warn her of what the consequences might be. All she had felt able to do, one evening at the end of the rehearsal, was to take Bella on one side and compliment her on her performance, adding: 'If there's ever anything I can do for you, or any advice or anything you need, I hope that you will ask. Even if it's after we've stopped seeing each other regularly like this. You've got my telephone number; so if you need help, please tell me.'

'How sweet of you, Irene,' Bella had said, looking surprised and sounding rather patronizing.

Irene had been able to imagine the thoughts that must have been going through her head: what could a fat, middle-aged woman like you possibly do for someone as thin, beautiful and poised for success as me?

You'll learn, Irene had said silently. I'd just like you to learn more easily than I have done.

Hearing Fin snuffling beside her, she wondered if Richard and Bella were together at that moment and, if so, whether Richard's wife knew about it and what she thought. Irene had never met her, but throughout the weeks of rehearsal her sympathy for the unknown woman had been growing. At first she had accepted Richard's impatience with his marriage without question, but watching him work, and work on Bella, she had changed her mind.

Irene had accepted long since that her old daydreams of a fulfilling, happy life with Richard could never have been realized, even if Fin had not hijacked her, but she was coming to think that no-one had ever lived in the sort of happy marriage she had imagined might be possible. Her own battles with Fin were beginning to seem less uniquely frightful than she had once believed, and she occasionally admitted to herself that she might have made an unnecessary fuss about them. But she had still not found a way of communicating with him that did not involve hostility on both sides. Whenever she suppressed her own, he merely strengthened his, as though seeing a weakness in her made him drive forwards to take advantage of it.

He turned over in his sleep, grunting, and she edged away from him, wondering what he would think of the play when he saw it and how much of it he would understand.

She and Richard had had a serious disagreement over the way the last scene should be played. Her ending had been one of disillusion and sadness; Richard's was triumphant. Irene still preferred her own interpretation of what she had written, but she had allowed herself to be persuaded to accept the box-office appeal of a happyish ending. He in turn had accepted some of her comments and criticisms and had even told her that she had made him see things he had never before understood.

The introduction of lighting, sound effects and real props had made the play seem more real to Irene and she had put up with banishment from the technical rehearsals with good grace. Then had come the dress rehearsal. Seeing the whole play acted in full costume on a real stage had been a worrying business, full of mistakes and dull patches and difficulties of all sorts, but she had been comforted by the theatrical folklore that said a good dress led inevitably to a flop and vice versa. She was hanging on to that belief with great difficulty as her pillows grew lumpier beneath her and Fin started to snore.

To her surprise, Richard had seemed more vulnerable after the dress rehearsal than at any previous stage of their collaboration, and she found herself comforting him for a change, telling him over and over again that the work he had done on the play had improved it; that she had benefited from everything he had said; that she was sure the first performance would go well.

Something made it possible for her to sleep for a while, but she woke out of a nightmare that slipped away from her even as she opened her eyes. All that was left was a sense of looming disaster and a great thirst. She fetched a glass of water from the bathroom and lay down again to sleep fitfully for a little longer.

When she woke for the fifth time, she sighed in frustration and looked at her bedside clock. It was just past six. She felt so awful by then that she thought she might be sick and got out of bed to run to the bathroom. She did not vomit, although she coughed and retched as hot saliva rushed into her mouth.

When she was confident that she had subdued the spasms and was not going to throw up after all, she pulled one of the dressing gowns off the bathroom hooks and put it on. Its vibrant print, which looked as though it had been taken from one of 'Le Douanier' Rousseau's paintings, did not suit her haggard face, but for once she did not care how she looked.

Downstairs in the kitchen would be coffee, she thought, and even toast. She wished that Helena still lived in the house so that they could talk. Helena's good sense and unfailing affection had always calmed her when she was in a state.

In default of Helena's company, Irene made herself several slices of thick white toast, which she spread with butter and golden syrup and ate until her need for comfort was assuaged. Just as she was thinking that she ought to go to bed again and try to get some more sleep, she heard the sound of bare feet on the stairs outside and a moment later saw Jane's face looking round the kitchen door.

'Hi, Mum,' she said with her usual careless greeting. 'Are you drinking coffee?'

'No, tea. I was too thirsty for coffee after pigging on toast and treacle. But if you'd like some I can easily make a pot.'

'Don't worry. I'll do it.'

To Irene's surprise, Jane ignored the jar of instant coffee she pillaged at all hours of the day and night and proceeded to make a large pot of real coffee, even heating milk to go with it. She took great care to warm both the coffee pot and the milk jug before fetching two of the best breakfast cups, the only ones left from a wedding-present set, and warming those too.

'Darling Jane, thank you,' said Irene as her daughter poured out the coffee.

'Pleasure. Did you get any sleep at all?'

'Some. Not a lot. What about you? Why are you up so early?'

'I heard you moving about and thought I'd see how you are. Were you sick?'

'No. But I'm sorry to have woken you, particularly in such a revolting way.'

'You didn't. I was working.'

'At this hour?' Irene began to understand her daughter's irritatingly frequent assaults on the instant coffee jar and the biscuit tin, both of which had needed replenishing almost daily. 'Jane, you're not overdoing it, are you?'

She shrugged. 'I don't think so. Mike says that one needs a first to get anything but a run-of-the-mill job in the City these days; and he also says that one needs to be able to do with very little sleep. I'm only getting into training for that.'

'Helena's Mike?'

'Yes. I like him, you know.'

'So do I, but if he's going to ruin your health by making you work this hard I may have to change my mind about him. I didn't realize you knew him that well or listened to him so carefully.'

Jane flushed and shook her head, but she looked pleased.

'Is Hella all right, d'you think?' she asked after a pause.

'Yes, I do,' said Irene, winding a strand of hair round and round one of her fingers. 'I think she got into one of her panics a while back, but she seems all right now. Why?'

'I'm not sure. She seems a bit stirred up to me. Different. Most of the time she's much nicer than before; brighter, too, but sometimes she's a bit *distraite*. I don't think it can be just Mike.'

Watching her mother's face change, Jane said with some of her old truculence: 'Now what have I done?'

'Nothing. No, honestly. It's just that Helena's been seeing something of her real mother for the last few months. I think it's the only thing that's any different in her life, so it's probably that.'

'And you mind?'

'There's no earthly reason why she shouldn't see the woman, and all sorts of terrifically good reasons why she should. And if it's making her happy even for some of the time then I'm glad.'

'But you do mind, don't you, even so?'

'Yes.'

'Can I ask why?'

Irene looked at her daughter, who had bothered to get up and share the horrible early morning hours with her, and knew she could not say 'because she's the only person apart from Ivo who has never deliberately tried to hurt me'.

'I suppose,' she said after she had taken the time to drink some coffee and think up some words that might express what she felt and yet be acceptable, 'because I feel that it might spoil the friendship I have always had with Helena.'

'I can't see why it should. In any case, she's still revoltingly devoted to you, as far as I can see.'

'Revoltingly?'

Jane pushed her rough, unwashed brown hair behind her

prominent ears and then started to finger a large, infected spot on her chin. Irene only just stopped herself offering to buy some antiseptic skin tonic.

'I think so. She treats you – and talks about you – as though you were some kind of saint. If I were you, I'd find that pretty creepy.'

'Why?' asked Irene, hastily adding, 'darling?'

Jane laughed at her.

'Because it's so silly. Come on, Mum, get real. You must admit you're no saint.'

At last distracted from the play, Irene began to smile. She hoped that Jane had no idea about her little fiasco with Richard in Amsterdam and was talking merely about faults in her character. That was likely; after all, Jane had spent a good deal of time over the previous five or six years commenting on her mother's faults and telling her how best to correct them.

'Yes, I do know that,' Irene said, trying to feel amused and to forget the fury some of her daughter's patronizing lectures had provoked in the past, 'but I think most people would enjoy absolute love if it were offered.'

Jane looked at her most stubbornly critical and some of Irene's good intentions slipped.

'After all,' Irene added more coldly, 'when you're offered little but criticism by other people, it is extraordinarily restful – to put it no higher – to know that somewhere you are loved unconditionally.'

Jane looked at her without speaking. It was not a friendly look.

'Perhaps you're too much Fin's daughter to be able to feel that,' Irene went on without even thinking of resisting the temptation to hit back. 'Although I'd have thought that you must at least understand the principle.'

Jane shrugged. 'Perhaps. But then how would I know anything about unconditional love? It's Ivo who got all that was going.'

'Oh dear.' Irene's pathetically inept comment was the best she could produce. Before she could improve on it, Jane remembered why she had come downstairs.

'More coffee?' she said brightly, putting her hand on the pot. Irene quickly covered it with her own.

'Jane,' she began, looking over the coffee pot and wishing that they could deal with each other as simply as she and Helena did, instead of performing endless rituals of courtship and conflict. Whether the rituals were benevolently intended or thoroughly malevolent, they had always been hard work and they had led, at least for Irene, to weeks of regret, self-justification, anger and unhappiness.

'Don't worry about it,' said Jane coolly. 'I've known for ages that you couldn't help it, and I don't blame you. After all, it's probably only biology that makes you favour your male offspring.'

'But I don't.' Irene's protest was instinctive. After a moment she said more slowly: 'Jane, you are and always have been unconditionally loved by me, however it may have seemed when we got across each other.'

Jane shook her head, apparently unwilling to say anything, but her expression was forbidding. The front door bell rang and she went to answer it, coming back a few moments later with a huge cellophane-wrapped bouquet of red, orange, and golden-yellow flowers, tied with a golden bow.

'Goodness,' said Irene, glad to be distracted from their painfully difficult conversation. 'They must be from Richard Orleton. How sweet of him! He must have so much else to think about at the moment.'

Jane pulled a small white envelope off the cellophane and handed it over.

Irene held the note far enough away for her long-sighted eyes to be able to read it properly.

'It isn't Richard. They're from Ivo. Isn't he an angel?'

'Vulgarly flashy if you ask me,' said Jane as she plonked the bouquet down on the table. 'Typical.'

Tempted to ask why Jane always had to spoil whatever pleasure her mother could garner, Irene looked up and saw the sullen expression with which Jane had often cloaked distress. It came to Irene that Jane could well have been thinking something like: *I got* up early and sat with you all through breakfast and made your coffee and listened to you and engaged with you. Isn't that worth more than a poxy bunch of flowers?

Yes, Irene said to herself, it is. And I'm not fair. I do value what Ivo does for me more highly than anything of Jane's. I don't know why. Perhaps I assume that she ought to be around to help and be nice to me, while he . . .

Irene did not complete the idea, ashamed that she, who had so often railed against Fin's unthinking sexism, should have demanded less of one child than the other simply because he was male. No wonder Jane had been truculent and grudging whenever she was asked to take a share of the domestic tasks that had been the whole of Irene's lot until she had started trying to write. And on top of that, Jane had had to see Irene valuing Helena's affection and help more highly, too. For the first time Irene asked herself whether Helena and Ivo had been so much kinder to her than Jane simply because she had been kinder to them.

She ignored the bouquet and watched Jane's face. The sulkiness was being transformed into a coldness that was extraordinarily like Fin's.

'Jane?'

'Yes?'

'Lovely as flowers are, they're not as important as company at a time like this. It's been quite extraordinarily good to have had you here this morning.'

Irene got up, walked round the table and, in spite of Jane's look of horror, kissed her cheek lightly. Without waiting for any response, Irene picked up the bouquet and took it to the sink. There she ripped off the ribbons and cellophane and dumped them in the rubbish bin before arranging the flowers in a tall white china vase. Still without looking at Jane, she carried it into the dining room and put it in the middle of the sideboard, where the strong colours lit up the gloom in a thoroughly satisfactory manner.

When Irene got back to the kitchen, she saw that Jane had fetched the newspapers from the doormat and was concentrating on the front page of the *Independent*. Irene was not sure where to go from there, but as she was washing out the coffee pot in order to replenish it for Fin's breakfast, she heard Jane say: 'Thanks. You know.'

Irene turned to look at her. Jane was still staring down at the paper, but Irene took a risk and stroked her rough hair. Jane did not move. Irene felt a current of sympathy running between them that made her think that they had achieved something worthwhile that morning. And she had to admit that most of it had come from Jane's initiative. That must have taken some courage.

Hearing the sound of Fin's footsteps outside, Jane glanced up briefly towards her mother, looking wistful and very much younger than usual. Irene smiled down at her.

'You're both up early,' said Fin from the doorway. 'Didn't you sleep well?'

'Perfectly,' said Jane, shaking out the newspaper just as Irene admitted that she had woken several times.

'And on the very night you most needed rest. Poor you,' said Fin, sitting down in his usual place. 'If that's coffee you're drinking there, Jane, may I have some?'

'It had gone cold,' said Irene, who was pulling the plug out of the kettle. 'I'm making another pot. Would you like an egg?'

'Not today, I think. I am a trifle costive. But thank you. Toast will do me fine.'

When Irene had brought the newly refilled coffee pot and a rack of hot toast and sat down again, Fin produced a tight smile and said: 'Try not to worry too much, my dear. Whatever will be, will be, and thinking about what may happen to the play won't make the performance any different.'

'No, I know. But I can't stop myself listing all the things that could still go wrong.'

'You shouldn't. There must be just as many that could go right. More perhaps. You know, I'm very much looking forward to seeing the play tonight.'

Irene was not, but she did not say so. She felt she could easily put up with not knowing that it had gone well if she could be protected from the risk of knowing it had failed. Then with a splendid, if unspoken, oath she had learned from an American hard-boiled detective story, she told herself not to be such a coward.

For their own private reasons, she and Jane both gave Fin the kind of silent breakfast he preferred. When Jane had eventually gone back to her books, Fin laid *The Times* down and asked Irene whether she would like to have lunch with him. Surprised by the unprecedented offer, she said: 'But aren't you in court today?'

'Yes. But I have to eat, and you might find it easier to relax if you're taken away from here for a while and given some good food and wine. What do you say?'

'That I'd like it very much indeed. Thank you, Fin.'

He looked nearly as surprised by her warmth as she felt, but he nodded and told her he was glad.

'I must get off now, though. If you want distraction, why not watch the trial this morning? It's quite an interesting one. My clerk can bring you round to meet me when we adjourn. I'll tell him to look out for you.'

'It's an idea, but I might not make it in time, Fin. I'm getting my hair properly put up so that at least I'll look rich and confident tonight, and there are various other things to be done. But I'll be there for lunch. What time will you adjourn?'

'Between half past twelve and one, I expect. I can't say exactly. If you're late I'll have to start, but you can join in at whatever point I've reached. I'll see you later.'

Irene sat on in the kitchen, sipping cold coffee and letting herself enjoy the after-effects of Fin's unexpected friendliness. She wondered whether it was only coincidence or whether he could have felt the unusually affectionate atmosphere that had grown up between herself and Jane and become infected by it.

Later, full of an enjoyable sense of benevolence, Irene rummaged in her desk for the batch of free tickets Richard had sent her for the play that night. Having checked that there were enough for all the people she had already invited to go with her, she then put one of the spares in an envelope with a note that said:

*Dear Miranda, I am not at all sure how to put this, but I wondered whether you might like a ticket to the first night of my play,* The House on the Canal. *I'm afraid that it's very short notice, and you will probably be doing something else tonight in any case. But Helena is coming with her young man and so it occurred to me that possibly you might like to come along, too. I gather that you have been seeing something of her recently.*

*My son, Ivo, and Helena have arranged for us all to go out to dinner afterwards with Richard Orleton, the director, and if you would like to join us I am sure he can ask the restaurant for another place.*

*I should like it very much if you were able to come. Yours sincerely, Irene Webton.*

# Chapter Nineteen

The first person Helena saw when she arrived at the theatre was Miranda. She was waiting alone in the red and gold foyer, standing at the foot of the flaring, red-carpeted staircase, calmly reading the *New Law Journal* and apparently quite at ease.

'Don't look so horrified,' she said as she looked up from the magazine and saw her daughter's expression. 'Your stepmother invited me herself. I'm here legitimately.'

'Goodness!' said Helena gracelessly. 'I mean, how very nice!'

Miranda laughed and bent down to tuck the magazine into the briefcase at her feet. 'Yes, isn't it? When I got back from court today, my clerk handed me an envelope Irene had apparently delivered herself with a charming note inviting me tonight and a ticket. She even said that I was welcome to come to the dinner that you and Ivo have arranged for her afterwards.'

Helena did not think that her expression had changed, but Miranda quickly said: 'Don't worry. I won't go that far. And I won't embarrass you, I promise.'

Helena shook her head. 'You couldn't. If I looked worried, it's only that I'm anxious Irene shouldn't have any extra stress tonight. So much hangs on this evening for her that I know she's likely to be in a great state. That's all. It's not – really – that I want to keep you out of anything. Honestly.'

'I know. I was teasing you. You're looking very lovely tonight. I'm pr—'

'Thank you,' said Helena before Miranda could finish the word. She was wearing the clothes she had chosen for the dinner Irene and Fin had given for Geoffrey Duxford. 'So are you.'

Miranda was always well dressed, but that evening she looked even more striking than usual. She was wearing a knee-length black dress that had been modelled on a man's dinner jacket. It was superbly cut and showed off all the delicacy of bone and feature that Helena had inherited from her. Around her neck, hanging between the severe silk revers of the dress, was a flamboyant gold pendant enamelled in emerald and scarlet with a large baroque pearl hanging from it. She looked rich and successful but delicately restrained. Helena hoped very much that Irene would not take the restraint as a comment on her own much bolder style.

When Irene arrived she looked so spectacular that it seemed unlikely that anyone else's appearance could worry her at all. Her dress was made of a cloth that looked like running water with the setting sun reflected on it. Peering more closely, Helena realized that it was silk that had been treated in some way that made it almost as supple as jersey and yet not nearly as clinging. Of a colour somewhere between copper and gold, it made the most of Irene's splendid shoulders and breasts and then diverged from her body to flow past her waist.

When she saw Helena, Irene opened her arms. Helena kissed her and was hugged. She hoped that if Miranda could see what was happening, she would not mind too much.

'That's a wonderful dress,' Helena said when Irene had let her go. 'Did you have it specially made?'

'Yes. I think it's worked. Even Fin likes it, if you can believe that. And they promised me that this sort of silk won't scrunkle up and crease when I sit in it, so it should still look all right in the interval, which is important. How are you, Helena?'

'I'm fine. You?'

'Hanging on. I tried to go backstage to wish them all broken legs and whatever else theatrical superstition allows, but Richard sent me away.'

'That seems pretty high-handed. Did you mind?'

Irene laughed, but she did not sound amused. 'He said that one look at my wild eyes and chewed lips would make them all lose whatever confidence they've managed to scrape together and that I was to get away quick before any of them saw me.'

'I'm sure it'll go well,' said Helena, trying to answer the real things that Irene had not managed to say. 'You told me you were pleased with the previews – and that Richard was; a man like him would never pretend about something as important as that. They must have been good.'

'To be perfectly frank, I think Richard would say anything at this stage if he thought it might avert disaster.'

'Don't talk about disaster.' For once Helena had no fear of it herself and added confidently, 'It's not allowed.'

'Isn't it? It seems the only thing to talk about,' said Irene, crossing her fingers and wishing that she could dredge up some of the old fiery anger to carry her through. The trouble was, there did not seem to be anyone with whom she could be angry. 'You know, I never realized it was going to be like this. I thought much the worst part would be writing the wretched thing. But this is torture. I don't know how long I can hang on.'

'You'll manage.' Helena stood up on her toes to kiss Irene's cheek. 'You're brave and tough, and you look gorgeous.'

'Oh, Helena, what would I do without you?'

'Plenty. Oh, goody, there's Jane,' said Helena, waving at her sister, who had walked through the main doors beside Fin.

Helena kissed them both and then heard Irene's voice saying: 'Miranda. How good of you to come this evening. It means a lot.'

Helena turned to watch them. Irene towered over Miranda, who seemed quite untroubled by her supplanter. There was no sign of the hatred she had once admitted.

'It's exceptionally kind of you to have invited me, Irene,' she said, offering her hand. Irene took it, but she could not make herself hold it for long. 'This is my daughter,' she said, urgently beckoning Jane forward. Fin waited beside Helena.

'How do you do?' said Miranda, concentrating on Jane and never once looking at Fin.

Knowing that they must have discussed Irene and the play many times in the past year, Helena admired both her parents for leaving all the initiative with Irene, but at the same time she was angry with them both for adding such constraint to Irene's most important evening. Helena turned her back and asked her father about his current trial, which had always been the easiest way to make him talk.

When Ivo appeared everyone's embarrassment seemed to fade away. He looked as relaxed as ever and was seductively affectionate towards his whole family, even Miranda, whom he treated as though she were a particularly beloved aunt. When Helena looked to see how Irene was taking that, she was relieved to see that Irene looked merely amused. A few minutes later Mike appeared, and Helena herself began to relax.

He was quickly followed by a whole group of people who were obviously well known to Irene. Helena did her best to be polite to everyone who was introduced to her, in case they were members of the press or the sort of opinion-formers who could help the play, but she would have much preferred to stay in a corner with Mike or even her mother.

She had worked her way round the foyer by the time the bell rang to summon everyone to the auditorium and she was standing next to Irene again.

'It'll be fine,' she whispered as she felt Irene shudder.

Irene turned for a moment, apparently unaware of who had spoken. Seeing Helena, she sighed.

'I wish it was over.'

'I know. But we must go in now and you must look confident. Can you smile? Great. Well done! Here's Fin. Are you taking her in?'

'Naturally.' Fin offered his arm to Irene in a more flamboyant gesture than Helena would have expected. Irene squared her shoulders, arranged her face and strode forward beside him.

'I gather you're sitting between me and Mike,' said Miranda from behind Helena.

'Yes.'

'He's gone ahead to buy programmes. He said he'd see us there. I like him, you know, very much.'

'Good. I'm sorry I haven't ever . . .'

'Ssh. I know why you didn't. Don't worry about it. This evening must be quite a strain for you. Don't think I don't realize how difficult it is to amalgamate the different parts of your life. I'm glad to be here, and very glad to have made his acquaintance. I don't need anything else.'

'It must make me seem very mean,' said Helena, disliking the ferment of emotion that spoiled the picture she wanted to have of herself, a picture of sense rather than sensibility, of calm and self-knowledge, of someone who dealt kindly and efficiently with other people's needs rather than being at the mercy of her own.

'No, it doesn't.' Miranda settled herself in her seat. 'Just wary. And I've already told you that I understand your wariness; I share it all. Now, what's this play about?'

Thinking of Irene's inarticulate description, Helena passed on as much as she could remember and was relieved when Mike edged into the row carrying the programmes. He gave one to Miranda and then slid past them both to his own seat. Miranda opened her programme, freeing Helena, who turned at once to Mike.

'How was the day?'

'Not bad. Although I kept being distracted by my memories of how sweet you looked tucked up under your duvet this morning,' he said.

The house lights dimmed before Helena could answer, but she leaned towards him and let her shoulder touch his. There was a prolonged rustle as people dropped programmes in their laps and crossed or uncrossed their legs. As the last of the lights turned orange and faded into nothing, Helena looked along the row and caught sight of Irene's face. It looked so defenceless that she longed to leap into her seat and beseech the audience to be fair and to do their best to like what they were about to see. She sat still with her hands tightly clasped in her lap. Mike dropped one of his over them in a brief but comforting gesture of reassurance.

Once the first scene had got under way, Helena realized how little she had understood of Irene's explanation of the play. It seemed to be about a woman, an elegant, unhappy middle-aged

244

woman, who was stuck in a fogbound airport with a mountain of baggage that was obviously important but also a dreadful nuisance to her. Waiting for the announcement of her flight, checking that her bags and cases were all still there and all still locked, she fell into conversation with another passenger, gradually telling him about her journey.

It had started some time ago in the States and was to end in Amsterdam, if she could ever get there. All sorts of things had delayed her before the fog had closed the airport and she was beginning to despair of ever reaching her destination.

The scene changed then to Amsterdam itself, to a room in a house beside a canal, empty except for a woman. She seemed very young, still almost a schoolgirl. From what Irene had told her, Helena knew that the girl and the much older woman were the same person, and she wondered how quickly the rest of the audience would catch on.

Helena soon understood that the girl was living in Amsterdam at the end of the Second World War. She had spent the war itself running errands for the resistance and putting herself and her family at tremendous risk, but they had all survived. The Allies had liberated the city only three days before the unconditional surrender of all the German forces was confirmed.

The citizens of Amsterdam ought to have been rewarded for the years of terror with peace and plenty, but they were almost starving.

Into the cold, miserable world came a charismatic American officer. Much older than Maria, he appeared like a dream conjured up by her need. He was generous, attentive and full of admiration for the courage she had shown during the occupation.

When the scene changed once more to the airport lounge, full of angry, tired, hungry people and the older Maria sitting beside her baggage, Helena began to understand what was going to happen. She glanced at her father to see whether he, too, understood what Irene had been doing. He looked pleasantly attentive but quite untroubled.

After the interval the scenes alternated between the past and the present. The older Maria talked of the exile in which she had been living for forty years while her younger self was tempted by the ease and plenty her American offered her. Along with the rest of the audience, Helena could see that Maria was making herself believe that she had fallen in love because that was the only way she could accept the escape her American was offering her. At last, just after the fog had lifted from the airport allowing the elder Maria to continue her journey, her younger self could be seen agreeing to marry her lover and follow him to the States.

Helena found herself gripping her hands together again as the curtain rose for the final scene. Maria was standing at the side of the stage with all her baggage beside her, staring at the house where she had once lived. She took a step towards the bridge that led over the canal to the house itself and was instantly set upon by a gang of unidentifiable young tourists. As they hit and kicked her, stripped her of all her jewellery and flung her handbag into the canal, her younger self emerged from the house arm in arm with the American and walked away from it without a backward look.

Bruised and bleeding the older woman eventually dragged herself across the bridge, opened the door of the house and walked in to find it absolutely empty. The rest of the stage darkened and bright light flooded the house. The triumphant music of Dvorak's symphony 'From the New World' filled the theatre.

When the final curtain fell, taking with it the tension that had kept the audience quite still for the past half hour, a splatter of clapping broke out, punctuated with several suspicious sniffs and coughings. The clapping quickened and became louder until it was an undifferentiated roar of approval.

Feeling an irritated movement from Miranda at her left, Helena looked sideways and saw her brushing one slender finger under the lashes of her lower eyelid. Helena herself was not at all sure how she felt. Perhaps the strongest emotion was surprise. It was not because the deceptively simple play seemed so competent. She had known that a man of Richard Orleton's reputation would never have taken on one that was not well written, or indeed produced it in any way that was not supremely professional. But the cleverness of the staging, of the dialogue, and of the way the very few characters had taken the audience into their emotions without explaining anything seemed quite unexpected.

It had all looked wonderful, too, and the girl had been entrancing in her excited yearning for an easier life and in her almost convincing love for her much older, richer suitor. The older actress had managed her part well, too. It would have been easy, Helena could see, to have made her appear bitter and unsympathetic. Instead her mixture of self-control and regret, her frequently expressed gratitude to the man who had both saved her and stolen her life, gave her a nearly tragic status.

Helena leaned forward so that she could look along the row of clapping friends and relations, trying to catch Irene's eye. When her stepmother did look at her, Helena smiled as widely as she could and gestured with both thumbs rigidly upwards. Irene raised her eyebrows. Helena nodded vigorously. Irene blushed lightly, smiled, and sat back in her chair, moving out of Helena's sight.

'Very instructive,' murmured Miranda, just as Mike was leaning towards Helena to say: 'I think that was pretty impressive. A woman of many talents, your stepmother.'

'She is, isn't she? I'm glad you approve.'

'Yes. But I wonder what your father thinks of it. She makes it jolly clear that . . .'

'Shh,' said Helena. 'I don't think it's quite as simple as that.'

The rest of the evening passed in a blur for Helena. With all Irene's other guests, she went backstage to meet and congratulate the actors, and later emerged into the street to help find enough taxis to transport the family and close friends to the restaurant she and Ivo had chosen. They had debated whether to invite the cast to join them and had eventually consulted Irene. After some discussion with Richard, who had already arranged a dinner for everyone connected with the play after the first of the previews, Irene had decided that the actors would be happier on their own. She was planning to give a party specifically for them later in the week.

Miranda, however, had eventually accepted the invitation to join the rest of them for dinner and was sitting between Richard Orleton and Ivo with Helena opposite her between Fin and Mike. Irene had taken the head of the table and radiated triumphant happiness. Miranda looked smaller and paler and more severe as dinner progressed. Helena ate too much, heard too much noise, and felt her waistband tighten uncomfortably as a sharpening sensation of emotional indigestion clawed at her insides.

Mike left before coffee was served, apologizing to Irene and explaining that he had a breakfast meeting out of London early the following morning and had to get to bed in good time. When he had gone, Helena turned to her father and asked what he had thought of the play.

'Rather duller than I had expected, I'm afraid,' he said very quietly so that Irene could not hear, 'but I was glad to see that so many people enjoyed it. And it looked pretty enough. That designer fellow had got Amsterdam to a T, I thought, as well as the beastly squalor of an airport waiting room.'

'Dull?' echoed Helena, wanting to say: but didn't you see what she meant?

'I'm afraid so.' He smiled at her. 'But then I like rather more going on in plays than a middle-aged woman moaning.'

Outraged but not surprised by his lack of perception, Helena was about to start explaining to him just exactly what the play had been about when he added: 'You're looking quite well. Does it still satisfy you, the carpentry?'

'Yes, thank you.' She ignored the implied insult to her and to her work with the ease of experience. 'And it's increasingly profitable, too.'

'I'm glad of that.' Fin looked at her and for a moment she thought she could detect affection, even warmth, in him. 'Your mother's rather proud of you, you know. I'm glad you're seeing something of her these days.'

At that moment Miranda got to her feet, distracting both of them, and said: 'Irene, I had better go, too. I have a brief to read tonight. Thank you for letting me come. It's been most . . . instructive.'

'I'm glad. Would you be angelic and see Helena home for me?

I don't trust her to take a taxi and I don't want her walking at this time of night dressed up like a Christmas tree.'

'I couldn't agree more. I'll be delighted to take her,' said Miranda, sounding polite rather than warm.

Helena was about to protest that she was quite capable of getting herself home and did not need to be sent to bed like a child, but then she caught her mother's eye and realized that there had been more to Irene's request than anxiety about her safety. Wanting to get both herself and Miranda out of the restaurant before anyone said anything they might regret, Helena scrambled up from her chair, tripping over her handbag, and went to the head of the table to kiss Irene and compliment her once again.

Irene put up a hand to cup her face and smiled with absolute trust and unshadowed love.

'Promise me you won't walk tonight, Helena. It's not safe.'

'No, all right. We'll share a cab. It was a wonderful evening, and I think the play's a triumph. I hope the reviews will be good.'

'They will be,' said a confident male voice.

Helena looked up and saw Richard Orleton nodding to her from his position on Irene's right.

'How can you tell?' asked Miranda, who was standing holding on to the back of her chair.

'The way the critics look as they start to scribble the outline of their reviews during the interval. I've watched them too often to be mistaken. All the omens are good. And it won't be long now before we get the proof.'

'I am glad.'

Helena had a word with Ivo about the best way to deal with the bill, and he amazed her by saying that their father had decided to pay for everything himself. Helena just looked at him. Ivo's eyes took on a devilish glint as he smiled and nodded.

'I know, but don't look too surprised. It's not polite. Go on home. You look knackered. I'll deal with anything that crops up and ring you in the morning to report.'

Helena hoped she had said enough to all the people she should have acknowledged and left the noisy restaurant with a sense of relief.

'I know you don't need my help getting home,' said Miranda as the door closed behind them, 'but shall we share a taxi? After all, it's the same direction for both of us. He can drop me off first and carry on to Clerkenwell.'

'Why not? Did you mind that? The instruction to see me home, I mean.'

'No. That, I thought, was quite touching.'

As Helena looked round in surprise at the sarcastic tone of voice, Miranda hurriedly added: 'I must say that I didn't much like that director of hers.'

'Richard Orleton? No, nor did I,' said Helena. She was not going to pass on any of Irene's confidences, but she was not averse to a little frank discussion of a man she had found both arrogant and unattractive. 'And I thought his behaviour to that poor little actress was vile. Talk about possessiveness!'

'And criticism,' agreed Miranda, signalling to a taxi that still had its orange light glowing. 'If it hadn't been for your Mike's tactful intervention, I think she might even have burst into tears. He really does seem like a good man.'

'Only seems?'

Miranda gave a short laugh. 'I haven't enough evidence to put it more strongly than that. I liked what I've seen of him, but I know nothing about him. I didn't even know his name until this evening. "Seems" is as far as I can safely go.'

'And now that you do know his name, will you be checking out the ownership of *his* house?' Helena said, shocked to hear how sharp she sounded, but unable to help it.

'I'm sorry.'

'What about?'

'I'm not sure except that it sounds as though you are very angry with me for what I told you about Ivo.'

'Don't you want to know why?'

'Only if you want to tell me.'

Helena sighed. 'Why is it that whenever we meet and are getting on particularly well everything degenerates into argument? Is it you or is it me?'

'I wasn't aware that we did always argue,' said Miranda, sounding as though she had never given in to any kind of emotion in her life.

'Nearly always when it's going extra well, not otherwise,' Helena said, looking away from her mother. She was hugely relieved to see that they were approaching John Street. 'Here we are.'

Miranda opened her handbag and took out a twenty-pound note.

'No, no. I'm paying for this,' said Helena, trying to smile. 'After all, as you pointed out, your house is on my route home, and I would have taken a cab this way in any case. Thank you for coming this evening.'

'I'm not sure that it was an unqualified success,' said Miranda, still in the same emotionless voice. 'Good night.'

'Good night.' Helena hoped that she did not sound as sulkily childish as she felt. 'I'll be in touch.'

'Yes. Good. Sleep well.'

For the rest of the short drive to Clerkenwell, Helena cursed herself for her clumsiness, for her irritability, for her lack of generosity to her mother, who, she was almost sure, was doing everything she could to establish friendly relations between them.

Back in the house, she forced herself to telephone Miranda and when she answered said directly: 'I am sorry I was so unpleasant just now. Will you try to ignore it?'

'Yes,' said Miranda, sounding once again like a woman who might occasionally feel things. 'I probably invited it, although I hadn't meant to. The play stirred me up rather.'

'Did it? I mean, why?'

There was a short laugh that sounded anything but amused. 'It seemed to me that your devoted and beloved stepmother was telling me that since I had run away from you and Fin all those years ago out of selfishness and cowardice, I was not to think that there was anything left for me in either of your lives, and so I had better keep out of the way.'

'I don't think that's what she meant at all,' said Helena in a rush. 'Quite the opposite, in fact. No, that's not quite what I mean either. I thought that she was exploring her own fury with Fin for having offered her security when she needed it and thought she'd never get it.'

'Why on earth should that make her angry?'

'Because it was a temptation she was too young and ignorant to resist, but she didn't understand at the time how much it would cost her, you know, that she was selling her life in a way. Didn't you see that at all? It seemed really clear to me. And then when she tried to get back to the life she should have gone on living, first of all she was stopped by her family's needs and then by the mugging (I'm not quite sure what, if anything, that mirrors in Irene's life), and then when she did finally get back she found that there was nothing there for her after all.'

Remembering that Irene had written the play before she had gone to Amsterdam with Richard and discovered the emptiness of all her fantasies about him and what his love might have done for her, Helena had a sudden doubt about her own interpretation.

'That sounds quite plausible,' said Miranda. 'But in that case why the triumphant music and the floods of light? I took that to be a yah-boo-sucks message specifically directed at me.'

'I'm not sure.' Helena took a moment to think. 'She'd always given me the impression that it was a sad play. I wonder if you could be right? No, I'm sure you're not. Why should Irene do something like that? That would be spiteful and she's never been that. Angry often, but never spiteful. Honestly, that wouldn't be like her at all. Perhaps the triumph came from the freedom. I mean, if there's nothing for you in the past, nothing to hold you back there, you become free to go forward. That would be a reason to be pretty triumphant, wouldn't it?'

'I'll take your word for it. I suppose that I have got into the habit of seeing several of her actions as directed at me. Perhaps I've been more self-centred than I realized.'

'Actions,' said Helena, suddenly worried. 'What do you mean?'

'It doesn't matter. It's late, you're tired and I genuinely do have a brief I must read. Good night, my dear. Sleep well. And try not to worry too much. It never does any good. And it wreaks havoc with the complexion.'

# Chapter Twenty

The reviews were good, not as splendid as Richard Orleton had suggested they might be, but good enough to make Irene feel that she might yet have the freedom she craved. Combined with the drawing power of Peter Callfield's name, they helped the box office to fill the theatre for several weeks in advance.

Helena went back for the Thursday matinée to test her interpretation of the play against her mother's and emerged, blinking in the soft light of the warm September evening, certain that she had been right.

That gave her an unusual sense of confidence; not, she told herself, that she had proved a better judge than Miranda, but because her reading of the play suggested that the virulent war between Fin and Irene might not have been her fault after all. If the dissatisfaction that had made Irene so unhappy – and therefore so angry with Fin – had been caused by her loss of the world she had thought she wanted rather than by having to care for someone else's child, then the grown-up version of that child might at last be able to shed her disabling sense of fault.

Standing on the pavement outside the theatre, hardly aware of the angry rush-hour crowds, the bored tourists, and the smelly traffic, Helena felt an aura of liberation. It was as though her whole body had expanded and yet become nearly weightless. She could move more easily than she had ever done; her lips curved into a smile; she breathed deeply and wanted to burst out singing. Letting the joy spring up through her, unknotting the tensions of years, she tried to remember what she was supposed to be doing. Eventually she had to get out her diary to see that she was due to meet an old friend for a drink before going home to change for dinner with Mike and one of his most important clients.

It was the first such occasion to which he had invited her, and she had been both pleased and alarmed to think that their relationship was about to move on to a more public phase. When she had tried to explain what she felt without sounding either obstructive or weedy, Mike had misunderstood her and assured her that she was unlikely to be bored, even though it was to be a business dinner, since the client concerned was an enormously civilized man with a particular interest in antiques.

'In fact,' Mike had said, 'it was he who first interested me in collecting. You'll like him, Helena. I've wanted you to meet him for some time, not least because it's possible that he might be able to put some work your way. Asking you to come too isn't pure selfishness on my part. He could do you some good. If you got on well he could bring in more and distinctly richer clients than the old faithfuls like Katharine Lidstone.'

I'm sure it's not selfishness, thought Helena as she caught a bus back to Clerkenwell, but even if it were, it wouldn't matter. Not now. Nothing matters now. All the same, it would be nice if the important, antique-collecting client decided to cancel so that Mike and I could have an evening on our own.

When she got home and saw that there were two messages waiting for her, she wondered whether the force of her wish might have reached the client and made him back out of the arrangement. Laughing at her mixture of sentimentality and superstition, she pressed the 'play' button on the machine.

'It's Irene here,' came her stepmother's voice, more agitated than Helena had ever heard it. 'Could you ring me, please? As soon as you get in. I need ... 'Bye.'

There was a beep, a click and then the same voice: 'Helena, where are you? Have you heard? Please, please ring me as soon as you possibly can. *Please*. Oh, where are you? Sorry, but do ring when you can. Please.'

Without waiting for anything else, Helena pressed the automatic dialling button for Irene's number. She must have been sitting beside the telephone for she answered immediately, reciting her number in the same breathless, shaking voice in which she had left the messages. Helena thought that there was something else in the sound as well, a wariness that suggested Irene of all people might be afraid.

'Irene? It's me, Helena. What's happened?'

'Oh God! Helena, it's too horrible. I can't . . . It's Ivo.'

The last of the joy in Helena was expelled by a sudden, ferocious griping in her stomach. 'What's happened to him?'

'He's been arrested.'

Helena sat heavily down on the floor, where she hugged her ribs with her free hand and pressed the telephone receiver to her ear so hard that it hurt.

It can't be, it can't be, it can't be, she said to herself. What have I done? Ivo hasn't done anything. I was wrong; I know I was; it was just one of my panics; there wasn't anything for the police to find. There can't have been. Ivo? He couldn't really have been doing it. Does Irene know it was me? Does Ivo? What will happen to us all now?

'Why?' she whispered at last as she dammed the torrent of anxieties. 'What do they think he's done?'

'They say he's been making Ecstasy,' said Irene, obviously holding on to her voice and her self control only with the greatest difficulty. 'In that farmhouse in Oxfordshire where we thought he was the caretaker for some rich collector of whatever it was.'

'I don't understand.' Helena's arms had relaxed and her voice came more easily.

Ecstasy? she thought. It's absurd. Ivo's always despised drugs and drug-takers. Anyway, he wouldn't be so stupid.

She pushed her left hand through her hair and then bit the thumbnail.

'How do they know?' she asked aloud. 'I mean, what evidence have they got?'

'I don't know,' Irene wailed. 'Fin's got the best possible solicitor to Ivo and he's being interviewed now. I don't know any more than that. We're waiting. I had to talk to someone. Helena . . .'

'Has he been charged?'

'Yes: with manufacturing and supplying a Class A controlled substance.'

'But how could he have done anything like that? Ivo of all people. I can't believe it. I really can't.'

'They say ... Fin said it's not all that difficult for a chemist to make it. I ...'

'But Ivo? Surely not.' The mixture of guilt, fear and a shocking kind of excitement, which disgusted her, was making Helena's head buzz and feel dangerously unstable on her neck. 'What ...? I mean, how is Fin ...? Oh, I don't know what I mean. Shall I come round? Would that help?'

'Can you? Fin's had to be in court today; a drugs case, too, which must be hell for him. He said he'd go to the police station as soon as he could to wait until they let Ivo out on bail and bring him back here.'

'Will they?'

'They must. He's not the sort who'll do any of the things that mean you can't get bail. They must see that. The solicitor will get them to see it. Fin will bring him back here, but, then ... Oh, God! Helena, do you suppose it could possibly be true? And if it is, what'll happen to him?'

'I've no idea. It seems impossible. Who's with you? Where's Jane?'

'She went back yesterday, before it all happened. There isn't anyone here. I'm waiting for Fin to bring Ivo back.'

'But term hasn't started yet, has it?' Helena knew that Jane's whereabouts were not relevant to any of the thoughts or feelings that must have been driving Irene at that moment but she had to keep talking in order to stop herself blurting out her own part in Ivo's disaster.

'No, but she thought she'd go anyway. There were things she needed from the library that she couldn't get hold of anywhere in London.'

'Oh, I see. Right. Well, I'll be with you as soon as I can.'

Helena took a couple of minutes to ring Mike, whose secretary said that he was in a meeting.

'Damn! Could you please tell him that I won't be able to come to the dinner tonight?' said Helena. 'Tell him I'm really sorry, but there's a family crisis and I have to go to my stepmother's now. I'll ring him when I can, as soon as I can. Will you tell him that I'm seriously sorry, but that I can't help it?'

'Certainly.'

Banging down the receiver, Helena reactivated the burglar alarm, locked the house behind her and ran to her van. She could not think of anything but Irene, Ivo and what might happen to them all as she drove to Knightsbridge. Later she assumed that she must have stopped at red lights and used her brakes and indicator and steering wheel at all the right moments, but she was not conscious of any of them at the time.

She let herself into the house in Herbert Crescent and stood for a moment in silence. The hall seemed even darker than usual, and for once it was quite flowerless. She called Irene's name, had no answer and started opening doors to look for her. There was no-one in the kitchen, the dining room or the drawing room.

Pushing open the door of Irene's study last, Helena saw her sitting in the swivel chair in front of her desk. She was very pale and her whole body shook. Her eyes stared intently at Helena and it took her a moment to realize that Irene had not even registered her presence.

'Hello,' she said gently.

Irene started and then smiled. She looked dreadful, still wearing the scarlet and black dressing gown she must have put on when the telephone rang at half past six that morning. It was flapping open over a heavily creased white nightgown, on which she had spilled coffee. Her hair had been pinned up earlier in the day, but half of it had come out of the pins. Helena thought that she looked as though she ought to be dancing in the mad scene in *Giselle* or wandering across a stage as the sleepwalking Lady Macbeth.

'Fin rang,' Irene said in a voice that sounded almost lifeless. 'They've got some real evidence.'

'They can't have.' All Helena's fears of what Ivo might or might not have been involved with rushed back to taunt her. 'What sort of evidence?'

'Things they found in the farmhouse.'

'But the house is someone else's,' protested Helena, forgetting for a moment that it was not.

When she did remember, she realized at last how Ivo had been able to afford it. She wondered how much Miranda had really known of his activities, and whether that first piece of information had been designed to lead to precisely what had happened. Helena shuddered as she considered the possibility that Miranda might have orchestrated the whole drama as revenge against Irene. It was difficult to believe that anyone could have been so cruelly manipulative, but it would be stupid to pretend that it was impossible.

'Mightn't he just have been an accessory?' she asked hopefully.

Irene shook her head. More of her hair came out of its pins. She laid her face in her hands. Her shoulders shook. Helena had never seen Irene cry before and did not know how to deal with it. She put her right hand on Irene's back and felt her flinch.

'I'm sorry,' she whispered, taking her hand away.

At that Irene looked up. Her face was streaked with tears and remnants of the previous day's mascara.

'It's not your fault,' said Irene, trying to smile at her. 'There are a lot of people who may have to take some of the guilt for this, but you're not one of them.'

Helena waited, unable to say anything. She had never found it hard to blame herself for any disaster that struck the people she loved, and the memory of her call to Crimestoppers made it even easier than usual.

'I just can't work out where it was we went so dreadfully wrong,' said Irene after a while. 'Should I have let Fin smack him whenever he wanted to? Was it the way we argued when he was growing up? Did we discipline him too much or too little? Was it the money I used to send him secretly when he was at school? Or the way Fin always tried to keep him poor? What was it?'

'Irene.' Helena tried to sound sensible and as though she might know the answers to some of the questions. 'You mustn't blame yourself. Ivo's twenty-three. He's left home. He makes his own choices. You can't take responsibility for what he does a hundred miles away. You mustn't. You get let off responsibility for your children when they reach adulthood.'

'I thought I knew him.' Irene blinked and then sniffed. 'I thought he loved me. But I can't have known anything about him at all.'

'You sound as though you're sure he did it,' said Helena. 'The police do make mistakes, you know. Perhaps Ivo was only a front for someone else.'

'Even if he was, he'll be sent down for it. The courts are savage with everyone when it comes to Ecstasy. He's bound to have to do time.'

'I suppose so, but presumably it'll be somewhere like Ford. Surely Ivo's just the sort of person who goes there rather than one of the grim Victorian horrors.'

'Not straight away,' said Irene. There was unmistakable fear in her huge dark eyes. 'They nearly always send them to one of the tough places first to give them a shock. Even if he gets to Ford later, how will he bear it? He's so young, so . . .'

Helena sat down on the small sofa that stood against the wall next to Irene's desk and turned the swivel chair so that Irene was facing her.

'Listen. Ivo is tough. We've always known that. And incredibly charming. He'll make them all like him wherever he is and whoever they are. It's one of the things he's always been able to do. And it's not as though he'll go down for one of the really dangerous things. I mean he won't have to be a Rule 22 prisoner or whatever it's called. He hasn't killed a child or raped them or anything. He'll probably be a bit of a hero. You mustn't have nightmares about what'll happen to him. No-one's going to beat Ivo up, or . . . or do anything like that. He'll make the screws like him and at the same time persuade the other inmates that he's the most rebellious, most powerful one among them all; just as he did at school.'

'Did he?'

'Yes, he did. Look, Irene, try not to worry so much. What was it that writer said? I can't even remember who it was, but something about prison being not much worse than a second-rate public school.'

Helena tried to laugh, but her own imagination was showing her all sorts of pictures of what might happen to Ivo in prison. Most of them were born of fiction she had read and television films she had seen, but they were none the less awful for that.

'No. But what will he do for the rest of his life? With something like that hanging over him?' Irene sobbed once and mopped her eyes on the hem of her nightgown. 'He's only twenty-three. Helena, I can't bear it. He's thrown his life away, just like I . . . I wanted him to have everything, but he's thrown it away.'

'I know.' Helena took her hand and tried to think of something comforting to say, but there was nothing.

Irene held her hand, sniffing and blinking away the tears that kept on filling her eyes and seeping down over her cheekbones. 'Sorry. I know it must be awful for you, too.'

'And Fin and Jane,' said Helena as a way of controlling her ludicrous, destructive urge to confess to Irene that it was she who had made the police search Ivo's farmhouse. She knew that it was only self-indulgence that was urging her to speak; her confession would do no good whatever to Irene and would take away a lot that she valued. There would be no possibility of forgiveness, and the only reason to confess would be in order to be forgiven.

'Jane.' Irene sounded so harsh that Helena shuddered. 'D'you know? When I rang to tell her what had happened she didn't ask any questions or sympathize with him or anything like that. She just said: "Now perhaps you'll listen to me sometimes and see that *I* might have some value too. All my life I've had perfect Ivo dinned into me. Now perhaps you'll have the grace to admit that he's not perfect." At least, I think it was something like that.'

'Poor Jane,' said Helena, jerked away from her guilt for a moment.

Irene looked at her and drew back, letting her hand go. There was hostility in her eyes, even dislike.

'What did you say to her?' Helena asked quickly, needing to re-establish friendly contact as soon as possible.

'Nothing. I couldn't. She banged the telephone down before I could say anything.'

'But you do see what she means, don't you?' Screwing up her courage, Helena made herself add: 'Irene, she has got a point, hasn't she? I mean, if Ivo really has done this?'

'So you resented him, too, did you? I must say, you hid it a great deal better than she did.' Irene's voice was quiet but still very cold.

'No,' said Helena, feeling as though she were biting down hard onto a holed tooth. 'I have never resented Ivo. I've always loved him; you must know that. But didn't we all ignore Jane except when she was being difficult and then tell her off? That's my memory of it all.'

'But she *was* difficult,' wailed Irene, forgetting all the insights she had had into Jane's state of mind on the morning of the play. 'And Ivo was always so nice, so helpful, such fun. Of course we . . . Oh, what does any of it matter now?'

'And such a liar, too, perhaps?' said Helena, recognizing Irene's attempts to justify her anger with Jane.

She did not know what to say or do to help. Eventually she made some tea for them both and tried to talk about the good parts of the past, about the things Ivo had said and done throughout his life that were undeniably kind, but none of it helped. In the end, recognizing that there was nothing she could do for Irene, she decided to do something for herself.

'Do you know why the police ever came to suspect Ivo in the first place?'

'All we know is that they received information. Fin said that's not surprising. One of the bigger operators probably wanted him out of the way and put the police on to him.'

Well, that's something, said Helena to herself. At least they're not going to try to find out who did it. As though the reassurance made her think more clearly she began to feel anger instead of guilt. She might have given in to panic, but Ivo had broken the law. For once he was the one who ought to carry the blame, not her.

'They may have been watching him for ages. In fact,' Irene

paused, looking both surprised and ashamed. 'In fact it could have been his name on some list or other that alerted the Customs officer's attention when I flew back from Amsterdam.'

'What are you talking about?'

'Didn't I tell you? When Richard and I came back from our trip last May, we were stopped and searched for drugs. He was furious at first, although I thought it was reasonable. And then I was furious when he told me that he did sometimes use marijuana. You see, I assumed it was his fault we were searched. But perhaps it happened because they were already suspicious of Ivo and his name was on some list. After all my air ticket was in the name of I. Webton. Oh, hell!'

Helena could not think of any way to comfort her. At half past eight they both heard the sound of a key in the front door and then Fin's voice, so stern that no-one who had not known him extremely well would have discerned the unhappiness in it: 'Go to your mother.' There was the sound of Ivo's voice, the words undistinguishable, and then Fin spoke again: 'Go and see her and then you may go upstairs.'

Helena got up at once. 'Look, Irene, I'll get out of the way.'

She brushed past Ivo as she left the study, but she would not look at him.

'Helena, my dear, how good of you to come,' said Fin, almost smiling at her as he put his briefcase down on the hall chest where the rugs were kept. 'I might have known you would. You've always been a good girl.'

He looked towards the study door, which Ivo had firmly closed, and led the way into the kitchen. He emptied the stale water from the kettle, refilled it and switched it on.

'How did Irene seem to you?' he asked, not looking at Helena.

'Worried,' she said, sitting down on one of the old-fashioned, plastic-seated Festival of Britain chairs that she had always hated. 'And angry, I think, and ashamed, and all the things you might expect. What about you?'

Fin turned and leaned against the worktop. He looked older, and the skin of his chin and neck seemed even dryer and more folded in on itself than usual. Helena felt sorry for him, but she did not know how to comfort him. He had never asked for her help or responded to any overture she had ever made. She realised that she did not know him at all.

'I'm not sure that I know,' he said at last.

'What?' Helena had not meant to sound so irritable and shook her head. 'Sorry. Do you think he did do it?'

'Oh, yes, he did it all right,' said Fin grimly, looking much less pathetic. Helena began to feel just a little sorry for Ivo.

'You sound angry with him.'

'Of course I'm angry,' said Fin, sounding quite as irritable as Helena had been. 'And all the other things you ascribed to Irene. I'm so angry that I can hardly see, but until I can understand why he did it I can't tell which of all my feelings is legitimate.'

'And you feel only legitimate emotions, do you?' she asked, staring at him. 'Lucky you.'

'What? No, of course not. Don't be silly.'

There's no need to sound so impatient, she thought, loathing the way he had once more cast her in the role of the unsympathetic child, the one who could not be bothered even to try to understand what he meant, or do what he wanted, the one in the way, the one who caused all the trouble; the one he disliked.

'And you, Helena: what are you feeling?'

She shrugged and tried to shrug off the sullenness, too. It would not help and it made her feel exactly like the useless child he had always thought she was.

'Rage, fear, sympathy, and . . .'

'And what?'

Unable to confess to excitement, she let her eyelids close in order to hide her thoughts. She heard Fin move and when she looked again saw that he was methodically making a pot of tea in the way he had been taught nearly sixty years earlier.

'My mother always said that tea is the only thing to drink in a crisis,' he said, sounding at his most conversational. 'She was probably right. Milk? I can't remember.'

'Yes, please, but no sugar or anything.'

He put a mug in front of her and poured tea into it before pushing a milk bottle across the table towards her.

'Some of Jane's satisfaction perhaps?' he asked. When Helena kept silent, he added really quite gently: 'It wouldn't be surprising, you know. You must have been very jealous of Ivo when he came to displace you.'

She shook her head, and drank. The steam from the tea condensed on her eyes and made them water.

'Miranda says . . .'

'Says what?' Helena demanded angrily. 'You mean you've been to see her today of all days?'

'She's appearing in one of the courts at the Old Bailey,' he said stiffly. 'When she heard what had happened she sent me a note.'

'And then you saw her,' said Helena, outraged at the thought of Irene alone in Herbert Crescent while Fin sought solace from Miranda.

'Sometimes I need support, too, you know,' he said mildly enough. 'I know that all your loyalty has always been given to your stepmother, but your mother and I . . .' He shook his head as though his hair were full of water.

'Is it so surprising when Irene is the only one who's ever really cared what happens to me?'

Fin looked shocked, then hurt, but he did not answer.

'I owe her everything. Even you must see that.'

He nodded, but it was not enough for Helena. All she could think of to do for Irene just then was make Fin admit how important she was so that he might treat her properly at last.

'He says he did it for money. Just for money and for pleasure.'

Fin and Helena both turned to see Irene standing in the doorway, looking more than ever like the mad tragic heroine of an opera or a ballet.

'He isn't even ashamed of it, just furious with whoever it was who turned the police on him. I don't know him any more. There is nothing in him that I recognize at all. And then I look at him and he's just Ivo. I . . .'

To Helena's astonishment, Fin got stiffly to his feet and took

Irene in his arms, cradling her against him, stroking her untidy hair. She was as tall as he and much bulkier and yet he seemed the acme of protectiveness.

'Oh, Fin, I don't think I can bear it.'

'Come upstairs, my darling love,' said Fin, swinging round so that he could urge her forward with one arm behind her back, the other smoothing the hair away from her messy, tear-stained face. Neither of them looked back.

Helena sat at the kitchen table, thinking to herself: he loves her; he actually loves her after all. And she him. Why have they baited each other all these years?

Finding no answer to her own question, still reeling from the astonishing revelation of their affection, Helena sat waiting for someone to appear and tell her to stay or go. She could not think what to do and it did not seem possible to slink off home and leave them all to their distress. She had always looked after them all; she could not just go.

The sun set and the room grew greyer and greyer but she made no move to switch on the lights. The tea in the mug between her hands was quite cold when she saw the kitchen door move at last. She had heard no-one on the stairs.

The door opened more widely and she saw Ivo peering round it. He looked put out to see her there.

'I thought you'd gone. Where are the parents?'

'Upstairs. I haven't gone home because it didn't seem quite the right thing to do in such a crisis. Are you hungry? I'm sure there's something you could have. Shall I have a look?'

He laughed and switched on the lights, making Helena blink in their brightness.

'Yes, but, criminal though I apparently am, I'm not incapable of opening a tin of beans.'

He moved to the larder, took out a can, found the tin opener and a saucepan. Helena watched as he made himself four pieces of toast, spread them thickly with butter, emptied the heated beans onto two of them and brought the plateful to the kitchen table, where he proceeded to eat.

'It doesn't seem to have affected your appetite,' she said eventually.

He looked up in surprise and then smiled. She saw what Irene had meant. He did look exactly the same as he had always done, with the same affection shining out of his dark eyes.

'Oh yes it has. It's made me a lot hungrier than usual. I'd have been down here sooner if I hadn't wanted to make sure the parents were out of the way first. There's nothing to say and I can't take all these questions. Why, why, why? On and on. I'm sick of it.'

'Are there any answers?'

'Plenty.'

Helena wanted to ask him all sorts of things, but she was not sure he would have replied to any of them.

'How long has it been going on?' she said at last.

He shook his head. 'Don't you start, Hella, please. I've been fielding questions all day. I don't want to talk about it and you don't want to hear. Believe me. Let's talk about something else. Tell me about Mike. Jane seems to like him and so does my mother.'

'I'm not sure there's anything to tell,' Helena said, deciding that she did not want to share anything about Mike with Ivo any longer. 'I was supposed to be dining with him tonight, but . . .'

'You were summoned to deal with the fallout, were you? Sorry about that.' He scraped up the last of the tomato sauce on his plate, put his knife and fork together tidily and said: 'I'm knackered. I'm going to bed.'

She put out a hand to stop him leaving. He took it between both of his for a moment.

'You're all sweaty,' he said. 'You're not afraid of me, are you?'

'Of you? No.'

'You don't need to be scared for me either.' He bent down and kissed her cheek. 'I'll do all right, you know. I'm a survivor.'

'Before you go, Ivo, tell me one thing.'

'If I must.'

'The desk. Where *did* it come from?'

'I told you,' he said, looking surprised. 'From my banking friend who decided it didn't fit with his modern Italian furniture.'

She shrugged. 'You mean the story was true?'

'Yes. Of course. Well, in essentials.'

'Ah. Only in essentials. I see. Which bit wasn't essential, then?'

Ivo smiled in a mixture of amusement, pity and mischief. 'The bank manager. True to all my father's precepts, I've never borrowed any money in my life. My trouble these last two years has been disposing of the bloody stuff, not acquiring it. The desk was amazingly expensive, but still a relatively good deal, I think.'

'Was it the one that had been stolen, the one I saw written up in *Find?*'

'I've no idea. All I know is that my mate George bought it at auction about four months before I took it off his hands. He made a tidy profit out of me, but that's fair enough. I was planning to flog it for even more once you'd tarted it up.'

'Oh, I see. So the aunt who bequeathed it to him wasn't one of the essentials of the story either?'

'No. Is that it or is there anything else you can't stop yourself asking?'

'There is one other thing,' said Helena slowly. 'I've been wondering whether you ever worried at all about the people who took your drugs.'

Ivo shrugged. 'Why should I? Do car manufacturers worry about the fools who drive so badly that they kill each other? No, of course they don't. The market's supposed to rule all our lives these days. Well, there's a market for what I produced and I satisfied it. The fact that it's made up of idiots who'll cheerfully risk their lives for a few hours of excitement or whatever it is they think E will give them isn't my problem.'

'But it's against the law.'

'So?'

'Don't you think that's important?'

'Of course not.' He laughed. 'As you know perfectly well, I've never shared your terror of breaking rules. And I needed the money.'

'I don't believe you care as little as that,' said Helena. 'I can't.' Ivo shrugged again and then laid his hand flat against his neck. 'Too bad. I'm off. I've had it up to here with questions. 'Night.'

When he had left her, Helena stopped trying to make sense of any of it. She patiently cleaned up after him, as she had always done, tidying away the evidence of his supper. Then she tore a piece of paper off the roll Irene kept for shopping lists and wrote a short note to explain why she had gone and that she would be available at any time of the day or night if Irene should need her.

# Chapter Twenty-One

Upstairs Irene was lying in bed, with Fin sitting in a chair at her side loosely holding her hand. They had not talked much, but the simple physical contact between them and the peace were extraordinarily comforting. They both heard the sound of Ivo and Helena moving about downstairs, but neither of them said anything. When Ivo's footsteps had passed the bedroom door as he went up to his own room and Helena had shut the front door, Irene looked towards Fin.

'How is all this going to affect you in your work?'

He frowned and wiped his face with his free hand.

'I'm not altogether sure. I may have to resign. I thought I wouldn't do anything for a week or two and then perhaps have a word with Geoffrey; see what he thinks. I'd trust his judgement on something like this.'

'Resignation might be a bit dramatic, don't you think? You love the law. It would be horribly unfair to make you leave it just because your son . . .'

'I don't suppose anyone would try to make me go. But having to sentence dealers and users might put me in a difficult position.' Fin stared at her left hand and the small Victorian ring he had given her when she had agreed to marry him. 'And parents who neglect and misuse their children,' he added.

'That's nonsense,' Irene said, sounding stronger than she had all day. 'You did neither.'

Fin dropped her hand. She sat up and pushed her hair away from her face.

'I mean it, Fin. That's idiotically exaggerated. You were a good father.'

'I thought,' he said, not looking anywhere near her face, 'that you would tell me that it was my insistence on keeping them short of money that made Ivo do this.'

Irene simply shook her head.

'Why not?'

'Why haven't you told me that it was my lack of discipline?' asked Irene. 'Or perhaps my "wild talk" of freedom and the importance of individuals finding their own morality and all the other things that used to annoy you so?'

'I'm not sure.' He did look at her then and for the first time in years saw not the tormenting spoiler of his peace but the eager, vital, warmly affectionate girl who had burst into his grey, lonely world and transformed it. 'Perhaps because this is so important that it makes our . . . our bickering seem so trivial.'

'It hasn't ever seemed trivial to me,' said Irene unhappily. 'There have been times when it's seemed so huge and important that I haven't been able to think of anything else. I've gritted my teeth waiting for the next bout, hating it, dreading it, knowing that it'll come, unable to stop it. I was buggered if I was ever going to give in unless you admitted what you were doing to me.'

'Yes, I know. I mean it's seemed like that to me too.' He frowned. 'The cruelty of some of the things you've said, the need to make you see things my way and behave have occasionally made me almost ill.'

'And very angry.' It was not a question.

'Yes.' He smiled, not altogether happily, and for only the second time Irene remarked something of Helena in him. Recognizing the tightness of the small muscles above his nose, which she had seen often in Helena when she was screwing herself up to deal with something that worried her, Irene wondered why she had never noticed it before.

'So angry,' he went on, 'that there were times when I was surprised I managed not to break something. Like you.'

'Break something like me, or feel like me in wanting to break things?' she asked, almost certain that she knew what his answer would be.

'The second.' He sighed.

'What?'

'I was just wondering,' he said, looking down at her face as though he, too, were seeing properly for the first time in years, 'how it happened; how we ever got like that.'

'Just at this moment, I can't imagine,' she said, grabbing his hand again, 'but at the time it seemed inevitable.'

She looked at the tiredness of his eyes, the lines around his chin and all the marks of pain and disillusion and sadness. The coldness, the anger, the withdrawal, and the deliberate provocation had all been wiped away by his likeness to the one person left whom she had never doubted that she loved.

'It seemed so important to win,' she said, sounding surprised by her own discoveries. Like Fin, she was trying to understand instead of simply react to what happened. 'I suppose I thought I'd never be able to be happy unless I could make you offer some kind of formal surrender.'

'And reparations?'

'Yes,' she admitted. 'Those too.'

'For what? I mean, what exactly? I know the general drift of it, and if I didn't the play would have shown me, but now that we're talking, perhaps you could give me some detail.'

'Oh,' she said, planning to brush it off with an insouciant, witty phrase that would not hurt him any more. Then she realized that there was too much at stake and that she would have to tell him. 'For stealing my chance of having a real life, for keeping me from all the things I really wanted to do, for turning me into someone I was never meant to be.'

He did not say anything, but the pain in his face was comment enough.

'And you?' she said, stroking his arm. 'What was it I did that needed so much punishment?'

For a moment she thought that he was not going to admit that he had ever felt like that or done anything deliberately to punish her, and the enormous amount of territory she had just given up to him extended itself before her as though in a nightmare battlefield of dead trees, corpses, mud and shell holes. Fin's face tightened up as it had always done before his worst salvoes.

'For being here – in the way – when Miranda wanted to come back. I think.'

'As easy as that,' Irene said as the rebellious, hurt, angry parts of her mind wanted to shriek out at him: that wasn't my fault; I wasn't the one who seduced anyone; you did that; then you asked me to marry you; you are an unutterable shit for having blamed me for what *you* made me do.

'I don't know that "easy" was quite the right word,' said Fin with a surprising return of his Helena-like smile. 'Neither the emotion nor the admitting of it was in the least easy. I don't suppose yours were either.'

No, but mine were more reasonable than yours, said the angry voice over and over again, until Irene told it savagely to remember what she had learned from the rehearsals of her play.

'It's been such a waste, Irene. Although it seems obvious now, I hadn't any idea of what I was doing or why at the time. All I knew was what you were doing. But now that I know – and you know – can we try again? A bit more honestly this time?'

'All right, Fin,' she said quietly, as the antagonistic voices in her mind at last gave her permission to cease fire, 'let's try.'

Upstairs, Ivo, perhaps bored with creeping about the house as though he had to apologize for his existence, or perhaps unable any longer to pretend that he did not care about what was going to happen to him, turned on his CD player and let loose 'The Ride of the Valkyries' played at full blast.

Helena was locking the van when she heard heavy footsteps hurrying towards her.

That's all I need, she thought, pulling her shoulder bag round so that it hung at the front of her body. A mugger on top of everything else. Perhaps the scene in Irene's play didn't reflect

273

anything in her past but was just a prophecy of this. Oh, well, what does it matter now? What does anything matter any more?

She did not even look in the direction of the steps, just finished locking the door of the van and turned towards the house.

'Helena!'

At the sound of the familiar voice, she did turn to see Mike, pounding along the pavement towards her. In a way, after everything she had been thinking as she drove back from Knightsbridge, he seemed a more worrying prospect than any mugger. She pushed the bag back to hang at her side and waited for him, her keys dangling from her hands.

'Hi,' she said.

'What happened? What is it that was wrong? You look frightful.' He took her arm and urged her towards her house. 'Is it Irene? Your father?'

Helena shook her head. 'How was the dinner?' she said conversationally, trying to pretend that everything was still normal and the thoughts that had been biting into what was left of her serenity had never been formed. 'Did it go all right? I was so sorry to have to duck out like that. I hope your client wasn't angry.'

'It was fine. Never mind that now. Helena, please tell me what's happened.'

They had reached her front door and she was fully occupied undoing all the locks and dealing with the alarm. That done, she dropped her bag on the floor and headed straight for the kitchen. She took an opened bottle of white wine from the fridge, poured some into two glasses and handed one of them to Mike.

Almost unable to contain his impatience, he accepted it, but he did not drink. Instead he switched on the light and examined her pinched, angry, frightened face.

'So?' he said at last. 'What's making you look as though you've lost your shirt?'

'My brother, Ivo, has been charged with making and selling Ecstasy,' she said in a formal, neatly articulated voice as though she were speaking to a room full of strangers.

'Is that all?' said Mike. He drank some of the wine. 'I thought someone must have died at least.'

'All?' She was standing stiffly in her chair with the full glass held between her hands like an offering.

'Yes.' Mike made her sit down at the table and then pulled out a chair for himself. 'Making drugs, using them, dealing in them is stupid, dangerous, wicked even if you think in terms like that, but it's manageable. It doesn't mean your brother is a psychopath or even a devil, just a greedy law-breaker. That's really not so bad, Helena.'

'I suppose that could be true,' she said after a long pause, during which she had been thinking: it sounds as though Mike understands; is that possible?

'He'll have to take his punishment, but he'll get out of prison eventually, and then he'll find a life for himself. He's clever, healthy, probably bloody tough. He'll make it. You don't need to look so tragic. You haven't actually lost anything important, you know.'

'I'm not so sure about that.' She looked at him and knew that she had to say it. 'All the way home I've been thinking that if Ivo, whom I've known all his life, could turn out to be even more criminal than the worst of my panicky, neurotic anxieties suggested, then perhaps you ...'

'Perhaps I what?' asked Mike wrathfully, beginning to understand at last.

'Perhaps you aren't as you've always seemed,' she said, trying not to sound either provocative or stupid. 'I don't mean that I think you've been making drugs, but what do I know about you?'

For a moment he looked bitterly hurt and she hated herself. Then he seemed to get some kind of control and took her hands.

'You don't know anything more about me than I know about you. I love you. You've said you love me. That's all we can actually know. We have to risk the rest.'

'Then we'll never be safe.'

'Safety isn't everything, Helena.'

She looked at him with the denial clear in her unhappy eyes.

# Epilogue

The long delay before Ivo's trial made Irene feel as though she were trapped in an unending nightmare. She tried to find pleasure in the fact that *The House on the Canal* was doing so well that Richard was talking about a transfer to the West End, but it seemed unimportant in comparison with what might be done to Ivo – and what he had done. She made huge efforts to keep the family's life as normal as possible, just as she sat down at her desk every morning to work fruitlessly on ideas for a new play. There were days when she felt that she could not keep going any longer, and she was almost always certain that she would never again be able to write anything worthwhile.

When she confided that to Richard, he told her with callous sympathy that her anguish would probably make her a better writer in the end but that she ought to wait to embark on another play until she had got a grip on her feelings. Her fury at his bracing attitude to her distress aroused enough of her old spark to give her a glimpse of a future in which she might be free of the nightmare, but it did not last long. There was so much guilt in her, and anger and fear, that the idea of controlling any of them seemed to be an impossible dream.

Ivo had been committed for trial in the Crown Court and granted bail. Fin, who had stood surety for him, had insisted that he leave Oxford and come to live in Herbert Crescent, but Irene had very little consolation from that. Ivo talked to her occasionally, but never about anything that mattered. When he was at home he spent most of his time up in his room, apparently working on his thesis against the day when he could return to Oxford to complete his doctorate.

Irene's truce with Fin was holding, but he looked so ill and unhappy that there were times when she almost wished that they were back in the middle of a raging fight. They had once discussed what Ivo might be facing, but the maximum penalty for what he had done was so horrifying that neither of them wanted to torment the other by talking about it again.

Ivo knew what it was, too, but the only time Irene had ventured to raise it with him he had snapped at her, sounding not only furious but also contemptuous. The discovery of just what he was capable of doing, and how little she had understood him, had shocked her so much that she was afraid to find out what might lie behind his contempt. She had turned away from him in silence and left him alone.

He ate most of his meals out, occasionally admitting to having been with a girlfriend who had never been introduced to either of his parents, but he did sometimes appear for dinner at home. The conversation on those evenings was particularly stilted. All Irene wanted Ivo to talk about was why he had done it, how he had reconciled it with everything she had tried to bring him up to believe, and whether anything she – or Fin – could have done might have stopped him. She wanted to ask Ivo who his friends had been at school and university and whether any of them had forced, blackmailed or seduced him into setting up the drug factory. Most of the time it seemed impossible to her that her son could have done such a thing off his own bat, but there was no evidence that anyone else had ever been involved.

She told Richard that too, as she told him most things. He was easier to confide in than anyone else she knew. He had heard the whole story, knew who all the characters were, and yet was not emotionally involved in anyway. One day she told him about the horror of her discovery that Ivo was so different from the son she thought she had borne. Richard listened patiently and then said: 'In a way, you ought to be proud of him. There aren't all that many 23-year-olds who can set up and run such a profitable business.

He's made himself a tidy little fortune. Even if he's convicted he'll be out of prison again in no time and then he can turn his entrepreneurial skills to something legal. He'll do well enough; you'll see. I really don't think you need be quite so tragic about it. It's not as bad as you think.'

After that lunch Irene did not see Richard again for several weeks and she turned once more to Helena. She was her usual unfailingly kind self but could do little to help. Nothing she could say or do could take away any of the desperation Irene felt, and Helena's own emotions were so complicated and so powerful that they got in the way of the old easy communication the two of them had once enjoyed.

Helena also found the waiting intolerable. She felt as though the whole family were living in limbo, not sure what they were facing but always afraid. Mike was steadfast in his support and they had had no more unhappy misunderstandings. He had asked her once whether she would be prepared to marry or move in with him and she had thanked him but said that she could not decide anything until after the trial. Later she had castigated herself for her selfishness, but Mike had seemed to understand and he had not raised the subject again. She was deeply grateful to him for that as well as for everything else.

Together they saw a certain amount of Miranda and a lot of Jane, who found the house in Herbert Crescent even more difficult to live in than usual. On the evening after Jane had taken the train back to Durham for the spring term, Helena and Mike went to Miranda's house for dinner and Helena at last plucked up the courage to ask what sentence Ivo was likely to get.

'It's impossible to say for certain,' Miranda said, refilling their wine glasses. 'The maximum for supplying a Class A drug is life imprisonment, and as you know Ecstasy is a Class A drug.'

Helena felt as though she had been punched. Some of the elliptical comments Fin had made about Ivo's future began to make more sense to her than when she had first heard them, as did his increasingly bleak expression and greying complexion.

'I'm afraid so,' Miranda went on, seeing that Helena could not speak. 'It's not mandatory, but it is possible. I thought you knew or I'd have told you months ago. I can't think of any mitigating circumstances that Ivo's counsel can raise except that it's a first offence and that he is of previous good character. It all depends on the judge.'

'Surely,' said Mike, who was sitting opposite Helena and wishing that he could wrap his arms round her and hang on to her so that he could stop her drowning in the waves of anxiety that he knew were washing over her again, 'no-one's going to send a fellow judge's child to prison for life?'

Miranda shrugged delicately. She was almost as uninvolved as Richard. Fin's unspoken rage and fear aroused her sympathy, as did Helena's misery, but she herself did not care very much what happened to Ivo. Her opinion, which she had expressed only to Mike in private, was that Ivo was a nasty piece of work who had conned almost everyone he had ever met and that even if he never tried making drugs again he was unlikely ever to be entirely honest in anything he did.

'It all depends,' she said, turning to Helena even though it was Mike who had asked the question. 'Some of them might not; others might think that someone brought up with all Ivo's advantages and knowledge ought to be punished more severely than some uneducated product of a hopeless inner city housing estate.'

'I wonder if Irene knows it could be life,' said Helena, who had not been listening.

'Of course she does,' answered Miranda impatiently.

'No wonder she looks as though she's on the rack.' There was a note in Helena's voice that made Mike glance quickly at Miranda, nod to her, and then say brightly that he thought it was about time for him and Helena to be getting home.

The trial eventually took place in March. After long discussions with Fin, the solicitor and his counsel, Ivo had decided to plead guilty and express profound remorse in the hope of a lighter sentence than he might get if he fought every inch of the way and put the Crown to the expense of a long trial.

On the day he was due to be sentenced his family was sitting in the public gallery, looking down at him. There were no clouds at all that morning, which Helena tried to believe was a good omen, and sunlight poured into the court from windows high up in its walls. As Ivo stood between his warders in the dock he seemed to be gilded in brightness, his dark hair outlined by light, his skin glowing, and his eyes looking soft and honest.

He had hardly ever raised them during the proceedings and then only when he had been looking at the judge, acknowledging his fault with a beautifully calculated air of regret. The judge was a youngish, dark-haired, caustic-sounding man with a strong northern accent, who had looked anything but sympathetic through most of the proceedings, but even he had occasionally responded to Ivo's performance.

He took off his spectacles and laid them on the papers in front of him before calmly looking across the court towards the dock. Mike took hold of Helena's hand.

'Ivo Henry Webton, you have pleaded guilty to a charge of manufacturing and supplying a Class A drug.'

The voice was calm enough to give Helena another scintilla of hope. She turned her hand in Mike's and held on tight.

'This is such a serious offence that, although it is your first, only a custodial sentence is suitable.'

Irene leaned against Fin and waited. In spite of the importance of keeping his dignity in that of all places, Fin put his arm round her. Irene softened her muscles so that he could feel her gratitude.

Jane looked at them coolly for a moment and then turned back to watch the judge again.

'Ecstasy is an extremely dangerous drug, which has led not only to illness and distress in the people who take it, but also to many deaths. Your counsel has spoken most eloquently of your regret for the pain you have caused and of the remorse you will feel for the rest of your life. He has also spoken of your previous good character, your intelligence and hard work, and your potential for leading a useful life as a law-abiding citizen.

'Praiseworthy though your academic career has been, it cannot excuse or mitigate the seriousness of your crime. Indeed, with your background and your brains, it makes that seriousness even greater. You were fully aware that what you were doing was wrong; you went to great lengths to disguise your activities and the profits that you gained from them. You had no material, medical or psychiatric reason to do what you did. You did it from wickedness and a desire for profit. I have therefore no option but to sentence you to life imprisonment. Take him down.'

Mike's hand gripped Helena's wrist as her other hand shot up to cover her mouth. She was afraid that she might be sick. Hearing a gasp, she looked towards Irene and saw that she was holding Fin in her arms. His face was terrifyingly grey, his breathing laboured and both hands were clasped to his chest. Jane went to hold his head, hissing at him: 'Breathe. Breathe. Come on.'

'I'll get an ambulance,' said Mike, already on his feet. 'Keep them as calm as you can, Helena.'

A court official in a black gown was clearing the public gallery of all the other spectators, who lagged past the group around Fin, staring avidly. When the official had got them all out of the way, she urged Irene to lay Fin down flat on the floor and proceeded very efficiently to give him heart massage. Irene got to her feet and swayed. Helena moved forwards but Jane got there first and persuaded her mother to sit down and put her head between her knees.

Helena went to sit with them, holding Irene's left hand until two paramedics in green overalls arrived with a stretcher and a portable defibrillator. Mike had followed them, and he bent down to whisper to Helena.

'They're going to take him to St Michael's. There won't be room for everyone in the ambulance. I'll go and get the car and meet you in the street. Will you bring the others down with you?'

Helena nodded. 'As soon as they've got him to the ambulance.'

Later, she and Mike followed the ambulance to the hospital and then stayed with Irene and Jane in casualty until they were told that Fin, who had been given all the latest clot-busting drugs, had been taken up to the intensive care unit. The nurse who brought them the news added that Irene would be allowed to see Fin in a few minutes.

'I'll be back in a second,' Helena said as soon as the nurse finished speaking.

Neither Irene nor Jane reacted, but Mike nodded. Helena left them, found a telephone box and rang the number of her mother's chambers.

'Is Mrs Webton there?' she asked when the clerk answered.

'Yes. May I say who's calling?'

'It's her daughter, Helena.'

A moment later they were connected.

'I've heard,' said Miranda. 'Life. I am so sorry, Helena.'

'It's not that. It's Fin. Have they told you yet?'

'Told me what?' Miranda's voice was sharp.

'He's had a heart attack. Not fatal. He's in St Michael's. We're all here at the moment and Irene's about to be allowed up to see him. I thought you might like to know.'

There was a pause and then Miranda said: 'That was very good of you. Will you  ...? I don't want to get in Irene's way, but I'd like to see him, too, when I can. Will you let me know as soon as it's feasible? And if anything happens before then.'

'Yes, I will.'

Helena went back to the others and heard Irene saying to Jane: 'And I didn't even look at him as they were taking him down to the cells. Jane, what is he going to think?'

'That he's been an unutterable fool and that you're deeply ashamed of him, I hope,' she said. Then, seeing Irene's face, she added less harshly: 'They will have told him what happened to Dad. They're not inhuman. He'll understand. And you can write to him, too. And you'll be able to visit soon.'

Helena waited, but neither Jane nor Irene said anything else. They just looked at each other with all the old antagonism fighting the kinder feelings they had been beginning to allow themselves. They did not seem to know what to do next. Helena moved to join them.

'Life sounds awful, Irene,' she said, hoping to help, 'but I'm sure he can appeal. Anyway somebody said it's usually a bit less than ten years with good behaviour. And Ivo will behave better than anyone. You know he will.'

Jane looked at her in silence and shook her head.

'It's not as easy as that,' Irene said stiffly, as though her face was hurting. 'It depends on the tariff the judge has put on it – and on the Home Secretary of the day, who could be anyone, with any sort of prejudice or vote-catching need to keep drug-dealers in prison. You know . . .' Her voice quivered and she shook her head as though trying to force some kind of control into her mind. Then she shrugged, recognizing that there was nothing she could do. Tears seeped out over her lashes and she lay back against the plastic chair and let her eyes close.

Even Helena, who ached to comfort her, understood that there was nothing to be said and managed to hold her tongue.

Two days later, when Fin had begun to recover some of his strength, but was still in intensive care, Helena met her mother in the foyer outside the unit. Miranda had just left his side and Helena was on her way to see him, bearing a bunch of small yellow roses.

'You look terrible,' said Miranda. 'What is it?'

'My brother has been sentenced to life imprisonment and my father's had a heart attack. He may – probably will – have another. Isn't that enough?'

'No. I don't think it is. D'you want to talk about the rest?'

'Not very much.'

'Is Mike around?'

'Well, he's in the office just now, but he's around in every other sense. I mean, he hasn't dumped me or anything because Ivo's gone to prison.'

Miranda smiled. 'I never thought he would. So tell me.'

Helena hesitated. There were things that had to be said, but she did not know how to begin or whether anything would be different if she did find a way to say them.

'Come and sit down,' said Miranda, for once sounding almost as maternal as Irene. 'Tell me.'

'It's more asking than telling,' said Helena reluctantly. She put the roses on one of the grey chairs and sat down on another. Miranda seated herself beside her.

'Then ask. I'll tell you anything I can.'

'Did you know what Ivo was doing when you got the Land Registry certificate?'

'No,' said Miranda at once. 'As I told you, I was fairly sure that he was up to something, but I had no idea it was as serious as this.'

'You do know that it's because of me he was found out?'

'I rather assumed it must have been and admired your courage.'

'It wasn't courage,' said Helena, looking at the far wall. 'If it had been, I might not be feeling quite so dreadful now. It was pure funk. I'd got myself into such a state of terror that I couldn't bear to go on without knowing for sure. I had to find out. And so I . . . I shopped him.' She held tightly on to her knees.

'Who knows that?'

'Only Mike. And now you.'

'And you blame me for my part in making you afraid of what Ivo might be doing.' Miranda sounded so sad that Helena had to look at her.

'No,' she said at last. 'I've come to see that blaming people doesn't do anyone any good.'

'And yet you're blaming yourself, aren't you? For Ivo's sentence and for Fin's heart attack.'

'How do you know that?'

'Because I know you. And because I know a lot about self-blame.'

'Do you?'

'Oh yes. Do you think that it is possible to give birth to a child and then leave her without blaming yourself?'

'I don't know,' said Helena, looking away again.

'Helena?'

'I can't talk about it.'

'I think we must,' said Miranda. 'If we don't do it now, I don't think we ever will, and if we don't, we won't either of us be able to . . .'

'What?' asked Helena.

'Heal, perhaps?'

It made sense. Helena picked up the roses and started pulling the petals off one of them. Miranda gently held her hand and took the flowers away.

'What was it I did that made you go?' Helena was so surprised by the ease with which the question emerged after all that she was able to look at her mother again.

'Nothing,' said Miranda passionately, taking both her daughter's hands. 'Is that what you've wanted to say all this time?'

Helena nodded.

'I thought it was some kind of accusation. Helena, you should . . . No, I should have said it. Listen to me now. You were a child and you behaved as a child. Nothing you did was the reason for my going. It could not have been. I was not a good mother of a small child; for one thing I was ignorant and clumsy. For another, I had very little support from Fin. Looking back, I can see that was because he was ignorant, too. And like a lot of other people, he assumed that mothers are automatically fitted to care for their babies. But they're not. Some lucky individuals seem to know what to do by instinct and are able to accept their baby's obstinacy as something natural, something that is not directed at them. The rest of us have to struggle. And it *is* a struggle.'

Helena shivered.

'But it's not the baby's fault,' said Miranda, 'however bad the struggle and however much it takes from the mother.'

'I wasn't a baby when you went.'

'No. But you were only three, which comes to much the same. And I didn't go because of you. I went because I wanted to show Fin what it was like. That's all. I never meant to go for ever. I just wanted him to have the responsibility for a few weeks so that he could see why I couldn't cope without his help. He'd always thought his career was more important than mine; it was certainly more successful.'

'Well, he was older,' said Helena angrily. 'He must have been at it for longer. No wonder it was more successful then.'

'True.' Miranda longed to be able to thank Helena for her instinctive partisanship, but there were other things that had to be said first. 'But he didn't see it quite like that. His view was that since he was more successful and more important, no need of mine could be expected to take anything from him that he wanted to give to his work. I eventually understood that he had absolutely no idea how powerful the needs were. I decided to show him. That's all.'

'So you left.'

'Yes. Planning to go back as soon as I could. But by then Irene was installed.'

'It was ages before she married him. You had to go through the whole business of the divorce. Couldn't you have told him before that happened? Explained to him before it got nearly so far?'

'I had what in those days was called a nervous breakdown. It was some time before I was back on an even keel and could understand what had been happening. By then the three of you seemed so cosy, so well installed. There wasn't much I could do.'

'Did you try to do anything?' Helena was hurting and she knew that it was making her sound accusatory, but she could not help it.

'Yes. I needed to put things straight with Fin at least. I told him why I'd done what I'd done. He told me that Irene was pregnant. We talked it all over very calmly and sensibly and agreed that we couldn't unpick anything, not least because you were at last settled again and apparently happy. Fin told me that you never said anything about me and appeared to believe that Irene was your mother. It was extremely hard, but we didn't see that we had any option.'

'I do love her, you know, and she has almost always been my mother,' said Helena with difficulty, understanding at last why Fin had turned on Irene around the time Ivo was born.

'I know. And although I've bitterly resented her for that, I'm grateful, too. At the time I could not care for you and she did – much better than I had ever done.' Miranda was still holding her daughter's hands. 'D'you think now that you might be able to have us both?'

One of the lift doors opposite the chairs opened and Irene emerged at a run, stopping when she saw the two of them holding hands. Her hair was falling down her back and she was breathless but there was more light in her eyes than there had been for months.

'Have they told you?' she said.

'What?' asked Helena, pulling her hands out of Miranda's. 'They haven't told us anything. We've been talking out here and no-one's come anywhere near us.'

'Fin's going to be moved down to an ordinary ward this afternoon,' said Irene in triumph. 'They even think that he'll be able to come home in about a week.'

'I'm so glad, Irene,' said Miranda.

'Thanks.' Irene took a great breath, let it out and smiled at them both. 'I thought he'd never get out of this place. I was sure he was going to die here.'

'But he's not,' said Miranda firmly.

'No. He'll have to live very carefully, and probably retire, which he'll hate. And it doesn't make Ivo's hideous situation any better, but it does seem like the first step out of the horror.' Irene looked at them, and a glimpse of her old exuberant self could be seen in her dark eyes. 'I hope bloody Richard is right and all this does improve my work. Otherwise . . .'

Miranda gasped and looked so shocked that Helena was afraid she might say something unforgivable to Irene. After a tense second or two it seemed that Miranda had recognized the real courage that lay behind Irene's bravado and she kept quiet.

'I'm going in to see him now. D'you want to come?' said Irene, adding when Miranda stood up to go with her: 'Helena?'

'You two go on ahead. I want to tell Mike.'

'About Fin?'

'Yes. But other things, too.'

'We'll see you later, then,' said Miranda. Irene blew Helena a kiss.

She watched them go and then took the mobile telephone Mike had given her out of her bag and dialled the number of his direct line.

He said his name, sounding quite different from the man she knew so well.

'It's me,' she said.

'How's Fin?' said Mike, immediately sounding like himself again.

'Pretty weak still, but they've told Irene they're about to move him down to an ordinary ward, which must be good. I'd thought ... Well, you know what I'd thought.'

'Yes.'

'Mike?'

'Yes.'

'I ...'

'What is it, Helena? Is something else wrong?'

'No. Quite the opposite, but I don't quite know how to put it. Perhaps it ought to wait until this evening. You must be very busy.'

'Yes, but not too busy for this. It sounds important.'

'I just wanted to say that something's happened that makes me free.'

'Free of me?' he said warily.

'No,' she said with great urgency. 'Free *for* you.'

'That's all right then,' he said, and she heard him laugh. 'That's great. When can I see you?'

'Whenever you want.'

'I'll come to the hospital. Wait there.'

## THE END